Her premonitions have the potential to resolve the past . . . or they may destroy her family's future

Tessa and Walter have, by all appearances, the perfect marriage. And they seem to be ideal parents for their somewhat rebellious teen-age daughter, Regina. Without warning, however, their comfortable lives are thrown into turmoil when a disturbing customer comes into the salon where Tessa works as a manicurist. Suddenly, Tessa's world is turned upside down as revelations come to light about the mother she thought had abandoned her in childhood and the second sight that she so guardedly seeks to keep from others. A magical novel of secrets revealed and a family in turmoil, searching together for new beginnings.

"Schieber has painted a fine portrait of the struggles and challenges of being different in an unforgiving world. Her characters are authentic and touching. Using language that is at once both straightforward and evocative, Schieber writes a story that you will recognize and remember long after you read the last page."
—Karen Chase, award-winning author of *Kazimierz Square*, *Bear*, *Land of Stone*, and *Jamali-Kamali*

"Phyllis Schieber once again shows how elegant storytelling can be. THE MANICURIST will remain on a top shelf in my library. This book will stir your emotions, excite you with its twists and delight you to the point of tears. A must-read."
—Susan Wingate, author of the award-winning novels, *Drowning* and *Bobby's Diner*

The Manicurist

by

Phyllis Schieber

Bell Bridge Books

This is a work of fiction. Names, characters, places and incidents are either the products of the author's imagination or are used fictitiously. Any resemblance to actual persons (living or dead,) events or locations is entirely coincidental.

Bell Bridge Books
PO BOX 300921
Memphis, TN 38130
ISBN: 978-1-61194-045-9

Bell Bridge Books is an Imprint of BelleBooks, Inc.

We at BelleBooks enjoy hearing from readers.
Visit our websites – www.BelleBooks.com and www.BellBridgeBooks.com.

10 9 8 7 6 5 4 3 2

Cover design: Debra Dixon
Interior design: Hank Smith
Photo credits:
Hand - © Stanislav Perov | Dreamstime.com
Background © Rolffimages | Dreamstime.com

:Lmt:01:

To Claire . . . for so many reasons.

Acknowledgments

I would have been unable to navigate any aspect of my career without the support, resilience, and sharp wit of my agent, Harvey Klinger. His belief in my work sustains me. The enthusiasm and professionalism of Deborah Smith, at Bell Bridge Books, made the process a genuine pleasure. I am also thankful to Debra Dixon and everyone else at Bell Bridge Books—especially Lynn Coddington, my editor. She was so generous with her time and her praise and brought a new focus and clarity to the narrative.

Writing is a solitary and often lonely pursuit. With that said, it is imperative to have the keen eyes of another writer, one whose skill and talent you admire, always at readiness to provide input. Candy Schulman did that for me with consistent and wholehearted interest and attention to detail, confirming that the craft of writing well is the true art.

I am also thankful to Claudia Hall who read my chapters with insight, always cheering me on.

And, as always, I appreciate the constancy and support of my husband, Howard Yager. Our son, Isaac, continues to surprise and delight me, and it is that for which I am most grateful.

I do what I want with the spirits,
and they do what they want with me.
—Andre Pierre, Haitian artist

Chapter One

First meetings could be so telling. Tessa knew this as well, if not better, than most. She was almost always accurate, tallying her small conquests according to conscience. After all, some conclusions, especially about people, were simply obvious. So when Tessa looked up from her work station in response to the woman's question about whether or not she needed an appointment for a plain manicure, and felt a stirring that was as inviting as it was alarming, she was prepared for something, though what she could not say. Before Tessa could say anything, the woman, just as cheerfully as she had the first time, asked her question again.

"Do I need an appointment for a plain manicure?"

The woman was in her sixties, perhaps younger, or maybe older. Tortoise shell glasses hung around her neck on a braided silver chain. Strands of dark hair, sharply streaked with grey, escaped from a loose bun that was pierced with elaborately painted black enamel hair pins. She was plump, which probably explained the skirt with the elasticized waist, and she immediately endeared herself to Tessa for no other reason than she seemed so comfortable with her appearance.

"Yes," Tessa said. She stood for no apparent reason. "Usually, especially on a Saturday. The receptionist, Kara, will be able to help you."

"But today is Thursday." The woman eyed Tessa's black slacks, black sweater and black flats, a combination that imitated what all the other workers were wearing. "Are you the manicurist?"

The collision of feelings that Tessa had first experienced made her suspicious, and she reminded herself that as a general rule it was always best to honor instinct before emotion.

"Yes. I am," Tessa said, slightly flustered. "I'm the manicurist." Her pale cheeks felt hot, and she shook her head as though this could help her regain some composure. She wondered how this woman had managed to elude Kara. Anna Marie, the manager of Escape, a day spa, referred to Kara as St. Peter, insisting that no one could get by without some interrogation. "What I meant to say is that we don't encourage walk-ins, but it's been a slow day and I just happen to have a cancellation. And, well, you're here."

The woman smiled so genuinely that Tessa smiled also and stooped to help her with the mesh shopping bag that kept toppling over.

"Thank you," she said. "That's very kind of you. Very kind." She offered her hand and said, "I'm Fran Hill."

Tessa casually ignored Fran's hand and set the mesh shopping bag against the wall. It was brimming over with fresh produce. She smelled garlic, onions and parsley, and something else she could not quite make out in a blend so compelling that her stomach growled.

"Excuse me," she said, deliberately patting her belly with both hands as a way to discourage any further contact. "I'm Tessa Jordan. So do you want a manicure?"

"Yes. I definitely need a manicure today." She tried to make it seem as if she had never offered her hand in the first place and fiddled with the waistband of her skirt. "Have you had your lunch, Tessa Jordan?"

"Well, no. Not yet."

Fran sat and rummaged through the bag, mumbling softly to herself, but in a way that invited eavesdropping. "One of these days I'm going to finally clean this bag out. Just dump everything. Way too much stuff." Finally, she pulled a Barbie thermos from the depths of the bag and set it on Tessa's table.

"Wait a moment. Just a second," Fran said. "Here now." She produced a cloth napkin and a soup spoon. "Try this." She unscrewed the lid of the thermos and inhaled deeply as the aroma was released. "It does smell wonderful, doesn't it? Eat right from the thermos. I have gallons of the stuff at home. Whenever I'm in a tizzy, I seem to make soup. Too much soup, always too much. I have to give it away, so I can make more."

Hesitantly, Tessa took the spoon from Fran. Tessa had been witness to some strange things in the salon, but Fran and her soup were unprecedented. There seemed to be no way to politely discourage this woman from imposing her soup on strangers.

"Go on," Fran said. "I promise you it isn't poisonous. Once you get to know me you'll understand my need to feed everyone."

Once I get to know her? Tessa swallowed and tried to discreetly sniff the soup. "But isn't this your lunch?"

"Oh goodness, no. I've already had my lunch."

"Weren't you bringing it somewhere?"

"Yes, certainly, I was," Fran said in a tone that suggested Tessa had asked a really funny question.

"Well, it does smell wonderful, and I am hungry." She held the spoon to her lips, and was about to take her first mouthful. Then she looked at Fran again, more carefully this time, and said, "Have we met before?"

"No," Fran said. "I don't believe we have. Go on now, have some soup."

The soup was quite unlike anything Tessa had ever eaten. The stock was flecked with bits of yellow corn and something else that wasn't bacon but gave the broth a smoky flavor. Tessa bit hungrily into chunks of chicken and fat lima beans.

While Tessa ate, Fran studied the nail polish display. She held each bottle up to the light, squinted and then examined the label on the bottom, and said the names aloud. *Keys To My Karma, Bubble Bath, Spring Bloom, I'm Not Really a Waitress.* She seemed more interested in the names than in the colors. Fran waited quietly, a bottle palmed in her hand, for Tessa to finish. When the last drop had been scraped from the thermos, Tessa wiped the spoon with the napkin and screwed the lid back on.

"Did you have something in mind?" Tessa asked.

"Excuse me?"

"A color," Tessa said. "Did you have a color in mind?"

Fran plucked a bottle of pale lilac polish from the display. "I like this, Peach Daiquiri," she said, handing the bottle to Tessa. "You don't think it's too young for me, do you?"

Tessa set the bottle down and considered not only the question but the woman who asked it. Tessa worried she would be unable to defend herself against Fran's intentions. Although Tessa was usually able to avert the onslaught of feeling that touch could deliver, Fran's will seemed very strong. It did not take much of either intelligence or vision to see that she had arrived with a purpose. Tessa stalled before beginning the manicure. She spent more time than necessary setting up her area and fussing with her tools. Fran watched these rituals without complaint. She had positioned the bottle of polish close to Tessa on the padded rest. Fran's hands remained on the table, anticipating Tessa's ministrations with patience. When Tessa saw this, she felt as if Fran had transformed the work station into an altar, a place where her jagged cuticles and careworn hands would be sanctified.

"Too young?" Tessa said. Her own hands felt unsteady. "I

wouldn't worry about that if I were you. Nail polish is supposed to be playful."

Fran smiled. "I suppose it's an odd question anyway coming from someone who uses a Barbie thermos."

"Yes, I suppose so." Tessa laughed and took Fran's hands, relieved by the absence of turbulence that could only be interpreted as a good sign. "Besides, I've always liked Barbie. I think she's unfairly criticized."

"I wholeheartedly agree," Fran said.

Tessa dipped a Q-Tip into a dish of warmed cream and slathered the pink concoction around the tired edges of each of Fran's nails. She rubbed the cream in well and examined each nail carefully, scowling at the cuticles.

"I prefer to just push the cuticles back, but I might have to trim some of these hanging pieces."

"Do what you have to do," Fran said.

Tessa took an orange stick and began to gently push back at the cuticles. Then she selected a pair of clippers from her tray and deftly trimmed the stray pieces of skin. She excused herself and returned with a heated washcloth. She pressed the palms of her own hands together as if in prayer.

"Like this, please," she said.

Fran obeyed. Tessa wrapped the warm cloth around Fran's hands and patted gently. After a few moments, Tessa removed the cloth and dropped it into a bin. She drew a deep breath and reached for Fran's left hand. First, Tessa massaged each finger and then moved to include Fran's entire hand. It was a large hand that immediately made Tessa suspect that Fran was comfortable with delicate work. It was Tessa's experience that people with small hands had notions about their own talents that far surpassed reality. The feel of Fran's hand was both solid and flexible. It suggested the sort of courage that was easily masked as perseverance. But Tessa knew better. This was a strong woman, and though Tessa usually tried to disregard what she felt when attending clients, her thumb pressed hard on the center of Fran's palm, probing for details.

"Are you looking for something?" Fran asked.

Tessa dropped Fran's hands.

"Oh, please," Fran said. She reached across the table and held Tessa by the wrist. "I'm sorry. I didn't mean to startle you. Continue. Please."

Tessa was suddenly very tired. It had been some time since she had felt so overwhelmed by simple contact.

"Are you all right?" Fran said.

"I'm fine," Tessa said. She felt confused, not at all herself. "I'm sorry."

"Don't be, please. It's all right."

"I know a bit of palmistry," Tessa said. "It's interesting in my line of work. To know palmistry, I mean."

"Of course," Fran said. "It must make the work more meaningful."

"It can."

"And it's so convenient. What you do and all. So lucky for you to have your skills so closely intertwined," Fran said.

"Yes, I guess it is lucky," Tessa said. "Though I don't really consider myself skilled in palmistry. I took it up as a hobby."

She was talking too much even though she was eager to change the subject, or to stay on it. She wasn't sure at all. All her wires had been crossed somehow, and the good feelings she had toward Fran were less generous now.

"I love to pry," Fran said. "Especially if I could go unnoticed."

She had said this as though they were confidants, and it chafed at Tessa's nerves. She was exasperated all over again.

"I wasn't prying."

"Yes, of course," Fran said quickly, trying to be conciliatory. She offered Tessa both hands at once, but Tessa tapped them, dismissing them. "How did you learn palmistry?"

"I guess you do love to pry," Tessa smiled. "And you're quite good at it."

"Tell me about myself," Fran said.

"I just did," Tessa said more pointedly than she had intended.

But she was curious about this woman, and reached for Fran's left hand, holding it in both her own. Fran's thumb was firmly jointed. She was, as Tessa had expected, a woman of rare will. Tessa assessed the length of Fran's fingers, noting that the third finger was unusually long.

"Do you paint?" Tessa asked.

"I used to. Oils," Fran said. "Miniatures. I don't anymore."

"I thought you might have some experience with delicate work."

"Most people assume I'm clumsy."

Tessa nodded and then scrutinized Fran's nails. They were shell-shaped and finely hued, but sorely neglected. She massaged Fran's hands again, one at a time, but this time without any reserve. She tugged at each finger, waiting for Fran to speak, knowing she would.

"Are you self-taught?" Fran finally asked.

Tessa ignored the question and continued to tug. "Do you prefer square or round?"

"You decide for me."

Tessa picked up the scissors and made one single cut across each nail, leaving each square. Then she selected a file and began to work, filing directly across the flat edge of the nail in one constant direction. Fran closed her eyes and seemed to be sleeping. She even kept her eyes closed when Tessa followed through all the same steps with the left hand. Neither of them spoke. Tessa first buffed, and then applied nail strengthener, and a base coat. Finally, Tessa unscrewed the bottle of polish and applied the first coat, using three strokes on each nail. One at the center of the nail, and then one stroke on either side. She applied a second coat, and still no word passed between them. Fran's eyes remained closed, giving Tessa full access to scrutinize every detail while maintaining a careful distance. She had few friends, mostly because the exchange of confidences that was eventually expected was not something Tessa easily shared. Yet now, in spite of Tessa's typical wariness, she wanted some assurance that she would see Fran again.

"You'll need at least twenty minutes to dry," Tessa said. Fran's eyes remained closed, but Tessa knew how to open them. "My mother taught me about palmistry. She felt it would be useful."

Fran's eyes flew open. Now, she stared at Tessa's face, but said nothing. Nothing at all.

"Do you like your nails?" Tessa asked almost too cheerfully. "The color is good for you."

"Yes, they're lovely," Fran said. She gave them a perfunctory glance. "Very shiny and all, but I can't wait twenty minutes. I simply can't wait that long. I really have to be going."

Tessa calmly watched as Fran soaked one cotton ball after another in nail polish remover and rapidly wiped the polish from each fingernail.

"There now," she said when she was done. "That's better." She blew on her damp nails and waved her hands about a bit. "I hope you're not angry."

"Not at all," Tessa said, though she was a bit stunned. She shrugged. "They're your nails and your money."

Fran stood and rummaged in her purse. She withdrew a five-dollar bill and placed it under the bottle of polish.

"Thank you," Tessa said. "That's very generous. And thank you for the soup."

Fran screwed the lid back on the Barbie thermos and dropped it into her satchel. She took a bobby pin off one of the nearby trays and secured a wayward strand of hair. The whole time, she kept her eyes on Tessa. Fran groped around in her coat pocket and withdrew a piece of tattered red ribbon.

"I found this. I want you to have it."

Tessa made no move to accept the offering.

"Take it," Fran said. "I understand it's good luck to find something red. I was told that you should never walk by anything red that you see on the street. You can wear it as an amulet if you like. It's supposed to protect you from enemies."

Tessa's mother, Ursula, had believed in amulets, curses and charms, yet nothing had been able to save her.

"I don't have any enemies," Tessa said. She kept her voice calm even though her heart was racing. "At least none that I know of."

Nodding ever so slightly, Fran dropped the piece of red ribbon on Tessa's work station. Fran was out the door before Tessa could find the courage to even ask what had brought her to the salon since it was evident she had not come to have her nails done. Tessa picked up the ribbon and ran out of the shop after Fran.

"Mrs. Hill!" Tessa called after her. "Take your ribbon!"

But Fran was already more than halfway down the street. If she heard Tessa, Fran chose not to answer. Tessa just watched from the doorway. It was hard to imagine what she was in such a hurry to get to, and Tessa felt almost envious about whatever gave Fran such a sense of urgency. Tessa strained for a last glimpse of Fran, but she was nowhere to be seen. Then, just as Tessa was about to turn away, she saw Fran, crossing the street against the light. The mesh shopping bag was dangling off her arm. One hand was held aloft to slow oncoming traffic, the other hand was pressed against her forehead as a visor to block out any glare as she scanned the ground for new treasures. And Tessa felt oddly relieved, as if what had been lost was now found.

Chapter Two

Soon after Tessa's seventh birthday, her mother took her on an adventure. At least, that's what Ursula called it, *an adventure.* She must have planned it carefully, which was unusual for her. Dennis, Tessa's father, was out of town on business, and Ursula's mother Lucy, who lived with them, was fast asleep when Ursula carried Tessa away in the middle of the night. Tessa remembered waking in the back seat of their car. Her mother had been cautious, belting her in carefully and tucking the blanket around her on all sides even though it was a warm night.

For the first few moments after waking Tessa said nothing, trying to get a sense of where they might be going and taking in her mother's mood. Ursula had an unlit cigarette dangling from her mouth and was listening to an Oldies' station. She was wearing a sleeveless fire engine red dress, and her elbow rested on the open window. Her arms were firm and tanned, and she seemed happy as she hummed along to the music. The next time she looked in the rear view mirror, she saw that Tessa's eyes were open.

"You up, angel?" Ursula said. Tessa sat up and nodded. Ursula told her not to worry. "We're going on an adventure."

What Tessa did not know, could not have known, was that their so-called adventure was precipitated by her father's desperate threat to file for sole custody of Tessa and to have Ursula permanently hospitalized unless she promised to take her medication consistently.

Ursula could not have known that it was an empty threat. Dennis would never have followed through even though he feared the worst, the very worst. He loved Ursula too much, and yet not enough. But that morning, Ursula was free. It was the summer, and everything was green and lazy. Ursula soon pulled over at a roadside diner. Before they got out of the car, Ursula helped Tessa change out of her pajamas and into shorts and a tee shirt. Ursula pulled everything, including socks and sneakers, from a big straw bag that was on the front seat. "I even brought your toothbrush and a tube of toothpaste. You can wash up in the bathroom before we have breakfast." She tousled Tessa's hair. "And Daddy says I'm not responsible."

Inside the diner, Ursula drank lots of black coffee and finally smoked her cigarette, taking one deep drag after another. She looked beautiful. Her hair was pushed out of her face and held back in a ponytail. Several of Tessa's fancy bobby pins kept the loose hairs in place. Ursula must have grabbed a handful of the pins for Tessa and stuck them along the sides of her own head for safekeeping. After they ate, Ursula lifted Tessa onto the hood of their car and combed her fine hair, arranging the pins in neat rows on each side of her head, congratulating herself out loud for thinking of everything. "I can handle this. I'm fine. I have everything under control."

For the first time since she woke, Tessa was afraid. Her mother's eyes were too bright, and her voice was too high.

Ursula recognized Tessa's apprehension and reassured her saying, "I'm fine. I just had one cup of coffee too many." Then she kissed Tessa once on each cheek. "We're going to see a friend of mine. She's from the center where I go for my appointments. She's nice. You'll like her. I promise, Tess." *Appointments.* That was the name they used for Ursula's visits to the psychiatrist. *Appointments.*

Minutes later they were off, driving up the New York State Thruway, passing villages and towns with names that Ursula said aloud, drawing out the syllables with exaggerated emphasis and making Tessa giggle. She was sitting up front now, and she kept checking the speedometer, just the way her father had taught her to do. *If Mommy goes above fifty, you scream. Fifty-five is the absolute limit, Tess. Thirty-five on the local streets. Got it?* Tessa breathed more easily when she saw they were cruising along at a safe speed.

Ursula knew what Tessa was doing, and she laughed and said, "You shouldn't spy on your mother like that."

But Ursula showed Tessa where to look on the map, and pretty soon they came up on the sign they were waiting for. Kingston. Route 28. Before long, they exited at Fleischmans, and Ursula followed some handwritten directions until she spotted the large, run-down house dotted with rickety fire escapes and said, "There it is!"

She seemed amazed that she had actually found the place. Mrs. Margaret's was a boarding house run by a stern local woman of the same name. Most of the guests were older women who escaped the sweltering heat of New York summers by buying a few weeks at Mrs. Margaret's. The accommodations were sparse, but there was plenty of company, and the mornings and evenings were cool and redolent with the scent of lilacs.

There were daisies growing along the dirt driveway, and a litter of new kittens trailed their mother. A large, white-haired woman came jauntily down the front steps, held out her arms to Ursula, and drew her into an embrace. "My dear Ursula, I hoped you were really coming. And this must be your Tessa," she said in a voice so heavily accented that Tessa thought the woman must be playing. Effortlessly, especially for her size and her age, the woman crouched down to make herself eye level with Tessa and shook hands with her. "I'm Amelia. Come. Everyone's getting ready to prepare for lunch. We have our cooked meal in the afternoon, just like when we were in Europe." She slapped her other hand over Tessa's, and pulled her against her sturdy body. "Come. We can get to know each other while we cook."

Ursula and Tessa followed Amelia into the huge kitchen.

There must have been ten women inside, all wearing aprons and chatting as they sliced and chopped and diced. There were multiple burners, and steam rose from the pots, while oil sizzled and hissed from frying pans.

"It's a communal kitchen," Amelia explained. "Some of us share the cooking, but others make their own meals each day. I made some borscht yesterday. We'll have it cold with boiled potatoes. We just have to fry the chicken cutlets. You can bread them, Tessa. I'll show you how. I made the cucumber salad early this morning with cukes and dill fresh from the garden."

Ursula was fumbling in her purse, looking for a cigarette, which she found and rolled between her thumb and forefinger. With her free hand, she tapped Tessa on the shoulder and said, "Mind if I step out for a smoke?"

Tessa shook her head, just a bit uncertainly.

"You help Amelia," Ursula said. "I'll be right back."

"Shouldn't we call Daddy and Grandma?" Tessa said. "They might be worried."

Ursula's voice had an edge when she answered, and she rolled the cigarette faster between her suddenly tense fingers.

"You just worry about yourself," she said.

Amelia put her hands on Tessa's shoulders and steered her in the direction of the sink where Tessa was instructed to wash her hands before she was placed at the big butcher block in the center of the busy kitchen. The other women were delighted to see a little girl, and they huddled around Tessa as if she were an exotic bird. One woman brought a stool over so Tessa could reach the butcher block more easily. Another woman draped an apron around Tessa's neck and folded the starched fabric over several times at the waist, winding the strings around three times before finally tying them in a big bow.

"My best apron," the woman said proudly.

"Thank you," Tessa said shyly.

All the attention was overwhelming. It was not long before Tessa forgot all about her father and her grandmother. She even forgot about her mother. The women had her buttering noodles, folding dough for *pierogen*, and frosting a cake. They called out warnings to watch her fingers and to keep the stool steady. Tessa nibbled on bread hot from the oven, savored bites of paprika-laden goulash, chewed mouthfuls of freshly grated cabbage slaw and sipped refreshing berry soup with dollops of homemade whipped cream. Before it was time to sit down to their meal, Tessa was sated.

She kept looking out the window for the swirls of smoke that she knew came from her mother's cigarette. Ursula did not come back inside for a long while. Finally, Tessa saw Amelia step outside. The smoke disappeared and Ursula followed Amelia back into the kitchen. It might just have been Tessa's imagination, but the kitchen grew quiet as soon as Ursula came back in. At first, the women eyed Ursula suspiciously, gauging her ability to care for their new little charge. And Ursula, who understood and appreciated their concern, smiled widely and genuinely at all of them before grasping a steaming potato dumpling between thumb and forefinger and taking a big bite. "This is incredible," she said.

Immediately, the bustle resumed. Ursula and Tessa were ushered into the dining hall and seated while platters of food passed before them as if they were visiting royalty. The day passed in a haze of wonderful food and endless stories about the countries the women had left behind.

Ursula was different while they were there. By the next day, she hardly smoked at all, and she slept through the night. Perhaps it was the comfort of so many women gathered in one place, doing what women did best, taking care of each other, that made the difference. Perhaps it was all the good food and the clean air. Perhaps it was the absence of her history to haunt her. After night fell, Ursula and Tessa swam naked in the lake. They played with the kittens, whom Tessa named after the women she liked best, Amelia, Margaret, Dorothy, Sophie and Lily. She thought fleetingly about her father and her grandmother, but they seemed far away to her.

One night, after she had been bathed by one woman, powdered

with scented talc by another, dressed and combed by still a third and, finally, read to by her own mother, Tessa fell into a deep and immediate sleep. But sometime in the middle of the night, she awoke.

Her father's voice was detached with controlled rage. "How could you, Ursula? It's no different from kidnapping."

Her grandmother was pleading with Ursula, trying to be conciliatory. "You should have phoned sooner. We were sick with worry, Ursula. You simply cannot stop taking your medication on your own and then just disappear."

When Tessa wandered in on them, rubbing her eyes, Dennis scooped her into his arms and pressed his face into her neck. "I'm sorry, Daddy," Tessa said. "I'm sorry you were worried."

Dennis could not hold back his tears. Lucy discreetly left the room.

Dennis went into the bedroom and took the blanket off the double bed that Ursula and Tessa had cozily shared with the kittens all week.

"I'm taking you home," he finally said.

Tessa cried. She wanted to stay. Her mother had been so calm and so happy all week. Tessa loved the kittens and Amelia and all the other women. And the food was so good, and so much fun to prepare.

"Let me stay, Daddy," she begged. "We're fine."

Ursula joined them in the bedroom and kept her eyes to the floor as she spoke. "I should have called. I'm sorry," she said. "I just didn't want it to end, the good feelings. I just didn't want them to end." And then Dennis pulled her so close that Tessa, between them now, could no longer tell where her mother's body began and her father's ended.

Chapter Three

Tessa waited for Fran to appear again, shopping bag in hand and wearing the same agreeable outfit. But Fran did not appear on Tuesday, nor did she materialize on either Friday or Saturday. By Sunday, Tessa was so confused by her own reaction that she decided to tell Walter about the strange woman who had come into the salon.

"I had the strangest client this week," she said. "She seemed to appear out of nowhere."

"Who was she?" he asked as though Tessa was deliberately withholding this significant piece of information.

As if on cue, Tessa sighed and said, "Never mind."

Walter narrowed his eyes and fixed his gaze on her with the sort of intentional restraint that comes from knowing someone well.

"You give up on me too easily, Tess."

She studied him with the sort of resoluteness she generally reserved for a particularly trying conversation with Regina.

"You need a haircut," she said.

"Ah," he said. "Diversion tactics. Very clever. I'm impressed."

He ran his hand through his almost completely grey hair. He was still handsome, still drew attention from women, both young and old. And while Tessa loved him, more than she had ever loved him, his pragmatism often infuriated her. No matter what they argued about, it always came back to these two issues: Walter's predisposition for prudence and clarity, and Tessa's reckless disregard for both, compounded by a lingering melancholy that left him with the feeling that he was in some way responsible.

"Well, *that's* something," she said. "It's not that easy to impress you."

When she had first identified Walter as the object of her love, everything had seemed possible. The world seemed renewed. But eventually she realized that no one, not even Walter, could change her past.

"I'm listening," he said. "Impress me some more."

"The woman who came into the salon," Tessa said, measuring

each word so that he would not misunderstand. "She seemed to know me . . . although I know I never met her before."

"How is that possible?"

She knew exactly what he feared. Her premonitions had the potential to alter the shape of their lives. He worked too hard to stay within the lines to invite any opportunity for variance. Walter did not want to know the future before it was upon him.

He had no investment in Tessa's intuitiveness. Any time she told him something that she sensed, he accused her of violating people's privacy. His response was not surprising. She had been groomed to hide her perceptions from everyone. Ursula knew better than anyone that it was an affliction to be out of the ordinary. She warned Tessa to keep her gift under her hat, often scribbling notes to her with "QT" in boldly exaggerated letters. It was advice that Tessa took to heart. She never allowed her presentiments to enter the forefront unless they were persistent, like the time she was having coffee with Janine, a neighbor, and an image of a pool and a toddler, floating face down in the water, began to hover near Janine's head. Almost faint with apprehension, Tessa asked Janine if she was thinking of putting in a pool. Janine laughed and said that she thought about a lot of things, but that, no, they weren't planning on it anytime soon. When Tessa asked if Janine knew anyone who had a pool, she said, yes, her sister-in-law had a pool. She was watching Janine's kids that morning. One of them, Malcolm, was only two.

"Call her," Tessa had said, trying to hide her panic. "Call her right now. I think the gate is unlocked."

For whatever reason, Janine did not question Tessa's urgency. Perhaps Janine was one of the few who understood and valued all ways of knowing, or perhaps she saw the fear in Tessa's eyes and responded. As Janine dialed her sister-in-law's number and began to speak, the images that had been floating above her head began to twirl. Tessa wanted to reach for them and contain them as if doing so would guarantee Malcom's safety.

"Mary? Is Malcom with you? He's outside with Leo? I think the gate to the pool is open." Janine had looked at Tessa. "I don't know. I just had a feeling. Hurry, would you? I'll hold on." She'd pressed her phone against her chest and in a faltering voice said, "She's gone to check." Janine held the phone to her ear and said, "Yes? Mary? Thank goodness. Don't cry. It's okay. Is Malcolm okay? Leo? I'll be there. Don't cry. It's okay."

Janine never asked Tessa how she knew though from then on Janine was mindful of Tessa in an almost reverential way. It seemed to Tessa that Janine could never do enough for her after that incident when all Tessa really wanted was to pretend that nothing out of the ordinary had happened. Of course, it was too late for that.

Later that evening, she had told Walter about the incident. He'd congratulated her and then said, "I thought you were going to put a stop to that."

Furious, Tessa asked him if he would have preferred that she let the little boy drown.

Walter had said, "Of course not," but they both knew he would have preferred that Tessa was not the one to divine the future.

It was a position to which he remained persistently loyal. Even now, the realization that Tessa felt something compelling about the strange woman worried Walter enough to make him take notice.

"How is anything possible?" she said.

She saw him bristle at this question. In some ways, Tessa knew, Walter was right to still distrust her. Though he insisted they were meant to be together, and that he had loved her from the start, she would never be certain if he would have loved her on his own, or if her crafty impositions on him had influenced their future.

"Who would know that better than you?" Walter said.

"No one, I guess," Tessa said. "No one understands the impossible better than I do. Is that the answer you're looking for?"

"I stopped looking for answers long ago," he said.

"Well," Tessa said, "maybe that was a mistake."

Tessa first saw Walter in a framed photograph on the piano in his parents' music room and immediately dreamed of seeing her own photograph included in the Jordan family gallery. Her own family gallery was scant and unsatisfying—a few snapshots of herself or her grandmother taken by friends at holiday gatherings with "Guess who?" scrawled in assorted unfamiliar handwriting. No one had ever bothered to date these pictures, making it even more difficult to place them. And while photographs of Tessa's smiling parents were displayed on the mantle in her grandmother's house, they seemed frozen in a time she could barely remember.

Mrs. Jordan, Kit to her friends, was Walter's mother, as well as the school nurse. When Tessa was a senior, she began to make constant trips to the infirmary. These visits had little to do with illness and more to do with the serious way Kit Jordan listened. Unlike Tessa's grandmother, Mrs. Jordan was always calm. Tessa complained of headaches and dizziness and was allowed to rest, sometimes with a cool compress on her forehead. Mrs. Jordan knew that Tessa's parents were dead before even checking a record. The rumors about Tessa's parents had almost mythical proportions in their village. And, as is the nature with all rumors, those about Tessa's parents were viciously exaggerated.

Tessa's losses had deeply touched Mrs. Jordan, and she offered the quiet, well-mannered girl a job babysitting her own Althea on Saturday nights. Althea protested that she didn't need a babysitter (after all, she was almost ten), but after meeting Tessa, Althea's objections stopped. They got along like friends, and Althea looked forward to their evenings together. Walter, Althea's older brother, was away in Chicago at law school, and Tessa began waiting for him to come home the moment she saw his photograph. She liked the way he seemed embarrassed by the camera's attention on him, yet still determined to have the last word. He had a sort of half-crooked smile that was disarmingly flirtatious—something that would allow her to later suggest it was he who had seduced her.

Tessa was seventeen then. She had been kissed by boys and had felt their excitement as they pushed against her, signaling their needs. But as soon as she saw the picture of Walter, she knew that everything up until then had been a rehearsal for her life with him. Walter would be hers. She thought only of him and waited. He would be everything to her. She would be everything to him. Everything. Together, they would have a perfect, normal family just like his. Her whole awful past would be vindicated by a blissful life with Walter Jordan and his flawless family.

Tessa knew exactly what Walter was worried about. It was always the same whenever anything occurred that referenced Tessa's insight. And even though he said very little on the subject of her mother, whatever he said, or didn't say, was always cautionary. He wasn't much of a talker, her Walter. Still, early in their marriage, he'd approached Lucy with his concerns. He wanted Tessa to thrust aside her preoccupation with Ursula's disappearance and focus on her own family. Walter told Lucy that he simply could not get through to Tessa. Lucy made repeated calls to Tessa, obviously at Walter's prompting, urging her granddaughter to remember her poor mother's end. "And think of the baby," Lucy pleaded. "Think of Regina." Tessa promised although she knew that no one had the power to conceal something if it chose to reveal itself.

And here they were, all these years later, still trying to make sense of that which could not be explained.

Walter tried to bring the conversation back to the unidentified client.

"I'm just attempting to understand why someone would come into the salon pretending not to know you when she does."

"There was just something about that woman," Tessa said. "I can't let go of it. She knows something."

"About what? Did you feel threatened by her?"

Tessa thought about Fran's soup and was immediately hungry for it again.

"No, I felt surprisingly relieved."

"I'm sure it was nothing," he said. "Just coincidence."

"Probably," Tessa allowed. "Just coincidence."

Unconvinced by her tone, he persisted. "How could she know you? Did you recognize her?"

"No. I just had the feeling that she knew me. Almost as if she'd been watching me for a long while."

"It's very unlikely," he said.

"I'm sure you're right," she said. "Very unlikely."

They looked at each other and looked away. Tessa picked up the newspaper and turned the pages though she stared off into the distance.

"If this is about your mother, Tess, I want you to let it go. Can you promise me you'll let it go?"

There it was. Walter had uttered the unmentionable.

"I don't make promises. You should know that by now."

"Make an exception." His tone was steely. Even he heard it and flinched, but he was staunch in his request. "Just this once."

The first time she met Walter he was home for Thanksgiving, and he had brought his girlfriend Charmaine. Tessa immediately noticed Charmaine's dark, exotic looks. Her hair hung like black satin across her broad shoulders and down her strong back. She was tall and athletically muscular; clearly, a woman who commanded attention.

Tessa ignored Charmaine and focused on Walter. It was as though he already belonged to her. *I want you*, she thought over and over. She said his name forwards and backwards, *Walter, Walter, Retlaw, Retlaw.* She repeated to herself, *I want you. I want you. Walter, Walter, Retlaw, Retlaw.* Her mother had kept a book of spells and charms hidden, but Tessa knew all about it. Dennis forbade Ursula to poke around in that magic nonsense, but she did anyway. It was such a relief from everything else she heard inside her head.

So when Kit Jordan told Tessa that they would not need her Saturday or Sunday, Tessa knew she had to act quickly. Soon Walter would return to Chicago. On Friday morning, Tessa brushed her fine, light brown hair and applied some mascara. She dabbed some blush on her cheeks. Her lips were good, full and surprisingly pink. And her nose was straight and strong, as was her jaw line, a complement to her long neck. She stared at her image in the mirror. She was still so colorless, so pale, next to Charmaine.

The Jordan home was in the most expensive part of the village, facing the Hudson River and the Palisades. As she walked, hating the cold and especially the winter wind blowing off the river, Tessa went over and over what she would say to Walter. The sun was so bright that Tessa made her hand a visor, shielding her eyes from its glare.

When Walter opened the door, he seemed momentarily confused, trying to place her.

"Theresa, isn't it?" he said. "Thea's nanny."

"Her babysitter. And it's Tessa, not Theresa." She hated herself for sounding so petulant. "It's not a very common name."

"I'm sorry. I'm not very good with names. Come in. Come in. It's freezing out."

He motioned her inside. She followed him, rubbing her arms through her coat.

"Everyone's out at the mall. Were they expecting you?"

"No. I wasn't expected." Tessa felt ridiculous. "I came to talk to you, Walter. I came to see you."

"Me?"

"May I hold your hands?" she asked.

"What for?" he said.

"Just for a moment."

"Are you going to read my palms?" His smile came and went as quickly as his next breath.

"That too," Tessa said with such conviction that Walter could think of nothing else to say.

He held out his hands, palms down, as most men often did, in what Tessa always saw as a final act of self-defense. Tessa took his hands and immediately turned them so his palms faced up. She rubbed each of her thumbs across the width of his smooth skin, jolted by what their touch roused. Her thumbs followed the same separate path across each upturned hand. First, she moved from his wrists slowly up towards the heel of his hand where she briefly lingered before cautiously exploring his Line of Life. She relaxed when she saw that it was both long and clear.

She closed her eyes to give her the courage she needed to venture across his Line of Heart. Yet even closed eyes could not divert the sudden pull she felt everywhere as she traced the course of her own future. He pulled back slightly, but she held on. She studied his palms. It was as she had expected. His Line of Heart seemed to spring from Saturn, just below the fleshy part of his middle finger, evidence that Walter could be self-centered. And there was more. His palms and fingers were slightly tapered. He would never be very good with money. Tessa found no surprises in Walter's hands. She had sensed all this about him the first time their hands grazed each other's in their cursory introduction. His imperfections did not concern her.

"Are you done?" Walter said.

"Yes," she said.

"Have your worst fears about me been confirmed?" he teased uneasily.

"Yes."

She could not yet tell him that palmistry was a ruse, a way to gain entry into the everyday world and quiet suspicions others might have about her. Palmistry merely verified what she already knew. Yet Tessa did not want to deceive Walter from the start, at least not completely.

"Sometimes I sense things about people," she said.

"I think they'll be back soon," he said nervously. "My mother, that is, and Charmaine and Thea."

"I sense things about you," she said, ignoring his warning.

"And I sense things about you," he said.

Walter, Walter, Retlaw, Retlaw.

It was as though he could hear Tessa's voice inside his head.

"Did you say something?" he asked.

Tessa shook her head.

"You're so pale," he said. "Do you feel well?"

"No. I'm fine. I'm always pale."

She worried that he was comparing her to Charmaine.

"Charmaine doesn't love you," Tessa said.

"I intend to marry Charmaine," he said, pulling himself up to his full height as if to defend himself against Tessa. "I've already told my mother. She's offered my grandmother's ring."

Tessa pretended she had not heard.

"I've never met anyone like you," he said.

"I know," she said so simply that it required no further response.

He touched her face, pausing briefly, before drawing back. In that fleeting, awkward moment, Tessa wondered if he was recalling Charmaine's exotically dark skin, her physical strength, and her self-confidence. Tessa knew she would have to rely on different attributes to win Walter.

"You lost both your parents in a car accident, didn't you?" he said.

"My father died in the accident. My mother disappeared," Tessa said. "I was told that she died some time later."

It was the first of many half-truths to come. She told herself it was different from lying. Looking back on that first time with Walter, Tessa wondered how different it might have been if she had told him the whole truth instead of a half-lie, half-truth—it didn't really matter which way she said it—not then and not later.

"Poor Tessa," he said.

"Yes," Tessa said. "Poor me."

"Maybe I've been too hasty about Charmaine."

"Maybe."

"Would you like to stay and have leftovers with us?"

"Yes," Tessa said. "I'd like that very much."

And there it was. The fairytale ending to the story Tessa had already written from start to finish. She had done nothing more than to allow Walter to play hero to her defenselessness. She had made herself vulnerable, allowed him to possess her. His family would embrace her, welcome her into the fold, and they would all live together, happily ever after. The ordinary existence she longed for was within reach at last.

Tessa and Walter had their own piano now; their own family photos as well, though none of them were of Walter's parents or sister. It was as though they had never existed. There were photographs of Regina at every stage of her babyhood. Several of her as a sweet infant swaddled in a pink blanket; another of her at six months, yawning widely and wearing a headband with a daisy on one side. And, Tessa's favorite, Regina smiling up at her from Grandma Lucy's arms. Regina's toddler years were captured in photographs of her in various Halloween costumes from the inevitable lime green lizard to the irresistibly endearing ballerina, followed by pictures of them at the beach with Regina in inflatable orange water wings. Tessa loved the photo of the three of them on a hiking excursion. Regina, strapped to Tessa's chest, facing forward, her chubby legs dangling from the carrier. Walter, standing behind Tessa, hunched forward with his arms wrapped around the two of them, making them appear to be some sort of mythical three-headed creature. They look indescribably content.

In later pictures, Regina, scowling and semi-toothless, her curls spilling out of a Yankee baseball cap, arms crossed defiantly, dares the camera with her flashing blue eyes. The photographs of her as an emerging adolescent, playing the role of Sarah Brown in a school production of *Guys and Dolls,* gave hints of the beauty that she would soon become.

Interspersed among these were pictures of Tessa as a serious child, standing between her parents or clinging to Ursula's side, arms wrapped around her mother's waist. One of Tessa's favorite pictures was her parents' wedding photo. Ursula, incandescent in a short, white eyelet dress, gazing up into the joyful expression on Dennis's face. They look luminous together, like every other young couple on their wedding day. It was this more than anything else that Tessa had always loved about the photograph. There was nothing in the photograph that foretold the future that would dismantle their anything but ordinary lives.

But Tessa could never deny how their futures had unfolded, just as she could not pretend that pushing forward with Fran might catapult them all into a place where no one wanted to be. Walter's love and commitment had been tested many times, and Tessa had to wonder how many more trials he could endure. She supposed they were about to find out.

"I think I have made a lot of exceptions for you," she said, giving the photographs a cursory glance. "And what if it is about my mother?"

"What are you saying?"

"I'm not saying anything. I'm just suggesting that there is something about this woman that can't be ignored."

"What exceptions have you made?"

"What?" Tessa said.

"You said you've made exceptions for me. What exceptions have you made?'

"I don't know. Lots."

"Name one," Walter said.

"I haven't turned you into a frog."

Walter laughed. "Well," he said. "The only explanation for that is that you don't know how."

"Don't bet on it," she said.

"I'm not a betting man."

"Now, *that's* not true either."

"I just want to say one thing," Walter said. "What if this woman never comes back to the salon?"

"That's not possible," Tessa said.

"But what *if*?" he persisted.

"She'll be back. It's only a matter of when."

"I wish you would let this go," he said. "You could make yourself unavailable."

Tessa didn't answer.

"Tess?"

She shook her head, not with spite, but with resignation. There was no choice, and there were no words to make that any more understandable.

Walter stood, looked down at her while his hand moved over her head, smoothing her silky hair. He bent all the way over and kissed the top of her head right where her part fell, exposing her scalp, and then left the room without looking at her or saying a word.

Once, a long time ago, Tessa had believed that Walter could change her life. She had believed that belonging to his perfect family would obliterate everything about her own flawed history. But the Jordans had never lived up to Tessa's expectations. On the contrary, they had betrayed her, leaving her with yet more loss to mourn. Photographs could be so deceptive, capturing a mere moment in time, not nearly substantial enough to invite assurances about the future.

Tessa walked over to the piano and looked at her parents'

wedding picture. Impulsively, she picked it up and held it towards the sunlight streaming in through the bay window. Perhaps there was something she had missed in her mother's eyes, her father's stance. But there was nothing. They were radiant, hopeful.

Gently, Tessa placed the photograph back on the piano. Something else was happening now. Tessa could feel the shift, the slight difference in the way everything felt. And it had everything and nothing to do with Fran.

Chapter Four

"Where's Dad?" Regina said.

Sometimes it was hard for Tessa to understand how Regina had turned out as she had. And sometimes Tessa knew it was the only way Regina could have turned out. Strangers were kind to her. Men trailed her like so many lost children. Even women wanted to be loved by her. But Regina could also be bristly, especially with her mother. Regina had always suspected that there was something about her mother that defied a simple explanation. And Tessa was as yet unable to help Regina find a way to believe that not everything had or required a simple *raison d'être* as Ursula had been fond of saying.

"He's here," Tessa said. "How was your day?"

Regina's face was framed in thick, blonde curls. A double set of dark eyelashes were, therefore, even more of a surprise. But then, Regina was a series of contradictions. Even her large, pale, blue eyes seemed an extraordinary achievement against her light, olive skin. Tessa gathered the sections of the Sunday paper and made a neat pile.

Before Regina could answer, Walter came in. He had avoided Tessa since their conversation earlier in the day, busying himself in the kitchen with the chili he had promised to prepare for dinner. It was one of the three meals he was expert at although Tessa did not consider beef chili and turkey chili two separate dishes.

Regina focused all her attention on him, pointedly disregarding Tessa.

"Hi Daddy."

Regina transformed Walter. Each time he set eyes on her, he was newly in love. And each time Tessa observed this, she fell in love with him all over again.

"I'm so glad you're home," he said, leading her to the couch. "What did you do with Marie?"

"I got a tattoo," Regina said.

"Oh, Regina," he said.

"Where?" Tessa said.

"At the place that just opened near the entrance to the highway," Regina said still averting her mother's gaze. "Marie got one, too."

"I mean where on your body," Tessa said. She tried to keep her voice level, but she felt her cheeks redden with anger. "I want to know where on your body."

"Calm down," Walter cautioned. "It's sort of after-the-fact, so let's deal with the reality."

Tessa glared at him.

"I don't want to be calm," she said. "I want an answer."

"It's no big deal, Mother. It's just a little tattoo. Here look." She stood, lifted her blouse and turned to display a bandage secured with tape at the base of her spine. "I got it this afternoon. I can take the bandage off now." She tugged at it gently, and it came off easily, revealing a tiny gold crown. "It's a crown. For a queen. Isn't that what why you named me Regina? It's just a little gold crown."

"We can see that," Tessa said.

"You should have asked permission," Walter said. "You know how we feel about tattoos."

"You would have said no," Regina said.

"That's correct," Walter said.

There was little conviction in his voice, and they all knew he would dismiss her imprudence. He always did. And it would be left to Tessa to deal with Regina's bold disregard for rules. It was always up to Tessa to mete out some form of punishment that would have little impact on Regina regardless. Regina always eventually did what she wanted to do, and Tessa ultimately saw her own role as protector rather than as disciplinarian. If she could not stop Regina, at least Tessa could try to keep her safe. Already, she worried about infection.

"I have a list of instructions about how to care for it in the next few days," Regina said, anticipating Tessa's concerns. "Will you help me, Mom? It needs to be washed, and I need to put cream on it a few times a day." Tentatively, Tessa reached out a finger and pressed it carefully alongside the fresh tattoo, knowing the area must still be sensitive. *I used to paint miniature oils.* Fran's voice had been filled with its own kind of longing. Regina's skin was warm. The crown seemed to throb beneath Tessa's grazing touch. Regina had been so congested as a baby. The doctors were frustrated. Nothing relieved her discomfort. One evening, Tessa had stripped her wheezing baby down to nothing but her bare skin, moving with certainty over Regina's struggling body, lightly pressing wherever instinct guided. Then Walter had called them healing hands, praising what he attributed to a mother's touch even though he knew it was more than that. Tessa quietly accepted his tribute, happy to have quelled Regina's wheezing, and to see her little body finally tranquil. They had all slept peacefully that night for the first time in weeks.

Regina dropped her shirt and spun around.

"Oh, Mom, please say you like it! Tell me you'll help me."

She wanted her mother's approval, but Tessa did not approve of either tattoos, or of deliberate disregard for her wishes. Still, she could not bear the thought of Regina getting an infection because her mother would not clean the wound. It would be up to Tessa since Walter had always been squeamish.

"It suits you," Tessa said. "I'll clean it for you before you go to sleep."

While Regina and Walter pondered this response in open-mouthed amazement, Tessa passed between them, ghost-like, and went upstairs.

She couldn't remember the last time she had given herself a manicure. Her tools occupied an entire shelf in the closet next to the bathroom. She chose carefully—a bottle of base coat, a buffer, cuticle clippers, cuticle cream, a nail file and an orange stick. Only the color of the polish gave her pause. There were samples of everything. Tessa closed her eyes and ran her hands just over the tops of the bottles, floating, estimating just how much energy to expend on choosing just the right color. Everything, even the most trivial matter, suddenly seemed like such a critical decision that she felt it necessary to parcel out her influence rather than use it all up at once on foolishness.

This was new to her. She had always just known where to touch Walter, how to mend Regina. Answers had always come to her through her fingertips. Her hands had always allowed her to interpret her world, make sense of what would otherwise be nothing more than white noise. And yet, now, the anticipation of Ursula's return made it feel necessary to hoard all feelings, all reserve power. Tessa expected she would need it all later to help decipher the years between then and now. She felt vulnerable, wide open to the elements, unable to even distinguish one color from the next. Just now, when her mother had come to say goodbye, Tessa wondered if she was ready after all. Her gift had no influence in matters of the heart. That, she now knew, was a domain unto itself. Tessa's greatest fear, after all, was whether or not she would be able to forgive an act of betrayal that still, all these years later, felt indefensible.

Fran had appeared the following Tuesday, looking disheveled, but earnest, and still clutching the same shopping bag. Tessa hoped for more soup, but there was none, and she felt momentarily rebuffed. Everything about the situation was odd—Tessa's need to see Fran and the uncharacteristic urge to talk intimately with a stranger. Tessa had even found herself wondering if Fran had been wandering the streets between now and her last visit, waiting for just the right moment to surface. Nothing about the events surrounding Fran made sense. Nevertheless, such enormous relief replaced all of Tessa's doubts when Fran finally walked into the salon that Tessa questioned her state of mind.

"I wondered when I would see you again," Tessa said.

"Did you?"

Fran set her shopping down with a flourish and began rummaging through it with such focus that Tessa was annoyed.

"What *are* you looking for?"

"Looking for?" Fran said. "I brought you a book, but now I can't seem to locate it."

"A book? What sort of book?"

"Never mind," Fran said. "It was just some silly book I thought you might like. You know one of those inspirational things. I don't know why I thought you'd like it, but it doesn't matter now anyway."

"What made you think I need to be inspired?" Tessa said.

"I think we all need to be inspired by something or someone, don't you?"

Tessa tapped the back of the chair, inviting Fran to sit.

"Frankly," Tessa said. "I never gave it much thought."

"Never gave what much thought?" Fran said.

"The need to be inspired. Isn't that what you were talking about?"

Fran slapped her forehead with an open palm, "Yes, of course. I'm so sorry. I get so easily distracted. Inspiration. Indeed."

"It's fine." Tessa pointed to Fran's hands. "Did you pick a color?"

"Yes." Fran pushed a bottle of orange polish towards Tessa. "I've been chewing on my cuticles lately." She winced. "Terrible habit."

"There are worse ones."

"I don't drink," Fran said.

Tessa laughed. "Well, *that's* good, I suppose."

"Though sometimes I wish I did."

Fran's hands felt heavy in Tessa's as she studied the damaged cuticles.

"Maybe you should drink instead," Tessa said. "You really went to town on these."

"Do you have any bad habits?" Fran said.

"I guess."

"Like?" Fran said.

"I can be very evasive," Tessa said sharply. "Sorry. I can also be a little gruff."

"No, that's fine. I ask questions that are far too personal."

Tessa began to minister to Fran's cuticles, rubbing oil into the skin with gentle, circular motions.

"Ah," Fran said, closing her eyes. "That feels lovely. Why did you get married?"

Tessa continued buffing the nails on Fran's left hand. "Talk about a personal question," Tessa said. She was a bit flustered, not so much by the question as by her willingness to answer. "Why do you ask?"

"No reason, really."

Tessa was skeptical, but she reasoned that her response would be in exchange for what Fran might eventually offer. It was a strange sort of trade, particularly since Tessa did not know what she was bartering for.

"I thought marriage would answer all my needs," Tessa said.

"A form of salvation?"

"In a way."

"How so?" Fran said.

"I was pregnant with Regina," Tessa said. She looked up to gauge Fran's reaction, but there was no judgment in her eyes. "I was very young, and I wanted my baby to have a family."

"What about love?" Fran said.

"Love? Of course, there was love." She considered her answer and added, "I very much wanted to be loved."

"Have you been?"

"Yes, I think so." She looked up again, trying to determine what it was about this confession that not only felt compulsory, but also an enormous relief. "My parents were in a car accident when I was a child. My grandmother raised me. I felt loved by all of them."

"That must have been very hard on you," Fran said. "You were so young to lose both your parents at the same time."

"Actually, my father died, and my mother disappeared. She called my grandmother once or twice, but no one actually ever saw her again. A few years later, we received word that she was dead."

"That must have been quite a shock," Fran said. Her voice was gentle, almost seductive. "It must have dashed all your hopes that she might still be alive."

"I don't know," Tessa said. She kept her head low over Fran's hands. A strand of hair fell into Tessa's eyes, and Fran, reflexively pulled her hand away from Tessa's hold and pushed the hair out of the way. It was such a motherly gesture, so reminiscent of how Ursula had always held bobby pins or barrettes in her mouth as she arranged Tessa's hair. *How can we see that pretty face when all that hair is in the way? Can you tell me that?* Tessa closed her eyes, just as she had done when she was little girl, remembering the feel of her mother's hands in her hair; her long, graceful fingers, and the slim braided gold wedding band that she never took off. Her nails were always perfectly manicured, beautifully painted in reds or pinks. Tessa had never felt so loved as when Ursula was tending to her.

Tessa opened her eyes with a jolt. "Actually," she said, so matter-of-factly that it was hard to hear herself, "it was a little easier after that, thinking she was dead, instead of just not interested in being my mother."

Fran's hands became so tense that Tessa had to tap lightly on her knuckles and tell her to relax. Finally, Fran let out a huge sigh and looked kindly at Tessa.

"It's hard to feel loved when you feel you've been abandoned," Fran said.

Tessa nodded, but she did not look up again. *Abandoned.*

"What about your husband?" Fran said. "Does he understand?"

Tessa dropped Fran's left hand and reached for the right hand, wishing the manicure was over. Usually, it was Tessa who listened while she worked, saying very little, concentrating almost exclusively on blocking out sensations. While occasionally Tessa interrupted a client's ramblings to make a suggestion (because it would have been irresponsible not to), she mostly kept what she saw close to her heart.

"No, he doesn't really understand," Tessa said. "But he loves me and wants me to be happy."

She peered at Fran's nails and seemed satisfied. The surface of the nails shone from the buffing, and she worried that she had been too vigorous. Carefully, Tessa dipped a cotton swab in baby oil to remove the excess dust from around the nails.

"And are you?" Fran said. "Happy?"

Tessa uncapped the bottle of base coat and reached for Fran's hand, but she resisted. She wanted Tessa's answer first. And although Tessa felt depleted from her admissions, it seemed vital to tell Fran as much as possible, though Tessa was not really sure why this was so. She pushed herself to answer because while she had thought about what she was about to say many times, this would be the first time she spoke the words aloud. A thrill went through Tessa as she rehearsed her answer in her head one last time.

"I thought I could reverse my history," Tessa said. "You know, change my future by changing my past. I thought that would make me happy forever. Of course, none of those things are possible—you can't reverse your history; you can't change your future by changing your past, and you certainly can't be happy forever." She smiled. "Can you?"

"No," Fran said. "Of course not." She extended her left hand and watched as Tessa applied the base coat. "You shouldn't be so hard on yourself. You were so young."

"I was born old," Tessa said. "My mother always said so."

She was almost certain this time that she saw Fran's eyes flicker with something more than compassion. Tessa frowned at the bottle of polish Fran had picked.

"Are you sure?" Tessa said. "It's really orange."

"I like it."

"All right then."

Fran cleared her throat and lowered her voice.

"I'm so sorry about your parents," Fran said. "It must have been very hard for you."

"Yes," Tessa said. "It was hard, but my grandmother did her best."

"I'm sure she did."

"Ursula was my grandmother's only child. Like me. Like my Regina."

"I see," Fran said. "And now?"

"Now what?" Tessa said.

"What do you think now, I mean about what your mother did."

"You mean running away?" Tessa said.

Tessa applied perfect, even strokes of polish on one hand before she answered.

"I think she thought she was being brave," Tessa said. "That was important to her for some reason. She seemed to feel that bravery made you noble. I had to promise that I would be brave. I guess she thought bravery would act as a talisman against the dangers of the world."

"And?"

"And she was wrong," Tessa said.

As a child, Tessa first had the usual aspirations of any little girl. She wanted to be a ballerina, then a teacher, then an actress. The day she announced she was going to become a Gypsy, Ursula turned rather abruptly from the sink and snapped, "You can't become a Gypsy, Tessa. You have to be born a Gypsy." Tessa had been startled. She felt very suited to the life of a Gypsy. After considerable thought, she solved the problem. She told her mother that she would marry a Gypsy boy. It was a rather grownup solution, and Tessa was proud of herself. But Ursula said, "I think not, sweetie." Then, when she saw Tessa's disappointment, Ursula relented, and prophetically added that it was almost impossible to know what was in store for anyone.

Tessa took to covering her head with colorful pieces of cloth that she found in her grandmother's sewing bag. Ursula also contributed a large gold hoop earring that Tessa eagerly snapped on to her left ear. She tied cloth around her waist, accenting her narrow little girl hips. Ordinary blouses and skirts were somehow changed into peasant costumes. Miraculously, all the blouses puffed at the waist, and all the skirts swirled when Tessa walked. Even Ursula had to laugh when she saw her daughter running barefoot through the house, a blur of colors that trumpeted her arrival before she descended, only to quietly contemplate her future as a Gypsy.

One morning, Ursula presented Tessa with a gift. She held out a closed fist to Tessa and smiled.

"For you," Ursula said.

She opened her hand and dropped a necklace into Tessa's cupped palms.

"It's beautiful," Tessa said.

It was a necklace of multi-hued crystal beads that Ursula had bought at the dime store, but Tessa knew its real value even though she was just a child. She held the necklace up to the window, and together they watched as the light reflected off the glass beads. Ursula took the necklace from Tessa and gently placed it around her neck.

"My sweet little Gypsy," Ursula said.

Tessa stepped back and spun and whirled between the shafts of colored light that moved with her. Ursula watched in silence. Suddenly, she began to imitate her daughter's movements. Together, they became one iridescent set of wings in a desperate search for sanctuary.

"Tessa," Ursula said as she dove and swooped. "I have to stop."

Tessa's heart raced. Her skin was clammy with the sweat of exhilaration, but she wanted to go on. She wanted more. Her mother pulled her to a standstill and took her by the shoulders.

"I'm glad when you're happy," Ursula said.

Tessa slowed her breath and wondered why her mother looked so sad. She almost always looked sad lately.

"I never know what to say to you," Ursula said. "I always seem to say the wrong thing. I'm sorry. I never want to spoil your dreams."

With one hand on her new strand of beads, and the other on her heart to slow its beating, Tessa spoke over restrained tears.

"You never spoil anything. I don't have to be a Gypsy, Mama," Tessa said. "I can be a teacher or a ballerina. I can. I really can. I won't marry a Gypsy boy. I'll marry a regular boy. I promise, Mama."

Ursula kneeled and took Tessa's face in one hand. With the other hand, she tucked a few stray hairs under the challis cloth wrapped around Tessa's head.

"You can only be what you were meant to be," Ursula said. "Don't be afraid. I've always been afraid, and I don't want you to be that way. But you don't have to be afraid. You know things. You really know. I want you to be brave."

A surge of sorrow gripped Tessa so deep that she thought it might split her in two as if she were a tree struck by a bolt of lightning. With a sob, she seized her mother in a ferocious hug and flattened both sweaty palms against her back. Tessa could feel her mother's skin through the flimsy cloth of her blouse, and what she sensed sent tremors through her.

"Promise me you'll be brave," Ursula said. "Promise."

"I promise," Tessa said.

Then she just cried and cried because she felt too much. The abrupt awareness of these emotions was a jolt. So sharp against her chest was every breath she now took that it seemed certain her senses had been honed on denial.

"You can be a Gypsy," Ursula said. "You can be a brave Gypsy."

"I don't want to be a Gypsy anymore," Tessa said as she yanked the necklace from her neck with such force that it broke.

The glass beads tumbled onto the floor in a riotous display of luminous colors as Tessa and Ursula watched.

"It's a beautiful afternoon," Fran said.

"Beautiful," Tessa said without as much as a glance out the window. She was trying to apply the final top coat of polish, wanting very much to be done with Fran. After all her disclosures, Tessa had reverted to her usual one-word answers. "Warm."

"Are you all right?" Fran said.

"Yes," Tessa said. She tightly screwed the lid on the bottle and set it in its place. "Done!"

"I'm sorry if I pried too much," Fran said. "Did I?"

"No."

"Are you certain?"

"Yes."

"My son, Philip, sometimes disappears. He usually phones, but this time he didn't, and I'm trying not to worry."

There was no way to respond with one word. Tessa knew she had been baited, but she could not resist. *Runaway. Fugitive. Deserter.* Those were the names Tessa had heard tacked on in the same breath her mother's name was mentioned.

"You mean he's run away?"

"I don't think so," Fran said. "Well, maybe he has, but I'm not sure."

"My mother always ran away," Tessa said unexpectedly, surprising herself with such a blunt admission.

Fran shook her head in agreement, as if she knew this already and while Tessa had stated the likeness with calm recognition, she felt a chill run through her, a warning that she could no more easily ignore than her dreams. She looked closely at Fran's expression. It was serene. There was no suggestion of her past in the soft fold of flesh beneath her chin. No indication of what her son had run from in the finely etched lines around her eyes. *Runaway. Fugitive. Deserter.* But as much as she had tried to defend herself, Tessa had felt the turmoil in Fran's touch.

"I guess we're all runaways of a sort," Fran said.

Tessa began to tighten all the caps on the bottles. It was part of her ritual at the end of the day. And while she still had several more clients to see, she felt the need for some immediate closure. She had said much too much already.

Chapter Five

Tessa was always puzzled at how few truly understood it was a blessing to escape tragedy, and an even greater blessing when things turned out well. She believed that the future was largely predicated on chance. One could strive to rearrange the universe, and yet nothing would alter what must happen. Delay it perhaps, but rarely change it. For any number of reasons, Tessa saw life, especially life with Ursula, as one seemingly endless Greek tragedy.

Ursula's favorite fairy tale was *Sleeping Beauty*. For a time, she read it to Tessa almost every day. In her own naive way, Tessa knew it was strange that the story they read and reread was not one that she wanted to hear, but one that Ursula favored. But Tessa never objected. Instead, she listened to Ursula read about how all the spinning wheels in the kingdom where Aurora Rose lived were collected and burned. Her poor parents, the king and the queen, hoped this would avert the witch's evil curse. The fires had burned throughout the kingdom. And Ursula had sobbed as she read aloud, already knowing the worst.

Poor little Tessa was incredulous each time that the king and the queen believed there was any hope that Aurora Rose would escape the curse of the wicked witch. Tessa always knew that there was no hope, no escape. The fairy tale was just another warning in a daily succession of omens. So when Aurora Rose heeded the seductive voice of the wicked witch and touched the needle on the spinning wheel, Tessa was stunned at Ursula's sorrow, wondering how she could have expected it to turn out any differently. But Tessa tried to comfort her mother though she knew nothing would ease her pain. Together, they stared at the picture of the bright red blood spurting from Aurora Rose's fingertip. "I warned you! I told you not to touch it!" Ursula moaned. Each time the princess was rescued from her eternal slumber, Ursula celebrated. But by that time, Tessa and Ursula were equally exhausted. Ursula stretched out on the living room rug and slept while Tessa curled up beside her, looking for some relief from the madness of life with her mother.

"Hey," Regina said.

"Hey."

Tessa was making dinner, chopping vegetables for a stir-fry. She smiled at her daughter, happy to see her.

"Isn't it early for dinner?" Regina said.

"I got home from work early and thought I'd get started. "

"Business slow?

"No, but I had two cancellations, so I decided to call it a day. How was your French test?"

"*Bon. Merci pour la demande.*"

"Impressive. What are you reading in English these days? Anything good?"

"Yes." Regina took a piece of red pepper and chewed on it thoughtfully for a moment. "Why the inquisition?"

"Inquisition? I was just trying to show some interest."

"So you're not really interested?"

"No, not really," Tessa said, her face completely expressionless. She held it for a minute before laughing. "Gotcha."

"Gotcha nothing." Regina said. "Like I would believe that for a second."

"You're not nearly as fascinating as you think you are," Tessa said. "I'm far more interesting."

"Well, I have something to tell you that might change your mind about that," Regina took a bottle of water from the refrigerator. "You'd better sit down."

"Oh?"

Tessa measured water and then brown rice into the pot before she looked up. "I'm listening." She reached for a wok from the pot rack. "What's going on?"

"I need your full attention."

"Oh, I'm sorry." Tessa set the pot down on the stove, checked the rice, and then immediately took a seat at the counter. "I'm listening. Are you going to sit?"

"In a minute." Regina was rummaging through her knapsack for something, emptying a dizzying assortment of notebooks, yellow legal pads, an iPod, a crumpled pack of Camels, mascara, lipsticks, eye pencils, tissues, a cell phone and, finally, a cream colored envelope with a printed return address. "Here it is."

"Here is what?" Tessa said. She was debating whether or not to deal with the issue of the crumpled cigarette pack. "Is that my lipstick?"

"Maybe." Regina tossed the letter onto the counter. "It's a letter from Aunt Althea."

"Really?" The senior Jordans had disappeared from their lives soon after Walter's graduation from law school. They sold their home and fled to Irvine, California. It was a devastating blow to Tessa on many levels. The Jordans, especially Kit, had embraced Tessa with so much warmth when she first met them. And Tessa had welcomed the attention, spending time with Althea even when Kit didn't ask. Kit had helped Tessa navigate the thorny issues of adolescence with more insight than her own weary grandmother could often manage.

When the Jordans abandoned Tessa and Walter, and then baby Regina, it seemed to Tessa that she had lost her family all over again. And while she loved Walter for establishing his loyalties from the onset, she often wished that he had been just a little more forgiving. In the beginning, Althea wrote them furtive notes, begging to be rescued, but it was not until she came back East to attend college that they saw her again. By then, she had been sufficiently poisoned by her parents' stories.

On her first visit, Althea paled whenever Tessa glanced her way. Poor Althea evidently believed that Tessa had bewitched Walter and irrevocably ruined the Jordan family. When Tessa confronted her young sister-in-law, reminding her of what good friends they had been and reassuring her that no harm would ever come to her, Althea nearly fainted. By the third visit, Althea began to hyperventilate as soon as Tessa entered the room, so Walter suggested they put an end to everyone's misery. As a result, the only family Regina knew was her great-grandmother, Grandma Lucy, who grew so frail that she was once actually knocked over in a snowstorm. Soon after that, she moved to Florida.

Every winter, Tessa, Walter and Regina made a pilgrimage to Boca Raton. Regina always insisted on bringing a snowball in one of her lunch boxes. They would wrap the snowball in foil and pack it in ice. When Lucy died, shortly before Regina's twelfth birthday, Tessa flew down alone to close up the apartment and to bring back her grandmother's body to be buried in the family plot alongside Tessa's father. As Tessa sorted through piles of old newspapers, coupons, and boxes of Lucy's medical records and investments, she found a shoe box filled with all the pieces of foil Regina had used to wrap her precious snowballs. The foil had been conscientiously smoothed and flattened first. More than anything else, this made Tessa cry.

"Really," Regina said. "Do you want to read it?"

Tessa reached for the envelope and peered at the return address. "San Francisco? Well, that's interesting. What does she say?"

"Read it."

First Tessa touched the dark brown embossed address, running her finger along the raised lettering, hoping to pick up something that might prepare her for what was inside. When she felt Regina closely watching, Tessa reached inside for the folded notepaper. It was only then that Tessa felt a slight flutter, more like a warning than an alarm. Althea's handwriting had not changed. Tessa could still recall the evenly slanted script that she had admired when she helped Althea with homework assignments. The top of the stationery was embossed with her initials: AJJ. Althea Jodi Jordan. Walter had called his sister AJ when she was very little, but she disliked the nickname as she got older, believing it was too boyish.

> *Dear Regina,*
>
> *I know you must be surprised to hear from me after such a long silence. I am sorry that I have not been a very good aunt. I am living in San Francisco, where I work as a curator for the San Francisco Museum of Modern Art. I moved out here to attend graduate school and stayed on. I wanted to put some distance between myself and my parents, and San Francisco always seemed so romantic to me. I was involved in a serious relationship for several years, but that has recently ended.*
>
> *Lately, I have been thinking a lot about you and your parents. I am coming to New York on some business and would like to see you—of course, only if your parents approve. I understand if they do not want you to see me, but I am hopeful that the years might have eased any bad feelings.*
>
> *I am guessing that you must be a junior in high school. I know so little about you that it is shameful. My email address and cell phone number are below. If my intrusion on your life makes you uncomfortable, you don't have to explain.*

Tessa looked up, expecting to find Regina staring at her, but she was calmly gazing out the window. Without comment, Tessa returned to the letter.

*Otherwise, it would be lovely to see you. I miss my brother
terribly.
I will be in New York the week before Christmas, so that gives
you plenty of time to come up with an excuse! Seriously, please
be assured that if I don't hear from you, I will understand.
Althea*

Tessa folded the letter along the crease and followed Regina's gaze
out the window. It was overcast. A man walking a dog stopped in front
of the house. An empty blue plastic bag from the morning paper was
tied in readiness to the leash. A jogger sprinted past the dog and its
owner, surprising both and causing the man to briefly lose his balance
and nearly fall over the dog. The jogger looked back over his shoulder
and seemed to shout out an apology of sorts that the man waved away,
evidently irritated. For as long as she could remember, Tessa had
watched similar dramas unfold outside this window. They had been a
relief from the dramas that took place on a daily basis inside her home.

"She sounds regretful," Tessa said. "Don't you think so?"

Regina turned away from the window, shrugged and said, "Do
you ever hear from her?"

"No," she said. "Not to my knowledge. Unless Dad does and
doesn't tell me."

"Would he do that?" Regina sounded skeptical. "Would he keep
that from you?"

"Possibly. People keep stuff from each other, honey. It's human
nature."

"I know that, but even something big like a letter from his sister?"

"Especially something like a letter from his sister."

Tessa didn't want to say how much she really kept to herself. Nor
did she want to reveal that Walter had once confided that sometimes
when he was with her, he felt as if he had walked into a room where all
the pictures on the wall had been tilted to one side. He could choose to
rearrange them or to walk with his head to one side. He said he had
come to terms with the reality that it was easier to keep his head to one
side. When Tessa said it was a silly analogy, he shrugged and tilted his
head all the way over his shoulder in mock exaggeration. To his credit,
he laughed with Tessa, but they both knew the seriousness of his
dilemma.

"Why is everything in this family such a mystery?" Regina said.

"Don't be so melodramatic," Tessa said. "No one has a normal family. Except maybe for Mia and Casey. We just *think* people do."

Mia was Tessa's closest girlfriend, and Casey was her husband. They had a son, Kyle, and a daughter, Megan. They lived in Portland, Oregon. Walter always accused Tessa of putting them on a pedestal, which she did, but rightfully so she maintained.

"But why did Dad's family move away?"

"I told you. Dad's father had a good job offer in California. It was a handy excuse to get away."

"Were they afraid of you?" Regina said.

"I hope so." Tessa winked, but she was not blithe about the subject of Walter's family. "I think this is an area that is best left unexplored. Evidently, Althea doesn't seem to miss me very much."

"I didn't write to Aunt Althea, Mom. Remember?"

"Yes, I remember."

Regina knew only the basics. She had no idea that when Walter graduated from law school, his parents gave him five thousand dollars and a new car. They promised him a Caribbean cruise and the down payment on his own condominium if he would join his father's practice and leave Tessa and Regina. His parents assured him that both girls would be well taken of and that his future was far more important than theirs. Although Tessa had looked bewildered and injured, the Jordans were indifferent. We can assure you, they insisted, we know what we're talking about. Think about your future. Tessa held the infant Regina so tightly that she squealed while Tessa searched Walter's face for any indecision. But he merely offered his father a thin smile and took Regina from Tessa's arms. His mother wept aloud. "All the stories were true," his mother wailed. "I should have listened. Now she's put you under a spell and ruined your future." Tessa waited, holding her breath as Walter said, "Tessa and Regina are my future." Mr. Jordan seethed, countering with his own prediction. "You'll regret this decision," he snarled.

Regina cried on cue as if she understood this insult to her mother, and Tessa waited to see if his father's words had ignited some recognition of the truth in Walter. There was nothing. Only love was in Walter's eyes, and Tessa turned away, humbled by his devotion. But when Walter then announced that he had no intention of practicing law, Tessa was astonished. She marveled at how easily he had already begun to exclude her. He had said nothing to her about this resolution. "I've decided to teach and to write poetry," Walter said. "A poet?" his father said. "Why not an Indian chief or a candlestick maker?" Tessa felt her knees go weak. *I went too far,* she told herself. She had encroached on his sensibilities with a vengeance, violated all natural boundaries, and now she would have to answer for her folly. None of that was true, of course. Walter had become a lawyer to please his father, but that no longer seemed possible. In a way, Tessa had freed Walter to be whatever he wanted to be, but she had been afraid that day. She had no viable skills to speak of, and they had a baby. But Walter had seemed so confident that day, so genuinely happy that she kept still.

"Why didn't they accept you?" Regina said.

"You know why," Tessa said. "We've been through this with you several times. I think they believed the gossip about my mother, and they thought I had some sort of power beyond being an intuitive."

"But there's more. There has to be." Regina peeled a banana and bit into it. "I know they didn't want Dad to marry you, and I know they were angry about me, but it all seems so, I don't know, bitter. Aren't families supposed to be loving and forgiving?"

"In a perfect world," Tessa said.

"That's what you always say."

"Because it's an answer that always fits."

"I haven't seen or heard from Aunt Althea since I was in grade school. Now, all of a sudden, this letter comes. What could have changed?"

"No one ever stopped her from calling or visiting," Tessa said. "It was her choice."

"But why? Isn't the timing strange?"

Tessa hesitated a moment, but only a moment. "I don't see the world that way," she said. "Synchronicity occurs with me on a regular basis. You think it's strange, but I think that not cooperating with the flow of events is even stranger. Althea's letter is actually perfectly timed. It's up to us now to uncover the meaning of what seem to be unrelated events, knowing that nothing is unrelated."

Regina bristled. "What's that supposed to mean, Mom? That's exactly what I'm talking about. You always talk in riddles. And this house . . . " She held out her hand as if the answer was in the room. "Doesn't it ever make you uncomfortable that we live here?" They lived in the house where Tessa had grown up with her parents, and then lived with her grandmother. The community had grown since Tessa was a child, and though some people still talked about Ursula and Dennis, no one treated the Jordans unkindly. They had used some of Tessa's inheritance to update the kitchen and the bathrooms, redo the deck and close it in, and even buy new furniture.

The house was small, but it was sweet and easy to maintain, and Tessa took pleasure in the familiarity. Her grandmother's biscuit recipe was taped to the inside of the cupboard where she had kept baking ingredients and where Tessa now did the very same. Although they had replaced the wallpaper with the tiny bouquets of red tea roses in the room Lucy had called the parlor, Tessa could see herself, seated next to her mother on the green silk divan, learning palmistry under her mother's tutelage. "Tell everyone it's only a parlor game," Ursula said. "Never identify your gift to anyone. People will try to take advantage of you."

There were those moments alone with Ursula when she was not overwhelmed by the manifestations of her illness, moments when she could speak candidly to Tessa and let her know that it was a source of pride to her that her daughter knew things about people she had no normal means of knowing. The house still held Ursula's energy, and there were times when Tessa could feel the mark of her mother's efforts to create some sort of harmonious balance between what she felt and what she knew to be true even if the source of what Ursula knew was from an entirely different place than Tessa's.

"No," Tessa said. "In fact, I'm quite comfortable here."

"Why don't you read palms anymore, Mom?"

"Whoa, I didn't see that coming." Tessa went back to her cooking, checking the rice, pouring some sesame oil into the wok. "Care to explain?"

"I don't know. What difference does it make?"

"No difference really."

"So?" Regina said. "What's the answer?"

"Well, first of all, it began to feel a little awkward."

"How so?"

Regina leaned against the counter, folding her arms across her chest as if to announce her readiness to hear Tessa's explanation. But Tessa could feel her daughter's reluctance, almost see it hovering above her head, circling Regina's curls as if to shield her from truths that might forever change her perceptions. Tessa was mindful of this presence, yet she also felt the need to pull Regina further along the precipice where she had finally dared to tread.

"Sometimes," Tessa said, "it felt as if I was recording a phone conversation without telling the other person. It made me feel dishonest."

"I could see that," Regina said. She smiled. "And let's not forget Dad, right?"

"Oh *that*." Tessa forgot herself then and said, "Poor Dad."

Shortly after they married, Walter saw that his father's predictions had come true. Tessa was indeed different, and it made Walter wary. He saw how Tessa recognized what was at the core of someone's sorrow, and he saw how she could make it better. Walter was a realistic thinker, the kind that society embraces, a top-down thinker who always did well in school. He liked getting the right answer. Someone like Walter would always be suspicious of someone like Tessa. She could never explain how she came by her answers. Instead, she learned to keep what she saw to herself.

Over the years, she honed her skills in private. Palmistry was merely a socially acceptable way to share what she already knew. But Walter found it all intolerable. Once, in a fit of anger, he had called her readings opportunistic, accusing her of taking advantage of others. He had denounced her as a carnival attraction, a roadside anomaly. He had no tolerance for what others sought in her, and he insisted that she put a stop to all that was certain to otherwise destroy their lives. Hard pressed to even talk about it, Walter tried to ignore the whole damned thing.

That was his way of referring to what Tessa could do: the whole damned thing.

Walter's standard approach was to ignore as much as he could. He hoped if he ignored something long enough, it would go away. But nothing ever went away. Tessa simply learned how to filter out what she sensed as if it were more noise pollution. Walter made her even more guarded of what she could do. And the irony of that was that Ursula never had. Tessa understood synchronicity now with an even deeper respect. The less she had allowed herself to acknowledge what she knew, the fainter her ability to sense and interpret the world around her had grown. Until now.

But Regina did not know her parents' history, so her persistence was not only understandable, but logical. She was like her father. They both need to show their work, to be able to explain how they had arrived at their answers.

"Don't you think he overreacts?" Regina said.

"Maybe," Tessa said.

"Maybe?"

"I don't think it's for me to say." Tessa said. "Anyway, I think Dad has probable cause to overreact if indeed he does."

"Are you going to tell him about the letter?" Regina said.

"It's your letter, Reg. It's your decision. And it's your choice whether or not you want to answer Althea."

"What would you do? Would you answer her?"

Tessa shivered a little though it was not cold in the kitchen. Her mother had always told her that when you shivered like that it was because a spirit was crossing your path. Tessa had always assumed the spirits must be malevolent, but she later realized she had filled in that part all on her own. It made sense, after all, to suppose such a thing when you had a mother who collected demon masks because she hoped to familiarize herself with her own demons.

"Mom?"

All Tessa had ever wanted was to be a good mother. It seemed to her that if she could be a good mother to Regina it would counteract all the terrible childhood memories that Ursula, through no fault of her own, had created. Once Tessa had cried out, "I wish you weren't my mother," and Ursula had been first hurt, then angry, and then hurt again before she rallied all her strength to dispense some small bit of wisdom for Tessa to take with her into the future. "Just remember," Ursula said, "even a bad mother is better than no mother at all." She made Tessa repeat the words, causing their hollowness to resonate. Even Ursula in one of her worst moments knew it was bad advice.

And now Regina wanted counsel from her mother, and Tessa hesitated because she was unsure of how to answer.

"Why don't you ask your father what he thinks?" Tessa said.

"Because I'm asking you."

"Okay, then. I would answer her. I would send her an email. That's easier than a phone call."

"Maybe a bad aunt is better than no aunt at all."

Sometimes Tessa wondered if she were merely playing out the inevitable sequence of events that was already scripted. It was so easy to jump to conclusions. That was what Ursula had always maintained. At first, the doctors had treated her for acute depression, but when medication after medication failed to alleviate her depression, she concluded (quite logically some authorities would agree) that perhaps she was sad because she had good reason to be sad. Ursula referred to her condition as "the proper sorrows of the soul," an expression she learned had been coined by a monk in the fourteenth century. "I have normal sadness," Ursula always said. Sometimes, she would sigh, wistful and self-deprecating all at once, and add, "It's the most normal thing about me." In the end, Ursula's normal sadness was too great for her to manage on her own, and she knew it better than anyone.

"Well," Tessa said. "I don't know about that, but maybe your Aunt Althea will be the sort of aunt you always wanted."

"And maybe she won't," Regina said.

"Your choice. Did you cut your bangs?"

"I did. What do you think?" Regina smoothed them down with her hand. "Are they uneven?"

"Next time let me do it," Tessa said. She reached over and planted a big smooch on Regina's cheek. "You're gorgeous no matter what."

"You have to say that. You're my mother."

"Indeed I am," Tessa said. She yawned. "I could sleep right now."

Regina laughed. "You always say that. You are weird."

"Let me have a look at that tattoo."

Obligingly, Regina lifted her sweater and turned around. Tessa tugged gently at Regina's jeans, exposing the tiny crown that was not only fully healed, but seemed to have taken such luminosity that it startled.

"I don't remember it looking quite so, oh, I don't know, three-dimensional."

"Does it?" Regina was still holding up her sweater, looking over her shoulder and trying to get a glimpse of her tattoo from that angle. "Do you like it?"

Tessa was riveted by the tattoo, so much so that she felt uncomfortably depleted just by viewing it.

"I do," she said. "It's so you."

Regina dropped her sweater and suggested that maybe Tessa should get a tattoo as well. Something visionary. A third eye or something like that.

"I'll consider it, "Tessa said.

"Call me when it's time to eat."

"I will."

It had started to rain, lightly but steadily, which would not have been surprising if the sun was not still shining. Ursula had once surreptitiously confided to Tessa that if it rained when the sun was shining it meant that a witch was getting married. And now, just as she had then, Tessa waited for the rain to let up or the sun to disappear. She knew far too much about incongruities to marvel at them.

Chapter Six

"That smells good."

"Does it?" Tessa tilted her head, proffering her cheek to meet Walter's kiss. "You must be hungry."

"I am." He reached over her and pinched a piece of chicken between his thumb and forefinger. "No lunch for a change. We worked straight through." He chewed and licked his fingers, and Tessa smiled because she still loved him.

"Everything is ready."

"Is Regina home?"

"She's in her room, doing homework. Or so she says."

Walter wiped his hands on the dishtowel, something that generally bothered her beyond belief, but she kept quiet, pacing herself. She would need Walter as her ally, and she knew he would be reluctant to minister to her needs once she fully disclosed her intentions.

"Is she okay?" Walter said. He tossed the dishtowel on the counter and opened the refrigerator, gazing contemplatively into its interior, often prompting Tessa to ask what he expected to find. "Perfect. Beer. I could use a cold beer. Want one?" Without waiting for an answer, he twisted off the top. "Do we have any salsa and chips?

"I'll have a sip of yours." She checked the rice, covered the pan with the chicken, and stirred the tofu. "I think there's some salsa in the fridge and some chips in the cupboard. She took a swig of beer from the bottle he volunteered. As he looked for the chips, she produced the salsa. "Was your day productive?"

In spite of his brief foray into teaching and his semi-successful attempts at poetry (he had published a few chapbooks that generated high praise from reviewers and readers alike), Walter loved law. He had inched his way back, renewing his license annually and maintaining his most valuable connections. By the time Regina was five, he was working for Legal Aid. From time to time, he would announce that he was going to leave and look in the private sector, but they both knew he wasn't cut out for that world. He loved his work, loved to be a hero of the beleaguered, and neither he nor Tessa had ever been greedy. In fact, the only area where they consistently could not find common ground was Tessa's work. He wanted her to find a different profession, one more suited to her abilities. They had suffered heated arguments over this with Tessa accusing him of snobbery. She knew, of course, that it was not condescension that drove him, but his wish that she not be exposed to the temptation to sharpen her intuitiveness. When she asked him what he would have her do instead, he fumbled his way through some halfhearted suggestions that included becoming a dental hygienist. Perhaps, Tessa surmised, he felt she was safer in people's mouths than if she held their hands. Their differences drove them apart for months.

One day a man came to the salon to have his back waxed. He was very young, even younger than she, and astonishingly hairy. Tufts of reddish hair peeked out from under his cuffs and showed through the top of his shirt. In spite of this, Tessa had discouraged him from waxing. She had pulled her long, thin fingers through the hair on his back and tugged gently, urging him to leave the hair as it was. It had been a long while since she had wanted a man so fervently. She could already feel the comfort of his heaviness securing her. As he lay down on top of her, she felt as if she were coupling with some mythological creature that was half-man, half-beast. "Minotaur," she murmured to him as she rubbed the hair on his arms. She allowed him to enter her because it was the only way she could find an excuse to sleep beneath his hairy body, which was all she had wanted to do in the first place. After a few weeks, he complained that she was a lifeless partner, and she lost her human blanket.

She told Walter, which was a mistake, and he threatened to leave her. Their fights were bitter and irreconcilable. One day she came home to find a note explaining that he could not make his peace with her deception. He had moved into a hotel for a few days. He needed time to think. She phoned him and tried to explain what it was about the man that had drawn her to him, but Walter, not surprisingly, was unable to understand not only her duplicity, but her calm rationalization, the brashness of her explanation. Tessa saw her own folly in expecting him to understand and promised to be like everyone else. Sobbing, she swore she would never again act on her impulses or indulge her eccentricities.

Three days later, Walter came home. She helped him unpack his bag and promised to be the wife and the partner he wanted. Walter was mollified, but the real source of his distress was Tessa's chronic sadness, her unwillingness to relinquish her hold over a past that could not be changed, and his grief that he could not make up to her what she had lost. He stayed with Tessa because he loved her, and because he believed she needed him to take care of her. "She's not one of your injured birds," his mother had snapped at him in one of her final pleas to break it off with Tessa, a reference to his childhood preoccupation with rescuing wounded wildlife. "You can't repair a girl like Tessa. She's too damaged." Of course, Walter had been staunch in his position. "But she's exactly like one of my injured birds." If the truth be known, however, Walter often wondered if his mother had been right about Tessa's inability to be restored.

Somehow they got through that awful period though Tessa wondered if he had pacified his injured ego with one of the many young law interns who passed through his office on a rotating basis. Each one was younger and prettier than the one before. Neither attribute really troubled Tessa; it was their intelligence and competence that threatened her. Their confidence made her shy, and she was awkward where she would have normally been self-assured. Regina was a convenient shield, proof of Tessa's worth as a productive human being. Once an intern (who could not have been much older than Tessa) noted that Tessa was so young to be a mother, and Tessa took it as an affront rather than as a compliment. Later, when Walter defended the intern's comment, Tessa lashed out at him and accused him of cheating on her, betraying their love with his lustful inclinations. She threw plates at him and threatened to leave and take Regina with her, someplace far away where he would never find either of them. Tessa's outbursts frightened him, but not as much as the thought that she would never be happy. He longed for stability and calm, neither of which had been consistently present in his life since the day he met Tessa.

They had been in a period of tranquility until recently. Walter seemed to savor these days, as if he knew they would not, could not, last. He had learned to ease into these interludes without question. Perhaps because of this, his senses were more alert than others, and he knew when the end of a good cycle was imminent. Stubbornly, he chose to ignore the impending warning signs and held on for dear life, hoping against hope to be wrong.

"Productive?" Walter said now. "Well, I guess so. I'm not sure anymore what that even means. There's just no way to stay ahead of the number of cases. It's endless. And the system is so backlogged that it's depressing."

She took another swig of beer and handed him the bottle. He shoved another chip loaded with salsa into his mouth and chewed contemplatively.

"I guess the only thing to do," he said, "is to keep your finger in the dam."

Tessa wiped some salsa off the corner of his mouth and kissed him lightly.

"What was that for?" he said.

"I appreciate your optimism."

"Oh?"

"Sooner or later, that stop-gap measure just ain't gonna work. Still, I guess it's good to have hope."

"And then what?"

"You know the answer," Tessa said mildly. She began to set the table, arranging the plates and folding the napkins, placing one alongside each plate. "It's always the same." She looked up at him and felt a twinge of remorse, but she brushed it aside. She had to. "Then all hell breaks loose."

Walter considered her prophetic words, nodded, then set his empty bottle of beer on the counter, took his tie from the back of the chair and left the kitchen.

"Tell Reggie dinner is served in ten minutes," Tessa called after him.

She waited for him to answer . . . even though she knew there was nothing to say.

They were almost done with dinner when Regina reached into the pocket of her jeans and pulled out the letter from Althea. Walter had already started to scrape and stack the dishes when he noticed the envelope Regina tossed onto the table.

"What's that?" he said.

"A letter." She pushed the envelope toward him. "Look at it."

Walter turned to Tessa as though she was already responsible for whatever calamity was about to befall all of them. Tessa, always a slow eater, was carefully spearing a piece of cooked pepper onto her fork, but she stopped as soon as she felt Walter's eyes on her.

"What do you know about this?" Walter said.

Tessa pointed at herself. "Me? Why do you ask me? I didn't write the letter. And I'm not the one showing it to you."

"I don't like surprises, "Walter said. "They never come to any good."

"It's a letter from your sister," Regina said. She pushed the letter closer to him. "Look at it."

"From Althea?"

"Why do people always do that?" Regina said though not to either of her parents. "Do you have any other sisters? Of course it's from Althea."

Walter didn't answer. Instead, he looked to Tessa for some explanation. "How long have you have known about this?"

"Since an hour or so before you came home."

"Why didn't you tell me?"

"Because it wasn't for me to tell," Tessa said. She finally ate the piece of pepper and then set about to pierce a rather large piece of broccoli. The vegetables were nice and crisp, just the way she liked them. "It's not my letter."

"You should have prepared me," Walter insisted. "You know that I don't like surprises."

"Why do you assume it's something bad?" Regina asked.

"Because it can't be anything good," Walter said. "Not if it's from my family."

"Well, that's encouraging," Regina said. "Do you want to read it or not?"

"Not," Walter said. He ignored the letter and waited for Tessa to eat the last piece of chicken on her plate. "Done?"

"I guess I am now," she said. "What's the rush?"

"I have some work to finish tonight."

"That's it?" Regina said. "You're not going to read the letter or even ask me what she has to say."

"I'm not interested," Walter said. He added Tessa's plate to the stack and stood. "I'm not Pandora. I have restraint."

Regina looked expectantly at Tessa, but she was as complacent as only someone who had first-hand experience with Walter's lack of curiosity could be. It was probably the single quality about him she understood least. If no one persisted, not only would he never read Althea's letter, but he would never ask about it again. Tessa initially found his self-control admirable, but she had come to see it differently over the years.

"Restraint?" Regina said. "I think you're a coward." Her face was flushed with the audaciousness of her accusation. "She's your sister. Aren't you the least bit curious?"

"Reggie!" Tessa said.

"It's okay," Walter placed a hand on top of Tessa's and turned to Regina. "No, I'm not at all curious. She made her choice long ago. But I don't appreciate you calling me a coward. You have no idea what my full history is with my family."

"I'm available any time you want to tell me anything at all about them."

"As far as I'm concerned, you know everything you need to know, Reggie," Walter said. He put the dishes in the sink and let the water run over them. "I don't see what the point is in talking about it."

"People change, Daddy."

"Actually, I don't agree with that."

"Althea is coming to New York. I want to see her." Regina took the glasses over to the sink and rested her head against her father's shoulder. "I'm sorry, Dad. I didn't mean to be so, whatever I was." She rubbed her cheek against his arm, and he kissed the top of her head. "It's sort of weird not having any family at all. "

"I can understand how you feel," Walter said. "You know, the grass isn't always greener on the other side."

Regina groaned as she always did when her father offered some tired cliché in lieu of a genuine answer.

"It's the truth, Reg," he said. "We always think other people have better lives than ours, but it isn't true."

"Some people must have better lives," Regina said.

"Tessa?" Walter said. "Anything to contribute?"

"No," Tessa said. "This is between you and Reggie."

"Oh, forget you," he said.

"Mom said I could do whatever I want, and I want to see Aunt Althea."

"I did say that," Tessa agreed. "And I meant it, too." She stood and scraped some crumbs from the table with one hand into her scooped palm. "I think it should be her choice."

She got up and took the kettle from the stove and went to stand next to Walter, waiting for him to move aside and give her an opportunity to fill it with water. He finally stepped aside, rather stiffly, and turned to give her access to the faucet. She was able to slip in and fill the kettle. The three of them were so close in proximity that for a moment Tessa felt a false sense of security. Their physical closeness was deceptive. They could not have been any more divided at the moment.

"See?" Regina said with a rush of victory in her tone. "I told you so."

"Indeed you did," Walter said. He placed the last dish in the dishwasher and turned to Tessa. "Are you making coffee?"

"Sure," Tessa said.

"Thanks," he said.

"There's some pie left," Tessa said.

"That's it?" Regina said. "Now we're going to have pie and forget about Althea?"

"No one's forgotten about Althea," Walter said. "If you want to see her, that's your choice. I certainly can't stop you."

"I want her to come here," Regina said. "For dinner. For a family dinner. And I want both of you to welcome her."

"Reggie," Walter said.

"We can do that, honey," Tessa said. She locked eyes with Walter. Neither of them blinked for several seconds. "You let her know that we would be happy to see her. Okay?"

"You let her know," Regina said. "I have her email address."

"That sounds reasonable," Walter said. "Your mother will be glad to do that. Right, Tess?"

Tessa set mugs out on the table. She knew what Walter was trying to do, but she would not be put off.

"I'll email her. I was once very close to her. I often miss her."

Regina pulled her father away from the sink and put an arm around each of her parents.

"Isn't this nice?" she said. "We can be a regular, normal family, can't we?"

"Depends on your standard of normal," Tessa said.

"We can be anything you want us to be," Walter said with more sarcasm than he had intended.

As soon as he saw Regina's disappointment, he was immediately sorry. "I'll do my best. I promise. It's just been a long time. A lot happened that I don't particularly want to revisit."

"That's in the past," Regina said. She kissed him on the cheek. "Everything is going to be fine."

"That's the spirit," Tessa said.

"I think I'll have my pie in my room if you don't mind. I have a paper to finish for tomorrow."

She looked happy, a little girl who had gotten her way. As soon as she left the room, Walter turned on Tessa. "You're going to invite Althea here for dinner?"

"Why not?" Tessa measured coffee into the Chemex and then poured boiling water into the filter. "Althea can't hurt me."

"What about Regina? Are you so sure she can't hurt Regina?"

"How would she hurt Regina?"

"We've spent a lifetime trying to protect Regina from the past."

"No, you've spent your life doing that. We're not criminals. It's ridiculous." She watched the water drip through the filter and waited before adding more. "We're haven't done anything wrong."

Walter took the Half and Half and set it on the table. He cut them each a conservative slice of pie. Careful, careful Walter. He was careful about everything. She filled their cups and sat down.

"I think Regina is right," she said. "We need to do this with Althea."

"Have you forgotten how terrified she was of you? They were all terrified of you," he said. "And they probably still are. I always took your side. Even when I had my doubts, I was on your side. But now . . ."

He was clearly agitated, clearly aware that he had more than likely said too much. There were no backsies in the game they were playing. They both owned the words now. Tessa had just been lifting her cup to her mouth as his words punctuated the space between them. Pausing to let the import of his admission settle over them, Tessa inclined her head faintly and with a very small smile said, "Well, you've been holding that in for a long time. Feel better?"

She had hoped to make him laugh, but when he averted her gaze a flicker of recognition went through Tessa. He was afraid of her too, still afraid evidently.

"And so are you," she said. "Terrified of me. After all this time, you're terrified of me."

He poured too much creamer into his mug of coffee and just sat there, staring down at the table. Tessa was sorry for him. She had hurt him, and now he was afraid she would hurt him again.

"I won't hurt you again." She placed a hand on top of his. "I promise. And I won't hurt Regina."

"I don't want to go back there, Tess." He looked up. His eyes were moist. "It was too hard. I don't want to lose Althea all over again. I haven't seen my parents in ten years."

"I know."

"They call me. Did you know that they call me?"

"No. I didn't know that."

"I don't get feelings the way you do. I had to choose, and I chose you and Regina. Things are pretty black and white in my world." He cleared his throat, took a sip of coffee and set the mug back down. "But I know something bad is going to happen. I don't know when, and I don't know what it is, but I know the catalyst for it is your mother."

Tessa nodded as she listened.

"You know how you hear those stories about bad things that happen to folks when they build a house on an old Native American cemetery? "

She loved that he said folks instead of people, but she kept it to herself and just nodded.

"I'm having that poltergeist feeling," he said. "It's coming at me in full force."

"Poltergeist?" Tessa said. "Is it my mother or Althea you're conjuring?"

"Be serious. This is serious. Do we need Althea back in our lives? Do we need to open the gates for your mother's return? Can't we keep them all out?"

Just as she was about to explain to him that you could burn all the spinning wheels in the kingdom and it would do nothing to change destiny, his cell phone rang. He answered it, listened, rolled his eyes at her and mouthed sorry as he left the room to take the call in his study. And Tessa pushed her mug aside and rested her head on folded arms. When Walter came back into the kitchen, she was gone.

They had arranged for Walter to drop off the car in the morning at the mechanic. The shop was near the station. He would drop Regina at school, take the train to work, and pick up the car in the evening. Tessa would take a cab to work. She had completely forgotten their arrangement until he reminded her in the morning. They said nothing to each other about what had happened the night before. Over breakfast, they talked about the car. When he bent over to kiss Tessa goodbye, he rested his hand on her shoulder. She patted his hand.

"Have a good day," she said.

"You too," he said. "We never finished our conversation."

"We never do."

He laughed, pretended to shoot himself with a finger aimed at his head and said, "I'll call you later." He turned and shouted, "Reggie! Time!"

Regina came down at a maddeningly slow pace, grabbed an apple and a yogurt drink from the refrigerator and took the five dollars Tessa held out. Tessa was rewarded with a peck on the cheek. Walter winked at Tessa as though they had shared a secret.

After they were gone, Tessa left the dishes and hurried to dress. She called the taxi service, went back to the kitchen to finish her coffee and put the dishes in the sink, all the while keeping an eye out the window for the taxi. She hated when they honked.

The driver, who must have been new, turned out to be blissfully silent, and Tessa was prepared to tip him generously for this until he started up a conversation. Ironically, he said experience had taught him that most people didn't like to talk much first thing in the morning. He was clearly foreign with a name that sounded like Dharma (but wasn't), and a melodic accent. Tessa inquired about neither.

But their hands grazed as she gave him the money, and she felt an urgent need to sustain contact. His skin was surprisingly supple, and she pressed against his palm with her fingers, holding his hand firmly, causing him to momentarily raise one eyebrow. A sharp pain suddenly pounded in her right temple and then, just as quickly, left. Tessa was relieved.

His wife was ill. The doctor suspected cancer. But it was a false alarm. It would turn out to be nothing more than a cyst. Tessa did not know any of these details, but she had felt, with startling clarity, the man's anguish and the source of his disquiet. She told him not to worry. "Your wife will be fine," she said.

The cabdriver stared at her. Then he bent his head all the way over to kiss the top of Tessa's hand. She patted his head, enjoying the luxuriousness of his thick, silky-smooth hair, and left the cab.

It was as simple as that sometimes. She could feel someone's pain as easily as her own. But more often than not, Tessa's ability to see what others could not seemed to have been diffused by resistance and disregard—her own, as well as others. She had grown comfortable with feeling less, likening herself to a dormant volcano and noting that there was no particular timeframe to classify dormancy. Regina had once done a report on Mount Vesuvius. It had not erupted since 1944, but volcanologists thought it could become active again. Tessa had listened, showing enough interest to satisfy, though all she could think about was her own potential to erupt. She actually believed that Walter would have sooner preferred molten lava flowing through his bedroom than a wife whose intuitiveness could jeopardize their existence.

That morning Tessa concentrated on her work with unusual intensity, fueled by the exchange with the cab driver. She listened as she filed and buffed and polished. Her head was tilted at the ideal angle for receiving, and she held each pair of hands with a light touch, eliminating as many barriers as possible. She eagerly massaged hand after hand, pressing into skin with confidence. Her own grasp seemed to take on new strength as she waited to withdraw the future from her clients' flesh. She worked at half-hour intervals, remembering to ask each client a pertinent question. *How was your grandson's recital? Did your interview go well? Is the deck almost done? Did you find a dress for the wedding?* The women were impatient for their turns. Tessa saw the way each client cast a furtive glance at her watch or looked out over the top of a magazine to see how much longer before she could take her seat. They all felt something in the air around Tessa. But Tessa saw nothing. She applied coat after coat of polish in mostly tasteful choices, except for one or two dreadful applications of yellow and blue, and a shade of lavender that was so lavender it could not have been called anything else.

Tessa warmed washcloth after washcloth in the microwave and said, "Put your hands together like this" so many times that the words seemed to come in a stream of connected vowels and consonants that made no sense whatsoever to her ears. She had been drawn into an impossible game of Hide and Seek with herself. By the end of the day, she understood. It was never up to her to choose in the first place.

Chapter Seven

Tessa had once spent an entire week rubbing a peach pit against a rock to make her mother a ring. When the pit finally gave, Tessa dislodged the small seed and swallowed it whole even though it was rumored to be poisonous. She felt courageous for facing this danger, but believed it was worth the risk. Her mother would feel protected whenever she wore the ring because Tessa's mysterious rite had secured a special bond between them. Ursula would understand this, appreciating the symbolism completely and fully as only she knew how.

When Tessa presented the ring to Ursula, she solemnly slipped it over her pinky finger, swearing to wear it forever and ever. The only time she would leave it behind would be if she needed a way to let Tessa know that something terrible had happened. It would be their secret symbol, like the Masons' handshake, Ursula explained. Even though Tessa had no idea what her mother was referring to, she listened carefully, nodding at the appropriate intervals. Eventually Ursula looped a piece of leather through the hole and, true to her word, always wore the ring as a necklace. If they were ever doing something neither of them really wanted to be doing but did not want outsiders to know, Ursula would touch the peach pit and smile at Tessa. It was their code, their exclusive secret.

The last time Tessa saw Ursula, she'd been wearing the ring. She was standing outside their house, arguing with Dennis, shouting, "I don't want you to come with me! Just leave me alone." Tessa peered at her parents from behind the living room drapes until her grandmother told her to come away from there. "Let them work it out," she said. "They will. They always do."

But Tessa already knew this time was different, and it was not only because fury had transformed her mother's face. Ursula appeared to be completely unhinged, and Dennis looked terrified. When Ursula dashed for the driver's side and tried to lock the door, Dennis was too fast. Tessa saw him fling open the door and shove Ursula over to the passenger side. Whatever Tessa had sensed was confirmed when she saw her mother wipe at the fogged passenger's window with her gloved hand, so that she might catch a final glimpse of Tessa. Ursula must have known Tessa was watching. But it was snowing so heavily that Tessa could not be sure if her mother saw her, waving madly and mouthing goodbye and goodbye until her breath fogged the window all over again. Tessa felt as if she were seeing her parents inside a snow globe, like the one with the ballerina in the pink tutu that was a gift from Ursula. Tessa almost asked why a ballerina in a pink tutu would be dancing in the snow before she realized it was this absurdity that had likely captivated her mother's attention. Instead, Tessa quietly agreed that the ballerina did look very pretty pirouetting through the falling snow.

Even after Tessa drew the drapes and covered her ears with her hands, her father's anguished pleas still echoed in the quiet. She ran to her bedroom, picked up the snow globe and shook it and shook it until the ballerina was entirely obscured except for a speck of pink that would not be concealed. That night was the last time Tessa ever saw her parents.

The peach pit ring was the first thing Tessa asked about when Lucy told her about the accident. Had anyone found it at the accident scene? Lucy, bewildered at the question, just kept shaking her head. She did not know about the symbolism of the peach pit ring, or about Tessa's dream. It had been accurate in almost every detail, except for the peach pit ring. In Tessa's dream, Ursula had left the ring behind as a sign. But there was nothing left behind, only Dennis' body, and Tessa's belief that she could have changed the future if she had heeded her dream. That evening, Tessa took her snow globe to the bathroom, held it over the sink, and forced it open. After all the liquid drained out, Tessa placed the globe back on her dresser.

"Walter?"

He was in the bathroom with the water running full force.

"Walter?"

The water stopped. The toilet flushed. He came out of the bathroom. He was naked and rubbed his wet hair with a towel.

"Is something wrong?" he said.

"Do you remember Charmaine?"

Walter stopped rubbing and took the towel he had been using to dry his hair and wrapped it around his waist. He remembered.

"Charmaine?" he said. "Yes. I remember her. Why do you ask?"

"I just wondered. Did you ever speak to her again after we got married?"

His expression was blank though his even tone when he answered suggested how guarded he felt he must be with Tessa.

"I think so. Maybe once or twice."

"When?" Tessa sat up in bed. "When I was pregnant?"

"I think so," he said. "I don't really remember. What is this all about now?"

"I was just wondering. Did you ever see her?"

"No," Walter said. "I never saw her again, Tess. Why do you ask?"

"I'm not sure either," she said. She met his level stare with one of her own. Neither of them smiled. "Don't look so grim, Walter." She smiled. "Come to bed now."

Walter obliged, but he did not move close to her as he usually did. He wrapped himself in the top sheet, leaving the quilt for Tessa. Tessa reached out a hand to place it on Walter's bare back and spread her fingers wide against his skin as if she felt the need to latch onto something solid.

"Tessa?" Walter said. "You asleep?"

"Almost," she murmured.

"Why did you ask if I spoke to Charmaine when you were pregnant?"

Fatigue was pulling her into the lushness of its core, but she resisted its lure and turned her full attention on him.

"Did you ever chase your shadow when you were a child?" she said.

He laughed nervously and turned toward her, gripping her wrist and placing her palm against his face. When he spoke, his words seemed to reverberate against her skin. "Yes, I chased my shadow."

"Did you ever catch it?"

She timed his breaths. It was a new means of communication. A Morse code of breaths, both short and long, some light and some heavy. He stuck out his tongue, like a frog, and Tessa wondered if her husband detected anything more than the salty sting of her sweat. She wondered if he could taste her fears.

"No," he said.

The answer struck against her skin, making her tense with expectation.

"No," he repeated. "I never caught my shadow."

He did not ask her anything, and she knew it was because he was always mindful with her, always readying himself for the unforeseen. In the stillness, she reached for him.

"You're like a succubus," he murmured.

"Do you want me to stop?"

"No. No. Don't stop."

He brought his tongue out again, gliding it between her fingers until her own breath quickened as his did against her hand. Then, as though he were shedding his skin, Walter moved out from under the sheet and pulled her beneath his body. Effortlessly, Tessa circled him with her arms and legs.

"I can catch my shadow, Walter," she whispered into his neck.

Walter's body lost its intent. Tessa knew that it didn't matter how much she tried to veil what she had to say in allegory, Walter already knew.

"What's going on, Tess?"

She wondered if she could distract him, make him forget that she ever initiated the conversation. Walter was so easily seduced.

"Tessa?" He moved away from her, sensing that she might try to dissuade him. "Tell me what's going on."

For a moment, she thought that she might lie to him. It would have been so much easier to lie to him. But the furrow between his eyebrows touched her—it signaled his distress. And though she knew what she had to tell him would only deepen the furrow, coerce his worries to a place front and center in his consciousness, she had to tell him.

"My mother is alive."

Walter had been quietly deferential when her hands quieted the baby Regina. He had even taken note when she subtly suggested an alternative to some new undertaking he was considering. But these occurrences were rare and hardly discussed. Walter never asked her guidance that would have called on her insights. He never sought redemption, only love. The poet in Walter, no matter how faulty, understood that there were feelings that could never be touched by words. And, on the contrary, Tessa understood that there were often no words for what she felt.

Instead of answering right away, Walter stared up at the ceiling. He closed his eyes when he spoke and said, "Jesus. Not this again, Tess."

Immediately, she sat up, hugged her knees and said, "You say that as though she's been alive before."

"Has she ever been dead? I mean really gone and dead. Ever?"

"Not for me, no, never really for me."

"You're inviting disaster into our lives," Walter said.

"I didn't invite it. It just happened to drop by."

"Of course. Things just happen to you. How foolish of me."

"Ah, sarcasm. Such an inviting prelude to effective dialogue." She let her knees go and almost toppled over. A nervous laugh rose in her throat like a tickle, and she made throat clearing noises instead of giving in. "Please try to understand."

"That's not fair," Walter said.

Just the other morning, he had reached for her favorite blue ceramic mug to fill it with freshly made coffee. The handle had come off in his hand as if someone were playing a trick on him, like a chair whose legs had been sawed off and then repositioned, creating a trap. Tessa had gasped, alarmed, as they had watched the bowl of the mug fall to the floor and shatter. When Tessa asked what happened, in a tone that suggested he would have an explanation, Walter had looked forlorn and said, "I guess it just wore out." They were quiet then, momentarily unsure what the other had heard in the summation that sounded more like a verdict than an observation.

"I'm warning you, Tessa, you have to let this go. I won't have you ruining our lives because you can't come to grips with the reality of your mother's illness. If she is in fact alive, it can mean only one thing—she abandoned you. We're better off without her. I feel the same way about Althea, yet you were so quick to give Regina the green light. I don't understand why you would invite the very people who caused us so much misery back into our lives, but I intend to stop it."

"Are you threatening me?"

Walter pulled back the cover and got out of bed. He was naked. Even when she hated him, she had always loved him naked. He followed her gaze and grabbed the sheet from the bed, covering himself like some archetypal virgin bride. He looked so silly, she thought.

"Threatening you? What are you talking about?" He shook his head. "Look at me. Am I a threatening person?"

"No, no, you're not. Not at all. I just need to feel close to you right now, and you won't allow it."

"I'm not so sure being close to you is the best thing for me." He clutched the corner of the sheet with one hand and ran his other hand through his hair. "Being close to you has had disastrous results in the past."

"Really?" she said. "Tell me more."

When Tessa stood, she did nothing to hide her nakedness. She was as slender as the day they had met. Walking kept her calves muscular, and lifting weights had made her arms sinewy rather than thin. Her skin was still pale; a faint pattern of veins gave her body the only color she had except for her oddly dark nipples. She turned and looked for her nightgown among the bedclothes.

"Tess," he said.

"What?"

"We have to be absolutely honest with each other."

"Absolutely honest? That never seems like a good idea to me."

"I may have pretended not to know what was going on, but I always knew."

"Meaning?"

"Why did you ask about Charmaine?"

"She just passed through my mind." Tessa found her nightshirt and slipped it over her head. "Evidently, she passes through your mind from time to time too."

"That's ridiculous, and you know it, Tess. Don't even go there."

"Why is that, Walter? Are you afraid I might put a spell on you?"

He didn't look afraid, only curious.

Tessa waved her hand at him. "Maybe I'll make you disappear." She made a poof sound and stepped toward him. "Abracadabra!"

"Funny," Walter said. "Really funny."

"Just because I picked up a little skill in magic from my mother doesn't give you the right to always use it against me."

"A cookie recipe is a little something you pick up from your mother, not magic potions. Your mother dabbled in mental illness, and you were a victim. It's time you got the story straight."

He turned away, dropped the sheet and stepped into a pair of old sweats. The grey ones, his favorites. They were like his security blanket, Tessa always teased. She waited for him to turn back to her, but he didn't. He sat back down on the bed, put his head in his hands and kept talking.

"Wasn't I always part of your plan to obliterate the damage done by your crazy mother and your dead father?"

Tessa narrowed her eyes and controlled her breathing, keeping herself calm. Their fights always went back to the same issues in one form or another. She forced herself not to cry, bracing herself for the conclusion of this confrontation. First, Walter would be remorseful; next, she would be unforgiving.

"I'm sorry," he said. "I know your mother was ill. It wasn't your fault, but it wasn't mine either. I'm sorry."

They were so predictable, Tessa thought, shaking her head.

"You have nothing to be sorry for," she said. "I pulled you into my life without sufficient warning." She sat beside him and rested her head on his shoulder. "I'm the one who should be apologizing. " She took his hand, and they interlaced their fingers. "The only certainty is that my mother is still ill."

His pulled his hand away, not spitefully, but with intention.

"I can't have this destroy our lives, Tess," he said. "We're always recovering from something. Since the day I met you, we've been trying to get past this."

"You say that as if I'm the enemy. I'm not the enemy."

"No?" Walter said. "Then who are you?"

She wanted to tell him she was the daughter of the woman who had been slain in the spirit. The daughter of the woman whose unpredictable life had impacted all of them. Ursula was the source of a chain reaction. Tessa had to live with the knowledge that she was the daughter of the woman who had believed it was better to leave her only child motherless than to have her grow up with the mother she had.

"I'm Ursula's daughter," she said.

It had been so long since she had said these words aloud that they felt foreign to her, and she was quietly proud that she had not stumbled over their pronunciation.

Walter started to say something and then stopped himself. He picked up his tee shirt from the floor. She stared at the swirls of hair on his belly, fleshier now than when it had first caught her attention, but still appealing. He hesitated, giving her one more chance to add something, anything that would make him stay. But she kept her eyes down, her mouth set. He left, closing the door behind him with deliberate care. Regina was asleep down the hall. Tessa refused to call after him. Now that she had revealed her identity, finally marked her place in the world, there was nothing else to say.

Religion had not been a consistent part of Tessa's childhood except for Ursula's random attachments to obscure religious traditions. Neither of her parents seemed seriously affiliated with any one particular faith although she suspected that her father might have been Jewish. He refused to have a Christmas tree in the house, and Tessa remembered that her parents had quarreled over this from year to year.

One Sunday morning, Tessa awoke, knowing that her mother was not home. The stillness was so acute that Tessa was certain her father was also awake in his bed, listening as closely as she was to the silence that had replaced Ursula. Finally, he had called out to her in his soft voice, "Tessa? You up?" When she called back to him, he said, "C'mon, baby. I'll get breakfast." His diction was so careful that no one could ever guess where he was originally from. Later, it seemed to Tessa that he had been determined to wipe out all traces of his past, and that whatever original accent he concealed was part of that subterfuge.

In her worn red and white striped pajamas, Tessa watched her father set about to prepare breakfast, surprising her with his know-how. He was tall and lean and very pleasant to look at. And while Tessa took after Dennis, he insisted she favored her mother. Maybe he just knew that Tessa would have preferred to look like her mother, or maybe the resemblance he stressed had nothing to do with Ursula's deep set grey eyes and richly hued olive skin.

Tessa watched as he held two brown eggs in the palm of his hand and cracked one after the other into a bowl of flour that he had measured out, carefully running the flat side of a knife along the top of the cup for precision. He added oil and salt and milk and then stirred the mixture. His shirt sleeves were rolled up and, for the first time, Tessa noticed that one arm was thinner than the other. He had a dishcloth tucked into the waist of his trousers, and he slowly wiped his hands on the cloth before speaking.

"Can you get me the griddle, honey?" he said.

Tessa could not have been more than five or six, but she must have already helped prepare hundreds of pancakes under her mother's watchful eyes. Tessa found the griddle in the cupboard and shyly handed it to her father.

"The secret of great pancakes is the temperature of the griddle," he said. "If you get it just right even the first batch comes out good."

"Is Mommy coming home?" Tessa said.

He didn't answer, but his eyes held Tessa's worried gaze for just a moment. Then, he turned up the flame under the griddle as high as it would go. The sudden smell of gas was quickly replaced by the aroma of the countless pancakes that had seasoned the iron griddle. Blue flames licked around its sides, and Tessa's father stared, waiting, a dancer anticipating his cue. Suddenly, he lowered the flame and poured four perfect circles of batter onto the griddle. He readied himself with a spatula, and as soon as the batter bubbled, he flipped each pancake high into the air and waited as it fell, one after the other, exactly back onto the appointed spot. It was miraculous.

"I was a cook in the army," he said.

It was the most intimate piece of information about his life that he had ever shared, but Tessa was too young to fully comprehend the extravagance of this disclosure.

"Is Mommy coming home?" Tessa was about to cry.

Her father pointed over to the dish rack for a plate, and she handed him one. Then he carefully removed the finished pancakes from the griddle and handed the plate back.

"Get yourself some syrup and butter while I make another batch," he said.

"What about Mommy?" she said.

He checked on the bubbling batter, adjusted the flame again and scratched the side of his unshaven face, leaving a streak of raw batter along his right cheek, Tessa noticed but said nothing.

"I don't know about Mommy," he said. "She gets funny like this once in awhile. You're too young to remember the last time, but she was gone about three days. She went off to find God."

The good and bad thing about Dennis was that he spoke the same way to everyone. It made no difference to him that Tessa was a little girl. He answered her question just the same as if she had been ten or twenty, or fifty or ninety.

"Did she find him?" Tessa said.

She held the butter dish in one hand and the bottle of maple syrup in the other and waited for an answer. Dennis frowned at the pancakes, adjusted the flame again and then steered Tessa to the table. He dressed the pancakes with butter and syrup and cut the stack into quarters before speaking.

"I think she found him and lost him again." He moved the plate toward her and handed her a fork. "Eat, baby. They're not as good when they're cold."

Tessa was surprised at how delicious the pancakes tasted. It did not seem right to enjoy them so much when her mother was gone. But the kitchen was warm, and she had her father all to herself. There was a peacefulness that Ursula's presence never allowed.

"Good?" he asked.

"Very good," she said.

He finished at the stove and set a plate of steaming pancakes on the table. He poured them each a glass of milk. Then he pulled up a chair right alongside hers and loaded up his plate, fixed his pancakes just as he had done for her, and ate. They finished their food in silence, wiping their sticky mouths at almost the exact intervals and making Dennis smile.

"Well, I guess you're my girl after all."

She smiled back because she did not know what to say, although she knew what to do. Her father's large hand did not fit inside her two small ones. Dennis did not resist. Tessa sandwiched his hand between hers as if she had caught some odd creature and could not decide what to do next. Another child might have been daunted by the mere weight of the limp hand, but Tessa set it down in her lap and stroked her father's palm with sure fingertips. They breathed rhythmically for a time until Dennis balled his hand into a fist and spoke.

"Don't," he said.

She was just a little girl who wanted her mother. She covered his fist with her own small hands as if she held a crystal ball.

"Mommy will be home soon," she said.

He kissed her forehead, touched by her need to reassure them both.

"That's good," he said.

By the time the dishes were cleared away and Tessa had brushed her teeth and dressed herself, they heard Ursula's key turn in the door. She looked calm and rested. More beautiful than either of them would ever remember her.

"I was slain in the spirit," she said.

Ever so slowly and tenderly, Dennis approached her, almost as though he were trying to capture a butterfly. Ursula remained motionless as he drew her against his quivering body and whispered something in her ear that Tessa strained to hear. She knew it had something to do with her because her mother nodded and walked purposefully to her side and kneeled.

"Did you eat?" she said.

"Daddy made pancakes," Tessa said.

"That's good." Ursula kissed her swiftly on the lips. Tessa liked the taste of her mother's lipstick. "Everything will be all right," Ursula said. "You'll see. Everything will be all right."

She was repeating the words Dennis had told her to say, but they were enough to console Tessa. She was just a little girl, and her mother was home. Nothing else mattered. Not even the feeling of dread she had experienced earlier when she touched her father's palm. The feeling was almost identical to the one she felt when she held her mother's hand for too long, like a warning burned into Tessa's own heart, a scar that would never heal.

Chapter Eight

Ursula collected spells and charms and mischievously entered them in a gingham-covered recipe file that was emblazoned with MOM'S FAVORITE RECIPES in primary colors. She compiled love potions, charms and spells because they were more tangible than the images and sounds in her head. *Light a stick of incense and hold it up straight. If the incense continues to burn for three minutes without dropping any ash, you have nothing to worry about. If it doesn't, it means he's up to something.* The charms and potions diverted attention from her madness; they were a way to make others believe her antics were the result of visionary wisdom—not the illness that had claimed her. And she truly wanted to help others. Ursula's heart was untainted by her illness. Once, after a long and terrible night of arguing with demons no one but Ursula could see, Tessa had watched her father bathe her mother's sweat-streaked face with a damp cloth as she writhed on the couch. Tessa heard him say, "I wish I could switch what's in your head with what's in your heart."

Strangely, however, Ursula's brews and mixes had worked more often than not. Maybe people just wanted to believe, or maybe it was Ursula, or maybe sometimes the magic was magic. *Make a stew of beef and lamb. Use plenty of marjoram and rosemary. But it's the garlic that really counts. It will keep the Evil Eye away. Don't forget to use salt. A generous pinch. When that's all done, file your nails over the stew just enough so a bit of the nail dust gets in. Then pluck a few hairs from all over your body and add it to the pot. No man will be able to resist you.* Tessa had stood on a little stool at their kitchen counter as her mother explained all this and mixed the savory concoction for dinner.

Together they watched as Dennis lifted forkful after forkful to his unsuspecting lips. Later that evening, Tessa saw her father sneak up behind Ursula and kiss her along her neck. She remembered the way her mother's arm had come up and wound itself around the back of Dennis's head, holding him against the place where her neck and shoulder met. They sent Tessa to bed early that night, and their laughter lulled her to sleep.

Just before she had met Walter, Tessa had felt the need to try one more time to see if her mother was really, really dead. She entered a notice in the paper on the obituary page, under *In Memoriam,* copying the style of other entries she had studied. *Emanuel—Ursula. Seven years and my heart is still aching. Send me a sign. I miss you so much. Tessa.* She had known it was futile, but she did it anyway. She had to. Just to be sure. For weeks, she waited for a sign. For a while, whenever the phone rang and no one was there, she picked up the receiver and said, "Mommy? Is it you?" Finally, she had made herself stop. And now, here she was, taking up exactly where she had left off.

Tessa knew she had to confront Fran. It was not coincidence that had brought her to the salon, nor was it mere happenstance that she had brought an offering in the form of a tattered red ribbon. It was clear to Tessa that Fran knew something about Ursula. It had been two weeks since Fran last came into the salon, and Tessa felt that if she waited any longer, she would lose her courage. It was the salon's policy to ask every client to fill out an information card in case it was necessary to cancel or reschedule an appointment. The information was stored on the computer. Tessa knew it was wrong to use the information for personal reasons, but she did it anyway. Ursula had always said, "Coincidence is the glue of dreams." She insisted that only genuinely crazy people dismissed coincidence as random occurrence. Ursula believed and understood that there was a whole world of intended occurrence that could not, should not, be ignored, and Tessa agreed.

Fran did not seem at all surprised to hear from Tessa. Nor was Tessa surprised when Fran invited her over for a coffee, even though it was a bit unnerving to discover how close she lived to the salon. Tessa walked to Fran's apartment in ten minutes.

"Thank you for coming over," Fran said. "May I take your coat?"

"Thank you for inviting me," Tessa said. "No, I'll just keep it on. I have to get back to see a client."

"Okay. Whatever you want."

It was strange to think of Fran walking past the salon, perhaps peering in and waiting for the right time, the right day to enter.

"So how long have you lived here?" Tessa said.

Boxes were piled up everywhere, more like a warehouse than a home.

"About a year, maybe a little more." Fran laughed. "I know it looks like I just moved in. Come on, then. The kitchen is the nicest room." She stretched out her arm, pointing the way. "I moved here from New Jersey after Thomas died. I felt as if I was rattling around in that big house. But there were so many things I couldn't part with, and now I don't know what to do with everything. I sold or gave away most of the furniture. I took all the things I could put in boxes with me."

Fran never mentioned her husband before or that she'd lived in New Jersey.

"We tend to accumulate far too many things," Tessa said.

"That's so true."

The kitchen was large for a small apartment. Fran had an oak table surrounded by five mismatched chairs.

"I'm afraid I'm addicted to garage sales." Fran smiled and pointed to a high-backed red chair that had sweet yellow flowers painted on its back and seat. "How does that saying go? One man's junk is another man's treasure? I guess it should be one person's. That would be so much more politically correct, wouldn't it? Here, try this one. It's the most comfortable. I don't always think about comfort when I buy something. I'm far more attracted to the odd piece, the one that no one else wants."

Tessa sat, but she was not really paying attention to Fran's chatter. There was too much to absorb.

"It's funny that I never saw you in the neighborhood before you came into the salon," Tessa said.

"Do you know everyone in this neighborhood?" Fran said.

Tessa had been fairly certain that her question would chafe at something in Fran, and her tone was proof.

"No, of course not. I was just wondering, that's all," Tessa said.

"I'm sorry. That was rude of me."

"That's all right."

"No," Fran said. "It isn't all right. I've been a bit on edge these last few weeks."

"Is it your son?" Tessa said. "You mentioned there were some difficulties."

"My son?" Fran filled the kettle with water and set it on the stove. "Well, that's part of it, of course."

"And the rest?"

"The rest?"

"Yes, the rest. You said you've been on edge."

Fran's back stiffened. She suddenly held herself differently, with greater reserve, more caution even. Tessa was exhausted by the effort of all this expectation and uncertainty. She felt her own body stiffen.

"You seem to be quite a bit on edge yourself," Fran said. "Are you feeling all right?"

Tessa's eyelids grew suddenly heavy. Her own mother had always been so tired. Tessa was tempted to close her eyes and drift off to sleep

"Tessa?" Fran gently touched her shoulder. "Are you all right?"

Mommy? Are you all right? You're scaring me. Say something. Please, Mommy.

Tessa opened her eyes and said, "Yes, I'm fine. I'm sorry."

The kettle began to whistle, startling them both. Fran took it from the stove and set it on a trivet.

"What can I offer you?" Fran asked. "Tea?"

"That's fine."

Fran's hand shook as she filled the teapot she had set down, splashing some of the hot water onto the table and forcing Tessa to stand and push away from the table rather abruptly.

"Sorry, sorry," Fran said. She dabbed at Tessa's lap with a dishtowel. "I'm usually quite calm."

Tessa took the towel from Fran, wiped the table and said, "I wish there were rules for how to proceed. It would help, wouldn't it?"

They had to look at each other because neither was able to turn from the moment. Fran's gaze was even, but kind when she asked, "What makes you believe that there are rules for everything?"

"Aren't there?"

"Only if you believe there is only one explanation for everything." Now Fran smiled. "Come sit with me and have some tea."

"Okay," Tessa said.

"Honey?"

"Just milk, please." Tessa chose a different chair this time. A green one with a seat cushioned in raspberry fabric and arms. Tessa supposed it was a side chair from a dining room set. She wondered what had happened to the rest of the set, leaving this one to be purchased independently. She settled into the chair comfortably and rested her forearms against the broad flat wood.

Sometimes she could read a life from an object simply by the imprints left behind. Ursula used to make her practice on the lockets, crosses, rings and watches that women left in her care, hopeful, always hopeful that the objects would become instruments of revelation. The women were mostly desperately in love, so in love, in fact, that they often never returned for either their treasured possessions or the answers they already had. And when it became clear to Ursula that Tessa could read objects the way an ordinary person pored over an ancient document for clues about the past, Ursula was sure the objects had been left for a reason. Jewelry, especially pieces worn daily, carried their owner's spirit. But Ursula carried her spirits with her all the time. They hosted in her mind, rejecting jewelry as frivolous. Ursula's spirits wanted her soul.

Tessa gently rubbed the worn wood of the chair's armrest, grateful for its prosaic history. She watched, without offering to help, as Fran made several trips, bringing two white mugs, a small cow creamer, a pot of honey, and finally a plate of sliced lemon cake. After setting everything down, she went back to the cupboard one more time for cake plates, one pink and one blue, and hastily rummaged in the silverware drawer for forks and spoons, also mismatched. A napkin holder from Sea World was already on the table.

"Sea World?" Tessa said as she took two napkins from the holder and folded one for Fran and one for herself. "A garage sale find or a souvenir?"

"No, I've been there. Have you?"

"Yes, several times, in fact. My grandmother moved down to Florida when the winters got too hard for her to get around here. She was happy there. I was glad though I missed her. She had a very hard and sad life. My mother's alleged death broke my grandmother's heart."

For a moment it seemed that they had come full circle to the place they both knew they had been inching toward. Tessa had taken the first daring step, and she held her breath, waiting for Fran's response.

"There now," Fran said as she surveyed the table. "I think we have everything. Shall I pour?"

"Please," Tessa said, more relieved than miffed. She opened a napkin and stretched it across her lap. "I'm very thirsty."

"Do you remember that I asked you why you got married? Yes? Well, I got married because I wanted babies," Fran said. She filled Tessa's cup first and moved the pitcher of cream toward her. "I wanted babies more than anything else."

Tessa drank greedily before answering. "Well, that seems sensible," she said, dabbing at her mouth with a napkin. "Babies are wonderful."

"Yes, but I couldn't conceive. I never counted on that. Not being able to have any of my own." She saw confusion transform Tessa's expression and added. "Philip is adopted. We adopted him as an infant. He was just days old. I was already forty. It was my last chance to be a mother."

"You must have felt very lucky to be able to adopt Philip."

"Yes and no. The situation was very complicated."

"I understand that adoptions can be very difficult," Tessa said. The information moved across her consciousness like a fire. "Was it a foreign adoption?"

Fran laughed and shook her head, "No, well, I guess it depends what you mean by *foreign*."

"What do you mean by foreign?"

"Never mind. I don't mean to be so cryptic. Tell me about your daughter." Fran placed a hand on Tessa's. "You said she was sixteen?"

"Seventeen." Tessa withdrew her hand and reached for a piece of cake. The pressure of Fran's hand made it hard to breathe. "She can be such a horror. Sometimes I can't wait for my Regina to be out and gone. And other times, I can't bear the thought of spending a day without her."

"I remember Philip at seventeen," Fran said. "It *was* horrible at times. But then they grow up, different problems take over, and you long for the troubles you left behind."

"Some people never seem to grow up," Tessa said.

"Like Peggy," Fran said. When she saw Tessa's blank look, Fran clapped her hands together and said, "You've never seen Peggy? I'm not sure how old she is. Probably older than you are. She's, you know, slow." Fran pointed to her head. "She wheels a stroller with a Cabbage Patch doll inside."

"No, I don't think I've ever seen her," Tessa said.

"You should keep an eye out for her," Fran said. "And be sure to talk to her. She's very chatty. I love the way she covers up her baby with a little pink blanket and stuffs the stroller full of toys. I've seen strangers stop, eager to admire the baby, and then freeze when they realize it's a doll, and Peggy is not who they thought she was either. It's something. And Peggy doesn't care one bit what anyone thinks. She's the mommy, and Rose is the baby. I always ask after Rose whenever I run into them. Once Peggy said that Rose had gas, so I suggested soy milk. Peggy assures me that Rose really likes me, and I believe her. Sometimes I watch them go off, Peggy singing, Rose staring ahead with the same fixed smile, and I'm jealous. I know they'll go home day after day. Nothing will ever change. Peggy's widowed father will have dinner ready for them. Peggy will bathe Rose in the kitchen sink and tuck her into a freshly laundered sleeper. Then Rose will be put to sleep in a cradle she'll never outgrow, and Peggy will never be lonely."

Tessa's mouth was so dry that she was unable to speak. Fran poured more tea into their cups, and they both drank quietly. Fran licked some honey from her spoon, and said, "Peggy's world is frozen in time. It's enviable, don't you think?"

"Only if you pick just the right moment," Tessa said.

"Yes, I suppose that's true."

"Tell me about Philip," Tessa said.

"I worry about him. He's been troubled lately, more so than usual. When he was a child, he trusted me. I could fix everything. I enjoyed the illusion of that power. It was magical." She leaned in toward Tessa and said, "A mother's love is the greatest magic of all, Tessa. There's so much power there. Don't you agree?"

Tessa withdrew involuntarily. Fran's energy suddenly seemed to overwhelm Tessa, and she said, rather half-heartedly, "Magic can be very destructive."

"Don't you have power over your Regina?" Fran said.

"Power is easily misused. Anyway, I think it's the other way around, especially these days." Tessa stood. She was still wearing her coat. "I really should get going. I'm sure Philip will be fine. He may be grown, but he still needs you."

"Not as much as I seem to need him."

"Well, that's only natural, don't you think?"

But Fran seemed not to hear. She was puzzling over her next question. Tessa could almost see the words forming, arranging themselves in some plausible form, already threatening her with their intent.

"Do you think there are any spells for that, Tessa?" she said. "Spells to keep mothers from needing their children after their children no longer need them?"

Moments after meeting Fran, Tessa sensed it was a harbinger of something that would not be ignored. But this was too much now. She felt enervated, devoured by what she could see and feel. Her mouth opened. She expected words would spill from between her parched lips, as if too much control had unleashed an overflow. Instead, she apprehended the words, swallowed them in great gulps of prudence.

"Why would I know about spells, Fran?" Tessa asked.

"I don't know," Fran said. "I don't know. I do know that babies grow up too fast."

You're growing up too fast. Ursula had hurled these words at Tessa over and over. So often, in fact, did Ursula accuse Tessa of what was only natural that she began to wonder how she could delay the inevitable if just to please her mother. For a long time after her mother's disappearance, Tessa naturally blamed herself. If only she had stopped growing, her mother would have never left.

"Why did you ask me about spells?" Tessa asked again.

"Why?" Fran brushed some crumbs from her sweater. "Do you know anything about the photon?"

Tessa shook her head.

"It's the tiniest packet of light." Fran held her thumb and forefinger up with just the most minuscule bit of space between them. "It can exist as either a wave or a particle, depending on how you look at it. Maybe that's the only way to explain coincidence, Tessa. A flaw in the tangled blur of cause and effect that we see when we look out at the world. That's the moment when the world looks back at us and there is no explanation for what we've experienced. It is a moment defined only by how we perceive it. Everything has suddenly changed, but nothing is different."

Coincidences are the glue of dreams.

"Are you telling me there is no such thing as a coincidence?"

"I'm telling you that I do not distrust the concept of coincidence. But I'm also telling you that in order to exist, a coincidence must first be perceived."

They stared at each other, not in an adversarial way, but as two weary travelers might, hopeful that they had finished the hardest part of their inevitable journey,

"I have to go," Tessa said without even looking at her watch. "It's late, and I have to get back to work."

"I understand," Fran said.

And Tessa believed her.

Tessa had lied. She knew Peggy. Everyone in the neighborhood knew Peggy and her baby Rose. There was no one explanation for why Tessa had lied to Fran. It had mostly been impulse, a way to maintain some control of her private life. And if Tessa had admitted to knowing Peggy, it would have also meant that she might disclose the details of their recent encounter. One evening as she was leaving the salon, Tessa had almost collided with her. It had grown cold, and the woman was fussing with a baby in its stroller. The baby was silent and motionless even as its mother tightened the pink blankets and rearranged the rattles and stuffed animals. A sack of groceries was in a basket in back of the stroller.

Their near-collision made some sort of conversation seem necessary, and Tessa had noted that Rose looked very warm under her blanket. It was the first time Tessa had ever spoken directly to Peggy. It was also the first time that Tessa had noticed that Peggy's face was slightly twisted to the right, and that she held her head at a peculiar angle. When she spoke, her bottom lip jutted toward the top. Her voice was garbled, but Tessa understood her without any difficulty.

"Baby Rose," Peggy said. "She's a girl."

Tessa had smiled and acknowledged that Rose was a beautiful name for a beautiful baby. Peggy had smiled shyly and said that Rose was her mother's name. The wind made them turn slightly in the opposite direction. Peggy clutched the stroller handle with two hands.

"You're a very good mother," Tessa said. "Rose is a lucky little girl."

Peggy's head moved rapidly back and shook uncontrollably for just a moment before she was able to place a reassuring hand on Tessa's coat sleeve.

"You're a good mother too," Peggy said.

It was exactly what Tessa had needed to hear.

The two women were standing in the middle of the street, the stroller causing passers-by to edge around them. Tessa said thank you, bent over the stroller, and with the top of her finger touched the hard, plastic cheek of the perpetually smiling Rose.

Tessa knew that in moments of coincidence the world seemed to be gently mocking the nonbeliever. She had never told anyone about that conversation with Peggy or about how Rose's cheek had seemed to yield when touched. Tessa could not be certain who was a believer and who was not, and so she lied to Fran. But Tessa was a believer because she could not be anything else.

Chapter Nine

She had lost heart. There was no denying it. And since Tessa had always believed that she lived to conquer her fears, she was disappointed in herself. Oh, of course, she tested her limits in the silliest ways, but she was aware of what she doing and why she was doing it. There was the trip to the market without a seat belt, and the occasional cigarette that she mooched off one of the girls in the salon. From time to time, she forced herself to stand too close to the edge of the platform while she waited for the train. All foolish (but not terribly risky) attempts to challenge the illusion of safety most everyone created to stave off the dangers that lurked around every corner. And around every corner in Tessa's world, Ursula was always there, waiting to reclaim her place in the life she had renounced.

Almost yearly since the accident, Tessa spotted some woman who might have been Ursula. Once it was a woman on the subway who stared at Tessa from across the car and made the sign of the cross over and over. There was something about the woman's stance. Her legs were positioned just slightly apart as she tried to keep her balance in the swaying car. Her hands, when she was not making the sign of the cross, hung limply at her sides, openly defying the pole for support. Tessa stared back. If it was Ursula, Tessa wanted her to know that she was not afraid. When the woman abruptly exited, Tessa almost followed her, but the condemnation in the eyes of the other passengers confused her because she could not tell if it was meant for her or for the woman.

Then just last winter, Tessa and Regina had been shopping in Manhattan. By evening, exhausted and cold, they waited for a cab. Regina was on the curb, huddled inside her coat, when Tessa turned, scanned the distance and noticed the woman watching them. It was hard to tell her age. She was swathed in layers of scarves and shawls that had been draped over two coats, one worn over the other. Both coats were black and shabby. But one bright purple scarf was tied around her head and then wrapped around her neck with such panache that Tessa immediately thought of her mother. The most ordinary dress took on elegance whenever Ursula added her touch.

The woman waited for Tessa to turn and then, unsmilingly, pressed a folded piece of paper into her hand. Their eyes met and held before they simultaneously turned to Regina. She had been watching. No one spoke. A cab mysteriously screeched to a halt, and just as mysteriously, the woman disappeared. In the cab, Tessa opened the piece of paper. *Esperanza carida. Angel. Angel. Angel.*

"What does it mean?" Regina had asked.

And Tessa had shrugged although she knew. Anticipate hope. Angel. Angel. Angel. Ursula had called her, my little angel.

Tessa said the woman was a stranger when Regina asked. But all that week and for many days afterwards, Tessa questioned the encounter. Anticipate hope. Angel. Angel. Angel. If only the woman had said how one should go about such a thing. Anticipate hope. Tessa had tried and failed. And now hope had been revived, and Tessa wanted to run from it.

Tessa decided to call Mia instead of running from hope. Mia Greene was Tessa's best friend. They had met in aesthetician school. Mia was everything Tessa was not. Mia was very tall, almost six feet. Her dark skin and black hair were a gift from her Cuban mother, and her Roman features her only legacy from her Italian father who left the family when Mia was only five. She was talkative, provocative, uninhibited; she used "fuck" as an all-purpose part of speech. When she laughed, everyone else laughed. Mia was a knee slapping laugher who couldn't resist repeating at least ten or twenty times whatever it was that had made her laugh in the first place. Just after graduation, Mia was hired to do hair and make-up on the set of a soap opera. It was good money, and the hours were reasonable.

Mia loved it. Tessa went down to the studio a few times to visit. It was exciting to see Mia in her trademark stilettos at work, towering over all the women and many of the men, shamelessly hopeful that she would be noticed and land a part, no matter how small, in one of the episodes. Mia never landed a part, but she met a handsome actor, Casey Nutley (Mia decided to definitely keep her own name), and three months later, they married and moved out to Portland, Oregon. Casey was sick of hustling the New York acting scene, and he definitely did not want to go to Los Angeles. They had been living out in Portland for almost fifteen years, and Tessa had been out there once. Walter and

Tessa had taken Regina to California for her tenth birthday and made a quick side trip to Portland so Tessa could see Mia.

From time to time, Mia came to New York to visit relatives, but she never had more than a day or two to spend with Tessa. Casey and Mia were busy with the drama school they had started for children. Mia did all the hair and make-up for the productions. They had two children of their own, a boy and a girl, Kyle and Megan, and they seemed like the happiest, most well-adjusted family that Tessa had ever known. Walter laughed whenever Tessa said that because he thought she was being naïve. "No such animal," he was fond of saying. "Even the Nutleys have their issues." Actually, Tessa thought he was a little jealous of Mia and Casey, and maybe just a little in love with Mia. Both made sense.

Mia and Tessa tried to talk a few times a month, but it was hard with the time difference to coordinate their schedules. When Tessa had time to herself, Mia didn't, and vice-versa. They had a shorthand that was preliminary to any real conversation. *Good time? Bad time? Yes? No? When then? Later? Tomorrow? What time? My time or your time?* It usually required planning to schedule a long talk, but Tessa needed to talk to Mia immediately. Tessa looked at her watch. Five o'clock. That meant it was two o'clock in Portland. Mia was probably still at work. The oldest group, the twelve to sixteen-year-olds were doing *Hair*, and Mia had last told Tessa that, "I am totally fucking psyched for this. You should so come out to see this show. Bring that stuffed shirt you call a husband and that vixen of a daughter. We'll have a blast." And Tessa said the same thing she always did, "Maybe. We'll see, okay?" They both knew she would never come.

Mia picked up on the first ring.

"Hey, Tessie."

"Mia?" Tessa said. "This has to be a good time."

"Then it is. Aren't you working today?'

"It's Monday. The salon is closed."

"Right, "Mia said. "Salons and bakeries. I always forget. So what's going on?"

"I'm in trouble, I think."

"No fucking way. You're pregnant?"

"No, nothing like that."

"You should have another kid, hon," Mia said. "You're young enough."

"Can we talk about this another time?" Tessa didn't wait for an answer. "Do you remember I told you about that strange woman who came into the salon?"

"The woman who brought you the red ribbon? The one who spooked you?"

"Yes, but she didn't spook me, Mia." Tessa laughed nervously. "Well, maybe just a little."

"More than just a little. Would you hang on?"

Tessa waited while Mia put her on hold. For a moment, Tessa was tempted to hang up. She had told Mia a lot about her childhood and her mother and even enough about the weird stuff to no longer be able to take it back, but it was so much work to confide in anyone. It always seemed to Tessa as if divulging a secret was like handing over a huge package and saying, "Here. Hold this for me, but I don't know when I'll be back." But Mia already knew more about Tessa than anyone else and never, not once, had she tried to get Tessa to divine the future for her. When Mia briefly struggled with whether or not to make the move to Portland, Tessa had said, "Go. Definitely go." It was the only time Mia had lowered her voice to a whisper (even though there was no one else in her apartment but the two of them) and said, "Do you see something, Tessie?" And Tessa had bent her head low and whispered back, "Only your happy face."

Now there was everything and nothing to tell Mia. It was all speculation right now. Tessa's only evidence was her gut feelings and a tattered piece of red ribbon. And besides, Mia couldn't really relate to Tessa's life. Everything always went right for Mia. She exuded good energy, and it always came back to her tenfold. The first time they met, Tessa imagined Mia with fairy wings and a wand, flying about and tapping everything and everyone with her wand, leaving fairy dust behind.

"Okay," Mia said, "I'm back." She inhaled right into the phone before she realized what she had done. "Shit."

"Are you smoking?"

"Shit, you're psychic," Mia said and laughed. "Now, *that's* funny." She inhaled again. "No matter now. I guess the proverbial cat is out of the bag. Relax, please, they're just clove."

"Clove cigarettes are still cigarettes, Mia, and you know it."

"Did you call to lecture me on the evils of nicotine?"

"No. I don't know why I called."

"Why?" Mia softened her voice. "Because even someone as guarded and suspicious and distant as you, needs to unburden herself from time to time. And who better to do that with than your old pal Mia?"

"I am not distant."

"You are, Tessie. Now spill."

She told Mia about the visit to Fran's place and how creepy it was that she lived so close to the salon. And then Tessa told her about the strange vibe she got when Fran talked about her son, and about how she had been leaving messages on Tessa's cell and how she hadn't returned any of the calls. She didn't forget Walter either. Tessa told Mia how Walter wanted it all to go away. Oh, and she told her about Althea and Regina, and how Walter didn't really want to see Althea.

"Did you email her?" Mia said.

"Not yet. I will."

"Well, you can't blame Walter for how he feels about Althea, or about how he feels about your mother."

"Why not? Why can't I blame him?"

"Okay, go ahead. Blame him for everything. I swear, Tessie, sometimes you're too weird."

"Sometimes I think you're right."

"Oh, honey, I didn't mean it like that. You know I love you."

And that was why Tessa had called Mia. Tessa knew Mia would say that no matter what Tessa said or told her. Unconditional love. The eternal quest. Mia told Tessa the same thing she had been telling her for years: follow your impulses. Run toward the light, not away from it.

"I'll try, Mia."

"Come for a visit. Just you. Come for five days. You could manage five fucking days."

"Is that alliteration?"

"Yes it is. Five fucking fabulous days!" Mia said. "I guarantee it. Come."

"After all this is over. I will. I promise I will."

"Okay. I'll take that. I never got an 'I promise' before," Mia said. "Are we square now?"

"Square. How are the kids? Casey?"

"Casey's great. He's happy with his work and with me. And the kids are cool. Kyle is learning how to blow glass, and Megan is in love, I think. We're all good."

"You all sound good," Tessa said. "Thanks for the ear."

"The ear and the heart and the soul, my friend." She blew smoke into the receiver. "How's Reggie?"

"She's fine," Tessa said. "Stop smoking."

"I'm trying. Oh fuck, what time is it?"

"Here or there?"

Mia laughed. "Either way I'm screwed. Got to run."

"Me too. I have a date with the grocery store."

"Love you," Mia said.

"Love you, too."

Before Mia had met Casey, she had lived in a tiny, fifth-floor walk-up in Greenwich Village. Tessa loved that apartment. It was so spare and filled with light. But what Tessa remembered most was the message on Mia's answering machine: "You have reached Mia. I'm not here now, but I'll be back. I'm out looking for love." Tessa was happy that Mia had found what she was looking for.

On her way to the car, Tessa replayed the messages from Fran. Tessa had saved them because in some way Fran's calm voice seemed to fortify her for what was ahead. The first message was almost cheerful, definitely unthreatening, but still firm. *Hi, Tessa, I'm sorry our last meeting ended so abruptly. Let's talk soon.*

The second message was more apologetic. *Tessa, it's Fran again. I don't mean to intrude, really I don't. But we need to talk. You know we do.*

And the last message was almost sad, tinged with a trace of hopefulness. *Tessa, it's Fran again. Are you okay? I've stayed away from the salon. Clearly, you prefer not to speak to me. I implore you to reconsider. Call me, please. Please, Tessa, call me.*

Tessa played the messages once, and then once again. She would call her later, after dinner. Mia was right. It was best to push forward with courage. Face your fears. That had always been Mia's motto. She believed that you could run, but you could not hide. And even if you could, Mia argued, what would be the point? Sooner or later, everything catches up to you. Tessa felt her past colliding with her present at record speed, and she braced herself for the onslaught.

When Tessa got home, she heard the water running in the upstairs bathroom.

"Regina?" she called out as she set the grocery bags on the counter. "Are you home?"

A toilet flushed.

"Reggie, honey? You there?"

"Mom?"

Regina's voice was weak. Tessa dropped her bag and hurried up the stairs to find Regina looking very pale. Her eyes were bright with fever, and she smiled wanly. Tessa grabbed her under the arms and said, "What's wrong?"

"I don't feel so good."

"I can see that. Come on, let's get you into bed and take your temperature. There's a lot of flu going around."

"I'm really, really thirsty."

"I'll get you some water. Come on now, baby. Let's get you to bed."

Regina was totally compliant. She let Tessa lead her to bed, and take off her shoes. While Tessa went to look for the thermometer, Regina dutifully changed into her sweats and a tee shirt. By the time Tessa returned with the thermometer and a bottle of cold water, Regina was already under her blanket and half asleep.

"Reggie, let me take your temperature." Tessa placed a cool hand on Regina's forehead and felt her fingers tingle, a sensation that typically heralded something waiting to be seen. But Tessa, relieved, saw nothing. Regina's eyes opened and closed. She looked like a little girl.

"I don't feel good," she moaned.

"It's the fever." Tessa said. She opened the bottle of water, grateful that Regina had either not sensed anything or was too sick to notice. "Drink some water." Gently, Tessa raised Regina's head. "Good girl. Drink some more. Good. Now let me put the thermometer under your tongue. Just like that. Just hold it there until the beeper sounds."

While they waited, Tessa gingerly pushed Regina's curls out of her face. She was so beautiful. Her face was blotchy with fever and damp with perspiration, but she was still beautiful. Just like Ursula had been no matter how her illness transformed her. Even when Ursula's eyes were hollow and her face swollen from medication, her beauty could not be disguised. It was there beneath the puffiness. At those times, however, Ursula's face seemed like a drawing in a coloring book; its original perimeters ignored, extended beyond its first intentions. But still beautiful. Always beautiful.

A chill went down Tessa's back even though it was warm in the room. What was that she had felt before? She closed her eyes, but she still saw nothing. There was just the faint tingling sensation in her fingers. The beeper on the thermometer sounded, and Tessa removed it. "101. Not too bad, but not too good."

Regina snored softly. Tessa went to dampen a washcloth and came back to find Regina wide awake.

"Hey," Tessa said. "I thought you were sleeping." She placed the damp washcloth on Regina's forehead. "You want some tea? Some soup? I think we have some ices."

Regina nodded.

"Ices? Good. Let me get you some Tylenol."

When Regina spoke, her voice was raspy. "What happened before? It was so weird. My head felt all tingly."

"It must be the fever," Tessa said automatically. She touched Regina's forehead again to prove her point. They both tensed, but nothing happened. "Does your throat hurt? No? Does anything hurt? I'm sure it's just flu of some kind, but your father will insist I call the doctor." She smiled. "I don't think it's necessary, but he's impossible when it comes to his girl." She pulled the cover up and around Regina and kissed her forehead. "Be right back."

When she returned with a tray loaded with supplies, Regina was fast asleep. Tessa set the tray down on the night table, and gently shook Regina. "C'mon, baby. I just want you to take two Tylenol. It'll bring the fever down."

Regina's eyelids fluttered, but her mouth remained closed.

Tessa tried again to rouse her. This time Regina opened her mouth, but not her eyes. Tessa lifted Regina's head, noting the dampness at the back of her neck. "Good girl. Now swallow. Perfect. You can sleep now." The ices were melting on the tray. "Just sleep."

As Tessa rose and reached for the tray, Regina's eyes flew open. She grabbed her mother's arm. "Don't go," she said.

"I won't," Tessa said. She sat back down on the bed and pressed the back of her hand to Regina's still hot cheeks, one after the other. "I'm here. I won't leave you. Just rest."

She felt like crying and fought the tightness in her throat. It was hard to know if it was because she felt so needed by Regina, or because of the vagueness that followed the earlier sensation. She simply felt overwhelmingly sad. Regina was still gripping her arm though she seemed to have fallen into a peaceful sleep. Tessa watched as she had done when Regina was an infant, reassured by the steady rise and fall of her chest.

The room grew dim, but Tessa, not wanting to disturb Regina, sat still even though her back began to ache. She reached for the cup of lemon ices, melting languorously, and lifted the spoon to her mouth, readying herself for the first taste of the sour sweetness.

"I thought that was for me," Regina said.

Tessa gasped. "You nearly gave me a heart attack."

"Sorry Mom."

"Want it?"

Tessa took the spoon off the tray and began to feed her small mouthfuls. Neither of them said anything until the cup was empty.

"Do you want more?" Tessa said.

"Not now. Thanks."

"How do you feel?"

"Pretty lousy. I thought I was going to die."

"Well, I'm glad you didn't."

"Me too."

"Do you want some water?" Tessa said.

"No. No water."

Regina closed her eyes and turned her head away. And that was when Tessa knew her daughter was hiding something. The sensation had been a portent of some disclosure that was imminent. Tessa waited. It was coming.

"There's something in my night table drawer that you might want to see," Regina said. She pointed as if Tessa did not know where the night table was. "In there. Open it."

Tessa opened the drawer and took out a pair of long black dinner gloves. They were very soft, some combination of cotton and satin. They were even more worn than Tessa remembered, but their scent was still present after all this time, flowery and inviting. The lump in Tessa's throat tightened.

The gloves had been one of Ursula's treasured Goodwill finds. Regina must have been rummaging in Tessa's bedroom dresser drawers where she kept the journals and other miscellaneous bits and pieces of Ursula's life . . . like the gloves. She kept these things in the deep corner of her bottom dresser drawer beneath a bunch of sweaters she never wore but kept because they created a convenient cache. Regina often wore Tessa's clothes without asking, but the gloves were different. Tessa kept the gloves separate in a satin pouch. Regina must have known the gloves were off-limits as soon as she discovered them. But she could not have known they were the only remnants of a

Goodwill shopping spree that had been one of Tessa's favorite ways to spend time with Ursula.

"I'm sorry, "Regina said. "I shouldn't have been snooping."

Tessa nodded, but she could not yet speak. She fingered the worn fabric, marveled at the pearl fastenings. When Ursula had been in a manic cycle, she had loved to shop at Goodwill for startling ensembles. She called the loose change and single dollars saved for these outings and stored in an old coffee can, her mad *mad* money. Even Dennis laughed when she said this. One of her favorite purchases had been this pair of long, black satiny dinner gloves with fake pearl buttons.

The day Ursula bought the gloves had been unusually successful. She found a black wool coat with a brown lamb's wool collar for five dollars. She picked a purple hat with a veil to go with the coat and a short red leather skirt. After a time, she settled on a sheer nylon blouse that had pink rose buttons. And though she had not been looking for gloves when she found them, she smiled, delighted, and said how perfectly they went with everything.

While Ursula squirmed and talked excitedly, Tessa helped her pull the gloves up over her forearms and fasten the pearl button at each elbow. When Tessa was finished, Ursula held out her hands at arms' length and said, "I just adore these gloves. Don't you?"

Tessa agreed. The gloves were spectacular. She touched the fake pearls and ran her hand over the soft, black cotton. Seeing Tessa's worshipful expression, Ursula pulled off the gloves and tossed them to Tessa.

"Let's find something snazzy to go with these gloves. They'll look even better on you." Ursula hugged Tessa until she squealed. Then Ursula said, "Enough. We have work to do." She found a short fake leopard skin jacket and a matching muff, and Tessa came up with a pair of orange bell-bottoms, a white cashmere sweater (with only a small hole under the left arm), and an orange beret. They watched as the clerk stuffed their purchases in a garbage bag she peeled off a roll.

As soon as they got home, they changed into their new outfits. Some hours later, when Dennis arrived, they were still fully outfitted. When Tessa tentatively asked her father if he liked their new clothes, he smiled a thin, tight smile. He knew better than anyone what the shopping spree suggested. Ursula would soon be catapulted into a depression, the cycle that always followed one of her manic phases. He was already steeling himself against the inevitable, wondering what he could do to stave off its onset. The next day, everything had mysteriously disappeared, except for the elbow length gloves. Anticipating his plan, Tessa had sneaked them away, adding them to her collection of keepsakes that would later remind her that there had been good days.

"These are your grandmother's gloves," Tessa told Regina now.

"I figured," Regina said. "They're not the sort of thing I imagined you'd ever buy."

"If it counts for anything, I approved the purchase." She decided against lecturing Regina about privacy. "How long have you had the gloves?"

"Not long. A few days." She drank thirstily from the bottle of water. "I was going to tell you. I know it was wrong to go through your stuff."

"Thank you. Were you looking for something, honey?"

"That's the funny part. I don't know what I was doing."

"Well, it's not important now. My mother bought these at Goodwill," Tessa said. "We always made up stories about the original owners. It was a game."

"They're beautiful," Regina said. "So soft."

"My mother claimed they belonged to a Civil War widow who vowed to dress in all black for the rest of her life." In her best Southern drawl she added, "Wearing black was an honorable tribute to a man who gave his life for his country." Tessa laughed. "Your grandmother loved talking in a Southern accent. She said it positively gave her goose bumps. She was a good storyteller."

"Why don't you like to talk about your mother?"

"Didn't I just talk about her?"

"You know what I mean," Regina said.

"I do know what you mean," Tessa said. "Sorry." Regina knew very little about Ursula. Stories about Ursula's life consisted of epochs that Tessa alternately tried to forget or to protect. Walter preferred that only the scantiest bits of information about Ursula be shared, and Tessa had adopted this secretiveness in deference to his wishes, as well as for her own comfort. Everything that had belonged to Ursula, including her notebooks, which told everything and nothing about the author, were packed away and stored in the attic. Only a few of these notebooks were hidden in Tessa's dresser drawers, covered with scarves and stockings and camisoles. Sometimes she needed to hold one of the notebooks, turning the pages without reading them. Sometimes she just missed her mother.

"Why do you always call her Ursula?" Regina said.

"I guess because I did so much of the mothering. It doesn't always feel natural to call her anything else." Tessa laughed and shook her head. "Besides, she wasn't your traditional sort of mother."

"Neither are you."

"No, I guess not."

"Tell me more about her," Regina said. She pulled the covers up to her chin. The Tylenol was working.

"I'm sorry I've always been so secretive. I just wanted to protect you," Tessa said. "That's why I didn't tell you much about her . . . or anything. I thought the most important thing was to defend you against the sort of madness that defined my childhood. The irony, of course, is that I've given you a childhood with so many similarities to my own. I hoped that if I burned all the spinning wheels in the kingdom, I could save you."

Regina reached for Tessa's hand, holding it briefly. And that was when Tessa knew that Regina had taken more than the gloves. She had found the hidden notebooks and taken one. Tessa felt it in Regina's touch. It was as though Tessa could see the notebook in Regina's hand.

"I don't need to be saved. Besides, it didn't even work in the fairy tale, Mom. How could it work in real life?"

"I don't even know where to begin," Tessa said.

"Was she a witch? Are the rumors true?"

"Where did you get that idea?"

"You know. Little pitchers have big ears."

They smiled at each other. Grandma Lucy had always said that whenever Regina was eavesdropping.

"No, she wasn't a witch though I'm certain she would rather have been. It's much more romantic to be a witch than to be bi-polar. She was manic-depressive, and she often had very, very dark moods. She would talk about death and how she wished she could die. Some days she did nothing but sleep. When she was manic, it was equally hard to live with her. She talked incessantly and reacted inappropriately to everything. It was as if someone had taken the brakes off a speeding car. I once saw her lift a couch by herself."

"Why did she do that?" Regina asked.

"I was helping her rearrange all the furniture in the house. We had to put the couch and all the chairs in the living room to face the front door because she was expecting visitors all the time. It was a whirlwind. No matter what you call it, she was very ill, and I was very young. I thought she was weak and that if she really loved me, she would have been well. It makes no sense, of course. No one wishes to be mentally ill. Sometimes everything was wonderful. She could be the ideal mother. She was beautiful and funny, and wise and brave. I loved her, but I hated her too."

"I'm sorry," Regina said. "It must have been awful for everyone."

"She never wanted to take her medication. She once claimed that when she medicated she had the same problem as some of the astronauts after they came back from the moon. She read an interview with an astronaut who said that after he returned from the moon, everything else was a letdown. I think she was always on the moon when she was off her meds. She hated how they made her feel, so she was either entirely off her meds or in the process of being regulated. Most of the time, she was just plain crazy. And I hated her when she was crazy."

"You just wanted everything to be normal," Regina said. She propped herself up and rested her head on her hand. "I can understand that. Was she ever happy?"

"Too happy," Tessa said.

"What was it like then? When she was too happy?"

"It was like riding a roller coaster, standing up. I can't describe it any other way. When she was manic, it was like living inside a cyclone. She hardly ever slept, and her behavior was unpredictable. Sometimes, it was exciting. I had a mother who let me go to school wearing a feathered boa over my jacket. She let me eat candy apples for breakfast, arguing that a fruit is a fruit. I loved her, so it was all right, you know?

Regina nodded. She knew exactly what her mother was saying.

"I knew something was wrong with her. She was horrified by cruelty and tried to fix it, to just make it go away. I think she had powers, but not the sort you might imagine. People like her just see the world differently. They feel far too much, and she felt far too much."

"It's so sad. For all of you, and for me too."

"I can see how it would make you sad. I'm sorry. Is this all too much information?"

"No, no, not at all. I want to know everything. I have to know everything."

"I was afraid all the time." Tessa held Regina's hand. "I was always in anticipation of the dark side of the moon. That's what my father called her lapses. The dark side of the moon. I would come home to a stranger. The depression completely transformed her. She wouldn't bathe or eat. She smoked incessantly then and drank cups and cups of coffee. Sometimes her breath was so bad from that combination that I imagined she had swallowed a demon. In a way, I guess she had. It tore at her insides, this demon of hers. Medication helped, but only when she took it. As soon as she was feeling good, she stopped, insisting she didn't need medication anymore. She swore that she was fine, that she was cured. And then, she'd slip into that awful darkness and couldn't find her way back. Once she tried to explain what it felt like. She said, 'I'm all alone in here. I can see you and see Daddy, but you can't save me. You can't get to me in time.' I thought she was wrong. We could save her if she called out to us. I tried to get her to practice. I'd tell her to just shout out our names, and we'd find her. She'd looked at me with her lost eyes and smiled. 'That's the problem. I can't remember your names once I'm trapped. I can't even speak.' You know what I did? I bought her a whistle. I thought that maybe if she used the whistle, we could save her. She could blow the whistle and know that she was never that alone. She would find her way home no matter what."

Tessa paused. There was so much to tell, and she was already exhausted.

"Go on," Regina said.

"After a time, things just got worse. She would disappear without warning or take me away without telling anyone. My father was frightened. We were all frightened."

"Why wasn't she in a hospital?" Regina said.

"She was, off and on. It was the most effective threat to get her to take her meds, but it wasn't always persuasive enough. Sometimes, she just had to be hospitalized. She was miserable when she was there."

"And she was miserable when she was home."

"Yes. Sometimes, she was," Tessa said.

"And then what?"

"Then there was the accident. I was told my father had died, and my mother was missing. Later on, my grandmother just announced that there had been word that my mother was dead."

"And you believed it?" Regina asked.

"I wanted to believe it. It was easier than believing she had abandoned me."

By now, the only light in the room came from outside the window. Tessa strained to see Regina's expression, but she could hear her breathing, feel her trying to absorb all this information. Unexpectedly, Regina sat up and turned on the light on her night table. They both squinted in the sudden light until Regina adjusted the intensity.

"And now you think she's alive," Regina said. "And close by, somehow?"

Tessa realized that Regina wanted to see her face when she answered. There was nowhere to hide anymore.

"I don't know," Tessa said. "Maybe, yes, I guess I do."

"Thank you for telling me all this," she said. "I know how hard it is for you."

"Your father will be furious when he finds out that I've told you all this. My mother is one area where he and I can never agree."

"I won't tell him," Regina offered.

"I will. I'll have to."

"I'm sorry." Regina yawned. "I don't know why I went searching. I shouldn't have. Look what I've done to you."

"Don't worry about me," Tessa said. "You just get some rest. Go to sleep."

Regina snuggled down under the covers and said, "There's more I have to tell you though."

"I know there is. You can tell me later."

Tessa turned out the light and waited for Regina to sleep, remembering how Ursula used to fervently cut and paste sections of articles into her notebooks. In one notebook, she had taken an article about Dr. Susan Snow, the granddaughter of the founder of the Maine chowder-making company, F.H. Snow's, who said, "Lobsters know when to let go. Most people struggle when a lobster bites them because they don't understand that it will eventually release its grasp."

Tessa had wondered, until now, what had caught Ursula's attention in those words. It was often hard to know what she thought even though she added elaborate diagrams, even maps to places she had never been. All Ursula's entries were dated, and all were marked with the name of the person she had in mind when she came across the piece. Ursula had written Tessa's name across the top of the excerpt from the article about Dr. Snow, the physician and lobster expert. The entry was dated two days before the accident.

The commentary that accompanied the article was succinct. *Don't struggle.*

The words had made little sense to Tessa when she first read them, but now she understood. It was pointless to struggle. She would know when she was ready. And Ursula would know when she could stay away no longer.

Chapter Ten

After Tessa's father died in the car accident and her mother's whereabouts were uncertain, Grandma Lucy had taken a large glass of water and the sugar bowl and set both on the table before Tessa. "Put some sugar in the water," Lucy had instructed. Tessa placed several heaping spoonfuls into the water. "Now stir," Lucy said. Tessa stirred and stirred. "Can you see the sugar?" Her grandmother seemed ancient then although she was only in her late sixties. Tessa shook her head. "But you know it's there, right?" Tessa nodded. "It's the same with your parents, Tessa. You can't see them, but they're there. They'll always love you and watch over you." Tessa had buried her face in her grandmother's lap and held back tears. She loved her grandmother and wanted to please her. "Thank you, Grandma," she said, lifting her head. Tessa knew it would be heartless to argue that it was not good enough to know that her parents would always watch over her and love her even if she could not see them. It simply was not good enough.

Tessa had hoped for Ursula's return and had imagined countless rationalizations for the delay. Her mother would never have left her. Tessa was convinced that Ursula simply did not remember the daughter she loved. Tessa held fast to this account until three years after Ursula's disappearance.

Then the day came when Grandmother Lucy took Tessa's hand and held it tightly. "Your mother is gone," she said. "We've received word."

Tessa did not ask any questions, and she did not cry. Her mother did not deserve tears. And later, when Tessa did finally cry, she told herself the tears were not for her mother at all, but for the time that had been wasted in false hopes.

"Your mother was not well. Not ever," Lucy said. "Try not to blame her. Your father thought he could make her be like everyone else, but no one could. Not your father, not me, not even you. You have to believe that."

But Tessa had not believed it then, and she did not really believe it now. Her mother had made a choice, and it seemed to Tessa (then and now) that Ursula had chosen to be herself, even at the cost of leaving Tessa behind. Perhaps Ursula had not really believed that a bad mother was better than no mother at all. Perhaps Ursula could not face the guilt over the pain she brought to her child's life, or perhaps she thought that life would be too unbearable without the dependability of mornings when she woke to a life that seemed designed by Disney animators.

The medication took all that away from her, gave her a much less spectacular, a much more ordinary existence. Banal. Mediocre. Ursula always said that those were the words that scared her. But she must have been more frightened at the thought of hurting Tessa.

In the end, Ursula must have believed that Tessa would be better off without a mother than with one who caused such suffering. *You wish I would just die, don't you?* Ursula had spat those words at Tessa, from time to time, shocking her with their truth. Tessa had sometimes wished her mother would die, and no matter how often her grandmother reassured her that no one was that powerful, Tessa could never be sure if her wish had come true or if Ursula had simply needed to find a way to navigate the space between madness and ordinary life.

In the hallway outside of Regina's room, Tessa stood quietly and listened to her child's hoarse snores. From the day Regina was born, Tessa wondered if her child had escaped the genetic markings of mental illness. Ever watchful, Tessa was always afraid that she could once again be fooled into believing that everything was fine, that there could really be a different outcome, a better one than what had already been determined. Ursula had fooled her. She had fooled them all. Before Ursula snatched the car keys from Dennis' hand and ran out to the car, she had seemed perfectly rational.

Tessa remembered how her mother had piled her plate high at dinner, eating everything, even having second helpings. Everyone had been encouraged that Ursula's appetite had been restored, believing that they were about to begin a good cycle, a long awaited time of calm. Dinner had been blessedly quiet that night as they savored the absence of turmoil. They had just weathered an unusually long stretch of Ursula's sleepless nights, of taking turns as they kept watch when she finally slept. The four of them had been together at dinner for the first time in a long while.

Tessa wondered at how unsuspecting they had all been, so ready to accept any sign that the worst might be over. If they could have stopped time that night, frozen themselves into that moment, an outsider would have seen a very normal family. Dennis in his favorite dark green corduroy slacks and a fisherman's sweater that had been an anniversary present from Ursula just that year, a real surprise since manic taste was always bad. And Ursula, her thick, black hair held away from her face with a red velvet headband, had looked especially beautiful. She was wearing the little silver frog earrings that Tessa had bought on a school trip to the Museum of Natural History.

Thinner than usual after this last bout of endless cigarettes and coffee coupled with little food or sleep, Ursula looked oddly radiant, like some exotic creature that had been preserved in a temperature-controlled environment under a glass dome. Her jumpy energy could easily have been confused with exhilaration. The edge of hysteria that typically made every move, every gesture suspect to those in her inner circle could have been misconstrued as a charming affectation. Ursula had bathed in something woodsy scented before dinner, and the fragrance seemed alive around her. She played the loving mother, devoted wife and grateful daughter to perfection. Even Lucy seemed to have cheerfully suspended her doubts, indulging the hope of a prosaic future.

Ursula had fooled them all.

Tessa never suspected the possibility that such an ordinary night could be the fateful night. She was only eleven-years-old. But if she had truly known that the decisive night was upon them, would she have been able to sound the alert? To give the warning that would have changed their lives? Would anyone have listened?

Dennis would surely have silenced her with a look. Lucy would have urged her to take another helping of something, anything to quiet her objections. Perhaps, only Ursula might have welcomed the interruption. But she never gave Tessa the slightest indication of what might be expected of her. Instead, Ursula had avoided Tessa's eyes throughout dinner, perhaps knowing that anything could be erroneously misconstrued as a signal.

Tessa felt certain that in Ursula's own convoluted logic she had feared that if time had stood still that night, she might have disrupted the future. Tessa might have been denied Walter, and might have longed all her life for a child just like Regina. Perhaps in her own deranged judgment, Ursula had known that she must help Tessa make the choice between seeing the future and changing it, and seeing the future and living in spite of it.

The future had arrived, yet Tessa continued to brood over those final days before the accident. There had been so many indications that Ursula was planning something. She had clipped an article about the Aborigines and pasted it into her Mysterious Sites journal, the one she kept exclusively for Tessa. There were narrative accounts of the geography and the history of every site, as well as Ursula's views on their intrinsic value: *Be sure to make a pilgrimage to western Arnhem Land in Australia. Long ago the Aborigines of this area developed a style of painting that is now known as X-ray art. The pictures not only portray the exterior forms of different creatures, but their skeleton and internal organs. Everything matters, Tessa. Look at everything before you make any judgments. Inside and outside. See it all.*

See all what? Tessa had wondered even though she knew now what Ursula had meant. That was not the problem. The problem was that Tessa could not understand what she saw at all anymore. So little made any sense. Ursula had once told Tessa about the enlightening hallucinations that followed hours in a sweat lodge, advising her to make the time to participate in this ancient ritual. *You should travel to where the Lakota Indians practiced this ancient ritual. See it all.* Ursula's voice was always urgent when she was manic. *See it all.*

In the dark hallway, Tessa now opened her eyes and turned around quickly, looking for her mother. See it all. Then she closed her eyes again. Nothing. Blackness. She wanted to cry out, *I can't see anything!* Instead, even though her mouth was shut, she heard her voice echo in the dark stillness.

"What did the doctor say?"

Tessa had left Walter a message on his cell phone, knowing he would be angry if she didn't tell him that Regina was home sick. He liked to be apprised of everything. That's the way he always said it, and always to Tessa's amusement.

"I didn't call the doctor," she said. "I gave her Tylenol. Her fever is down already. She's much better. I'll see how she is in the morning. I just checked her a few minutes ago."

"I think you should have called," he said.

"I know you do."

She knew she could have told him to call the doctor himself if he was so worried, but it would have been unnecessarily contentious. He was just being cautious He was always cautious, especially about

Regina. But it was the wrong time for caution although she was unable to say what it was time was for. Just more, she thought. Just a lot more. Maybe that was why she liked parades, she mused, all that fanfare and noise and hoopla. Sort of left no doubt that one was there and present in the moment. Unlike now, where each moment seemed endless and surreal.

"Tessa?"

"Yes?" She pulled a bag of garbage from the pail beneath the sink and twisted the ends into a firm knot before shutting the cabinet door with her knee and setting the bag down. "I'm sorry. I sort of drifted. We should go to the Thanksgiving Day parade this year. We used to go all the time when Reggie was little. It was such fun. Remember?" She looked up at him with teary eyes. "I think Regina would like to go."

The clock in the kitchen struck six, startling them both since it had not worked in forever. It was a gift from one of Tessa's clients. Each hour was represented by a picture of a different bird. When the hour rang, a bird's song filled the house. After awhile, nobody said, "Hurry up. It's almost three o'clock," or "I'll pick you up at seven-fifteen." Their whole language changed. It was, "Hurry up. It's almost cardinal," or "I'll pick you up at a quarter past blue jay." Eventually, the mechanism broke, and they went back to telling time the regular way, all vaguely disappointed though no one would admit it.

"It's half-past hummingbird," he said.

"We should get it fixed," she said. "We keep talking about it, but we never do it."

"Yes. We should."

They both stared at the clock before facing each other again. Walter smiled and reached out for Tessa, pulling her close. She wrapped her arms around his waist. He was a really good man.

"We'll go to the parade this year." He stepped back, holding her at arm's length. "Now tell me what's going on."

It was always so hard to know what Walter wanted to hear, or if he really wanted to hear anything at all. Conversations about Ursula and Dennis were, at best, always perfunctory. Walter credited Tessa's confessions with a sort of dull familiarity, but it was never anything more than obligatory recognition, like spotting a famous landmark at the end of a long day of sightseeing. It was enough just to say you had seen it. You didn't even really have to go inside as long as you took a picture of it. And it was typically enough for Walter to just listen. But not anymore. Nothing was enough anymore.

"I talked to Regina today about my mother. I think she has a right to know about her family." They had been holding hands, but now Tessa let go and stepped away from him. "It wasn't as hard as I thought it would be."

"I don't know what to say," he admitted. "I thought I would be angrier, but I feel surprisingly calm and that worries me even more." He laughed apologetically. "I know this isn't about me, but I feel sort of empty."

Tessa nodded, touched by his admission although it was not new to her.

"I need your help with this," she said. "I can't do it alone."

"I don't know how to help you with this," he said. "I can't understand what you see or what you feel. It frightens me. *You* frighten me."

There it was at last. His long overdue confession.

She did not know how to explain that it was difficult to distinguish between what she saw and her own memories. For that was how impressions came to her. Like her own memories, except they did not belong to her. She had tried to explain it to him many times. *I own the memories of others,* she told him. *I experience small flashes of recognition that have no connection to my own life, yet feel as if they do.* The accident had first appeared to her just like that, like a memory, rather than like something that was going to happen.

"I don't see much these days," she said. It was not a real lie, at least not completely. "It's as though I have to clear out the past to see the future."

"Is that supposed to console me?"

"Do you need to be consoled?"

"I need the truth. I guess that would console me."

"That's why I talked to Regina today."

"To console me?"

"To console you. To console me, Regina, all of us. To clear out the past," she said. "To tell the truth. It's all the same."

"How did Regina take it?"

Tessa stepped behind the chair he had so carefully fitted his jacket over. She smoothed the shoulders with flattened hands as though he were still inside. Walter watched her and then sort of slid into a chair. He looked so tired. She took a seat across from him.

"Surprisingly well," Tessa said. "She's been ready for a long time. She'd already met me halfway." Then she added, "There's a whole part to this story that I've never told anyone."

He waited.

"I knew about the accident before it happened," she said.

"Your parents' accident? You knew?" he said. "You knew the car was going to crash?"

"Not that night, no, but I knew there was going to be an accident." She covered her eyes with her hand. Why couldn't she get the facts straight? "I don't think I knew it was going to be that night." She looked up. "Or maybe I did. I was only eleven. I had a dream. I saw a car turned over in the snow. I had the dream several times. Ursula had the same dream actually. Maybe my father had it too. Who knows what people dream?"

"Why are you telling me this now?"

"Because it's all going to come together very soon now, and I don't want to have to go back and redo anything."

Walter tilted his head slightly, trying to show that he understood, but Tessa knew he was struggling to keep up.

"I'm sorry," she said. "I've made such a mess of everything. It's all very confusing. And now this business with Fran."

"I thought you resolved that."

"How? How would I have resolved it, Walter?"

"I don't know. Somehow, I thought you had."

Tessa shook her head slowly, as if this truth was just now dawning on her. "I haven't resolved anything."

"I want to help you," he said. "I really do, but I don't see what I could do."

"Just listen for now. You know the thing of it is that Ursula knew about my premonition. That was the part that was always the hardest for me. It's still the hardest. She never said anything to me about it. She just let it happen. I guess she believed that the universe had its own timetable."

"How could she have believed that?"

"How could she *not?*" Tessa could not hide her surprise. "Why is this so hard for you to understand?"

"I don't know. I just can't help but wonder how things could have been different."

"Different how?"

"I don't know. Just different."

She decided it was best not to tell Walter about the gloves that Regina had found or about the notebook that she was still hiding. He had enough to think about for now. Maybe she wouldn't tell him at all. But she had to tell him. She had promised herself that she would be honest with him. No more subterfuge. It suddenly seemed as if she had spent a lifetime invested in artifice, always trying to sidestep the past and always failing.

"I'm going up to check on Regina," Walter said.

"Good idea." She smiled. The moment to tell him anything more had passed anyway.

Walter stood. He seemed to want to say something, but he just looked at her and said nothing. And though Tessa wanted to help him, she could say nothing that might ease his concerns.

"How about some dinner?" she offered. "Pasta?"

Walter seemed grateful for that overture and answered almost too enthusiastically. She waited till she knew he was upstairs before going about the business of dinner. She put a pot of water to boil and warmed some leftover soup for Regina. The simplicity of these routines reassured that life could be easier than it seemed to be. When her cell phone rang, Tessa knew it was Fran and answered, aware of the absence of anxiety that usually accompanied hearing her voice.

"Tessa? It's Fran."

"Yes, I know."

"How are you?"

Tessa lowered the flame under the soup.

"I'm fine. How are you?"

Instead of answering, Fran said, "We need to talk."

"Yes. I know. I'm sorry. I've been busy."

"I know. I know," Fran said. "I understand."

"Soon," Tessa said. "I'll call you. I promise."

"When?" Fran asked.

"Soon."

"Well, I guess I'll have to take you at your word."

"That's very brave since you don't even know me."

The silence was brief, not nearly long enough for Tessa to prepare for what came next.

"In a way, I feel as if I've known you for years," Fran said.

"How's that?" Tessa said. She knew she was baiting Fran, trying to force a confrontation. The room felt as if it were spinning. She closed her eyes. *Breathe*, she told herself. *Breathe. Don't struggle.* "Tell me why you feel that way. Say it. I need to hear you say it."

"Your mother has told me so much about you that I feel as though I know you."

"I see." Tessa thought she might cry, but she felt strangely calm. "I thought as much."

"Yes, I know you did."

"Where is she?" Tessa said. "Is she with you?"

"She's not far."

Tessa thought it was a funny answer, but then it was a funny question.

Strange funny, not ha-ha funny. That would have been Ursula's clarification.

"I'll call you tomorrow," Tessa said. "My Regina isn't feeling well, so I want to first see how she is tomorrow."

"I understand."

"Thank you."

"Well, don't thank me yet," Fran said.

Tessa laughed in spite of herself, in spite of the gravity of what was to come. Fran politely said goodnight and hung up. Tessa, her knees suddenly weak, dropped into a chair with a resounding thud.

Ursula was close by, waiting to be claimed.

Walter and Regina were watching television in the big bed. That's what Regina had always called Tessa and Walter's bed. It was where Regina always slept when she didn't feel well, or if Walter was away on business, or if a storm or a bad dream frightened her.

"How are you feeling?" Tessa said. She sat on the bed, reaching out a hand to touch Regina's forehead. "Your fever is down. I brought you tea."

"Thanks, Mom." She took a few sips as Tessa held the cup. "I feel a little better. Just really, really tired."

Tessa looked at Walter. He was already half-asleep.

"He was snoring before," Regina said.

"I'm not surprised," Tessa said. "Would you like some soup? I made some pasta, too."

"I can hear you," Walter said. "My eyes may be closed, but I'm awake." He stuck his tongue out, and they both laughed. "See? Not at all dead."

Regina snuggled up against his side and said, "Nothing to eat. Can I have some more ices?"

"You can have anything you want," Tessa said. "What's your wish?"

"I wish I could sleep in this bed tonight and have more ices."

"That's it?" Walter said from under his drooping eyelids. "That's all you would wish for?"

"Yup," Regina said. She pulled the blanket up to her chin and yawned. "I'm so tired."

Ursula had kept a statue of the Virgin Mary submerged in a basin of blue tinted water. She used food dye, counting out the drops, until the water turned the shade of blue she desired. For a time, she dropped fistfuls of pennies into the azure water, announcing that every penny represents a wish, and now don't you forget it. Tessa heard the hiss of her mother's last word over and over and over. *Wish. Wish. Wish.* Ursula said the word over and over. Who knew where she was able to get so many pennies? When the water spilled over the top of the basin, Dennis quietly suggested that perhaps there were enough pennies, enough wishes.

"Try to sleep," Tessa said. "I'll bring up some ginger ale and some ices."

"I'm coming down," Walter said. "I'm tired too, but I wish for some pasta."

Wishes. Wishes. Wishes. There can never be enough wishes, Ursula insisted. She wept as Dennis spilled the water into the sink.

"I think I can make everyone's wishes come true tonight," Tessa said.

"Just tonight?" Walter said. "What happens to the wishes after tonight?"

All my wishes, wishes, wishes are gone now, Ursula said, pulling at her hair. All gone.

Tessa put up her hands in surrender.

"After tonight?" she said. "Who knows? Maybe tomorrow there will be no more wishes."

Walter and Regina laughed, but not Tessa. She slipped out of the bedroom, trying not to think about the promises she had made.

Chapter Eleven

Before Lucy came to live with them, it was part of Tessa's daily ritual to sit at her mother's bedside when she napped. Often it was the only peaceful time of their day. And sometimes, Tessa napped too, exhausted from the effort of pretending that everything was fine. Every day her father asked if it was too much for her, if keeping an eye on things until he came home kept her from having a normal life. He offered to hire someone, and they both knew he should. It wasn't the money, he insisted. And it wasn't. It was the fear of an outsider being privy to their secrets. Mostly, Tessa knew, it was the shame.

Tessa was persistent. She assured him that she could handle things for a few hours in the afternoon. And it wasn't like Ursula needed to be minded every day. It was just that when she did need minding, Tessa was so afraid that her mother would be hospitalized if the truth was discovered. Tessa often thought about the awful stillness of the house when her mother was not there. And the stillness was awful, as much for the pain of her absence, as for the shocking relief it brought to the rhythm of Tessa's days. That terrible and wonderful stillness compelled Tessa to keep up the charade and to subdue Dennis's concerns again and again.

Tessa remembered one afternoon; she had fallen asleep against her mother's side, luxuriating in her smell, in her soft skin, and in the quiet. Ursula's eyes suddenly flew open, and Tessa's did also, simultaneously. Ursula placed a hand against Tessa's chest to still her and said, "There's nothing to be afraid of. I'm sure of it. I dreamed I was walking skyward."

Tessa could still recall how she had listened, imagining her mother ascending an endless staircase into the clouds. Slowly, slowly, Tessa's heart had found its normal beat as she thought about a life uninterrupted by outbursts and hysteria. And as Tessa imagined this, she felt her mother watching her and turned to look into her sad eyes. Ursula reached out a shaking hand, took Tessa's chin between her thumb and forefinger and winked in that sweet, personal way that made Tessa feel more important than anyone else in the world. "I told you," Ursula said. "There's nothing to be afraid of."

A few weeks later Ursula almost set the kitchen on fire. She hadn't meant to, of course, but she was heating up soup for their lunch when the flames beneath the pot were so achingly beautiful that Ursula just had to make them as high and big as possible. That meant removing the pot and fanning the flame with a newspaper that caught on fire, prompting Ursula to throw the burning newspaper at the kitchen curtains, and so on and so on.

When Tessa thought about the events it almost made her laugh. It was like that song about the old woman who swallowed the fly. A chain of inevitable events, or so it seemed. Soon after, Dennis asked Lucy to live with them. There was no need anymore for Tessa to stay with Ursula during her afternoon nap. Tessa was released from her duties. She was free to join a club at school, to play soccer or volleyball, even to linger instead of coming straight home. Of course, she never did. And, more than likely, Ursula never dreamed about walking skyward again.

Tessa decided to take the day off and stay home with Regina. Her fever was gone, but she was still too weak to return to school. Regina had slept in the big bed, which meant that Walter had to sleep in Regina's room. It was no longer appropriate for Regina to sleep in the same bed as her father, but she enjoyed the comfort of the big bed and the presence of a parent though she would be reluctant to admit that. After Walter kissed Regina's forehead and Tessa's cheek, he seemed happy to retreat to some solitude. And Tessa and Regina watched sappy shows on the cable stations without Walter's predictable commentary.

Regina was still asleep when Tessa tiptoed downstairs to make coffee. She steamed the milk and frothed it, adding an extra scoop of coffee to the paper filter. Walter liked it strong in the morning, and so did she. Just as she was pouring the hot water into the Chemex, Walter came up behind her and lightly kissed her neck.

"Careful," Tessa said, but she smiled. "Did you sleep well?"

Walter yawned loudly as his answer. He was already showered, dressed and ready to leave after he had his coffee and some breakfast. "I guess. I just checked her. She's still fast asleep, but she doesn't feel as hot."

"It's the morning. Fever is always down in the morning."

"Still," Walter said. He put two slices of whole wheat bread in the toaster and took a jar of strawberry jam from the refrigerator. "Do you want toast?"

"Maybe. Just one slice though." She poured coffee into his mug and set it by his place at the table. "Thank you."

"Thank *you*," he said. "Is this tie okay?"

She turned to look. He was into a monochromatic look these days. Today's color was blue. It was a good choice for him. "Perfect," she said.

When the toast was done, he slathered jam on both slices and put two more in the toaster.

"I just want one slice," Tessa said.

"You'll change your mind. You always do."

She shrugged and took bites of toast between sips of coffee. Walter sat beside her and bit heartily into his slice. He could eat a slice of toast in three mouthfuls while Tessa took forever. With one finger, she reached over to take a crumb off his lip. Playfully, he snapped at her finger.

"Silly," she said.

He held her by the wrist and looked into her eyes before he kissed her. She kissed him back, tasting the sweetness of the jam on his tongue.

"Strawberry," he said.

"Same here," she said.

She didn't protest when he slipped a hand under her tee shirt. They kissed again. This time Tessa wasn't sure it was the jam that made the kiss so sweet or the good feelings.

"Unfortunately," Walter said. "I have to go to work."

"Too bad for you," she teased.

"Too bad for *you*," he said.

"Shall I make the toast to go?"

"Please. I'll take both if you don't want another slice."

"But I do."

He kissed her cheek and said, "See? I always know what you want."

If only she had told him about Ursula, she thought as she put jam on the toasted bread and cut it in half before wrapping it in a piece of waxed paper. It had been only one day, and already she was guilty of omission.

She stood by the back door and waited, wrapped toast in hand, while he checked his briefcase one last time, grabbed his overcoat and bent to give her a final kiss.

"Take your toast," she said.

"Call me when she wakes up."

"I will."

"You're a good mother. Do you know that?"

She was taken aback by this compliment. It was so perfectly timed, so just what she wanted and needed to hear that it made her weepy. "Oh," she said. "Thank you." Her eyes welled up, and she felt foolishly sentimental.

"Apparently I don't tell you that often enough," Walter said. "I'm sorry. You really are a good mom. Reggie is lucky."

Still clutching the wrapped piece of toast, Tessa wound her arms around Walter's neck and gripped him tightly.

"Whoa there," he said. "You're choking me." He laughed and tried to disengage himself from her hold. "I always forget how strong you are. Are you crying?" He used his thumbs to wipe at her moist cheeks. "Why, Tess?"

She shrugged helplessly and laughed. "I don't know. You took me by surprise. It doesn't matter. Go. You'll be late. I want to get in the shower before Regina wakes up. Maybe she'll be hungry."

"I hope so. Call me."

Tessa waited in the doorway till he backed the car out of the driveway. He waved and honked lightly before he accelerated and sped off. She remembered holding Regina's hand and waving it for her at Walter until the car was a mere speck in the distance. "Bye, bye, Daddy," Tessa would say, repeating it over and over until Regina could finally piece the words together. "Bye, bye, Daddy." Then, Tessa had been secretly glad when Walter left for the day, and she had Regina all to herself. When Walter was home, Regina had eyes only for her daddy.

But Tessa never put together a private world like the one that Ursula had created for herself and Tessa, a world Ursula insisted must be hidden from Dennis. "We can't tell Daddy about this, right?" Ursula always said. To a little girl who was most afraid of losing her mother, yes was the only possible answer.

It made sense then that when Ursula began collecting statues of saints that she hid in the closet, away from Dennis, Tessa knew enough to keep quiet. Ursula took them out and spoke to them when he was at work. And Tessa said nothing when Ursula dragged her along to the storefront church where the dark-skinned worshippers spoke in a fervent, almost frenzied, manner, to the Voodoo counterparts of Catholic saints. Ursula prayed to Ezili Freda, the equivalent of Mother Dolorosa, warning Tessa that the Voodoo mistress was very powerful. "She's the Goddess of Love and Luxury," Ursula said. "She's my patron goddess now. I serve her."

Tessa mostly just watched except for one time when she had prayed to Ezili Freda to make Ursula happy. "You must not displease Ezili Freda," Ursula warned. "She is a powerful mambo who loves fine clothes, jewels, perfume and lace. Her favorite colors are pink and white, and her favorite perfume is Anais-Anais." Ursula always doused herself in this before they made an offering. Tessa learned that Ezili Freda loved sweets, especially drinks made with orange syrup and grenadine.

Tessa would come home from school on a Thursday to find Ursula cooking rice with cinnamon milk or making fried bananas with sugar. Her body would be tense with excitement. "Hurry," Ursula urged. "I waited for you. We're bringing this to Ezili Freda. Thursday is her sacred day." Lucy even came with them occasionally because she was too afraid to let Ursula take Tessa alone. They would drive to the Bronx church where the other worshipers welcomed them with smiles and hugs. "I've brought this for Mistress EF," Ursula said, showing them her offerings. If there was no time to cook, Ursula brought several packs of Virginia Slims and laid them at the statue's feet.

Ezili Freda was beautiful, but tears were fixed on her mocha colored skin. "Why is she so sad?" Tessa wanted to know. Ursula clasped her closed fists to her chest and shut her eyes and explained, "The love Ezili Freda seeks is forever unreturned, and this makes her cry. She can't stop. She can never stop." Tessa held on to her mother's skirt as she rocked and wailed in front of Ezili Freda's image. Ursula's impassioned motions pulled Tessa along. She kept her eyes wide open though, unlike Ursula and the other worshipers who prayed and moaned with tightly shut eyes. Tessa wanted to see Ezili Freda, wanted to see if the gifts of lace and sweets and Anais-Anais were enough to make her any happier. But she was never any happier and neither was Ursula, at least not for very long.

Regina was still asleep when Tessa checked in on her before showering, and she was still asleep when Tessa was done. After she dressed, Tessa went downstairs and decided to make farina, hoping

Regina would be hungry when she woke. As Tessa stirred the farina, she could almost see her mother as she cooked rice with cinnamon milk. "Cook! Cook!" she would shout at the pot of rice and milk. Sometimes she would weep uncontrollably, pushing her face into the curve of her arm as she tried not to look, thinking in some way this would make the ingredients cook faster. "Do you see?" Ursula would ask Tessa. "Do you see how hard it is for me?" Tessa would nod and try to calm her mother before taking the wooden spoon from her trembling hand, avoiding looking at her because it was so reminiscent of Ezili Freda and her forever sad face.

"Mom? You home?"

Regina's sleepy voice sounded stronger than it had the day before, and Tessa happily turned off the flame beneath the cereal and hurried up the stairs. Regina was sitting up in bed with the covers pulled up to her chin. She looked pale, but her eyes were no longer bright with fever.

"Well," Tessa said. "How are you?"

"Hungry and thirsty."

Tessa sat down on the bed and held her palm against Regina's forehead.

"Cool," Tessa said. "On so many levels."

Regina smiled and said, "Do we have farina?"

"It's ready and waiting. Should I bring some up?"

"No. I'll come down. I need to pee. And I think I could drink a quart of orange juice." She got out from under the quilt and shivered a little. "Did you call the attendance number at school?"

"I did." Tessa got up and took her robe from the closet and brought it to Regina. "And put some slippers or socks on. The floor downstairs is cold."

"I will. First I have to pee."

She took the robe and shuffled to the bathroom while Tessa waited outside the door. When Regina came out, she looked a bit better. She had washed her face and tried to pull her hair back with one of Tessa's clips, but her curls escaped almost willfully.

"Come here," Tessa said. "Let me fix your hair."

With uncharacteristic compliance, Regina sat on the closed toilet seat and let Tessa pull a brush through her unruly curls.

"Am I hurting you?"

"Not yet," Regina said. "Do you want the hairclip?"

"Not yet." Tessa was enjoying the excuse to touch her daughter. She gathered all of Regina's hair in one hand and held the brush in the other, using long, steady strokes to get through the thick curls. She could feel Regina relax as she allowed her head to fall back. Her eyes were half-closed, and she rested her head in her mother's hand. "Let me have that hairclip, honey."

Regina held it out without opening her eyes. Tessa coiled Regina's hair and firmly fastened the clip close to the top of her head.

"Perfect," Tessa said. "Now put something on your feet and come downstairs and eat."

"Did you take the day off for me?"

"I did."

"Cool. Thanks."

"Oh, any excuse to play hooky. You should know that."

"Don't you like your work anymore?" Regina tried to stick an escaped strand of hair into the clip. "I thought you love what you do."

"I love you more. And leave your hair alone." Tessa slapped at her hand. "Oh, we have to call Dad. I told him we would call when you woke up."

"Okay. I'll call him."

Tessa went down ahead and turned a low heat under the farina to warm it. By the time Regina slid into a chair, a bowl of hot cereal was waiting for her. She was talking to Walter on her cell as she placed several pats of butter into her cereal and then sprinkled it generously with granulated brown sugar. Tessa filled a large glass with orange juice and then poured herself another cup of coffee.

"Much better, Dad. I'm having farina with a pound of butter. Uh-huh. Yes, and lots of sugar. Love you, too. Here's Mom."

After Tessa reassured Walter that Regina looked positively well, she said goodbye and handed the phone back to Regina.

"Did you ever write to Aunt Althea?" Regina said.

"Of course I did. I told you I would."

"She never wrote back?"

"Nope." Tessa took a bite of her cold toast. "Not a word."

"Were you nice to her?"

"I'm always nice, honey."

"That's not entirely true."

"Oh, really?" Tessa said. "And here I thought I was such a spectacular person."

Regina made a face, and Tessa laughed.

"Will you write to her again?" Regina licked the last bit of farina off her spoon and drank some juice while she waited for an answer. "Well? Will you?"

Tessa hesitated because she genuinely didn't know how to answer. She reached out a hand to smooth Regina's curls, but instead Regina intercepted, took her mother's hand and held it, staring into her eyes.

It was such an unanticipated gesture that Tessa froze, suddenly uncertain of Regina's intent. But in that moment when their hands met, Tessa understood as she had so many times before that nothing really happened by chance, or did it? So much could change in a day, in a moment. Last week, Tessa had seen a young mother setting out with her child in a stroller to cross in the middle of the street. As Tessa held her breath, she saw the mother, suddenly remembering something (perhaps a letter that had to be mailed), turn back. In that exact moment that she turned, a truck careened around the corner. The mother and her child were saved. Was it destiny that guided the mother's decision to turn back? Or did she turn back because she had somehow, perhaps in a forgotten dream, been given a glimpse of the future? Most would say it was merely good fortune, but Tessa could not be certain.

As she held Regina's hand, it seemed to Tessa that everything was about timing. When she had first set her heart on Walter, was it because she knew that it would take Regina (not any other child, but Regina), to bring Ursula back to their lives? Did anything ever really happen suddenly?

Each day, Tessa held the hands of women whose futures were often visible. Tessa wondered what would happen if she told a client not to take the much anticipated trip to Bermuda because her husband was in danger. Would the woman listen? Perhaps, Tessa rationalized, it was the woman's destiny to grapple for the rest of her life with the knowledge that she should have prevented her husband from swimming after he complained of what he was sure was nothing more than mild indigestion. If Tessa told the hopeful bride-to-be that her intended would not make her forget the passion she had felt for her previous lover, would the wedding be called off? Was it possible that the bride had chosen her bland and unimaginative intended because he would never interfere with her fiery memories of the man she continued to love, but could never have?

Tessa was haunted by what she knew and never told. What if she had spoken up and saved the husband from drowning? What if she had urged the bride to forgive her former lover and marry him instead? What if, after all, Tessa had interceded, and the results were equally devastating. What if she was wrong?

"Mom? Is there more cereal?"

"Yes, of course. I'll get it for you."

"You didn't answer me about Aunt Althea. Will you write to her again?"

"Yes, I'll write to her again."

"When?"

"Later today."

"Promise?"

"You can watch me write to her."

Regina laughed and said, "Maybe I will." She pulled the sleeves of her sweatshirt down over her hands and then wrapped her arms around herself. "Mom, can we talk about Ursula's gloves?"

"What about them?" Tessa ladled more cereal into Regina's bowl. "I told you everything I know."

"But there's more I haven't told you."

"Yes, now I remember. The notebook."

"How did you know about the notebook?" Regina said.

"You told me." Tessa kept her expression impassive. "Don't you remember?"

Regina looked uncertain, and Tessa was contrite. Lying still came too easily to her, but at least she knew the difference between the truth and a lie. She was still unsure if she had merely dreamed that her mother was crying for her, or if she had heard the cries and ignored them. It seemed important now to be able to make that differentiation, but Tessa could not remember. Some things did not want to be remembered. Like why she had not stopped her parents from getting in the car that snowy night so long ago.

"Will you tell me everything from the beginning?" Regina asked.

How far back was the beginning? Tessa tried to arrange her thoughts in some sequence that Regina would understand. When did Tessa first recognize that Ursula was not like the other mothers? Was it the time she ran through the sprinkler in the park with her clothes on? Or was it the time she woke Tessa in the middle of a rainy summer night to hunt salamanders in the woods? Tessa would have to answer no, for none of those events made her think that her mother was anything other than amazing. It was miraculous to have a mother like Ursula, and Tessa loved her with an unrestrained heart.

It was the other times, the times that Ursula was distant and remote, eluding conversation and balking at the suggestion of showering while snarling obscenities at Tessa. Poor Tessa would run, terrified, from the room, covering her ears with her hands as her father had told her to do. The tirades grew worse the more Ursula suspected that the gift she struggled to fabricate came to Tessa without effort. At these times, Ursula would not touch Tessa, claiming to be in fear of her own life in the presence of such power. She said this with so much cruelty that Tessa cowered and cried, begging to be forgiven, pleading that it was not her fault. Still, Ursula coldly denied her. Ursula's eyes became dark hollows in which Tessa could not find any trace of her mother.

"The beginning?" Tessa said. "I'm not sure I can remember that far back."

"Yes you can," Regina said.

"Maybe I don't want to."

"You have to, Mom.

So this was how Tessa decided to make Regina an accessory to her own legacy. It might not have been the right decision, but Tessa made it without regret. She knew that all childhoods were replete with some disappointment and some pain. Mostly, those feelings could be easily influenced. Sharp words were willingly displaced by good memories. The sporadic shame of her mother's neglect, the times she forgot to pick her up from school or sent in tins of smoked sprats and jars of cocktail onions when it was her turn to be snack mother could be forgotten. For every dreadful memory, for every indifferent act, Tessa could remember something good. But it was what she had done, what she had known and failed to prevent, that tore at her like her mother's nails had against her own flesh when the demons could not be held at bay. And it was that Ursula had also known, and also done nothing, making them accomplices in their own tragedy. Tessa was not about to let that happen again.

"Yes," Tessa agreed. "You're right. I do."

Chapter Twelve

"I'm waiting," Regina said. "You promised."

"Which part first?" Tessa rinsed the dishes and loaded them into the dishwasher. The bowl was encrusted with leftover farina, and she scraped it with a rubber-gloved finger. "The part about her notebook?"

"I never told you about the notebook, Mom. I'm positive."

Tessa sighed and said, "No. You didn't. I'm sorry."

"Why did you lie?"

"I don't know, Reg." She turned away from the sink. "I don't know why I do anything I do." Another lie. The truth was just too hard sometimes.

"I'm not afraid of the truth," Regina said.

"Well, you should be."

"Your mother knew that you had dreamed about the accident, didn't she?"

"Yes. She apparently had the same dream."

"Did she record all her dreams?" Regina sounded skeptical. "The details were incredible. It must have taken forever."

"She was meticulous about some things."

"Do any of those spells really work?"

Regina curled her legs beneath her and pulled her sweatshirt down over her knees. She stared at Tessa, anticipating some form of confession.

"She seemed to think so," Tessa said. "Let me see your nails."

"What?"

"Your nails. Let me see them."

Tessa could not tell from looking at Regina's hands what parts of which boys' bodies they had stroked and pressed. It was not clear how adept her hands were at unknotting a chain or applying eyeliner. Nor were there any telltale signs of how much surreptitious pleasure they might have brought to their owner. They were simply a pair of hands with flaking black-over-dark red nails and rough cuticles. Tessa was rather fond of the trend in mindfully chipped nails that the girls

Regina's age favored, but she felt obliged to ask Regina if she would like a manicure.

"Now?" Regina said.

"Yes, now."

"But they're so perfectly chipped. I had to peel some of the polish off to get them to look this way."

"I know," Tessa said. "It's bad for your nails to do that. But then you know that already."

"I do," Regina said.

Tessa looked deeply into Regina's beautiful face. She was so pale, and a trace of blue eyeliner that was the same shade as the veins on her eyelids was still visible. It gave her an oddly defenseless appearance, made her seem accessible in a way that was not typically her style. It was almost as if her eyelids had been turned inside out like the models of the human body she had once liked to build. For a time, her room was cluttered with plastic reproductions of the eye, the hand, the brain, and once the entire Visible Man *and* the Visible Woman, their organs exposed for all to judge. Regina had painted each artery and vein with breathless precision, spent hours laboring over a spleen or a femur and kept everyone in suspense while she fit together the pieces. But it was the model of the heart that had compelled Tessa most. She had often hoped it would always be so simple for Regina to rule the ways of the heart, to take the pieces apart and put them together with such care, with such understanding.

"So no manicure," Tessa said.

"Not today."

"I brought home a bottle of an amazing purple polish."

Regina shook her head, looking down as she worked off some polish on her pinky nail. When she looked up, her expression was solemn.

"Is Ursula's illness genetic?" she said. "Am I like my grandmother?"

"Now where did that come from?" Tessa said. "Why would you ask such a question?"

"Isn't it a reasonable question?"

"Yes, I'm sorry. It's a very reasonable question, but you're not crazy. Moody, yes." She smiled. "But not crazy."

"How do you know?"

"Because I know."

"Do you remember Brandon?"

"Yes. He was a very nice young man."

"He told me I was crazy."

"Well, he's wrong. Men like to tell women that when they won't do what they want them to do."

Regina laughed. "Well, it doesn't matter. I'm through with men."

Tessa nodded. She understood. *Regina. Queen Regina.* She could not have turned out any differently. "I'm sorry. Brandon seemed so nice."

"Well, he wasn't so nice."

"Don't get angry."

"I can't help it," Regina said. "Anyway, I don't really care that much." She shrugged halfheartedly. "Are you afraid of your mother?"

"Yes. I guess so."

"Are you sure she's alive?" Regina asked.

"Is she really alive?" Tessa asked Regina. "Well, I haven't seen her yet, so I couldn't say for sure."

Regina went back into the big bed for a nap while Tessa finished loading the dishwasher. When she was finished cleaning up, she went upstairs to check on Regina and found her wide awake, staring at the ceiling.

"I thought you were going to take a nap," Tessa said.

"Are you sure she wasn't a witch, Mom?" Regina said. "Some of those spells seem really convincing."

Tessa sat down on the bed and pulled the covers tight around Regina, practically swaddling her with the blanket. Regina did nothing to resist. In fact, she seemed to relax, just as she had as an infant.

"No, she wasn't a witch. Life might have been easier as a witch, but she wasn't one."

"It would have been pretty cool to have a grandmother who was a witch." She yawned loudly. "I'm so tired, but I can't sleep. I can't stop thinking about her."

"I know you can't." Tessa whispered. "Neither can I." She stroked Regina's hair, humming gently as she watched Regina's eyelids flutter, determined to resist sleep just as she had when she was a baby. "Try to sleep."

"Are you a witch?" Regina murmured. Her eyes were half-closed. "Once I thought you were."

"No, baby, I'm not a witch." She stared down at her

Regina yawned again, snuggling down under the comforter. "I want to meet my grandmother," she said. "Will you let me?"

"I'll try."

"Promise?"

"You know that I don't make promises."

"I know, I know," Regina said.

And then, just like that, she was asleep.

Tip-toeing, Tessa left the room and went down to the kitchen where she reheated her coffee in the microwave and sat down to call Fran.

"I've been waiting for you to call," Fran said.

"I'm sorry."

"I should be sorry. I don't know how I could have made this easier for you, but there must have been some way."

"When can we meet to talk?"

"Do you want to see your mother?"

"Yes, but not yet. I'm not ready."

"I see," Fran said. She seemed to be stalling. Her voice was low and hesitant. "I see."

"Do you? Do you really see?" Tessa felt unreasonably irritated. Her coffee was still cold and she put the mug back in the microwave, impatiently drumming her fingers on the countertop as she waited for Fran to say something, anything, but she remained silent, cautiously anticipating Tessa's next move. "Can you genuinely believe that you can understand how I feel? I don't know what she's told you, but whatever she has, you can only trust some of it. I don't think you have any idea who my mother is or what she has struggled with all her life."

"But I do know," Fran said.

"How long have you known her?"

"Long enough."

The timer on the microwave went off, startling Tessa, but not as such as Fran's reply had. While Tessa tried to think of a rejoinder, Fran surprised her again with a question.

"Do you believe in love?" Fran said.

Tessa added some Half and Half to her coffee and swirled her cup, a habit that typically annoyed Walter for no reason at all. "Yes, of course I believe in love. I think that everything is about love. You know, wanting it or not wanting it. Having it or not having it. But always about love in some way."

"Good, that's good. I'm glad to hear you say that because you have to know how much your mother loves you."

"I don't want to hear this now."

"Listen to me, Tessa. I don't know you, but I know that the remarkable thing about love is it can exist on its own. We've all loved someone who didn't return our love the way we hoped it would be returned. We love our children even when they seem to hate us and tell us so. We love men who disappoint us and break our hearts. Love is an isolated emotion. It thrives on its own volition. It fuels itself. Don't you think that's remarkable?"

"Yes, but not as remarkable as knowing my mother is within reach."

"Well, then there's that, too, isn't there?" Fran said. "Then trust in the belief that love renews us."

"Or it destroys us, right?"

"It can, yes."

"When can we meet?" Tessa said.

They agreed to meet in the morning. No, Tessa did not want to go to Fran's place. The coffee shop where they had met before would be fine. Ten o'clock was perfect.

"How is she?" Tessa said.

"She struggles," Fran said gently. "But she's managing."

"Well, that's good. Tell her that I asked for her."

"I will, dear. She's eager to see you." Fran cleared her throat. "She doesn't want anything from you, Tessa. Only to be forgiven."

Tessa shut her eyes tightly, hoping to suppress the image of how her mother had cornered her more than once, shrieking, "You want something from me. You all want something from me, but I have nothing to give you."

Each time, Tessa would cringe and sob, repeating that it wasn't true. "I only want you to be happier," she had cried. She had really wanted to say that she only wanted her mother not to be so crazy. Ursula never believed her anyway, calling her a liar and a fraud, part of a conspiracy.

Eyes open or shut, Tessa could do nothing to free herself from her memories. But instead of being softened by Fran's words, Tessa only felt belligerent and antagonistic. She had the awful desire to bully Fran.

"What makes her think that I don't want something from her?" Tessa said.

"I don't know how to answer that question," Fran said quietly. "I can't speak for Ursula. I'll see you tomorrow."

"Yes you will," Tessa said. "Indeed you will."

With Regina still asleep, Tessa decided to write an email to Althea. It seemed to Tessa that she was at a critical junction. The past was pushing its way into her life in a way that demanded she take hold of it. Ursula and Althea. Tessa had loved them both, and they had both abandoned her. The irony was painful. Tessa needed to assume some control over how they would resume their places.

It was strange to think of Althea as an adult with a life and a career all her own. And it was equally strange to realize how many years had passed since they had last seen each other. Careful to choose words that could not be misunderstood, Tessa asked after her in-laws with the same restraint Tessa had felt in Althea's email to Regina. The whole process of inching toward each other was exhausting, but Tessa had promised Regina, and now was not the time to renege on a pledge.

Tessa made it a point not to make any references to the past. She asked after Althea's work, observed that curating sounded like interesting work, and acknowledged that it had been too many years since they last met. Tessa said she hoped Althea would make good on her promise to call before she came to New York and allow them to host her for lunch or dinner, or whatever was most comfortable. She knew Regina was eager to see her aunt and, of course, Walter missed his family.

She deleted that last part—it sounded falsely hollow even to her. Instead, Tessa reiterated her invitation to join them at their house. You remember where we live, don't you? Tessa deleted that because it sounded too hostile. Quickly, she wrapped up the email with a friendly goodbye and gave best regards to all. That seemed generic enough not to provoke any misunderstanding. When she was done, she forwarded the email to Regina, leaned back in the chair, closed her eyes and wished she could sleep. She was afraid to sleep in the day when her dreams were always more disturbing.

Ursula had insisted that she dreamed like a person who had been born blind. "I don't see images in my dreams," she said. She claimed that her dreams were defined by taste and touch and smell. She might not see burnt toast, but she could describe how it smelled. But what Tessa remembered most was how so many of her mother's dream narratives were about the misfortunes she endured on cars or buses or planes. Any form of travel became the mainstay of her terrors. In her dreams, Ursula was always on her way to somewhere, and she was always getting lost. Years later, Tessa realized that her mother's comparisons were entirely reasonable. A blind person had to navigate a dark world, just like the world Ursula fumbled her way through. "I might as well walk around with my eyes closed," she had once wailed. "I can't see anything anyway."

Fran had said that Ursula did not want anything from her, but Tessa had never been worried about that. She worried more that she would be unable to forgive her mother for disappearing and that the bitterness of that loss would make it impossible to be compassionate. Tessa knew that compassion could be in short supply for someone like Ursula.

The only time Dennis had left them alone for a night had been disastrous. Reluctantly, he had agreed to attend a convention in Atlantic City. "Just one night," he told Ursula and Tessa. "They want me to go for three nights, but I agreed to one night only." Tessa, born an adult, had told him not to worry. Ursula had been on a good run then, and they all felt certain one night was safe. That evening, Ursula even helped him pick out the right tie for his shirt and suit and folded and readied everything for his overnight bag. Tessa sat on the bed and watched them, hopeful that they could really be like every other family. They looked just like any other family. The next morning, Ursula, in her bathrobe, scrambled eggs for everyone and made perfect toast. Tessa noted the look her parents exchanged when they kissed. They generated heat, and Tessa basked in it.

When her father walked her down to the bus, he casually handed her a piece of paper with the name and number of the hotel where he would be staying that night. He told her to call him no matter what time it was if she needed anything at all. And young as Tessa was she understood everything that her father didn't say. Later that afternoon, when the bus dropped her off, Tessa walked the half block home with the full certainty that something was wrong. She had the distinct impression that she was walking in her mother's footprints. Behind her eyes, Tessa saw her mother, alone and confused, wandering unfamiliar streets. But anger rose in Tessa rather than fear. She was furious that her mother had done something that would breach the flawlessness of the night before and the promise of the morning. Ursula always ruined everything.

As Tessa approached the house, she saw that the front door was ajar. Her fingers tingled as soon as she made contact with the heavy brass doorknob. She didn't even bother to call out for her mother. Instead, Tessa opened her lunch bag, removed the half of the peanut butter and jelly sandwich that she hadn't eaten, poured herself a glass of milk, took two oatmeal cookies from the Cookie Monster cookie jar, and sat down at the kitchen table. From her pocket, she took the piece of paper her father had given her and smoothed it out on the table, staring at his writing while she ate.

Tessa never called him. She locked the front door, went upstairs, changed her clothes and did her homework. When her father called at dinnertime, she told him that Mommy was taking a nap and that everything was fine. They were having macaroni and cheese for dinner. She even told him a funny joke that she had heard in school that day. *Knock Knock! Who's there? Lettuce. Lettuce who? Lettuce in or you'll be sorry!* Dennis laughed, and the relief Tessa heard in his voice made her feel very grown-up. She had handled things. She felt proud.

In retrospect, Tessa wondered how he could have been so naïve. When she talked to Walter about those years, he had surmised that it was desperation rather than naiveté that had enabled Dennis's decisions. That day, however, it was only after Tessa hung up with her father that she saw her mother's shoes on the mat near the front door. Ursula always took her shoes off when she came in from outside and slipped into a pair of soft black leather flats that she wore only in the house. They were on the mat as well.

Of course, it was entirely possible that she had worn different shoes, but it was unlikely. Tessa just knew it. She knew it as well as she had known from the beginning that something was wrong. It was a feeling that began as a sort of quiet unease and then became familiar as though it had been there all along. She didn't know how to explain it back then, but years later when she and Walter and Regina came home from a two-week vacation on Cape Cod, Tessa turned to Walter and said, and "It feels just like this." Everything in the house looked different, and it felt strange to be in her own home that didn't feel like her own home at all.

By the time Ursula found her way back that night, it was well past ten. Tessa was sitting on the steps in the foyer of the center hall colonial that would one day be hers. She sat upright and very still, staring at the front door, anticipating her mother's return. When the door finally opened, Tessa immediately looked at her mother's feet. It was not quite winter yet, but it was cold enough out that a woman without shoes should not have gone unnoticed. Ursula's feet were black with dirt, and her soles were lacerated and bloody. "Why didn't you come and find me?" she said pathetically.

Grim, but not without tenderness, Tessa led her to the kitchen, helped her out of her coat and sat her in a chair. Ursula's face and hands were dirty as well. Within minutes, Tessa had prepared a mug of chamomile tea and filled a basin with warm soapy water that she placed on the floor. While Ursula sipped her tea, Tessa carefully guided her mother's torn feet into the basin of water. Next, Tessa wrung a wet washcloth in the sink and wiped away the dirt on her mother's hands and face.

"You knew, didn't you?" Ursula said. Her head was thrust back slightly, giving Tessa access to her soiled neck. Tessa didn't answer as she dabbed at her mother's forehead. From between cracked lips, Ursula said, "What good is it to know?"

Wordlessly, Tessa continued to clean her mother's face. And while she didn't say so, Tessa thought to herself, no good at all.

"Thanks, Mom."

Regina suddenly surprised Tessa by wrapping her arms around her from behind and planting a loud kiss on her cheek.

"I must have done something right," Tessa said. "You're clearly happy with me." She spun around in the chair and Regina, very uncharacteristically, sat on her mother's lap. "My, my how you've grown." Tessa said. She laughed and shifted her weight, trying to help Regina get comfortable. "To what do I owe this great honor?"

"The email to Aunt Althea."

"Oh, that little gem of evasive writing."

Regina was much too big for her mother's lap. In fact, it would have made more sense the other way around, but Tessa loved the weight of Regina and hugged her tightly.

"Well, I appreciate it," Regina said. "I just hope she visits and likes us."

"Ouch," Tessa said, trying to shift Regina to a better spot. "Careful what you wish for. Next thing you know, Aunt Althea will be moving in with us."

"So? We have the space."

"Great. She can have your room. Ouch, ouch, ouch. I think you have to get up. You're way too big."

Regina got up and leaned against the desk.

"How do you feel?" Tessa said.

"So much better. Nearly perfect except for feeling tired." She stood up straight and stretched. "I have to do some homework. I'm already behind."

"Then hop to it."

But Regina did not move. She shifted uneasily from foot to foot, and Tessa wondered what could be next.

"When you go to meet Ursula, can I come with you?"

Tessa shook her head and reached out for Regina who moved toward her simultaneously. "Please, be patient. You know your Aunt Althea used to ask me a million questions about my mother. In those years, I was still quite a sensation in this village. The stories about my father's death and my mother's disappearance made for great local gossip. I was at the center of that for most of my adolescence."

"I'm sorry, but what does that have to do with me?"

"Nothing, I guess. I don't know. I was just thinking out loud." She squeezed Regina's hands. She was small boned, like Ursula. "I still have trouble making sense of a lot of what happened with Ursula."

"People still talk about her sometimes, you know?"

"I know."

"Does it bother you?"

"No, not anymore. Not really, anyway."

"I heard you once tell Mia that you bewitched Dad into falling in love with you."

Tessa ran her fingers over Regina's bony knuckles. She must have overheard countless pieces of information, storing them away, unsure of what to do with them.

"That's funny." Tessa shrugged. "Well, we love each other."

"I know you do." Regina hesitated, seeming to gather some courage for the next question. "But did you? I mean, could you if you'd wanted to? Could you have bewitched him?"

"What do you want, Regina?" It sounded sharper than she had intended, and Tessa softened her voice and said, "If you want something from me, just tell me."

"I want to know why you didn't find her if all along you knew she was still alive."

Regina's face was flushed again, but this time it was not the work of a fever. Her fists were clenched just like when she was a little girl in the throes of a tantrum. Tessa almost laughed at the memory, but she caught herself. Then, she had swooped Regina up in her arms, blowing lightly on her face, whispering, "Mommy is making all your anger go away." She would point at the air. "See it, there? The little wisps of smoke? That's your anger. See it? Gone!" Regina would laugh in spite of herself and wind her arms around Tessa's neck. It had been so easy then.

"Not even I could find someone who didn't want to be found," Tessa said.

Regina seemed unconvinced, but she agreed anyway. Her mouth was set in a resolute line that could not mask her frustration. For now, there was nothing more to say or to do, though Tessa knew it was temporary. Regina wasn't one to be held in abeyance for long. Along with a small boned frame, she had inherited that from Ursula as well.

Chapter Thirteen

In spite of Regina's quizzical looks and intermittent efforts to bring the dinner conversation around to Ursula or Althea, Tessa rambled on somewhat inanely about whatever came to mind. She told Walter and Regina about an eight-foot alligator that had walked into a woman's house in Tampa, Florida. The poor woman had come into the kitchen only to find the huge beast, thrashing about, evidently in search of food.

"What did she do?" Walter said.

"She called 911," Tessa said.

"They must have thought it was some sort of prank," Regina said.

"Maybe," Tessa said. "I don't know."

She had already lost interest. Then she asked Walter if the law intern in his office had given birth. Walter said he thought so, and why did she want to know, anyway?

Tessa said, "So I can buy a present, of course. What did she have?"

"A baby," Walter said. He was already scraping plates and stacking them. "Does it matter?"

Regina rolled her eyes at Tessa, who smiled, happy to be allies again.

"Well, only if she doesn't mind dressing her son in a pink dress," Tessa said.

"Why would she do that?" Walter said.

"Forget it, Mom." Regina gave Walter a threatening look. "I'm not done." She held onto her plate, discouraging his efforts to add it to the stack. "Get something in yellow."

"That's an idea," Walter said. "A yellow dress." He laughed when Tessa and Regina exchanged exact looks of disbelief. "Ha! You see? You think I'm totally stupid, but I'm not!"

"Indeed," Tessa said, but she smiled and handed Walter her plate. She had barely eaten. "You win, as always."

"Do I detect a sore loser in our midst?" Walter said. "What do you think, Reggie?"

"I'm Switzerland," Regina said. "I don't want to get involved. " She got up and took her own plate to the sink. "I have some work to finish."

"No dessert?" Tessa said. "I made some baked apples."

"Maybe," Regina said.

"Walter?" Tessa asked.

"Definitely," he said. "Not maybe like our indecisive girl here."

Regina stood still at the sink until Walter nudged her aside so he could fill the kettle with water.

"I wrote an email to Althea," Tessa said.

"Really?" he said. "Well, good for you. That must have taken some courage."

"Not really." Tessa was a bit thrown by his reaction. "I don't see how courage has anything to do with it."

"No? That's interesting," he said. "I would have thought you'd be reluctant to reconnect with Althea after all these years and after everything that happened."

"What happened?" Regina said.

"Nothing," Tessa said. "Nothing happened." She scowled at Walter. "I thought we talked about this."

"Indeed," Walter said. He took three mugs from the cupboard. "Preferences?"

"Green," Regina said.

"Same for me." Tessa looked at Regina. "I thought you had work to do."

"I do, but I can't miss this."

"Miss it," Tessa said.

While Walter filled the mugs with hot water, Tessa watched. No one spoke until Regina, looking from her mother to her father, finally said, "Okay. I get it. I think I'll have my tea in my room. If you guys don't mind, that is." She pretended to be offended. "I really need to finish up a paper and study my Spanish." She took her mug, said good luck, and disappeared.

"Good luck?" Walter called after her. "What does that mean?" He turned to Tessa. "Why did she wish me good luck?"

"How do you know she wasn't wishing me good luck?"

He regarded Tessa suspiciously, but clearly had no intentions of taking her on. "So tell me more about Althea."

"Nothing to tell. I just broke the ice. I can forward you a copy of the email."

He sipped at his tea and said nothing.

"Regina seems all better," Tessa said.

"Yes, she seems back to herself . . .whatever that means."

They could hear Regina's muted laughter.

"I thought she had to study," Walter said.

"She will. Don't worry," Tessa said. "I spoke with Fran today." Using her thumb and forefinger, she removed a tea leaf from her tongue and placed it on her napkin. When she looked up, Walter was looking at her with unblinking eyes. It made her nervous, the way he stared. "I'm going to have coffee with her tomorrow morning." Walter sipped his tea. "Would you say something, please? It's infuriating when you give me the silent treatment."

"I would think you would prefer it."

"Why would I prefer it?"

He set his mug down and leaned back in the chair, clasping his hands behind his head and stretching his long legs out full length. Breathing in deeply, he let out a long sigh as if he needed to brace himself for what was ahead. Almost immediately, he narrowed his eyes, pursed his lips, and focused his full attention on Tessa.

"Aren't you going to answer me?" Tessa asked.

"I just did."

"I thought you said you wanted to help me."

"I do. I want to help you get over this. You know how I feel about your mother. I don't know what you're thinking. Emails to Althea, and now a meeting with this Fran character, which is clearly a precursor to a reunion with your mother, and you question my intentions? That strikes me as absurd."

"A reunion? You make it sound so festive."

"Maybe it will be. I hope so for your sake."

"What did you want me to do about Althea? Regina is so determined."

"Really? And where do you imagine she gets that from?"

"I need your help," Tessa said. "I can't do this alone."

"I'm not going anywhere. "

"But I need more than that. I need to be able to talk to you about it without feeling judged."

"I'm not judging you," he said. "That's preposterous. I think you're crazy, but that's an opinion, not a judgment."

Tessa took a sip of tea, hoping it would quiet her stomach. The tea was very hot, and she burned her lip. She felt like crying.

"Can't you see how upset I am?" she said. "I burned my lip."

"Do you want some ice?"

"No. I want you to be reasonable."

"Why can't you let it go?"

"I can't," she said.

"You'll be sorry. It portents disaster on every level."

"How do you know? What if she's changed?"

"Althea or your mother?"

"Stop it." Tessa tried not to raise her voice. "You're being stubborn."

"I'm just trying to stay alive," Walter said. He was deliberately calm. "And you don't always make that easy for me. Althea waited too long. It's over for me. It's just the way I am, and you should know that better than anyone else. Why is this so hard to understand? Your mother chose not to be part of your life. Now she suddenly wants entry. Why should you give it to her? Do you think she's cured? She's crazy. She was always crazy, and she's still crazy. What makes it so hard for you to accept that?"

"What makes it so easy for you to let people you love go?"

He shook his head. "I don't let them go. I just don't fight to keep them if they don't want me."

"Maybe she wants you now. Maybe Althea is ready to reconcile. Wouldn't you like a chance to make amends?"

"With a hysteric and a crazy woman?"

"I wouldn't call Althea a hysteric. She was very young and very impressionable. And don't call my mother *crazy*," Tessa said. "I resent that label, especially when someone else uses it."

Tessa knew she was being unreasonable, but she had always protected her mother. Walter looked skeptical, but he dropped it. He drained his tea cup and asked her if she was coming up.

"In a few minutes," she said. "I just have to make a grocery list."

He kissed her with such gentleness that it moved her, but not enough to share her grief. She waited until she heard his shoes drop on the wooden floor with a resounding thud until she put her head in the crook of her arm and wept. She hated having a crazy mother. She just hated it.

Regina was well enough to go to school the next day. She came flying downstairs, took three bites of a bagel, and then stuffed a yogurt drink into her knapsack while urging Walter to hurry or she would be late for her first period class. He took one more sip of coffee and another spoonful of oatmeal.

"I'll wait for you in the car," Regina said. "Hurry, Dad. Bye, Mom! Don't be nervous." She made a kissing noise at Tessa. "Tell me everything later."

Tessa make a kissing noise back and snuck a banana into Regina's knapsack as she made her way out the door.

"I'm not nervous, honey. Make sure you eat some lunch."

"Well," Walter said. He had filled a thermal car mug with coffee. "You okay?"

"I'm okay," she said. "Go on. Regina will start honking the horn."

"I'm sorry if I fell asleep on you last night."

"Don't be sorry." She stood on her tiptoes and kissed him. "You were tired. There wasn't anything else to talk about."

"Well, I'm not so sure about that."

"Go. I'm fine."

"Will you call me?" Walter said.

"I don't know," Tessa said.

"No more chances?"

"I'll give you many chances. Go."

Walter kissed her cheek and hurried out to the car. Tessa saw Regina laughing at something her father said. They looked like a picture-perfect family.

The coffee shop crowd was thinning out as Tessa stepped inside and relished the blast of warm air. She had layered up against the cold and began to unwind the scarf from around her neck as she searched for Fran.

"Over here!" Fran said. She was standing, waving exaggeratedly with both hands. "Right here, Tessa."

Tessa lifted her chin slightly, subtly acknowledging Fran's energetic greeting, and made her way to the back of the diner.

"Am I late?" Tessa glanced at her watch, but it was not even ten. "No, I'm still early."

"I was very early," Fran said. "Overzealous, I guess."

"Apparently so, from that double hand waving."

"My son used to hate when I did that. I embarrassed him all the time."

Immediately Tessa felt lightheaded, assaulted by a multitude of conflicting feelings. She closed her eyes, imagined herself swooning like some Victorian woman, clutching her vinaigrette pendant, inhaling the vapors on the hidden sponge.

Ursula had worn such an antique piece. It had been an anniversary gift from Dennis, but Ursula had lost it on one of her mysterious sojourns. Tessa thought it was strange to think of the vinaigrette pendant after so many years when she had completely forgotten about it—until now. Thinking she heard a baby crying, she turned. But there were no babies in the coffee shop. No women wearing vinaigrette pendants though Tessa sniffed the air. It smelled like ammonia, exactly what Ursula had used on the new sponge she placed in her pendant. "My va—pors," she had drawled. "I need my vapors."

"Is something wrong?" Fran said. "You're trembling."

Tessa opened her eyes. It seemed as though she had been standing for hours. Wearily, she slid into the booth across from Fran. "Am I?" she said. "Maybe I'm catching whatever Regina had."

The waitress came and took their orders, returning quickly with a pot of hot water, a mug, and a teabag. Tessa put her hands around the teapot. Fran poured some cream into her coffee and took several small sips in succession.

"How are you?" Fran said. "Aside from being cold, that is." She smiled. "Is Regina feeling better?"

"Oh, I'm fine. Just a bit tired. Regina is much better today. She went to school this morning."

"It's amazing how children bounce back."

"Yes, amazing."

Fran had let her hair loose. It was shorter than Tessa had thought. Several wisps of hair framed her face, making her look far younger than she had before. She was wearing elongated silver hoops with a sizeable blue bead at the bottom. Tessa noticed that Fran's nails were bare. She had probably never worn polish before she came to the salon. Nail polish simply did not suit Fran. She blushed under Tessa's scrutiny.

"I'm famished," Fran said. "I left without eating anything. Nervous, I guess."

"Nervous? Why?"

"You know why. Don't be coy."

Tessa had not expected Fran to be quite so direct.

"I didn't mean to be coy. I'm sorry."

"That's okay. It's just that we're on the brink here, aren't we? Everything in our lives could change after this meeting."

"You make it seem very dramatic," Tessa said.

"Isn't it? Dramatic, that is."

"I don't know yet. That remains to be seen, I think."

The waitress arrived with Fran's order, and Fran immediately picked up a piece of her buttered toast and took a large bite while simultaneously lifting a forkful of scrambled egg to her mouth.

"Sorry," Fran said. "I should have waited for you."

"That's fine. Go ahead. I'm not that hungry. I had something before I left."

"You're so thin."

"It's hereditary I guess."

They both stopped what they were doing to consider the implications of this information. Fran seemed to summon up some courage before pursuing Tessa's statement.

"Your mother is still quite thin," Fran said. She blushed as if there was more she wanted to say. "And she is still very beautiful."

"Still? So you've known her a long time."

Fran lowered her fork and placed it on her plate. Then she took her napkin from her lap and dabbed at the corners of her mouth before she spoke.

"Shall we get right down to it?" she said.

"No, let's wait," Tessa said. "That is if you don't mind. You don't, do you?"

"No." Fran shook her head as she spoke. "I don't mind at all."

"So. How old is your son?" She tried to sound casual. "You said you were forty when you adopted him."

"That's correct." Fran said. "I wasn't young."

"So Philip must be in his twenties."

"He'll be twenty-five on his next birthday."

Hot water splashed onto Tessa's hand, but she barely reacted. Instead, she watched Fran's left eyelid twitch and counted the beats between the flutters. One, two, three. Twitch. One, two, three. Twitch. One, two, three. Twitch. When Fran saw Tessa watching her, she pressed the pad of her index finger to her eyelid and held it there.

"Why are you so tense whenever I ask about Philip?" Tessa said.

Fran lowered her head, took her finger off her eyelid and sat up straighter than before.

"Is something wrong with Philip?" Tessa said.

They were hard words. Tessa said them in her head first, felt the hardness before she said them aloud, noting the preliminary satisfaction it gave her knowing she would hurt Fran. Tessa's heart fluttered just a bit because somehow she accepted that she did not mind being cruel. Even if this knowledge brought her shame, Tessa made no effort to either renounce her bad behavior or to reframe her question. Instead, Tessa did what she did best: she waited.

She knew how to wait. It came from years of practice as a child. Her grandmother had called her the stillest child in the universe. Unable to accept Ursula's death, Tessa had devised countless tests to bring her mother back. If Tessa could count twenty red cars in five minutes, Ursula would return. If Tessa could sit motionless for two hours, her mother would reappear. The trials become more and more complicated and required enormous efforts of patience and will for a little girl, even one as unusual as Tessa. She stayed awake for an entire night; wrote her name, Tessa Emanuel Tessa Emanuel Tessa Emanuel, fifty times without lifting her pen from the paper; stared at an object for five minutes without blinking.

For a time, Tessa refused to wear new clothes because she was afraid her mother might not recognize her. It was important to keep everything as it had been. Finally, when Tessa's jeans were above her ankles and her tee shirts grew so short that they revealed her bare midriff, Grandmother Lucy put her foot down. Tessa wore the stiff new jeans and the brightly colored tee shirts to satisfy her grandmother, but only after Lucy promised to keep the old clothes. As soon as Tessa came home from school, she dutifully changed into her old clothes and sat on the steps for hours anyway, just in case Ursula wandered back and needed a marker to identify her past.

"I don't know how to answer that question," Fran said, holding up her hand.

Tessa saw that it was shaking. Reaching across the table, Tessa took Fran's hand and said, "Well, we might as well get on with it, right?" She smiled, tightly, but not unkindly. "Tell me what happened."

"It wasn't complicated at first," Fran said as if they had been talking about Philip's adoption all along. "We hired an attorney. He handled private adoptions. I wanted a boy if at all possible. I didn't think I'd be very good at raising a girl. I don't know why. I just didn't. The attorney put an ad in the paper. We offered to pay all medical expenses, plus a sum to the birth mother. It was all very legal, very up front." She paused. "Shall I go on?"

"Go on," Tessa said. "I'm listening."

"Philip's birth mother needed help. She was alone and very frightened. When I met her the first time, I thought *she* should be adopted." Fran laughed at herself, and then took a sip of coffee. "I mean it. I invited her to live with us until after the birth."

"Did she?"

"Yes," Fran said. "She did."

"And then what happened?" Tessa prompted.

"After a few days, it became clear that she was more than scared. She was troubled . . . ill. But I wanted that baby, so I told myself everything would be all right. You know how we do that? It's easy when it's something important you want." Fran covered her face with her hands. "If only I had been smarter, I might have prevented all this."

"All what?" Tessa said, already knowing and not knowing at the same time.

"We didn't know she was mentally ill," Fran said. "She left after Philip was born, promising to stay out of our lives. She was true to her word, but we had also made a promise."

Tessa just wanted the story to be over. When the story was over, she would go home. Tessa could leave and forget that any of this had ever happened.

The smell of ammonia was gone. She felt relieved as though Fran's story would take a different trajectory now, but it was simply more wishful thinking. The story had *happened*. It just had to be told now.

"We promised that if he ever wanted to meet her, we would help him. She would keep in touch every year to let us know her whereabouts. I made that promise, never believing that day would come."

"That day always comes," Tessa said.

It would never be over. She had really known that all along.

"Everything was fine until about three years ago," Fran continued. "Philip decided he wanted to find his birth mother. I knew it was a request that had to be honored no matter how I felt or what I knew about her. Thomas wanted me to discourage it, to forbid it. Of course, he knew what I knew, and so it made sense to want the whole process brought to a halt. He couldn't accept that once Philip made the request, it was already out of our hands."

"What did you know?" Tessa said.

Fran ignored the question.

"He was a remarkably good natured baby," she said. "So sociable. Everyone marveled at it."

When Fran lifted her eyes, Tessa felt the struggle of what Fran had lived with all these years.

"Say it," Tessa said.

"Philip's birth mother," Fran said. "Her name is Ursula Emanuel. She's Philip's birth mother, Tessa. You have a brother."

Tessa nodded and nodded and nodded, as her eyes overflowed with tears. She shivered, afraid she would never be warm again.

"I wanted to tell you," Fran said. "I wanted to tell you time and time again. I tried to find a way that wouldn't be so painful. What could I do? How could I have made this any easier?"

Once again, it was Tessa who was being called on to give solace, to lessen the grief and to assure that all would be well. Over and over in her young and tumultuous life, Tessa had been given this burdensome task.

"She's not well," Fran said.

"I'm sorry to hear that," Tessa said stiffly.

"She only told me the full story a few months ago," Fran said. "That's when I felt I should contact you. She was against it."

"Really?" Tessa said bitterly. "How thoughtful of her."

"It's not like that. She knows how much sadness she's brought you. That's why she never came back."

"Oh, she did it for *me*?" Tessa said. "Well, that's really something. And she thought abandoning me would relieve my misery? What about Philip? How much does he know?"

"He knows nothing. I swear to you."

"Does she know? Ursula. Does she know that you've found me?"

"Yes," Fran said. "She knows. She told me where to find you."

It did not take sorcery or genius to know what Tessa had always believed. All this time, all these years, her mother had been watching her. She might have grazed Tessa on the street or in the fruit store. Ursula might even have been in the salon for the Tuesday special. A wash and a set for twenty-five dollars. The salon was always packed on a Tuesday, and after awhile the faces of all those women became a blur. Ursula might have sat beneath a dryer, her hair wound in pink and blue and green curlers. On her way up to the counter to pay, she might have brushed against Tessa's shoulder without her ever knowing. Tessa shook her head. No. She would have known Ursula was near.

"I didn't mean to mislead you," Fran said.

"The first afternoon you came to see me in the salon, you gave me the red ribbon. What would you call that?"

"I wanted to help. I wanted to make things easier."

"This is what you call easy?" Tessa asked.

"Please, don't," Fran said. "There are things you don't know."

"Undoubtedly," Tessa said.

"Your mother became pregnant when she was taking medication. Haldol. It's a very potent drug. The pregnancy was unplanned, and she wanted to end it. She was terrified the baby would be hurt by the drugs. Your father didn't care. He wanted the baby no matter what. That's what they were fighting about the night of the accident."

Tessa thought about all the time she had spent waiting for a sign from her mother. For awhile, whenever the phone rang and no one was there, she picked up the receiver and said, "Mommy? Is it you?" Finally, she had made herself stop. She was not going to start again now.

"Tessa, I'm sorry. She was very ill."

"The red ribbon you gave me, and the words to go with it," Tessa said, "that was my mother's idea, wasn't it?"

"Yes," Fran said.

"And when I massaged your hands, you knew what I was doing. She told you, didn't she?"

"Yes. She told me you were special. She said you were sensitive."

"Sensitive? Talk about being coy."

"She's come a very long way since you last saw her."

"So have I," Tessa said.

Fran nodded and said, "I understand."

"What about Philip? How is he?"

"He struggles from time to time," Fran said. "He's different, but not like your mother and not like you either. He's sweet, but he has had a hard time fitting in." She leaned close to Tessa and lowered her voice even more. "He's your brother, Tessa."

It was suddenly quiet in the coffee shop as if in deference to Fran's announcement. Tessa reached into her purse for her wallet and took out a ten-dollar bill and placed it on the table.

"I have to go to work," she said.

"Tessa—"

"I have to go."

"Promise me you won't do anything before talking to me," Fran said.

"I don't make promises," Tessa said. "I never do."

Fran shook her head. "Well, I should have known. Neither does your mother."

Tessa gathered her things and hurried out of the coffee shop, wondering whether or not Philip made promises, or if he too was like his mother and sister.

Chapter Fourteen

Tessa didn't know how she was going to tell Walter about her meeting with Fran.

All day at work, Tessa could not stop thinking about the words of the spiritualist at Lily Dale. Tessa had insisted on a detour to Cassadaga, the world's largest center of spiritualism, while she and Walter were en route to Niagara on the honeymoon they were finally able to take when Regina was three-years-old. Tessa had promised him that she would never mention her mother again if he stopped at Lily Dale, and he promised never to ask what the spiritualist had shared with Tessa that night.

Walter had been true to his word as usual. He was remarkable in that way. Although she frequently accused him of having no sense of curiosity at all, she admired his integrity. Unlike her, he almost always meant what he said. Tessa knew her promise to never mention her mother again was a lie even as the words were out of her mouth.

The spiritualist (who had the unlikely name of Roz Levine) could not have been any kinder. She assured Tessa that if Ursula was present, she would do what she could to bring her through. Almost immediately, however, Roz knew that Ursula was very much alive. And then Roz wanted to know why Tessa had come to Lily Dale.

"Your energy is very clear, my dear," Roz said. "What do you really want from me?"

It was all Tessa could do to keep from crying on the spot. She balled up her hands into fists and dug her nails into her palms. "Where is she?" Tessa said. "I can't see her anywhere."

Roz took Tessa's hands and together they tried to find Ursula. It was useless. Ursula would not be seen.

There was no explanation, nor did Roz consider it unusual. Spirits, according to Roz, could be very willful.

"Her will is strong," Roz said. She smiled. "And you and I know that there is nothing greater than human will."

Tessa nodded, but her disappointment was transparent.

When she tried to pay Roz, she shook her head and said, "Professional courtesy."

She wished Tessa good luck in her search and then, just as Tessa was about to leave, added that perhaps it was best to let Ursula be. "Honor her choice," Roz said. "Sometimes we simply have to let go of what we want because it's the right thing to do."

Tessa thanked her again and left. She kicked at the stones on the graveled path as she walked back to the parking lot where Walter was waiting for her and told herself that perhaps Roz was right. It was time to let Ursula go. But Tessa could not let go then, and she could not let go now.

At the end of the day, Tessa began to tidy up her work station. She was tired and ready to go home, but there was still thirty-five minutes left and a walk-in was possible even though the spa discouraged the practice. And then Walter was standing in front of her. It took her a moment to place him. Then she realized it was her husband and not some man who just happened to look like him.

"What are you doing here?" she said as she leaned over her station to give him a kiss. "Is Regina okay?"

"She's fine. I didn't mean to scare you."

"Why are you here?"

"I thought you might like to stop for a coffee or a drink on the way home."

"Oh. You did?"

"Is that bad?"

"No, not at all. It's very sweet. I'm just surprised."

"By my spontaneity, or by the fact that I even remembered you were meeting that Fran person today?"

Tess laughed. "Both I guess."

"Double whammy." Walter looked pleased with himself. "So? Are we celebrating, or are we mourning?"

"What were you hoping for?"

"I think I would be celebrating what you would be mourning and mourning what you'd be celebrating." He seemed to be trying to gauge her expression. "So should I dust off my dark suit or chill the champagne?"

"I wish it were that simple."

"Don't we all?"

Tessa looked at the clock and said, "Let's go."

"You sure?"

"Positive. I'm thinking vodka and cranberry juice."

Walter grimaced and said, "I'll see your vodka and cranberry juice and raise you a cold beer." He held her coat for her. "It's pretty chilly out. Why don't we go to the place up the block? Then I can follow you home and make sure you're sober."

"I'm always sober. That's my problem."

She slipped her arm through his as they walked up the block. There were several bars in the neighborhood, and they were all fairly identical.

Walter held the door for her and she began to unbutton her coat as soon as she stepped inside. They slid onto stools at the bar and Walter ordered for them.

"Hungry?" he said.

"No, but you go ahead and have something if you need to." She touched his cheek. "Did you have any lunch?"

"I did. I can wait."

"It was nice of you to think of me." Tessa took a handful of nuts from a dish on the bar and looked at them carefully before she shrugged and tossed them all into her mouth. Ursula had always warned her against eating anything left open, but Tessa was feeling reckless. "My mother once told me that rats pee on these nuts."

"Really? So, your mother took you to bars?"

"Only for special occasions." Tessa smiled. "Didn't yours?"

He laughed, reached for some nuts, hesitated, and then cautiously nibbled on a cashew. The bartender set their drinks in front of them. He started to pour Walter's beer into a glass, but Walter covered the top of the glass with his hand. He preferred his beer out of the bottle. The bartender saluted him good-naturedly and took the glass away. Walter handed him a ten and told him to keep the change.

"Oh, what the hell," Walter said. He tossed back a generous serving of nuts and chased it with beer. "I might as well live dangerously." He winked at Tessa. "Right?"

"I suppose." She sipped at her drink. "I feel as though you've been living dangerously since the day you met me."

Walter didn't respond. Instead, he drank his beer slowly, keeping a steady eye on her face, waiting for her to say more. Tessa understood his strategy. There was really nothing for him to say—he had arranged their tryst to make it easier for both of them. She knew he didn't want Regina involved any more than she had to be in the unfolding drama.

"Well, as you might have guessed, she's quite alive."

"Go on."

"She's eager to see me, of course, and hopes to make amends." Tessa unwound her scarf, bunched it up in her lap, and pulled at some stray threads. She knew that he could see how nervous she was. "But that's the least of it." She sighed, took a deep breath, and then launched into the explanation that Walter had come to hear. "I have a brother. His name is Philip. Fran adopted him when he was an infant, and Ursula promised to stay out of their lives unless Philip wanted to meet her. Well, he did, and that's how all this happened."

Walter tilted his head back and finished his beer, caught the bartender's attention and held up the empty bottle. The bartender nodded, set another cold beer down. Walter waited for him to finish and then took a swig from the frosty bottle. It was quite lively in the bar for a weeknight, and Tessa nursed her drink, anticipating Walter's reaction. When none was forthcoming, she gently tapped his arm. He looked at her, almost as if he were surprised to see she was still there.

"Say something," Tessa said. "Please."

"Congratulations."

"*Congratulations?*"

"Yes, you have a brother." He threw an extra five-dollar bill down on the bar. "Are you ready? I want to go before I'm too drunk to drive."

"I think you may already be over the limit," Tessa said quietly.

Walter laughed darkly. "I don't really think you're in a position to talk to me about limits." He shook his head and was about to finish his beer when Tessa firmly wrapped her fingers around the neck of the bottle. "What's this all about?" He pried her fingers loose. "I'm just drinking to my new brother-in-law and my resurrected mother-in-law. Cheers."

"You're drunk," Tessa said.

"Don't be ridiculous. I'm not drunk."

"Well, then you're making an ass of yourself."

To his credit, Walter set the bottle on the bar and nodded contritely as he ran his hand through his hair. "Yes, I guess I am," he agreed.

Immediately, Tessa reached over and grabbed his arm with both hands. "This doesn't have to be a bad thing. What if Philip is fascinating? He could be a lovely uncle for Regina. And what if my mother is ready to step up and assume responsibility for the lives she damaged? Isn't any of that possible?"

She looked so hopeful, so eager to have him confirm what she said. Walter sighed and kissed her cheek, nodding as a compromise.

"If you say so. Sure. I'm always game for a happy ending. What the hell, huh? No harm in being hopeful."

She clapped her hands, relieved even by this. Relieved even though she knew that no matter what they agreed to, some things, like the closely guarded sadness of great losses, were simply eternal and unchanging.

Confident that Walter was indeed sober, Tessa drove leisurely behind his nearly ancient Volvo. Each time they stopped at a light, he waved to her in his rear view mirror, and she waved back. It was sweet and silly, but it reminded her of how he used to pay her toll whenever they drove somewhere in separate cars. It had seemed so gallant, so chivalrous to her younger self that she fell in love with him each time all over again. Regina called Walter's behavior old-fashioned, but she did not mean it at all as a compliment. Tessa said that being old-fashioned wasn't a curse, but Regina always looked skeptical.

As they approached the turn to their street, they hit one last light. Predictably, Walter looked into his rear view mirror and waved, and Tessa held up her gloved hand and wiggled her finger in the mirror. The sky was reassuringly clear, and Tessa felt happy though there was no real reason for her cheerfulness. Her husband's blinker announced his intent to turn, and she waited for the light to change, wanting to turn with him in synchronization, as if such an orchestrated move would insure a good outcome to the events of the day. It seemed as if her wish would come true. The streets were relatively deserted; no other cars were in sight. She took her foot off the brake, let herself hover over the gas pedal, and eased into the move just as the light changed. But it was all too good to be true. Another car seemed to come from nowhere and because it was going straight, it had the right of way.

Tessa knew that there would be news waiting for them at home. Not necessarily bad news, but definitely news of some sort. Therefore, it was no surprise when she found the front door ajar, and Walter and Regina waiting for her in the foyer.

He had not yet taken off his coat, and Regina, holding the portable phone in one hand and a yellow Post-it in the other, unsmilingly asked, "Who's Philip and why is he looking forward to meeting me?"

Tessa took the piece of paper and stared down at Regina's self-conscious print: Philip—917-555-0172.

"Let's go sit down," Tessa said. She made it a point not to look at Walter. "We should talk."

Chapter Fifteen

Walter made tea for everyone. It was a kind gesture, and Tessa gratefully acknowledged his thoughtfulness with a smile as he set a steaming mug in front of her. He did not return her smile, but he nodded as he let his gaze drift toward Regina. She was listening to Tessa explain how it was that Philip came to be.

"Wow," Regina said. "Instant family! It's like those sea monkeys that you just add water to and they come alive."

"Something like that," Tessa said. "Though I hesitate to think of my brother as a biological novelty."

"Well," Walter said, "let's reserve judgment until after we meet him." Tessa and Regina both looked at him disapprovingly. "It was just a joke," he said. "Evidently, a bad one."

"Timing is everything in life," Tessa said between pursed lips.

"I thought it was position," Regina said.

"And I always thought of sea monkeys as little time travelers trapped in their capsules on some weird journey into the future."

"You're too literal, Daddy."

"Perhaps," Walter said.

"So now what?" Regina scrutinized Tessa's face, searching for any information she might have been withholding. "When are we going to meet him?"

"I'm not sure that *we* is the right pronoun. I would like to meet him first, and then Dad and I will decide how to proceed."

"Are you afraid he's crazy, too?" Regina asked.

"No, not crazy. But I'm a little afraid, I guess. Don't you think I should be?"

Regina shrugged. "I guess."

"Just be patient," Tessa said. "I know it's hard to wait. Believe me, I know." She stood and kissed the top of Regina's head. "I'm going to phone Fran. I think the first thing I need to do is to speak with my mother."

"Really?" Walter said. "Just like that? Have you really thought this through?"

"What's to think through?" she said. "I'm going into the other room."

Fran answered right away, but her voice sounded distant, the words coming through intermittently, like the trans-Atlantic calls Tessa remembered her mother had made. Who had she called? *Here. Listen. That's Paris. That's what Paris sounds like. Say something, dearie. Say, oui, oui Cherie.* Tessa had pressed her ear to the phone and heard little more than static before passing the phone back to her mother. It had been so long since Tessa had even thought of those calls. Her mother's voice high with excitement. The memory moved through Tessa like small tremors from beneath the earth, and she felt faint with apprehension.

"Fran? It's Tessa."

"Tessa. Are you okay?"

"Yes, I'm fine."

"Philip just told me he phoned your house."

"He did."

"He said he spoke with Regina. I'm really sorry. I hope he didn't make any trouble for you."

"Trouble? No, he didn't make any trouble."

"Is Regina okay? She must have had a bit of a shock."

"I think we've all had more than a bit of a shock."

"I'm sorry. I'm really sorry. Philip can be impulsive."

"It's hereditary," Tessa said rather dryly. "I tend to be a little impulsive myself." She cleared her throat. "I actually called because I want Ursula's number."

"I'm happy to give it to you."

"Thank you."

"What about Philip?" Fran said. "What should I tell him?"

"Tell him to get in line."

Fran said that was very funny, though she did not laugh. Tessa was relieved anyway since the words came out of her mouth before she thought them through—impulsive, like her brother. She put the numbers into her cell phone as Fran called them off and said goodbye.

Tessa went back into the kitchen and found Walter and Regina poring over a take-out menu from the Chinese restaurant.

"Do you want anything?" Walter said. "Soup?"

"Surprise me," Tessa said before she caught the irony in her request. "That's funny, isn't it?"

"Hilarious," Walter said.

Regina looked up, and then looked back down at the menu. Over her bent head, Walter and Tessa exchanged looks, but neither of them said anything.

"I'm going to go upstairs and call Ursula," Tessa said.

Regina put down the menu and looked up.

"That's so cool. Can I come with you?"

"Of course not," Tessa said. She cupped Regina's chin and ran the back of her hand across her cheek. "I just need to do this alone."

"Are you sure?" Walter said.

"Pretty sure," Tessa said. She let go of Regina's chin. "Maybe I will have some wonton soup."

Tessa sat on the bed in her bedroom and held her cell phone in her lap. Forcing herself to concentrate, Tessa studied the numbers. The numbers were so ordinary it was hard to imagine that she could not have guessed them on her own all these years. Hard to imagine that anything so ordinary would give her entry to something so remarkable. Her mother. Ursula.

"Hello."

Ursula's voice was rough with years of too many cigarettes and too many sorrows. Tessa heard her mother drag hard on her cigarette and blow the smoke into the receiver. Their telephone at home had always reeked of the foul odor of stale smoke. Lucy had taken the phone apart each week and swabbed it with alcohol and perfume, but it was almost impossible to mask the sour smell that lingered like the hardships of their strange lives.

"I said hello."

Ursula was offended. The tone was recognizable. Local children often phoned their house and played cruel jokes on Ursula.

"It's Tessa."

"Tes-sa?" Ursula said.

She said it as if she did not know the name and was trying to pronounce it correctly.

"Yes. Tessa."

"And how are you Tes-sa?"

Hang up. Hang up the damned phone. She's crazy! Crazy! Hang up the phone.

"I'm very well. I have a daughter."

Non-sequiturs. It was one of the first labels Tessa heard the doctor assign to the odd conversations one shared with Ursula. *Does she speak in non-sequiturs?* The meanings of her responses were only clear to

Ursula. *Why doesn't anyone understand me?* And now Tessa found she was doing the very same thing her mother had done.

"Me too," Ursula said. Her voice was suddenly gentle, almost maternal. "I'm happy for you."

"Her name is Regina," Tessa said.

"I know. Regina. Regina. That's a lovely name, Tessa."

She said it right this time, even with a touch of whimsy as if she had been teasing Tessa all along.

"How are you?" Tessa said.

"I'm fine, Tessa."

"You have a son," Tessa said.

"And you have a brother, Tessa."

"Why do you keep using my name?"

"Because I want you to call me Mother, Tes-sa." Ursula's tone was patient, the way it had been when she was explaining something complicated to a younger Tessa. "Philip calls me Ursula. No one calls me Mother anymore."

It would have been so easy to be cruel. And also, in some ways, deserved. Ursula was guilty of abandoning her children. It was true that she was ill, but she was still guilty. But to call her "Mother" as though nothing had ever happened seemed impossible. Tessa simply could not say the word.

"I'm sorry," Tessa said.

"Yes, well, so am I."

For a moment, Tessa listened to her mother drag on her cigarette. Then she coughed for some time and gulped loudly on something that seemed to give her relief.

"My apologies," Ursula said.

"That's okay. Take your time."

"You were always such a good girl. Thank you."

Tessa's throat tightened. She had so many questions, but she could only think of one to ask.

"May I ask you something?" Tessa said.

"A question?" Ursula laughed. "You were always a girl of many questions. Go ahead. Ask me anything. Just one?"

"For now."

"Ask me anything. I have no more secrets."

"Who were you calling in Paris? When I was a little girl you used to call someone in Paris. Who was it?"

"I can't remember. I swear to you. I can't remember."

"How could you not remember?"

Ursula stammered, her nervousness evident when she said, "I just don't. I just don't."

Tessa knew her anger was irrational, but then so was love. She gripped the phone hard and tersely said, "What *do* you remember, Mother?"

Tessa could not see Ursula, who was protected from her daughter's view and cynicism. But Tessa heard the sorrow when her mother answered with heartbreaking compliance, "I remember you, Tessie. I remember you so well."

Growing up, Tessa never made any close friends because there was no way of knowing how Ursula would be on any given day. But in the fifth grade, Tessa could not resist the temptation of Marta. At first, they confined their friendship to the school bus and to the noisy cafeteria. Then, one day, Marta invited Tessa over. Tessa was excited, but not nearly so much as her grandmother, who clapped as though Tessa had just received an award. When the bus driver dropped the two girls off at Marta's house, Tessa ran up the stairs behind Marta and already wished to come home to this house every day instead of to her own. Marta's mother smiled warmly at Tessa. "And this must be Tessa," she said. "I've heard so much about you. Call me Bunny."

Inside was just as Tessa imagined it would be, only better. Bunny gave them milk and cookies, and when Marta excused herself, Bunny said, "I'm so glad she asked you over. She's been feeling a little shy since the accident." Tessa nodded knowingly although she had no idea what Bunny was talking about. When Marta returned, Bunny said, "Be sure to introduce Tessa to your dad."

Marta stiffened slightly and pulled Tessa towards the living room where her father was watching television. "Dad was in a car accident last year," Marta said. "He had a traumatic brain injury. He doesn't even remember how to pee. He's got to learn how to do everything all over again, like memorize the names of things and what everything is for. It's weird. His language is all gone. The doctor said it's as if Dad is in a foreign country." Then, her voice changed, becoming angrier, and she added, "More like another *planet*." Tessa understood her friend's anger.

Tessa eventually learned that the injury Marta's father had suffered to his brain made it impossible for him to express and to understand ideas. Lost. He was lost inside his own head. He simply could not make the connection between what had previously been everyday knowledge and the words to describe any of it.

That was exactly how Tessa felt as she spoke to Ursula. She could not connect the word for what she once called this woman with the woman on the phone. *Mother. Mommy. Mom.* The words moved through Tessa's head as she tried to attach them to Ursula's voice

"Tessa?" Ursula said, sounding even more anxious than before. "Are you still there?"

"I'm here."

"I'm sorry if I've upset you."

"You should stop smoking," Tessa said. "It's so bad for you."

"I have stopped," Ursula said. "Millions of times."

"But for good. You should stop for good."

"I'll try." Ursula sighed. "I promise."

"I thought you don't make promises," Tessa said.

"I'm turning over a new leaf," Ursula said brightly.

"I see . . . Mother."

"Thank you for calling me Mother."

"Yes, well, I have to go now."

"So soon?" Ursula caught herself. "Of course, you do. I know you must be very busy. Thank you for taking the time to phone me."

"I need some time," Tessa said.

"I understand," Ursula said.

She sounded so sad that Tessa felt she should offer her something more.

"Maybe you could stop by the salon one evening."

"I would like that very much."

"We'll talk again," Tessa said.

"Yes, of course. Goodbye, my darling girl."

Tessa could not say anything more. She sat quietly, eyes closed and remembered that when Marta's family had moved away, she had hoped that they moved to a new country where they would all be obliged to learn a new language. That way, Tessa had reasoned, Marta's father would no longer have to feel so separate from everyone else again.

Walter knocked on the door and opened it at the same time.

"Tessa?" Walter said.

"Hello." Tessa smiled and waved him to come further in. "I just realized that Philip is the name of the prince in *Sleeping Beauty*. Do you think that was intentional?"

"I don't know. Do you?"

"I don't know either," Tessa said. "I guess it doesn't really matter."

"I guess not," Walter said.

He sat on the edge of the bed and pulled Tessa close. Neither of them said anything as they held each other tightly, quietly anticipating everything else they did not know.

Chapter Sixteen

Whenever a client had a hard time deciding on a shade of polish, Tessa always tore off two or three small pieces of Scotch tape and positioned them over different fingernails. Clients were invariably impressed by this little trick. It made it seem as if there was nothing trivial about choosing just the right color nail polish. Tessa would apply a quick coat of three different colors to each of the taped nails, and the client would choose the perfect color.

If only there was an equally simple way to assess two or three potential outcomes, and then choose the best. If only Tessa could see the scenarios played out, preview the dialogues and the actions and then make a decision that would have no lasting consequences. She sighed deeply as she followed Walter down the stairs. He turned around, smiled at her reassuringly and winked. It was his way of letting her know that they would be fine. And although she smiled back, she wished she could be as sure.

In the kitchen, Regina had set the table and positioned the cartons of Chinese take-out. She was just arranging chopsticks at each place setting when her parents silently entered.

"Well, you guys look pretty grim," Regina said. "How was it?"

"It was pretty strange," Tessa said.

"What did she say?"

Tessa sifted through her conversation with Ursula for something to offer.

"She asked me to call her Mother."

Walter looked surprised. Tessa had not said anything about this to him. He fixed her with a questioning look and waited, saying nothing.

"What did you do?" Regina said.

"I called her Mother, of course."

"Was it hard?" Regina said.

"Not at all," Tessa said.

It was an outright lie. She was amused by the almost identical looks of relief that transformed their previously worried expressions, but also slightly ashamed. She knew it was perfectly childish of her to want and need their approval so badly, but it was more than that. It was simply too hard to explain how the word caught in her throat as hard and immovable as regrets.

"That was generous of you." Walter said. He kissed her cheek. "I'm proud of you."

"Me too," Regina said. "Did she ask about me?"

"Of course she did. " Tessa wound one of Regina's curls around her finger. "She knew all about you. Fran must have told her everything."

Regina pulled away, but Tessa held fast without even realizing it. Gently, Walter tapped her hand, and she looked at him, then at Regina, and then stepped back just as Regina pulled in the other direction.

"Ouch! Let go," Regina said.

"I thought I did," Tessa said. "I'm sorry."

"It's okay." Regina rubbed her head in the spot where Tessa had inadvertently tugged. It seemed so symbolic to Tessa: she was always holding on while someone was trying to let go.

"I'm really sorry." She kissed the spot of Regina's head where she was still energetically rubbing. "I wasn't paying attention. I told Ursula to come to the salon."

"The salon?" Walter said. "Why would you do that?"

"It felt safe. I don't know." Tessa shrugged. "I guess it felt too risky to have her come here."

"Risky? Isn't this her house?" Walter sounded incredulous. "Why wouldn't you have her come here?"

Regina's stare was accusatory. Tessa found it unbearable, but also undeserved. After all, what did Regina and Walter know about what she had suffered? Ursula's newly confirmed existence would compel confrontations with the past that could only be painful. Tessa felt she could not be faulted for her reluctance to run toward that with open arms.

"I just need some more time," Tessa said. She tried to keep her voice strong, her tone level. "You know, to get used to this."

"What if your time's up, Mother?"

Tessa overcame an overwhelming urge to slap Regina and reached for her instead. This time, however, Regina adeptly slipped out of her mother's grasp and stormed out of the room.

Walter had watched the drama without interference. As soon as the door to Regina's room slammed shut, he turned to Tessa. She was still staring in the direction of the staircase.

"You can't blame her," he said.

"Can't I?"

He opened a carton of the Chinese food and peered inside almost morosely. Tessa knew he was hungry and just wanted to put all this behind him and move on with their lives. It was what he had wanted for the past seventeen years.

"I don't know." Using his fingers, he picked up a dumpling and bit into it. "I'm sorry. I don't even know what to say anymore. But I think you should cut Regina some slack."

"You always think I should cut Regina some slack."

"Well, maybe it's time you listened."

"This isn't about Regina."

"It's about all of us." He dabbed at his chin with a paper napkin; some soy sauce had dripped down. "It's been about all of us since day one."

She shrugged. "I suppose."

"You suppose?" He laughed. "What do you want from her?"

"From Ursula?"

Walter nodded. He was wielding his chopsticks now, navigating strands of lo mein straight from the container.

"I can't answer that," Tessa said.

"That's bullshit, and you know it."

"It's not bullshit. And don't eat from the container."

Defiantly, he slurped some noodles at her and she, miraculously, laughed and took the chopsticks he offered. They passed containers back and forth, eating in silence until there was nothing left.

In the church in the East Bronx where Ursula took Tessa when she was still young enough not to question anything, there was a couple who had been together since they were children. They had met when their parents were part of a religious cult. By the time they reached adolescence, the two knew they wanted to be together forever. They eventually left the cult in a midnight escape, and found their way across the country where they married and raised a family of their own. Ursula was envious of them, not because of their evident, almost smug, satisfaction with each other, but because their path in life had prevented them from ever having experienced the anguish of a broken heart. "What must that be like?" Ursula said aloud to no one in particular. "What must it be like to never have experienced a broken heart?" She shook her head in disbelief, placed a flat palm against her breast, and said, "I was born with a broken heart." Tessa believed it then, and she believed it now.

That was the recollection that spurred Tessa to hasten her meeting with her mother. In spite of Walter's objection and Regina's reaction, Tessa wanted to meet her mother on neutral ground, in a place where they had no history. Too much had happened in the house where they had once lived together as mother and child. Too many memories seeped under the doors and in and out of the rooms where Tessa had teetered on the brink of terror or basked in the soothing pleasure of her mother's presence. Tessa especially loved the nights when Ursula would silently slip under the blanket and wrap her arms tightly around her. In the narrow twin bed, they seemed to be one person. When Tessa turned, Ursula turned with her. And when Ursula turned, Tessa allowed herself to be pulled along. "We're on a life raft," Ursula sometimes whispered. "Hold on, baby. Hold on."

No, Tessa told herself. She needed to be on firm ground when she saw her mother again. No life rafts this time.

The following morning, Regina was sullen and withdrawn. She ate a bowl of cold cereal without acknowledging Tessa other than a terse good morning in response to her mother's overture at conversation.

"Is today your history test?" Tessa said much too cheerfully even if they had not been in a litigious impasse. "I can't seem to keep my days straight."

Regina kept the bowl close to her mouth and shoveled in spoonful after spoonful of cornflakes.

"Do you want some toast?"

No response. Tessa took another sip of coffee.

"Look," Tessa said. "I know you're confused and angry at me, but this is my drama, and I have to play it out as I see fit. Can't you try to understand that?"

Regina lifted her head, rolled her eyes at Tessa, and said, "You can keep your drama to yourself, Mom. It's all yours." She took a last spoonful of cereal and got up to place the bowl in the sink. She ran some water into it and turned to her mother. "Tell Dad I'm walking to school." She took her coat from the knobbed wall rack in the mud room, grabbed her knapsack, hooked it over one shoulder and left. Seconds after she closed the door behind her, Regina popped her head back in and said, "I'm going to Marie's after school. I'll call you."

For awhile Tessa just stared at the door, waiting for Regina to come back one more time and tell her that she was sorry and that she understood and loved her no matter what.

The minute Walter left, Tessa called Mia. Since Regina had walked, Walter decided to do some work at home. It was after ten by the time he left. Tessa thought he would never leave.

"She could have told me that she loves me," Tessa said. "Don't you think?"

"Fat chance of that," Mia said.

"But why?" Tessa insisted. "Why can't they ever understand what we feel?"

"Did you ever understand your parents?" Mia sucked her breath in almost immediately after the words were out and said, "Ixnay on the questionay. Sorry."

Tessa laughed. For the first ten minutes, she had tried to bring Mia up to date with everything was happening.

"Consider it ixnayed," she said.

"Talking to you about family is like walking on a minefield."

"Careful where you step," Tessa said.

"I wonder if that's where the expression, look before you leap came from. Maybe some guy who worked in explosives made it up."

"Unlikely."

"You're probably right. So, now what?" Mia said. "Are you going to meet the brother? Hook up with the mother?"

"I guess so."

"You guess so."

"Well, I'm not sure of the order, but yes."

"I think it's for the best." Mia sounded very definite, exactly the way she did when she finally made an important decision. "You have to push through this and see it to its natural conclusion."

"There's nothing natural about my family." Tessa sighed. "It's a mess. Tell me, what should I do about Regina?"

"Do? I don't think there's anything to do, my friend. Just sit tight and see what she does."

"It doesn't make me very comfortable to give Regina the lead," Tessa said. "In fact, it feels downright scary."

"I don't see how you have a choice."

"Oh, that choice thing again."

"Sorry, but it's the way it is. You can't control how Regina feels, and it makes sense that she would feel the way she does."

"You sound just like Walter."

"Ouch," Mia said. She yawned loudly. Tessa had woken her at a little past seven, apologizing profusely and promising to make it up to her. "That was harsh."

"I shouldn't have woken you." Tessa said.

"Don't be silly. I had to get up anyway . . . in about two hours."

"Thanks, Mia. Thanks for always being there."

"You mean here, right? Not there."

"Whatever you say. I wish we lived in the same time zone."

Mia yawned again, this time even louder. "Me too. Believe me."

"I have to go. I'm late as it is."

"Love you," Mia said, blowing kisses into the phone. "Call me and let me know what's going on."

"I will. Love you too."

The salon was extremely busy that day. Tessa's appointment, a new client, Fiona West, was already waiting for her when she arrived, and she looked miffed. Tessa got one of the girls to take Mrs. West's coat and bring her a coffee. Apologizing again for her lateness, Tessa carefully examined her hands, complimenting her on her soft skin and nicely shaped nails. Mrs. West was probably in her seventies but very fit and well-preserved (a favorite expression of Mia's). Her silver grey hair was cut stylishly short, and her blue eyes looked out from behind a very contemporary pair of eyeglasses. It was evident that she was not given to chatting, and Tessa followed her lead, saying only what was necessary to help the manicure go smoothly. Square or round? Cut or push back the cuticles?

As Tessa worked, she barely glanced up, except to see that Mrs. West was absorbed in a magazine and seemed unaware that Tessa existed. Then Tessa began the massage. She squeezed a small amount of lemon scented moisturizing cream onto the top of her right hand and began to gently rub the cream into her skin, massaging toward the heart as she had been taught.

When Tessa turned Mrs. West's hand over and began working the palm, she stopped reading her magazine. She closed her eyes; her breathing became shallow. As Tessa applied careful pressure at the base of each finger and then worked her way down the palm to the wrist, she felt Mrs. West's pulse as if it were her own.

There had been many times when Tessa had felt a client's emotions and disregarded them, preferring to save herself rather than become immersed in the tangle of feeling that would more than likely threaten her own stability. Still, it often led Tessa to marvel at the audacity of the human spirit's stamina. After all, what must it take for a woman to get her nails done knowing that her husband no longer loved her? How was it possible to deliberate over the right shade of red when your child was gravely ill? Tessa tiptoed through these arenas of danger, circumnavigating the compulsion to become involved, to help in any small way. She simply had to curtail her senses in order to live. But this was different. In some odd way, this very conventional woman seemed to be some sort of messenger, and Tessa felt the need to pay close attention to her.

"You're quite good at this," Mrs. West said. Her eyelids fluttered. The hand Tessa had not yet massaged was resting on the table, palm up, completely still, almost reaching toward her. "I haven't felt this relaxed in such a long time."

Tessa nodded, pleased.

"You picked an interesting line of work," Mrs. West said. "Very clever of you."

The sudden sensation of heat that Tessa felt as her hands lightly separated Mrs. West's fingers was not remarkably intense. Tessa might even have disregarded the feeling if it were not for Mrs. West's comment. In concert, the two events created a synchronicity that demanded acknowledgement. Determined not to be intimidated, Tessa continued her work, concentrating on the area between the thumb and forefinger, but the intensity of feeling was almost unbearable.

Mrs. West opened her eyes, smiled broadly in an unexpected way and withdrew her hand, offering the other in exchange. "You're not used to being on the other end, are you?"

Guarded as ever, Tessa said, "I'm not sure what you mean."

"You're perspiring," Mrs. West said. "That's not like you."

It was true. Tessa rarely, if ever, perspired. She placed her thumb into the palm of Mrs. West's proffered hand, gently shaking it to measure its state of relaxation. She need not have bothered; Mrs. West was fully relaxed.

"It's pure chance," Mrs. West said.

"If indeed there is such a thing," Tessa said.

"Agreed." Mrs. West smiled. "Well, as long we've been thrown together . . . ."

Tessa inadvertently squeezed too hard, and Mrs. West arched her brow.

"Sorry," Tessa said.

Mrs. West tacitly accepted the apology, but withdrew her hands, first one then the other, nonetheless.

"I would like your full attention," she said. "Is that possible?"

Tessa felt little beads of sweat on her upper lip and concentrated on ignoring it. Walter always marveled that she was bone dry even after a round of energetic sex. It was a source of much curiosity to him.

"I'm listening," Tessa said. She felt a flutter of alarm. "Is there danger?"

She knew that it was not possible to tell someone that tomorrow morning she would trip over a ladder, or that she should have the party she was planning on a Sunday instead of a Saturday. It simply did not work that way.

"Oh, no," Mrs. West said, "nothing at all like that." She patted Tessa's hand, trying to reassure her. "I think I have to tell you what you already know." She paused. "You have a daughter? A teenager? A bit of a fireball, but I guess that's true of most teen girls. I have three daughters."

A calm settled over Tessa that could not have been more welcomed. The door to the salon opened, and a large delivery of cartons was wheeled in on a cart. Tessa could hear the deliveryman apologize. There were more boxes, and would it be alright to hold the door ajar for just a few moments longer? The cool air reached Tessa and her damp skin tingled, ever so fleetingly. She felt energized by the change in her body temperature, more aware, ready to take on what could not be avoided.

"She needs you to accept her decision," Mrs. West said. "Does that make sense?"

Of course it made sense. She had known as soon as Regina said she was going to Marie's after school. Tessa had known and pretended otherwise because it was easier that way.

"Yes," Tessa said. "Thank you."

"Don't be angry with her."

"I won't be."

"And be kind."

"Kind?" Tessa looked confused. "What does that mean?"

Mrs. West leaned forward conspiratorially and said, "I just always throw that in at the end. No harm, right?"

"No harm at all." Tessa said, laughing. She took Mrs. West's hands and squeezed them, tenderly this time. "Let me finish your manicure."

Oddly enough, neither of them spoke anymore. Mrs. West went back to her magazine, and Tessa gave her full concentration to the manicure. They parted amicably, but Tessa suspected she would never see Fiona West again. For the rest of the day, Tessa worked, surreptitiously watching the clock, wondering if Regina had been successful in finding her grandmother.

Chapter Seventeen

Walter's car wasn't in the driveway when Tessa pulled in, and she offered a quick prayer of thanks. She was still unsure of what to do first. Her immediate reaction had been to phone Ursula, but if Regina had gone there (wherever there was), it could have unfavorable consequences. Regina would see it as a vote of no-confidence, a sure sign that Tessa had no faith in her judgment. And, if the truth be told, Tessa found Regina's decision in this particular case very questionable no matter what Mrs. West said. But Regina had a right to want to make a connection with her family, no matter how strange the road to that place might be.

Tessa realized that Regina must have taken Ursula's number off the phone. It was probably the reason she had been so impassive over breakfast. She had never been a very good liar and withdrawal was always a telltale sign that she was hiding something. Tessa had been too overwrought that morning to pay close enough attention to the warning signs. And wasn't it always like that? She couldn't help but think that the very moment you let your guard down, something went wrong.

Or maybe not. Maybe this was exactly what should have happened, what needed to happen. Still, no matter how she tried to dress it up, Walter would not see it that way. There was no time to worry about him. She had to find out where Regina had gone and be sure that she was safe.

Fran picked up after the first ring.

"It's Tessa."

"I was expecting your call."

"Then you know about Regina?"

"Ursula phoned me."

"And you didn't call me?" Tessa did not try to mask her irritation. "What did she say?

"She said that Regina had phoned her and was coming to see her."

"Where does she live?"

"Not far," Fran said. "She won't hurt Regina."

"I'm not worried about that." Tessa was lying. She was worried about that even though she knew it was irrational. Ursula had never, not in her worst state, ever raised a hand to her. "I know Ursula wouldn't hurt Regina. She wouldn't hurt anyone." She wanted to cry, wanted to flail her arms and wail, releasing long guttural cries like the ones that had come from deep inside her gut when Regina was born. "I'm just worried. It's reasonable to be worried. Ursula's behavior can be unpredictable. She was quite erratic in her responses."

"She was nervous. She gets like that when she's nervous."

"Well, I was nervous too, but that's not the point. Is it?" Tessa thought she might sound fairly erratic herself and took a deep breath. "How far is not far?"

"About twenty minutes or so north."

"I see. Does she have her own place?"

"Yes. A small one bedroom."

"She manages on her own?" Tessa swallowed hard, struggling to fight back her tears. She could not conceive of how her mother could manage on her own.

"Yes," Fran said. "She manages very well."

A picture of her mother, her beautiful mother, sitting alone in an apartment, smoking, and staring into the darkness made Tessa reel with such sadness that it took her by surprise. All those years of longing and anger and bitterness were reduced to nothing by this single image. Tessa had believed that if she tried very hard, her mother's madness would never touch them, especially not Regina. But it had been no use. Night after night, Ursula was there, beside Tessa, just waiting. In the darkness that could never hide Ursula, Tessa always felt her mother's presence. And in the brightness of the day, Tessa could still never escape her own memories.

"Do you have her address?"

"I do, but . . . "

"But what?"

"I think, and please forgive me if I am intruding, but I think you should let them be."

"You don't know what Ursula is capable of." Tessa made her voice hard. "You think you do, but you don't. I was there! I saw it all. You have no idea what I lived through!"

Her body shook as she tried to find the words to explain what she had witnessed. She wanted to explain how one day she had come home from school to find her mother sitting on the bed, naked, surrounded by piles of sweaters, many still with the tags on. The sweaters were evidence of her manic phases. A gold sequined shrug, a hot pink turtleneck with a huge appliquéd flower on the chest, Christmas sweaters with bells, and several Halloween themed cardigans with the predictable pumpkins, cats, witches and goblins. After one manic shopping spree, Ursula had confided that, "Manic taste really is *always* bad." Tessa could not even imagine where her mother had been hiding all of them.

But, as young as she was, Tessa was even more startled by her mother's raw beauty. Although she had certainly seen her mother naked before, she had never before seemed so vulnerable. Her knees were drawn up to her chest; her breasts were flattened against the top of her thighs. She was fiercely clutching her legs and rocking back and forth, comforting herself. More often than not, no matter how dim the tunnels were that Ursula wandered into became, she always tried to allay Tessa's fears. And that day, true to form, as soon as Ursula saw Tessa, the rocking ceased. Ursula smiled and stood although she did not seem to remember that she was naked. Tessa stared at her mother's body. Her nipples were dark against her white skin. Because she was so thin, her breasts seemed even larger, disproportionate with her narrow hips and tiny waist. Her breasts stood high against her rib cage, the nipples erect in the cold room. Ursula did not shave under her arms, so when she stretched out to reach for Tessa, the patches of black hair were arresting.

But Ursula did not try to cover herself. She shivered and looked down at her naked body, shaking her head as if she could not believe her own foolishness. Then she closed her eyes, pointed a finger at the pile of sweaters and spun around several times before stopping.

Tessa had tried not to cry as she watched her mother take an emerald green sweater set from the pile and pull the soft wool shell over her head. It was too tight, and it flattened her breasts a bit, but it was flattering, even more provocative than her bare chest. Then she draped the cardigan around her shoulders and buttoned the simulated pearl button at the top. Ursula was naked now only from the waist down. Tessa looked away. Her mother seemed even more exposed than before, and Tessa was embarrassed.

Suddenly, as if a wonderful thought had occurred to her, Ursula made believe she was flying. The sleeves of her sweater were her wings, and she flapped and flapped her arms until it looked as if she could take off and leave the earth forever. It was as if she thought she might be able to distract Tessa from what she had witnessed; replace that memory with something better, something less frightening. How could she predict that when Tessa would remember that afternoon, as she did now, she would only feel the pain her mother must have later felt in knowing how she had failed to sufficiently protect her child. It was one of many times that Tessa was forced to see Ursula literally stripped of all that was considered sane and viable.

"No, you're quite right," Fran said. "I can't even imagine. Nevertheless, I have lived through my own tragedies, and I can tell you that every misfortune leaves it mark."

"I know that, but this is different. This is about my child. It's not about me."

"Regina can handle herself."

"How do you know? You don't even know her."

"I know because she's your daughter."

Tessa nodded into the phone. Fran was the mother Tessa had wished for. And she was more than likely the mother that Ursula had wanted to be.

"Thank you," Tessa said. "That's very kind of you."

"Oh, not at all, dear," Fran said. "You've been through so much, and I'm so sorry to be contributing to it even more. It was never my intent."

"I know that. Between a rock and a hard place."

"What's that?"

"That's how Ursula used to describe her life: between a rock and a hard place." Tessa tried to lighten the words by laughing. "I think it was an apt description."

"She's better now. She's really better."

"Is she still beautiful? I always wanted to be as beautiful as she was."

"She's aged quite a bit," Fran said. "She hasn't had an easy life."

"So you've said."

"So you know," Fran said very, very gently.

"What should I do now?" Tessa asked.

"Can you wait? Can you let them come to you?"

"I'll try. I'll give it a few more hours."

"And your husband?"

"I can't speak for him."

"Of course not. What will you tell him?"

Tessa hesitated. She walked over to the living room window and parted the laths to peek outside. It was so dark out. She shivered even though it was warm inside the house. The news had predicted the first snowfall of the season.

"Tessa?"

She had completely forgotten about Fran.

"Did you know that they predicted snow for tonight?" Tessa walked away from the window and curled her legs beneath her on the couch. "You were asking me about Walter. I don't have a plan. I'm not a very good planner. That may be one of my greatest shortcomings."

"Mine too, actually. " Fran said, unable to mask her regret. "There were times that I thought it was an advantage. But I guess I was just fooling myself."

"Probably," Tessa agreed. "I've made a career out of fooling myself."

Neither of them said anything, but the silence was not awkward.

Fran finally said, "Let me give you the address anyway."

"Yes, I'd like that."

Fran said the address slowly, giving Tessa a chance to write it down and then repeat it for accuracy.

"Everything will be fine," Fran said.

"If you say so," Tessa said. "I have to go."

"Will you keep me informed?" Fran said.

"Yes. Of course I will."

They said their final goodnights, and Tessa went back to the window though this time she did not look outside. She just stood there, waiting, anticipating Walter's arrival or a phone call from Regina. After a few moments, she realized that it was dark in the house, and she went from room to room, turning on lights. The fear inside her rose and then ebbed in response to whatever seemed to pass through her mind.

She remembered an article she had read about the archaeological unearthing of a pair of sandals from the first millennium. Scientists surmised that the sandals had belonged to a prostitute. The soles of the sandals were studded, so that with each step the ground would be marked with the invitation, *Follow me*. Oh, that Regina might have such a pair of footwear. Tessa would have found her easily.

Walter came home. She heard the car pull into the driveway. She heard the engine grow quiet as he turned off the ignition. The door slammed shut. There was a brief silence. He must have been reaching inside for his briefcase, taking an empty coffee cup from the holder, maybe the newspaper or his overcoat. She resisted the temptation to bolt. She kept her eyes closed and tried to attach images to what she heard. Walter with his briefcase under his arm; Walter placing one foot ahead of the other as he navigated the dark driveway (Tessa had forgotten to turn on the outside light), stopping to throw some litter into the trash; Walter reaching inside the mailbox for the mail (Tessa never remembered to take the mail out of the box), and then Walter putting his key in the door only to find (much to his constant dismay) that the door was unlocked. "Someone could just walk right in while you were in the shower or while Reggie was alone in the kitchen. Did you ever think about that?" he would ask. Of course she did. She wasn't stupid.

"Tess? Tess? I'm home."

She had seen a program on the Discovery channel about animals that were able to blend into the environment. Some of the more sophisticated hiders could even change their camouflage in accordance with a change in their surroundings. And some animals did not hide at all, but were able to throw predators off by disguising themselves as something dangerous or uninteresting. That would have been Tessa's wish: to be able to disguise herself as something uninteresting, something so easily overlooked that it would be as if she did not exist at all. She had been fascinated by the walking stick, an insect that looked so much like an ordinary twig that its predators could not distinguish the walking stick from its surroundings and simply moved past it, ignoring it. But Walter was not a predator, and she could not blend in with her surroundings any more than she could avoid the inevitable.

"I'm here," Tessa said. "In the living room."

"Hi." He kissed her cheek. "Why are all the lights on?"

"I don't know. I honestly don't know." She sat uncomfortably perched on the edge of the couch. Staring down at her hands, folded in her lap, Tessa felt oddly disoriented. Even her hands looked as though they belonged to someone else, and she turned them from side-to-side, examining the lines on her palms, and her short, unpainted nails. She could never have painted nails in her line of work. When she had to attend an event, she painted her nails and took off the polish when she came home. "It got dark so fast," she said, looking up into Walter's concerned face. "It was light, and then it was dark."

"Where's Regina?" Walter said. "Isn't it late for a school night?"

She often wondered if it were possible that his intuitiveness had been honed by years of living with her. Ursula had told her stories about people whose intuitiveness came to the forefront when there was a critical need, like a life or death situation that involved someone dear. Someone like Regina was to Walter.

"She's not home," Tessa said. She stood and took his hands. They were warm. "Regina went to see my mother." Reflexively, Walter tightened his grip. "I spoke to Fran. She said that Ursula had phoned to tell her that Regina called her. She must have taken the number off my cell phone. I haven't spoken with Regina. I was going to call her, but I thought I should let her do this, that we should let her do this."

Throughout Tessa's delivery, Walter had listened, nodding at intervals and appearing to be relatively calm. He had loosened his grip though he still held her hands. And in his touch, she felt such inordinate sadness that it made her want to cry. She could have more easily dealt with his anger than with his grief.

"Walter?" She pulled away one hand and placed it against his cheek. He already had the four o'clock shadow that Regina, as a little girl, had hated. She would shriek when he would come home from work and playfully rub his rough beard against her velvety cheek. It was one of their personal games. Now he leaned his cheek into Tessa's hand. "Walter. Say something, please."

"I should have been able to anticipate this," he said. "I should have been there to protect her."

"Protect her from my mother?"

"Yes." He dropped her other hand and stepped back, averting his eyes. "I don't want to be cruel."

"Then don't be," she said.

"How did we wind up here?" he said. "I thought it was all behind us."

Ursula had once read an article to Tessa about the various reasons for committing patients to mental asylums at the turn-of the-century. Excitedly, Ursula had rattled off the grounds to Tessa: religious excitement, loss of a lawsuit, parents who are cousins, fever, and desertion by a husband. Shaking her head, Ursula had whispered to Tessa that all the reasons seemed fabricated. "I'll bet all those poor people are just like me, but there wasn't a name for it then. It was easier to just lock everyone up and throw away the key." She held a strand of Tessa's hair between her thumb and forefinger and added, "I bet you wish that Daddy had been able to do that. You could've had someone like that nice lady in the bakery for a mother instead of a crazy person like me."

That day, it had been different from her usual diatribes. Ursula had been so sad that day. Like Walter was now. Maybe Ursula had been right about what would have been best for their family. And Walter should have married Charmaine. He would have had a normal life.

"Maybe this is just the way it all has to play out," Tessa said. "My mother won't hurt Regina."

"Regina's already hurt. That's the part I hate." He ran a hand along his jaw as if measuring the stubble. "I mean, what good was anything if I couldn't protect her from this?"

"There's nothing to protect her from. You can't go through life believing there is a way to sidestep catastrophe." She saw his expression and quickly added, "Not that this is a catastrophe. Regina had to do this. She couldn't wait for me because I might not have ever been ready."

"Where does Ursula live?"

She gave him the address and the phone number and watched as he stared at the piece of paper with the information.

"Should we go get her?" he said. "Shouldn't we call her?"

"I think we should give Regina a chance." She looked at her watch. It was after seven. "Let's wait till nine. If she doesn't call by then, I'll call Ursula."

He put his hand out to shake hers. It was an act of formality that surprised Tessa. She was not sure if she should be offended or amused, but she shook his hand, resisting the temptation to spit into her palm the way the boys used to when she was growing up.

"Deal," she said.

Walter did not reiterate the pledge. He just sat down to wait. And because she did not know what else to do, Tessa sat beside him.

At a quarter of nine, the doorbell rang. Walter and Tessa both jumped. She had heated up some leftovers for them, which they ate in front of the television. Neither of them was interested in any more talking, and the television helped pass the time.

"Who could that be?" Walter said. He was finishing his tea, looking even wearier than usual for this time of night. "Isn't it late for visitors?"

She was already up, standing at the sink, rinsing dishes and putting them in the dishwasher, so she dried her hands on a piece of paper toweling and went to the front door to see.

The tall, gangly stranger at the door looked very nervous. His shoulders were rounded as if he hoped (for no logical reason) to hide some of his height. And he was thin, far too thin for someone as tall as he. He was wearing a maroon hooded sweatshirt and matching sweatpants. The hood was pulled down low over his forehead, almost covering his eyes. But Tessa was not in the least bit afraid of this young man, especially when she saw that he was clutching a stress ball in one of his large hands.

"Hello," he said.

Almost as if he suddenly remembered his manners, he pulled the hood back to reveal his face. It was a pleasant enough face and Tessa might have left it at that if she had not recognized that the shape of his jaw was so much like her own. Almost immediately, her hand flew up to touch herself, confirming their sameness.

"Hello," she said.

"Are you Tessa?"

"Yes."

He grinned and shoved the stress ball into his pants pocket. Then he extended his hand to her and said, "I'm Philip Hill."

"Yes," Tessa said, taking his hand and shaking it firmly, encouraged by the rush of warmth their contact generated. "I recognize you."

He looked confused.

"Have we met before?"

Tessa shook her head and laughed. "No. We haven't met before." She felt Walter behind her, and saw Philip's expression change. "This is my husband, Walter Jordan."

"Hello," Philip said. With mastered shyness, he held out his hand to Walter. "I'm Philip."

"Of course you are," Walter said. He stepped to the side. "Please. Come in."

Tessa and Walter watched as Philip stooped before he entered even though it was not necessary. It was a funny habit, almost an affectation. He must have lived somewhere that had low ceilings or doorways.

As he followed Tessa to the kitchen with Walter trailing behind, Tessa smiled. *This is my brother. This is my baby brother.*

Chapter Eighteen

"What can I offer you?" Tessa said, guiding Philip to a chair. "Please, sit down. I'm so glad you came."

She blushed and put her hands to her face. Worried that she had made Philip ill at ease, she waited for his response. Walter had tactfully excused himself in order to give Tessa and Philip some time alone. But before he left, Walter tapped his watch with import. They had still not heard from Regina, and it was well past nine, but Tessa gave him a reassuring look. Walter shook his head in frustration and hastily left the room. She thought to call after him, but what would she say?

"Thanks," Philip finally said. "I don't want anything."

Tessa was pulled back into the moment and picked up the conversation seamlessly. "Nothing?"

"Well, I'd have some Ovaltine if you have it," he said.

"I'm sorry, no. But I make good hot chocolate." Tessa smiled. "I could fix you a sandwich."

He scratched his head, thinking. "Do you have provolone? Sliced from the deli, not the stuff in the package from the grocery."

Tessa smiled again and shook her head regretfully, knowing how odd such a specific request would strike a stranger and feeling immediately protective. It was not that he seemed helpless; it was more that he seemed exposed. She had the urge to lay Philip down on the kitchen floor as if he were some large, injured beast. She would treat his wounds with salve and calm his fears while speaking to him in a comforting voice. It was her time to take care of him. At least, that was how it felt to Tessa.

"I'm sorry, Philip," she said. "I don't have provolone of any kind."

"No? Well, maybe I will have some tea." He smiled, a little bashfully, and then a little self-deprecatingly added, "Any kind. Lipton's good."

She found his effort at humor surprisingly touching.

"All right then," she said. "At least sit, would you please?"

He pushed the chair away from the table because his long legs would not fit comfortably and folded his arms across his chest.

"I jog," he said.

"Do you? That seems very healthy." Her hand shook slightly as she filled the kettle at the sink. She could feel his gaze on her back. "I'm terribly lazy when it comes to exercise."

"I'm off my time," Philip said. "It's hard to run in the winter."

"The cold?"

"Uh-uh. I like the cold. I like snow." He furrowed his forehead. "I don't know why it's harder to run in the winter."

"Biorhythms or something," Tessa said. She set the kettle on the stove and turned to look at him.

"I know who you are," Philip said.

His stare was almost brazen, but it was not threatening.

"Yes. I know you do." She smiled. "And I know who you are."

"Well, you'd have to in that case, wouldn't you?"

"I suppose so."

"My mother told me everything." Philip saw the flicker of something in Tessa's expression and added, "My mother Fran."

"It must have been very emotional for you."

Philip's almost immediate response seemed to surprise them both.

"Do you have any other kind of cheese?" he asked.

Tessa wondered for a second if he were teasing her. Their father had been a tease.

But she saw that Philip was quite serious.

"I'm sure we have some cheddar. My Regina loves cheese. She's vegetarian. For a time, she didn't even eat dairy. But now she does." Tessa knew she was rambling. She took out a wrapped chunk of cheddar cheese from the refrigerator and showed it to Philip. "Is this good?"

"It's not low fat is it? I hate low fat."

"It's loaded with fat. I promise."

When Philip smiled, Tessa saw her father, their father. Philip's eyes became slits when he smiled fully, just as Dennis's had. And like Dennis, Philip's bottom lip curled over the top in a futile attempt to cover too large teeth.

Without waiting for his answer, Tessa sliced the cheese and took out a loaf of whole wheat bread from the bread box that had been in that kitchen since she was a little girl. *This was our mother's. This is the house I grew up in. This is the house you would have grown up in if the world didn't turn upside down in our mother's head.* She sliced a tomato and washed some lettuce, adding both to the sandwich.

"I just want you to know that it was very emotional for me," Tessa said. "You know, learning that Ursula was still alive and that I have a brother." She put the plate down in front of him. "I'm very glad to meet you."

He took a bite of the sandwich and then another before he said, "Did you make the tea?"

"Oh, damn, I forgot." She turned to check the kettle when she heard the front door close. "Excuse me a minute, Philip. I'll be right back." Quickly, she raised the flame under the kettle and called out to Walter as she rushed to the door. He was already outside, getting into his car. She shivered in the doorway. "Walter! Where are you going?"

He looked as though he might not even answer but simply drive away. Then he looked up at Tessa as he gripped the wheel in both hands.

"I'm going to get Regina."

"I figured as much."

"She's not answering her cell. I can't wait any longer."

"I understand."

"I left her a message and told her I was on my way."

"That was a good idea." She moved closer to the car. "You're a good father."

"Thank you."

Tessa leaned in through the open window and kissed him lightly on the lips.

"Are you okay in there with him?" Walter asked. "He seems a bit weird to me."

"Just a bit?"

They laughed together, and Walter turned the key in the ignition.

"Go inside," he said. "It's freezing."

"Call me?"

"Who else would I call?" He winked at her. "Go inside."

She nodded, but she waited until he had backed out of the driveway and into the street before she went back inside.

Philip was sipping a cup of tea. He had finished his sandwich.

"I hope you don't mind that I made it myself," he said, lifting his mug into the air. "I didn't know if you wanted a cup."

"I'm glad you helped yourself. I'll fix myself a cup." She was so tired. "What do you do?" The water in the kettle was still hot, and she dropped a tea bag into a mug. "Do you work?"

The tips of Philip's ears turned red, exactly the same way Tessa's did when she was embarrassed or caught off guard.

"I'm sorry," she said. "I didn't mean to pry. I was just making conversation."

"I'm a carpenter."

"Really? Your father was very good with his hands."

"You mean my biological father?"

"Yes, of course. I'm sorry. That was insensitive of me."

"No, it's just a little confusing. I'll get used to it." He paused. "Won't I?"

"I think so," Tessa said. "In fact, I know so."

She was worried about Regina. Had she had any dinner? Would Ursula pick a theme for their meal as she always had for Tessa? Sometimes there were only red foods for breakfast (apples, beets, cranberries or red velvet cake); miniature foods for lunch (tiny salamis, petit fours, cocktail franks or hors d'oeuvres), and foods with seeds for dinner (tomatoes, avocadoes, breadsticks, and cucumbers). The themes varied with Ursula's moods and could be entirely bizarre or unexpectedly quaint in their own way.

Nothing was ever a certainty with Ursula. One time as Ursula was coming down from a week long cycle of depression so severe that she had to be hospitalized, Tessa insisted on seeing her in spite of Dennis's objections. As Ursula slept, Tessa stretched out alongside her in the narrow hospital bed. "When will it all stop?" Tessa wanted to know. "When will it all go away, once and for all? I need to know." And Ursula, groggy from the drugs, still heard Tessa and said, "That's the thing of it, baby. It never goes away. That's the nightmare I never wake up from."

The shocking truth made Dennis and Tessa afraid to look at each other. Wordlessly, pretending that Ursula had never answered, they watched her fall back asleep until the nurse came in and said it was really time to leave.

Ursula had never hurt anyone. And she could no more be blamed for the torments that visited her unannounced and with unabashed fierceness than one could be blamed for wanting to be loved. Yet the visibility of what she suffered could be painful to the novice observer, and it was this that Tessa feared for with Regina. She would cast

Ursula as the beleaguered victim of drama, and not even Tessa could foretell how Ursula would play that part.

"Ursula won't hurt Regina," Philip said. "I know you're worried. You don't have to be."

Her father, their father, had been a kind man. Tessa could not remember him ever speaking to her harshly or using force. More than once, Ursula had berated him for this, mocked his gentle nature and told him that he was weak. But he was strong. He had never deserted them. Not even once.

"Thank you, Philip. I know you mean well, and I appreciate that, but it's all very complicated. So much has happened in such a short time that I think we're all reeling from it." She took several small sips of her tea. "And my Regina is a fiercely independent thinker."

Philip did not appear to be listening though she did not know him well enough to measure his expression. Tessa felt that he had somehow assigned himself to this mission. It would be up to him to set right all that had been wronged in their lives. And in her own way, Tessa wanted to believe that he could, in his own way, make a difference.

"I think Ursula wants to be a good mother," he continued. "She just got lost. Sometimes people need help finding their way back." Philip tilted his head to the side as though an idea had just occurred to him. "That could be your job, Tessa. You could help Ursula find her way back."

Tessa answered too quickly and with too little thought, something that was apparent to her only after the words escaped her mouth.

"I'm not too good with directions," she said

Part of her had wanted to make Philip smile, but she was really trying to sidestep his efforts to engage her in a relationship with Ursula. Either way, Philip seemed to miss the nuance even though what he said next surprised her.

"There are so many ways to interpret that," Philip said.

She laughed and saw how it pleased him. And then she wondered at how she had managed all these years without the intimacy of his companionship.

"Sometime, not now, I was hoping that you could tell me everything that happened," Philip said. "I want to hear your side of the story."

"I don't think my side of the story will illuminate much."

"And I don't see how that could be true."

"Really? What makes you say that?"

"An eyewitness account is a primary source. And primary sources are invaluable." His thin shoulders were hunched with the effort of making himself understood. "I don't want anyone to get hurt anymore," he said. "You know?"

"I know," she said so quickly that her sentence seemed to be a continuation of his last words. "I don't want you to confuse my hesitancy with disinterest."

"I understand." He brightened a bit. "There's nothing wrong with being careful. I think we're being very sensible, don't you?"

We. Tessa said, "Of course we are." *We.*

And then she said it again because the word was so new now that it included him.

Philip left just moments before Walter phoned from the car to tell her that he had spoken to Regina. She had come out of Ursula's apartment after he had phoned and said he was waiting outside to take her home. Regina had been respectful, but predictably inflexible. She was spending the night with Ursula. When Walter balked at the idea, Regina explained that Ursula was her grandmother and that they had a right to know each other. Tessa admitted that she was stunned at how calmly he had handled the situation.

"It's not at all what I would have expected from you," she said.

"Not what I expected from me either."

Tessa waited. She knew that he had more to say

"She was really so poised and in control that I felt all right," he said. "I can see that she needs to understand what happened to you and to your family, and I can't help her with any of that. It's going to have to be you. You're going to have to be the one to help her find her way back from this."

"That's what Philip just told me I had to do for Ursula. I don't know if I can rescue all these people, Fran, Ursula, Regina. Who will rescue me? Who will come back for me after everyone is safe?"

Much to her disappointment, Walter did not offer to be her hero, to be the one who would save her. She took the opportunity of the silence to tell him to drive carefully. In response, he asked about Philip.

"Do you remember the three-legged dog?" Tessa asked.

"Vaguely," Walter said.

Tessa suspected he was not being entirely truthful. The three-legged dog had roamed the neighborhood for a long time. He had once had a home. It was clear from the way he sought out strangers, wagging his tail and flashing bright eyes that grew duller over time. In spite of his missing leg, he was nimble and frisky. Except for his lopsided gait, there was no way to tell what he had suffered. But he broke Tessa's heart. She wept over him so profusely that Walter grew impatient. "It's just a dog," he said. "You're overreacting."

He was right, but his words did nothing to help her anxiety. Every day, she prayed that she would not see the dog. This way she could convince herself that he had found a new home, that he was safe and warm in front of a fire, his appetite for meat and love satiated. When days without seeing the dog passed, she was encouraged, and then suddenly worried again. She imagined he had been run over, flattened by a careless driver, left to die in the cold even though it was a warm fall. She could never have any peace without knowing his fate. Then, she would spot him, hobbling along in some part of the neighborhood that a four-legged dog would find it difficult to reach, and the cycle of despair would resume. Of course, she knew it was irrational, but that didn't change anything.

Winter arrived, and Tessa anticipated the snow with anxiety. What would happen to Dog? That was the name she gave him. Dog. Not Three-Legged Dog. Just Dog. One blustery night, they came home, and Dog was there. He was in front of their house, his three legs curled beneath him, peacefully sleeping. In a patch of earth, he had made a spot for himself between two bushes. The awning protected this one area of lawn. There was hardly any green anymore, but it was free of the snow, possibly even warm. Dog lifted his head when he heard them and tilted it to the side, deciding if he had to bolt, or if he was safe for the night. "Don't feed him," Walter warned. "We'll never get rid of him if you feed him." She had nodded and held Regina closer. She was a toddler then and still half asleep from the car ride. Tessa pulled Regina's hood around her warm face and kissed her eyelids. Walter went on ahead into the house, and Tessa watched Dog sleep. The snow fell and Regina snored against her shoulder. The cold froze the tears on Tessa's cheek. If you asked her, she probably could not have said what made her so unhappy, so filled with longing for what she could not say. Dog was gone in the morning, but the patch of ground where he had slept bore the impression of his curved body. They never saw him again after that day, and Tessa prayed that he had been taken in by a loving family. But she never stopped regretting that she had not fed him on that freezing winter night.

"Well," Tessa said. "Philip reminds me a little of the three-legged dog."

"So he breaks your heart?" Walter said. "Is that it?"

She was right. He remembered. He might even have wondered about Dog once in a while.

"Yes," Tessa said. "He breaks my heart."

"Then you'll have to rescue him as well."

Tessa asked the same question she'd asked earlier. "Who will rescue me?"

When no answer was forthcoming, Tessa was disappointed again though she let it go. Instead, she told him again to drive carefully. But when he came home and after he had some tea and went to bed, Tessa's unanswered question inserted itself between them as they got into bed.

"Sometimes," she said, taking the lead as she almost always did, "I wonder what I've done to you."

"You haven't done anything to me." He sighed and held his palms up in a somewhat apologetic manner. "At least not anything I didn't allow."

"A mixed message, if I ever heard one."

"Let's go to sleep," Walter finally said. "We can argue tomorrow."

"Well, *that's* something to look forward to," Tessa said.

Walter waited for her to slip under the quilt and settle down before he turned on his side, facing her, and said, "Did you ever wonder if perhaps your mother came back to rescue you?"

Almost at once, Tessa realized what had held him back earlier from offering to be her rescuer.

"Is that what you really think?" she said. "You think my mother has come back to save me?"

"Maybe I do."

"Why would you think that?" she asked even though she already knew the answer.

"I think it would be more to the point to ask me why I wouldn't think that," he said. "Your mother has demanded your attention for as long as I've known you."

"Am I supposed to apologize?" Tessa said.

"I'm not looking for an apology. I'm looking for some resolution—it's not going to go away. We have to deal with it."

We. There it was again. Tessa was touched, but she didn't know how to reassure him, or even how to thank him.

"I'm tired," he said. "I need to go to sleep."

"Walter?" she reached over and took his hand. He was already half-asleep, but he murmured something conciliatory even though most of it was inaudible. The heat from his hand was reassuring; it told her he was fully present, completely available. Still, it was up to her to give her mother entrance, to invite her into their lives. "I love you, Walter."

As she drifted off to sleep, she went over the last time she had seen her mother. The awful things Tessa had heard her say to Dennis. She replayed the images of her mother's hysteria, her sheer panic. Now of course with the insights of time, Tessa fully understood how fearful Ursula must have been of what she could pass along to her unborn child. *Keep my baby safe,* Tessa thought as she closed her eyes. But she could not be sure if it was her mother's voice or her own that she heard repeat the plaintive entreaty over and over, hopeful that it would be heard and fulfilled.

It was still dark when Tessa's eyes flew open. Momentarily, she was unsure of her surroundings, but Walter's loud snores quickly placed her. The time for revelations had come, certainly not without warning, but with a rush of complications that she had not predicted.

Philip wanted to know everything, and Tessa knew it was a way for him to reclaim the past that should have been his instead of the one he owned in its place. Now, with Ursula in their lives, she would be able to explain why it had been necessary to leave Tessa behind and to give Philip away. And Tessa would have to justify her part in the drama that had irrevocably changed their lives.

Walter stirred when she left the bed. Gingerly, she stepped into the hallway and padded down the hallway to Regina's room. It had been Tessa's room once. She opened the door and stood in the threshold. Regina's absence was palpable. The room was sheathed in darkness though Tessa could make out the objects in the room from memory: the dresser and night table that had been hers. Regina had repainted both pieces red, sanding them down and then applying two coats of a deep red that reminded Tessa of royalty. The tops of both pieces were covered with perfume bottles, random pieces of costume jewelry, discarded tights, barrettes, pencils, matches, books, half-filled glasses and an assortment of single earrings, dental floss, loose change and crumpled bills. It always seemed as if Regina had simply spilled her pockets out and fled. While Tessa could not see any of this in the dark, she knew it was there.

She knew it just as well as she knew that over the years Ursula's presence had been as vibrant as it was now, ever trusting that an opening would present itself and she might reenter her children's lives and take her rightful place without too much disruption.

She suddenly saw Ursula as neither a threat nor a savior, just as a woman who had been lost for a long time and had returned, needing to recapture some of what had been lost. Breathless with this realization, Tessa understood that all these years, she had not been looking for her mother after all. All these years, Tessa had been looking for forgiveness, and only Ursula could grant that. She was the one and only. And for the moment, that was enough for Tessa.

Chapter Nineteen

When Tessa answered the doorbell a little before noon, she saw Regina standing in the doorway, clutching the arm of a woman who seemed quite ordinary at first. She could have been anyone, but she was Ursula. *Mother. Mommy. Mom.* None of them seemed suitable for the stranger who covertly glanced at Tessa from under downcast eyes. Then, with boldness that was as unsettling as her previous reticence, Ursula squared her shoulders, raised her head and looked directly at Tessa.

"Hello, Tessa," Ursula said. "I'm glad to see you."

"Hello," Tessa said.

Now it was Tessa who could not meet Ursula's eyes and, instead, fixed her gaze on Ursula's shoes. They were black with laces, the sort of shoes that Ursula had once naughtily referred to as nun shoes. Rubber soled, Ursula had explained, so they can sneak up on the Devil. She swore she would never wear such shoes. Ever. Unable to say anything more to Ursula, Tessa smiled, tight-lipped, and turned to Regina.

"Are you all right?" Tessa asked. "How did you get here?"

"I'm fine," Regina said. "We took the train, and we walked from there." She glanced at Ursula and smiled encouragingly, then looked back at Tessa and said, with genuine earnestness, "I'm sorry if you were worried."

"I'm just glad you're all right," Tessa said. "I guess there were extenuating circumstances." She smiled. "I know all about those."

Suddenly, Ursula took a step forward as though her name had been called.

"I'm sorry too," Ursula said. She reached out a hand and seemed about to touch Tessa's sleeve, but then quickly reconsidered it after Tessa imperceptibly backed away. Instead, Ursula clasped her hands together and looked down, childlike in her evident chagrin. "I was afraid you wouldn't talk to me if I called."

"That's fine," Tessa said stiffly. Even she was aware that her response made little sense. She made no effort to either refute Ursula's statement or to agree with it, concentrating on formulating the words in her head before speaking, thinking again of Marta's father. Did he ever remember the words he needed to express love? Did he learn to put together the sentences that would, like some magical portal open to reveal his past? Tessa felt a kinship with him even though they had suffered different wounds.

"Please, both of you," she said. "Let's get out of the hallway. Come in. I think you both know the way."

Ursula and Regina exchanged looks and in that moment, Tessa saw what they already meant to each other. She felt such a profound rush of jealousy that she was ashamed. As she stepped aside to allow them to pass her, she stole furtive glances at her mother, looking for clues to how she felt about being back in the house where her past was inescapable. Tessa waited to see where they would sit before choosing a place. They paused. She observed how they paused in accord and was grudgingly alert to the careful way Regina's hand hovered near Ursula's elbow as if she might stumble and fall without support. Regina guided Ursula to the couch. Tessa sat across from them in a chair.

"May I get you anything?" Tessa said with stiffness noticeable even to her.

Regina rolled her eyes at the formalities, but she seemed surprisingly cheerful for someone who had taken a dive head first into her murky ancestral waters.

"I wish Dad was home. I wanted him to meet Grandma." Regina smiled shyly at Ursula who reached for her hand and squeezed. Ursula's broad smile lit up her tired expression and seemed to give her some confidence.

"It's been a long time since I've been home," Ursula said.

"Yes," Tessa said, resenting Ursula's use of the word "home" and feeling mean-spirited as a result. "It has been a very long time."

"You're all grown up." Ursula shook her head ruefully and said, "But you were always grown up."

Tessa wanted to say yes, thanks to you, but she just nodded, acknowledging the comment, and waited for Ursula to go on.

"I haven't been well," Ursula said by way of explanation.

She seemed able to read Tessa's thoughts, but then that had always been so.

"Yes, I heard," Tessa said. "Fran told me."

"Fran is an angel," Ursula said. "I don't know what I would have done without her. She rescued me from the abyss."

"The abyss?" Tessa said. "I didn't realize you knew her that long."

Remarkably, to both Tessa and Regina, Ursula laughed, giving credence to Tessa's wry comment. But Regina did not find anything funny about her mother's reply, and she glared at Tessa who glared back. She was actually lightheaded from the onslaught of so many feelings—anger, jealousy, resentment, fear, and love.

There was definitely still love. It was tempting to devour Ursula with all her senses, but Tessa found it painful to even look at her. Cursory appraisals of Ursula's appearance revealed a woman who made great efforts to fit in with her surroundings. She wore a grey wool skirt and a black sweater. Tessa suspected the hose were support since they were thicker and shinier than ordinary stockings. And Ursula wore no make-up. Not even lipstick. Her lips had once been full and supple. Now they were dry and finely lined. Her skin was unexpectedly wrinkled, especially around the mouth and eyes, and her nails were poorly tended and unpainted, making Tessa suspect that it was too much for Ursula to attend to too many details.

Tessa had given her first manicures to Ursula, using polish stolen from the local pharmacy. Whenever Ursula pocketed a bottle of some outlandishly colored polish, she would whisper in Tessa's ear that it was just for the thrill. Terrified, Tessa would nod, furtively scanning the store for anyone who might have witnessed her mother's petty larceny. Ursula always went back the following day and paid for the polish (either saying the bottle fell into her purse or that she forgot she was holding it), but Tessa still hated it. The fear of her mother getting caught was too great. The memory of that fear made Tessa's stomach lurch even now.

Most disturbing was the transformation of Ursula's once lustrous hair. It had grown thin and grey. Even worse was that it was cut short in a severe and unflattering style with blunt bangs across her forehead that squarely framed her face. Tessa had to stop herself from wrapping her mother's hair around her ears, just to soften the look somehow. Just to touch her.

"I have a job," Ursula offered. "I work in an office."

"Oh, I see," Tessa said. She felt Regina's eyes boring a hole through her and added, "That's good."

"My case coordinator helped me get the job," Ursula said.

"Wonderful," Tessa said. She wanted to cry. "That sounds very interesting. An office job, I mean. Not the part about your case coordinator." Catching Ursula's confused expression, Tessa added, "Though that part sounds very interesting as well."

"And I have my own apartment," Ursula said.

Her delivery seemed scripted. Tessa imagined Ursula rehearsing what she planned to say in case they ever met. And while Tessa had prepared for the inevitability of just such an encounter, now she had no idea what to say. She watched how Ursula's lips pinched together the way they had when she was desperate for a cigarette. Tessa was reminded of countless afternoons spent in this very room, listening to Ursula's tirades against Dennis who had, once again, hidden her pack of whichever brand she favored that week. Now, as it had then, her mouth seemed to draw on an invisible cigarette. When Ursula saw the recognition in Tessa's expression, Ursula smiled at her as if they were conspirators. Tessa looked away, pretending something else had caught her attention.

"I keep the apartment nice." Ursula's tone was defensive. "And I don't smoke anymore. I quit."

"It's a *very* nice apartment," Regina added. "Lots of light and really big rooms. And so clean."

Tessa thought Regina sounded like a nursery school teacher, praising a pupil. Her solicitous attitude toward Ursula touched Tessa. It was new to see her Regina, who could be so cool and distant toward her own mother for no reason other than whim, be so deferential, so ardently protective of a woman she had only just met. Mirroring her daughter's frequent irrational reactions, Tessa felt almost vicious in her need to avenge Regina's kindness.

"Well, that's good," Tessa said. "That certainly makes up for everything in my life."

No one moved. They were caught in an eerie game of Statues without a designated liberator. Tessa's expression was set in stony silence, a foil to the incongruous softening of Ursula's mouth. Regina was stunned into silence. It was Ursula who placed a hand on Regina's arm, a gentle reminder of something they seemed to have previously discussed. Tessa saw all this, and it fueled her anger even more. That she should be excluded from their small circle offended her sense of justice.

"I'm sorry," Ursula said. "I wish I could take back all the hurt I caused you, but I can't. No one can."

Tessa refused to grant the truth of the statement, even forcing herself not to blink.

"It's all right," Ursula said. "I think I know how you must feel." Her voice was low and breathy, closer to the voice of Tessa's memories. But still Tessa would not yield. Ursula patted Regina's hand again, directing her words to her. "This is very traumatic for your mother, as well it should be. I disappeared from her life, and now I've reappeared. That just can't be easy." She turned towards Tessa. "I just want you to know that I take my meds regularly now. I never skip a day. It's been about twenty years."

"Twenty-six years," Tessa interrupted pointedly.

"Really? That long?" Ursula said with an almost seductive dreaminess. "It feels even longer to me." She shifted her weight on the couch, pressing down on Regina's arm with one hand. "I know I have a lot to explain. When you let me, I will try to tell you everything. But I had to see you, Tessa. I just wanted to see you up close. You're still my beautiful angel."

Tessa recognized those words. They were as familiar to her as the pain of her loss. Nothing could make her ever forget. She faced her mother, made her face uncharacteristically hard and waited for whatever was yet to come.

"Mom?" Regina said. She was imploring Tessa to speak, to address what she perceived as an impassioned plea from Ursula. "Mom? Don't you want to say something?"

Tessa blinked in succession several times. Her eyes had begun to water, and she held her head high, fearful they would think she was crying. And, oh, she so wanted to cry, to bury her head in Ursula's wool skirt and ask her why she had left her with no word, no reason.

"I think you should go now," Tessa said. She looked right at Ursula. "It's too much for me. I need some more time." Images and bits and pieces of conversation in her head made her turn and look around as if there were others in the room, and she was afraid they would overhear her. "I don't feel well myself."

"This has been a lot for you, Tessa. I'm sorry. You were never very good with surprises. I'm sorry. I should have warned you, but I knew how worried you must be about Regina and —"

"How would you know?" Tessa said. Her voice was icy. She scared herself. "How would you know how it feels to worry about your child? Tell me how you would know?"

"Mom," Regina said. "Stop it." She stood and stepped in front of Ursula, protecting her from any potential of injury. "Please, stop it!"

Tessa and Ursula reached for Regina simultaneously, but she sidestepped them both and ran sobbing out of the room. Tessa rose to go after her, but Ursula rose as well and blocked her way.

"Let her go," Ursula said. "She needs to be alone."

"Who doesn't?" Tessa said.

This time Ursula's laugh was more relaxed, the honeyed laugh of Tessa's early childhood. It made Tessa soft with desire and longing for the times that were good; times Tessa only dimly remembered and often wondered if she had just imagined.

"She'll be fine," Ursula said earnestly. "You have nothing to fear."

"How do you know what I fear?" Tessa said.

"Fears are like skin. Fears and doubts. They cover us. All of us, Tessa."

Ursula looked past Tessa, concentrating on every word, as if looking at her face might be too distracting.

"I can't choose what I remember." Tessa said, trying to keep the despair out of her voice.

"Can't you, Tessa?"

Tessa nodded, mute with the implication of her mother's question.

"I fear the same things you do," Ursula continued without waiting for a response. "My doubts are yours."

"And back then," Tessa said. Her voice was trembling. "In that other time. What did you fear then?"

It seemed to Tessa that Ursula knew the question before it was asked. Her reply was so measured, so precise, that Tessa thought her mother had been holding the answer on her tongue, savoring the richness of the flavor, hoping to make it last.

"I feared that I would live forever," Ursula said. "I feared that I couldn't protect my children."

It was the first time Philip had been mentioned and oblique as the reference to him was, Tessa knew it had taken enormous courage for Ursula to include him.

"That seems like a contradiction," she said. "Even for you."

"I live in a contradictory world," Ursula said and smiled. "That's not a bad thing, so long as you accept it."

"And you do?"

"I try. I'm still learning."

"Me, too," Tessa said. "I try, too."

"I know."

"Philip is very sweet. He cares for you a great deal."

Ursula's eyes filled with tears. She was too overcome to speak. They were standing close enough to touch; neither of them moved. They were heedful that a space had opened between them. Ursula felt it, and Tessa knew she did. Ever cautious, neither of them moved toward the opportunity that would have been hers for the taking. It was too risky, and they both had too much to lose.

"I should go," Ursula finally said. She looked around the living room. "The house looks nice. You took good care of everything. I knew you would."

Tessa held Ursula's coat as she slipped into the arms. The space was closing. Something had to be said before the path was sealed forever with no markers to make the next leg of their journey easier. And Tessa knew that no matter what, the journey would have to be taken.

"Thank you," Tessa said. "Thank you for bringing Regina home."

"It's the least I could do." Ursula smiled that cocky half-smile that suggested she was not entirely serious. "I'd like to call her later. To make sure she's okay. Do you mind?" Then she gripped Tessa's hands in that crazed way that was all too reminiscent and said, "I have to talk to you very soon, Tessa. It's very important."

Ursula's flesh was damp and personal in a way that made Tessa withdraw. She had expected her mother's skin to be dry. The way it had always been. Soft and powdery. Tessa could not break away, although she tried. Ursula's grip was tight.

"Some other time," Tessa said.

"When?" Ursula said. "I must know."

"I'll call you."

"When?"

"Soon. I promise. Just give me a little time," Tessa said. "Just a little more time."

"All right," Ursula said reassuringly. "I can wait. And Regina? What about her?"

"I'll see to her. I'll tell her that you'll call her later," Tessa said, and then automatically added, "Don't worry. I'll take care of it."

"Thank you. For an unlucky person, I'm very lucky."

With concurrent movements, Ursula relaxed her grip and Tessa no longer resisted. It was almost impossible to tell which had occurred first. But it no longer mattered. They shared a memory. *Don't worry,*

Mommy. I'll take care of everything. They might have been the first full phrases Tessa ever uttered.

Ursula pressed a small white cloth bag into Tessa's hand. She knew what it was without asking. *One white feather, a gold coin, a piece of coal, a piece of rock crystal and some dust from a church altar. For protection. For when you need it, Tessa. Only for when you need it.* Ursula bent low over Tessa's hands and kissed them quickly, very quickly, while Tessa closed her eyes and waited for the tremors that passed through her to stop. And while she waited, Ursula slipped into the bone chilling cold without another word.

"Now I know," Tessa said aloud.

There was no one there to hear her or to ask what she meant by those words. But Tessa knew, and it would change everything.

"Why didn't you drive her to the station?" Regina said.

She had come into the kitchen where Tessa was quietly sipping a cup of tea and began to immediately interrogate her.

"I offered to," Tessa said very patiently. "I even offered to drive her home."

"This is her home."

Instead of answering, Tessa took a careful sip of tea.

"It is, you know," Regina said. "She could move right back in here and make us leave."

"Is that what she told you?"

"No." Regina pulled a chair away from the table and sat down with a thump. She folded her arms onto the table and rested her cheek on her arms. "I don't know what's wrong with me."

"There's nothing wrong with you, baby. Nothing at all."

"That's so not true, Mom."

"It's been a hard few days. Give yourself a break."

"Don't you feel the least bit sorry for her?" Regina picked up her head and sat up straight. "Doesn't she just break your heart?"

"She already did that," Tessa said.

"Ursula said you were clever and combative, even as a child."

"Combative? Clever I can see, but combative?"

"See?"

"I see noth-ing," Tessa said, stretching out the word for emphasis. "Noth-ing."

"That's not true either, is it, Mom?"

Instead of answering, Tessa said, "She's going to call you later."

"I already called her. I wanted to make sure she got home safely."

"That was very sweet of you."

"I'm a very sweet girl." Regina grinned almost ghoulishly. "See? Sweet?"

Tessa closed her eyes against the awful sight and turned her head away. When Regina reassured her that it was safe to look, she did and said, "What did you do last night?"

"We had dinner. She made spaghetti."

"She loves spaghetti."

"The sauce was good. And she made salad and garlic bread. And we had ice cream for dessert. Vanilla with—"

"Crumbled gingersnap cookies. Homemade. With real pieces of ginger."

"Yes. They were delicious."

"Well, she must be feeling well."

"There are pictures of you all over the apartment. And of your dad."

"Really? Grandma Lucy must have sent them to her."

"They were just trying to protect you," Regina said. "Ursula was really sick for such a long time."

Tessa dismissed her daughter's editorializing as well-intentioned and instead of answering asked another question. "Where did you sleep?"

"On the pullout in the living room. It was very comfortable. She wanted me to sleep in her bed and she would take the pullout, but I said no."

"What did she tell you about me?"

"Nothing really. Nothing directly, anyway. She mostly told me stories," Regina said. Her voice had taken on a dreamy quality. "At first, it seemed a little weird to me, but then I realized that she was telling me about herself. She kept a journal almost from the time she disappeared. She read to me from that. Practically everything in that journal was directed toward you and Philip. Uncle Philip. He *is* my uncle, isn't he?"

"Yes. He'd be your uncle."

Tessa thought it best to say as little as possible. And Tessa knew how to listen. She knew how to let her own thoughts entwine with the words of the person speaking to her so that it all seemed like one extraordinary canvas. After all, everything was connected. Did anything ever really happen without some purpose?

"Mom?" Regina waved her hand back and forth in front of Tessa's face. "Are you with me?"

"Yes, of course I'm here."

"Are *you* all right?"

"Are you all right?" Tessa peered into Regina's beautiful face. How she had created someone so beautiful, Tessa wondered. She searched Regina's face for something of herself and found that only the arched brows and the ever so slightly bucked teeth were an exact genetic match. "Are you hungry?"

Regina shook her head.

"I'm sorry," Tessa said. "I know you meant well. It's just that it was such a shock to see her, and I don't know how to sort out my feelings. It's been such a long time, and I couldn't possibly begin to explain everything I'm feeling."

"I just wanted everything to be perfect," Regina said. "I thought I could be the one to make it all right, *everything,* you know."

Tessa understood. Ursula had often slept with a small clock. She said the steady tick-tock encouraged her own heart to beat. She was so sure it would stop the moment she closed her eyes. But Tessa did not share that with Regina. It was necessary to proceed cautiously if she wanted to make Regina understand about that long ago night and how it had brought them to this day.

"I feel so sorry for her," Regina whispered. "I want to ask her so many questions, but she seems like she could break if I say the wrong thing."

Tessa lightly touched Regina's curls, savoring their softness, and said, "I often thought that in the perfect world there would be no uncertainty, no questions to be asked or answered."

"But it's not a perfect world," Regina said. She sounded exasperated. "Is that the moral of the story?"

"There is no moral to this story. Only revelation." She smiled. "It'll have to do for now."

"Why didn't you stop them that night?" Regina said.

"Stop them?" Tessa said.

"Yes, stop them. You knew what was going to happen, and you didn't stop it. You could have changed the future, and you chose not to."

"It's not that simple, Regina. Nothing ever is."

"Are you telling me you didn't know your mother was pregnant?"

After all these years, nothing was really clear in Tessa's head. But Regina needed answers.

"I'm sure I did on some level. It was never officially announced, but I do remember some reference to it. She couldn't have been very far along. You have to remember that I was just a child, a scared one at that. I didn't even know what to make of what I could see. I was never really sure. Still, I was as sure as I had ever been about anything that there would be disaster that night. I did know that. It's true. I felt its approach."

"You remember that you were very afraid."

"I was always afraid," Tessa said. "Maybe I don't want to remember. Maybe it's just too hard. You think you know your grandmother after just a few days? I lived in a crazy house. Ursula moved between two very different worlds, and we were all pulled along. There were the in-between times, the lulls. But the periods of calm didn't last. It was the other times that shaped the way we lived."

"So you did know," Regina insisted.

"Maybe I knew and chose not to stop it," Tessa said.

Regina paled and Tessa began to speak quickly, more eager to get it over with than anything else.

"Suppose for a moment that I wasn't supposed to stop it," Tessa said. "Suppose that it played itself out exactly as it needed to, and I understood that on some very primitive level."

"And Ursula?" Regina said. "She knew about the dream you kept having. I read it in her journal. How did she know about the dream?"

Tessa understood from this question that Ursula had revealed nothing to Regina about their collective dream. It was Ursula's first offering. It would be up to Tessa to decide what to disclose.

"Because she had the same dream," Tessa said.

"But why?" Regina said. "If she had the same dream, why did she let it happen?"

"I don't know. Maybe so she could find her way home and meet you," Tessa said. "Maybe so Philip could be raised in a stable family. So I could meet your father and have you because it seems that you're one who will make sense of this whole puzzle. It just goes on, Regina. It just goes on."

She waited for Regina to say something, believing she would understand some of what she had just been told.

"Marie's cat gave birth," Regina said. "Six of the cutest little kittens I've ever seen."

"Oh?" Tessa said. She wasn't at all sure where Regina was going with this information, but something about her matter-of-fact tone suggested that Regina was headed somewhere important.

"Marie found good homes for all of them. She was so worried at first," Regina said. She lowered her eyes before continuing with the story. "But when she came home from school, she found that the mother had bitten off her own tail." She lifted her face. Her voice was tremulous when she continued. "The vet said it was distress over the loss of her kittens. She had stopped eating and drinking as well. It happens, was all the vet could say. Not often, but it happens."

"Was Marie surprised?" Tessa said. She wanted to embrace Regina but she knew it was necessary to let her finish her story first. "She must have been shocked."

"Yes," Regina said. "She was a bit shocked, I guess."

"Were you?"

Regina had already thought about her answer. It was the reason the story had been told in the first place. And Tessa knew, as her mother had known that dreams and stories had to be finished, had to be told in their own way, in their own time. The day of the accident Ursula had told Tessa that plantation slaves sealed their marriage vows by jumping over a stick. Ursula found that extraordinary. The idea that when people were robbed of their rituals, they created new ones. People are resilient, Ursula emphasized. She told this and more to Tessa as though it were Tessa leaving on a long journey. "Remember everything I'm telling you," she said. And though Tessa never made them, it was the same day Ursula had passed along her ginger cookie recipe. "Here." She had pressed an index card into Tessa's hand. "Put this away for later." She had even warned Tessa to let them cool before removing them from the cookie sheet. "Otherwise, they'll fall apart." Such urgency in everything that day. So much confusion.

"I think I might have been before I read what Ursula wrote in her journal," Regina said.

"What did she write?" Tessa asked.

"A mother's love is the greatest magic," Regina said. "Did you know she wrote that in her journal?"

For just a moment, they were both silent, allowing the import of Ursula's words to unite them, the three of them, for the very first time. And then Tessa said, no, she didn't know. But she did understand.

And then she said "poor cat," and Regina agreed, as if the story had been about the cat after all.

Chapter Twenty

"So what's going on?"

Walter came in through the kitchen door, took off his coat and carefully fit it around the back of one of the wooden chairs. He had phoned first from his office and then again from the car. The second time he phoned, Tessa was no longer able to wait to tell him about Ursula. She gave him very few particulars. He listened quietly (too quietly Tessa felt), and then wanted to know why she hadn't phoned him immediately. Her excuse was reasonable: he had been in meetings all day. Fortunately, he seemed to accept that, but he pressed her for more information. Whenever she paused, he said, "And?" He wanted to hear every detail.

"Well," Tessa said. "She looks much older."

"Don't we all?"

Although she knew it was foolish to expect Walter to step into her skin and to know what she felt after so many years of estrangement from her mother, Tessa was disappointed by his lack of effort. She had hoped he would work harder to tease some information out of her. She needed help and none was forthcoming.

Tessa had eaten with Regina. They had fixed some grilled cheese sandwiches and heated some soup, working together in the kitchen, silently but comfortably, each too drained to say much more than could you pass me this or that. After dinner, Tessa said she would clean up, and Regina went to her room to do her homework.

Although Tessa was tired, she waited for Walter. It was almost nine by the time he arrived. She had left food for him, ready to be warmed. Sighing heavily, she pulled a bag of garbage from the pail and dropped the bag with a thud. The smallest output of energy drained her, and she sank wearily into the nearest chair.

"You look exhausted," Walter said, not unkindly at all.

"I am, but I'm okay." She looked up into his face. "I'm really fine."

"You seem very calm. Are you?"

"I said I'm fine."

"I'm not convinced," he said.

"Sorry." She heard the edge in her response and adjusted her tone. He was just showing concern. "There's soup."

"I'll have some in a minute. Where's Regina?"

"In her room. She had homework."

"How was she with Ursula?"

Tessa shook her head as if she could not believe what she was about to say, but was going to say it anyway.

"She was perfect."

"Perfect?" Walter looked skeptical. "What does that mean?"

"Well, she was attentive, gentle, loving and supportive, ad nauseam I might add."

"Really?"

"I was, admittedly, incredulous," Tessa said. "I didn't know what came over her."

"She's a good girl."

"I know she's a good girl, but this was, well, above and beyond."

"And how did Ursula respond?"

"Like a grandmother. She responded like a goddamned grandmother." Tessa waited for him to say something, but he seemed to be mulling this over. "Where the hell did she learn how to be a grandmother?"

Watching her closely, he crossed his arms over his chest and leaned against the refrigerator. She went to him, uncrossed his arms and leaned against him. She felt his heart beating, not faster or slower than usual, just beating. That comforted her, made her feel that things were normal in spite of how they seemed. Walter held her and rested his cheek on the top of her head. When he spoke, his breath rustled her hair so that it tickled, and she shuddered slightly against him.

"Tell me about her," he said.

Tessa played with the buttons on his shirt and said, "She looks worn."

She waited for him to ask her something else, anything else that would make it easier for her to know what to say. He was so rarely forthcoming on the subject of Ursula. His struggle was so evident, so poignant. So when he spoke, her heart fluttered with forgotten optimism.

"I don't know how to approach this with you," Walter admitted. "I'm at a loss." He rhythmically patted her back as if trying to comfort her, and then stopped, quite abruptly. "Anything I could say would be inadequate or inflammatory."

Tessa was encouraged by the heartfelt tone of his admission although it was not new to her. She knew that her needs often left him feeling stranded. That was how he described it. There were no markers, he claimed, to identify how to advance with her. So he remained in the same place as if he were a lost child, as if those were the instructions he had been given, and he wanted to prove his obedience. Mostly, Tessa suspected, he just wanted to be found. When Regina was a little girl, they always warned her that if you get lost, don't move. Don't look for us. We'll find you. Just stay put. And that was exactly what Walter did, what Walter was doing now, staying put and waiting to be found.

"I don't know how to help you with this," he said. "I can't understand what you see. It frightens me. And you were right. You still frighten me."

He let his arms fall, leaving Tessa feeling as though she had been dropped from a considerable height, like the water balloons Ursula had liked to throw from the attic window. The sound of them bursting, and the water spraying everywhere, had delighted her and thrilled Tessa.

"And what I know of Ursula terrifies me," he said.

If Tessa tried to explain, she would have told him that it was hard to distinguish between what she saw and her own memories. For that was how impressions came to her. Like her own memories, except they did not belong to her. *I own the memories of others*, she could have told him. *Like small flashes of recognition that have no connection to my own life, yet feel as if they do,* she would have said. Instead, she said nothing because when she did she would have to tell him the truth about the accident and how it had appeared to her as her own memory.

"Don't be afraid," Tessa said. "Ursula seems to be in control of her illness. She works in an office. She takes her meds and, according to Regina, maintains a very nice apartment."

"That's all very good to know," Walter said. "What I want to know, however, is if you're afraid."

"Of what?"

"Funny." He reached for her again and tightened his arms around her. "I'll repeat the question. Are you afraid?"

"I don't know how to answer that."

"Try."

She freed herself from his arms and sat, scowling at the table.

"I love it when you put on your lawyer hat," Tessa said.

"Sorry," Walter said.

Regina suddenly appeared in the doorway, arms crossed over her chest, making her look just like her father. Her hair was wet, and she was wearing pajamas. She smiled indulgently at them, two bad children caught in the act.

"Nice to see you," Walter said. "You saved us from ourselves."

"Hallelujah," Tessa said.

"Ah, sarcasm," Regina said, using a carefully modulated singsong voice. "Not a good healing tool."

Tessa had to laugh, hearing her own frequently repeated words flung back at her in mockery, and with such exact inflection that it was embarrassing to hear how ridiculous she must sound to Regina.

Clapping her hands together, Regina said. "Well, folks, my work seems to be done here."

"How was Ursula?" Walter said.

Regina's entire demeanor changed. She looked cautiously at Tessa and said, "She's good."

"Do you want to talk?" Walter said.

"I'm okay." Regina crossed the room and wrapped her arms around him. "I love you."

"I love you too," he said, hugging her. "I love you very much." He looked at Tessa over the top of Regina's head and winked.

"So now what?" Regina said. She was still leaning against her father, using all her influence to keep him on her side. "I'm sure Dad would like to meet Ursula."

"Would he?" Tessa said. "You know that for a fact?"

"Tess," Walter said. His tone was immediately cautionary. "Maybe we can talk about it."

"*I* don't know if *we* can," Tessa said. "I don't know."

"Tessa," Walter said, lowering his voice as he tried to soften Tessa's resistance. "Ursula needs you."

"How do you know what she needs?" Tessa said. "For someone who has just met this woman and someone who has never met her at all, you both know an awful lot."

"You just told me that she wasn't a threat to us," Walter said.

"It has nothing to do with her," Tessa said. "It's about me. And of course she isn't a threat."

"Ursula's scared of Mom," Regina said.

Tessa's looked from one to the other, measuring Walter's reaction while at the same time trying to get a sense of Regina's expectations. It was a lot to evaluate in a few moments.

"Ursula has no reason to be afraid of me," Tessa finally said.

"Yet," Regina said.

"That's simply unkind, Regina," Tessa said.

"This hasn't been easy for her either," Regina said. "She knew you wouldn't react well to her."

"Did she?" Tessa asked.

"*That's* simply sarcastic," Regina said.

"Regina," Walter said, making her name a warning. He had been listening, trying to remain neutral. "Take it down a notch."

"It's okay," Tessa said.

"Try to look at things from your mother's point of view," Walter said. His voice was low and persuasive. "All this has been a shock."

But Tessa saw from Regina's expression that she was unable to do that just yet, to see anything from anyone else's perspective, except Ursula's perhaps. Like Philip, Regina needed a reason for why all this had happened, why the outcome could not have been any different.

"This didn't happen to you," Tessa said. "It happened to me, and you got caught in it. We can't always protect the people we love. Ursula couldn't protect me, and I couldn't protect you. Love isn't always the answer. We want it to be. We think it can be, that it can solve everything, but it can't. One thing is certain. I'll never love you less. But that doesn't change how things will work out."

"But you always say that love is everything," Regina said. "You tell me that all the time."

"And it's true," Tessa said. "It *is* everything. It just isn't enough to change what has to be."

"Why didn't you save them?" Regina asked.

Her eyes were teary, but her tone belied the intensity of her pain. Tessa indulged the hint of sanctimoniousness that colored Regina's question as she pressed on for answers.

"Why didn't you try to stop them?" Regina's voice went up an octave. "You could have saved them and you didn't. Why?"

Tessa had prepared the answer to this question several times and in several versions.

"I guess I wasn't supposed to, or I would have," Tessa said. She met Walter's shocked expression with a cool, level gaze. Steady, she told herself. Deep breaths. "I don't have a definitive answer."

Walter placed his hands on Regina's shoulders, pressing down as if to secure her. She leaned back against him and then turned. His arms circled her, and he looked at Tessa, bewildered and (she thought) a little afraid because he also wanted to hear a different answer.

"Who knows what people dream? And maybe I wanted her to die. That's another possibility although that's too taboo to even address. I mean, after all, we're on sacred ground here. Would I be the first child to wish a parent dead?"

Regina flushed, and Walter shook his head, just once at first, but then again, more emphatically, before he ventured some response.

"I think this is more than a childish wish to get even with a parent," he said.

"So you're saying that I'm responsible for my father's death, and for my mother's decision to abandon her children."

"I don't know what I'm saying anymore," he said. "No, of course not . . ."

Walter looked miserable, but before Tessa could respond, Regina, her voice suddenly and surprisingly small, like the voice of a little girl, said, "Did you really want her to die? I mean really and truly?"

"Oh, Regina," Tessa said, crossing the room to pull her away from Walter and take her in her own arms. "I *really* and *truly* loved my mother, but I was trying to live in spite of her. I know it's natural to make hasty judgments." She inclined her head with import at Walter. "I know you really and truly understand what I'm talking about." Tessa kissed Regina's curly head and stepped back, holding her at arms' length. "I love you so much."

"How is it possible that your mother had the same dream?" Walter said.

"Is that the strangest story you ever heard?" Tessa said. "It must happen all the time. I think it would be a surprise if it didn't happen, especially to us."

"How can you be certain that it was the exact dream?"

"I can't be, but I believe it was, or at least some version of it," Tessa said. "I guess she thought she was protecting me. She was just trying to be a good mother, and I was too young and too hurt to see it. I didn't even believe she loved me."

Later, Tessa would remember how Walter and Regina seemed stunned at her rendering of the events that had shaped all their lives. Nevertheless, Tessa felt relieved, maybe even exonerated. At least she had spoken most of the truth. At least now they knew that in spite of love or because of it, anything was possible.

"Althea phoned me at the office today," Walter said.

Tessa bolted upright in bed and switched on the light.

"Why didn't you tell me?" she said.

"I'm telling you now." He squinted in the light. They had both been almost asleep when he must have decided it was news that should not wait until the morning. "There was too much happening. And I didn't want to get Regina's hopes up."

"What does that mean?"

"It was a weird conversation. She caught me completely off guard."

"How did she get your number at work?"

"I don't know. My parents? They know where I work." He squinted. "Could you shut off that light?"

Tessa obliged, but she remained sitting up.

"What did she say? Was she nice?"

"Nice? I guess. She was uncomfortable. That was obvious."

"Did you ask about your parents?"

Walter yawned loudly. "Of course. She said they're fine."

"Were you freaked out when you heard her voice?"

"I guess so. I don't know. What difference does it make?"

Tessa turned on the light again, and he squinted and put one of the pillows over his eyes.

"Jeez, what's the deal?"

"You gave me all this sanctimonious crap about my mother to make yourself look good in front of Regina, and you didn't say a word about Althea. What's the deal with *that?*"

She was shouting, and he told her to lower her voice.

"C'mon, it's late," he said. "Regina's probably sleeping. I'm tired. I'm just so fucking tired of all this *family* drama. I was perfectly content without your mother in the picture and without Althea."

"I can't believe you." Tessa pulled back the blanket and got out of bed. "I just can't believe you."

"It's late. It's been a long day. Come back to bed."

"No."

"At least hit that damned light."

"No."

"What do you want?" He sat up in bed. "Tell me so I can get to sleep."

"Tell me what she said."

"She said she is going to be in town next week, and she would like to have lunch or dinner with me."

"Just with you?"

Walter ran his hand through his hair, yawned and looked slightly desperate to end the conversation and get back to bed. "I guess so. I don't know."

"You don't know? How could you not know?"

He bristled. "I don't know."

"What did you say?" Tessa insisted. "Did you invite her over? What did you say?"

"I said I would get back to her. And I asked her not to call Regina until after I spoke to you."

"Why did you do that?"

"I don't want Althea dropping into our lives and stirring up a lot of feelings, and then leaving once she realizes it's more than she bargained for." He was shouting now, but he caught himself and lowered his voice almost to a whisper. "Why can't you see that? Even I can see it. Nothing could be more obvious."

"Why would it be more than she bargained for?" Tessa kept her voice low, but her tone was steely. "Because nothing has changed? Because she would still be afraid of me?"

"I don't know. Let's just drop this."

"I know you're not telling me everything," Tessa said.

He looked exhausted, and if Tessa had not been so angry, she would have felt remorse.

"Can we pick this up in the morning?" Walter said.

"Sure. The morning is good."

Tessa got under the blanket and reached over to turn off the light on her nightstand. She waited, listening to Walter's intermittent grunts of pleasure as he gratefully settled down. She was hopeful that something conciliatory would be forthcoming from him, something that would show he was sorry. Instead he was asleep instantly, snoring with complete self-satisfaction.

It was only a little past eleven. Quickly calculating in her head, Tessa realized it was just a little past nine in Portland. She could safely call Mia and tell her everything. Making her way downstairs, Tessa sat in the dark kitchen and prayed Mia would be available.

By the graces of the gods, Mia was free, alone and happy to hear from Tessa. It took only a few minutes to bring Mia up to date on everything.

"How long has it been since you've seen your mother?" Mia said.

"A long time. I don't know, twenty-six years?"

Mia let out a long, low whistle and said, "Long time, baby. Really long time."

"I don't know what to do. I used to know what to do in most every situation."

"That's impressive," Mia said.

"Not anymore," Tessa said. "I'm completely lost now. What should I do?"

"What do you want to do?" Mia asked.

"I want to be able to forgive her and welcome her back in my life, but I don't know if I can."

"Why?"

Everything was always very clear for Mia. She saw a problem, and she devised a solution. Common sense was her compass. There was no room for doubt in Mia's approach. And while Tessa was drawn to Mia for these very reasons, it was often difficult to assume her practical attitude without some resistance.

"Well, for one, she left me."

"Ancient history," Mia said.

Tessa could practically see Mia sweeping her hand in the air, waving away any doubts that might be lurking, threatening to undermine her no-nonsense plan of attack.

"Ancient for you, maybe," Tessa said. "Not so ancient for me."

"How many times did you tell me that she was ill?" Mia said. "I know I didn't imagine it. She was very ill, wasn't she?"

"Yes, she was very ill," Tessa agreed.

"And didn't you tell me that she thought she was doing the right thing?"

"Yes."

"And, haven't you spent your life since then believing that she was still alive, and waiting for her to come back?"

"I get it. I get it."

"Give her a chance," Mia said. "This can't be easy for her."

"You're right."

"What's Philip like?"

"The three-legged dog that hung around here for awhile when Reggie was a baby."

"Is that good or bad?"

Tessa sighed. "I swear I can't answer that yet. He's sweet, really, really sweet, but he sort of breaks my heart."

"Oh, everything breaks your heart."

"Well, I'm sensitive," Tessa said with exaggerated indignation.

"That's something I can't argue with," Mia said. "But you know, this business with Althea is the strangest part of the story. It's such a weird coincidence."

"First of all, that's redundant. And, more importantly, there are no coincidences. Haven't I at least taught you that?"

"Of course you have, but it's hard not to wonder about the timing."

"Wonder all you want."

It was very late for Tessa, and she stifled a yawn. She asked about everyone before saying goodnight. As always, Mia urged Tessa to come for a visit.

"As soon as all this settles down, grab Reggie and come for a few days. We can relax and have some laughs."

"I will. I really promise."

Mia blew kisses into the phone, something Tessa would never do. After she hung up, she cautiously peeked in at Regina, trying to imagine what those first few moments with Ursula had been like for each of them. Ursula had missed all of Regina's childhood. And Ursula loved babies. She wept for the women who asked her for advice on how to conceive. And Ursula worried about the souls of babies who died at birth. Once she told Tessa that the souls of babies who died at birth hovered around their mothers for a while. Ursula confided that occasionally she could see the souls of these poor little things. *Poor little things.* That's what Ursula called them. *Poor little things.* The memory made Tessa shiver. She closed the door to Regina's room and in the dark felt her way back to her bedroom, flailing at the space above her head, suddenly fearful of any stray souls lingering nearby.

Chapter Twenty-One

"I'm late for work," Walter said.

Tessa had barricaded him in the master bathroom, pressing herself against the door, refusing to let him out. Of course, he could have thrown his weight at the door and sent her flying, but of all the tribulations that had beset their marriage throughout the years, they had never been violent with each other.

"I'm not going to move away until you talk to me about Althea," Tessa said.

"This is silly. Step away from the door, or I'm going to open it."

"You won't do that." She had heard Regina's alarm go off and spoke softly. "I want an answer. I want to know what you plan to do."

"I don't have any plans," Walter confessed. "I was thinking about pretending that it never happened."

"Seriously?"

"Yes, seriously."

Exasperated, she relinquished her pressure on the door. Walter nearly fell on top of her. He had been leaning with all his weight, waiting for an opportunity, but not expecting it to come so quickly.

"For crying out loud, Tess, I almost killed myself." He stumbled past her and went to his closet, chose a freshly laundered white shirt and slipped it on. As he buttoned it, he said, "What would you like me to do?"

"Call Althea back and invite her for brunch this Sunday."

"She'll never show."

"Why do you say that?"

"Because I'm intuitive," he said.

Tessa had to laugh even though she told him he wasn't funny. Shrugging, he selected a red tie from the tie rack, but Tessa intercepted and chose a tie of alternating shades of blue with a hint of burgundy running through it.

"You're sure?" he said, eyeing the tie skeptically. "I'm wearing the gray suit."

"Actually, it's the only thing I am sure of."

"I wish you would let this go." He allowed her to do his tie. "Let me handle it my own way."

"Regina has her heart set on a family," she said.

"She has a family," he said, sticking his finger inside his collar to make sure he could move his neck. "I wish you would trust me."

"I do trust you, but not when it comes to good judgment."

"Semantics," he said, gently kissing her mouth. "It's a good thing I love you."

Long ago Tessa had surmised that love was a revolt against all reason. She remembered how women, young and old, had stealthily come to this very house seeking Ursula's potions, mostly cures for the mysteries of love and the heartaches that resulted. It was clear that nothing was more difficult than to make a stubborn heart yield to the will of another. Ursula's efforts were tireless, struggling as she did to replace the fragile core of her own existence, and failing to ever replenish what she gave away. Tessa leaned her head against Walter's chest. *If you lose someone you love and want to get him back all you have to do is take a needle and carefully prick the skin over your heart. Use the blood to write your name and your lover's name on a clean piece of silk. Make the letters as small as you can. Then take some ash and draw a circle around your names. Fold up the cloth and watch the sky for the first evening star. As soon as you see it, bury the cloth. The one you love will return and beg to be forgiven. But you must remember, Tessa, tell no one what you have done, or the spell will have the opposite effect.* Ursula read spells to Tessa as though they were bedtime stories. And Tessa listened, solemn and mindful. Now it was clear that her mother had known that even if her spells could rejuvenate love, it would never be for long. It was best to let go of a man who had lost interest. Better to find a new love. All Tessa had ever wanted was a spell that could make her feel less, until she met Walter.

"I know that you're not telling me everything," she said.

"Do you tell me everything?"

She yanked at his tie, playfully but with intent.

"I should have knocked you down when I had the chance." He smiled.

"Next time."

"There won't be a next time," he said.

They stared at each other, each waiting for the other to clarify the future.

"I have to get going," Walter finally said. "Is there coffee?"

"There's coffee."

"Am I taking Regina?"

"No. I'll take her. Mid-terms. She doesn't have to be in until ten."

"And you?"

"I'm good till eleven or so."

"Will you come downstairs and have some coffee with me?"

"Will you call Althea?"

She knew the answer, but she had to ask. And she knew that this time he would tell her what she had suspected all along. For a moment she felt as though she should write down the reason Walter would not call Althea the way a magician might ask audience members to pick a card from a deck and keep it hidden. But Tessa had nothing to prove.

"No, I won't call her."

Tessa waited. She heard the toilet flush. Regina was awake.

"She doesn't want to see you. She only wants to see me and Regina."

"Oh," Tessa said.

"That's it?" Walter said. "That's all you have to say?"

"I think so."

"Don't you want to know why?"

"I know why. We all know why."

"And it doesn't infuriate you?" He sat down on the bed and put his head in his hands. "I didn't even know what to say. I was speechless."

She sat beside him on the bed, close enough so that their shoulders were touching, breathing into him with a steady rhythm that she hoped would calm him. After a few moments of this, he seemed less agitated.

"I don't see how you can be so calm," he said. "Why did she write to Regina? It's so manipulative. Don't you think it's manipulative?"

"It's manipulative," Tessa agreed.

"She told me that you wrote her a very nice email, but she couldn't bring herself to respond. "

Tessa shrugged. "I did it for Regina."

"I know you did." He turned to look at her. "Did you see this coming?"

She shook her head. "No. I can't say that I did, not until today when you started acting all mysterious about Althea."

"I'm sorry," Walter said. "I apologize for my family. I don't know what else to say."

She bumped him with her shoulder. "And I apologize for my family. Well, for my mother, anyway."

"At least she has an excuse."

She stood and placed her hands on his head as though she was about to bless him, then took her hands away and hugged herself, rocking back and forth just momentarily before she came to a full stop.

"Rocking is institutional behavior," she said more to herself than to Walter. "So is smoking. Ursula used to do both."

He looked up into her face with such a poignant expression that it wrenched at her heart.

"Are we bad people?" he asked.

"Of course not!" Tessa sat on his lap and wrapped her arms around his neck. "We're very good people. What a thing to ask! Look at me."

In his typically good-natured way, he obliged, but he had trouble holding her gaze.

"What is it?" she asked.

"I just don't get it. I barely said anything to Althea. I should have told her off, but I sidestepped the whole thing because I was so shocked. I mean I told her that I'd get back to her."

"Will you?" Tessa smoothed his hair with her fingers. "What's your plan?"

"I told you. I plan to forget it ever happened." He craned his neck to see his watch on the arm that was wrapped around Tessa. "I have to go."

As she slid off his lap, she held onto his shoulder to steady herself. Walter turned his head and rubbed his cheek against her hand before he too stood.

"You'll have to talk to Regina about this," Tessa said. "You'll have to tell her the truth."

"Not the truth," he said. "The truth sucks."

"Indeed it does."

"I'll tell her. And I'm going to call Althea and tell her that unless she wants to see all of us, the reunion is off."

"You don't have to do that for me," Tessa said. "I would be fine if you wanted to see her."

"I don't."

"She seemed so normal in the letter she wrote to Regina," Tessa mused. "You'd think that I would be able to see through her."

"For any number of reasons," Walter said.

And Tessa laughed because it felt good to think that they were just like everyone else. Regular people with family problems.

"Maybe Althea just got scared," Tessa said. "It's been a long time, and she was very young and impressionable."

"Then why bother to write at all?" He shook his head, as if responding to his own statement. "It doesn't make any sense."

Tessa shrugged and said, "Regina will be hurt no matter what."

"I guess she'll have to know the truth sooner or later," Walter said.

"And what is the truth?"

"When I make it up, I'll tell you."

"Fair enough."

With playful intent, she held out her hand to seal the agreement, but he shook it with an unsettling solemnity. As he clasped her hand, his pain and distress moved through her, unconcealed, raw in its strength. And Walter did not resist as he might have at some other time. They seemed locked together in this moment, fearless in their determination for some clarity. But Walter was unable to see what Tessa saw with almost alarming simplicity. He did however observe the fleeting shift in her stance, the almost indiscernible change in her expression.

"What is it?" he said.

"It's nothing." She tried to pull away her hand, but he held fast. "It's getting late."

"We're all in this together. Now's not the time to hold back."

Slyly, she faked a sneeze and outmaneuvered him, managing to free herself from his grip.

"Let's have that coffee," she said.

"Are we okay?"

"So far, so good." She kissed his cheek. "You worry too much."

Regina was already in the kitchen, studying flash cards she had made for her biology exam. She barely looked up from her cereal when her parents came in. Over the top of her head, Walter winked at Tessa, who smiled faintly but did not wink back. She had been an accomplice too many times to feel comfortable in the role.

Fran called while Tessa was making the bed.

"I didn't wake you, did I?" Fran said.

"Oh no, not at all. I'm getting ready for work, and I have to drive Regina to school."

She felt overwhelmingly sorry for Fran, who had merely wanted to fix a wrong. Everything had spiraled out of control, which seemed to be the only way it could have concluded. This was the first time they had spoken since Fran had urged Tessa to allow Regina to have her time with Ursula.

"Good, good," Fran said. "I've been thinking about you. Are you coping with the recent events?"

"I think so. There's just so much going on right now." Tessa hesitated. She restrained the impulse to tell Fran about Althea. There was no reason to tell Fran, yet for a moment it seemed the most natural thing to do. "What about yourself? And Philip?" It was evident that Fran had put considerable preparation into what she wanted to say to Tessa. Fran went on with her own script, disregarding Tessa's questions.

"I didn't know it would get so complicated. I just wanted to help. You know, I actually thought I would be able to keep it simple."

"Did you really?"

There was a pause before Fran finally admitted the truth and said, "No. I guess I didn't. But I guess that if I had allowed myself to face what was about to unravel, I would never have gotten involved. And I had to get involved. So many lives were intertwined. It needed to be sorted out. And my son was in pain."

"I understand. I really do."

"Maybe you can recover some of what you lost with Ursula," Fran said.

She sounded so hopeful that Tessa felt she had to agree in some way, no matter how small.

"Maybe," she said. "I hope so. Tell me. How is Philip?"

"He struggles."

"I'm sorry," Tessa said.

"No, don't be sorry. It's who he is, and he's quite extraordinary. He's visiting with Ursula."

"Does that upset you?"

"No," Fran said. "He has a right to know her."

"But it must be painful for you," Tessa said.

Fran deftly changed the subject. "Was it very painful for you when you saw Ursula?"

Before today, Tessa would have been quick to answer no, of course not, there was no pain.

"Yes," she said. "It was painful."

"It's better that way, you know. Sometimes, you just have to feel the pain," Fran said.

"Sometimes, yes," Tessa agreed. "But not all the time."

"Ursula said something remarkable to me when we first met," Fran said. "She talked about you a lot. She has lots of memories, but surprisingly few regrets for someone who has had such a hard life. Sorry, I'm editorializing. It's a bad habit."

"It's all right," Tessa said. She felt remarkably calm. It was a relief. "This is hard . . ." She swept her hand as though she wanted to make a point, any point. "Tell me what she said, please."

"She said that she was trying hard to plan her past better," Fran said. "I thought it was an extraordinary way of summing up a life."

When Tessa could speak, she said thank you. It was clear that Ursula had been speaking to Tessa through Fran, knowing full well that when the time was right, Tessa would heed each word.

They went out for dinner that night. Walter, Tessa and Regina. A threesome. That was how Walter had always referred to them. A threesome. They were exhausted, each for different reasons, but still happy to be together.

"A lot of drama these last weeks," Walter said. He broke a breadstick in half and chewed on it thoughtfully. "It's amazing how things happen all at the same time."

"In threes," Regina said. "Grandma Lucy used to say that stuff happens in threes."

"Like us," Tessa said. "Three."

Walter was about to say something when the waitress took their orders. They came often to this local Italian restaurant. The owner, Roberto, the restaurant's namesake, always sent something special over to their table. Tonight it was homemade bruschetta on toasted garlic rounds. Walter ordered a bottle of the house wine. The waitress returned promptly and filled two glasses.

"Delicious," Regina said, sipping greedily from Walter's glass. "Even more delicious."

"One sip," Tessa warned. She placed a hand over the top of her glass. "And that's it."

"You know in Europe kids are allowed to drink wine all the time," Regina said.

"We don't live in Europe," Tessa said.

"Maybe we should move," Walter said. "You know, pull up roots and start new lives."

Tessa knew he was partially serious. There was something tempting about the idea of leaving behind the remnants of their disenchanted pasts. And it was exciting to think of themselves as expatriates in some distant land.

"You can't run away," Regina said. "Not now. Especially not now."

"Of course not," Walter said quickly. "I was just fantasizing."

A large bowl of family style salad was placed in the center of the table. Tessa served everyone. They were all hungry and ate steadily for several minutes. Before long, steaming plates of food arrived.

"So how was school today?" Walter asked. He wiped the corners of his mouth with his napkin. "How's that World Religions class? Are you still enjoying it?"

He had always been so much better than Tessa at making conversation. It was a skill she admired.

"It's really interesting," Regina said. "We talked about sand mandalas today. They're so cool."

"Tibetan, right?" Walter said,

"Yeah, it's an ancient art form of Tibetan Buddhism. They draw in three-dimensional forms of sand using colored powders. They're so beautiful."

Tessa kept eating. She knew all about sand mandalas. Ursula had once taken her to see the closing ceremony of a mandala. Several Tibetan monks worked around the clock in shifts to carry out the ancient ritual. Tessa was curious to hear what Regina took away from her introduction to this complex ritual.

"We learned that the mandala is constructed as a vehicle to generate compassion for the impermanence of life."

"Impressive," Walter said.

"It's also supposed to provide a cosmic healing of the environment," Tessa said.

Walter looked at her quizzically, but said nothing.

"You know about mandalas?" Regina said. "Cool."

"I know a little about a lot of stuff," Tessa said. "It gets me through."

"The monks pour millions of grains of sand over a period of four to five days. They use these metal funnels. The finished mandala is so beautiful. We saw pictures of them. I couldn't believe how magnificent they were. And then they dismantle them to show the impermanence of everything that exists. They just sweep up all that colored sand and pour it into a nearby river or stream, so that the water can carry healing energies throughout the world." Regina's voice was incredulous. "Isn't that amazing?"

"Amazing," Walter said. "I didn't know any of that."

"I couldn't help feeling sad though. I mean all that work, and then it's destroyed."

"The impermanence of everything that exists," Tessa said aloud but really to herself. She looked up to find Walter and Regina staring at her. "I guess if you reach a place in life where you can celebrate that truth, you've come a really long way."

"I guess," Regina said.

Walter raised his glass. "Here's to the monks."

Tessa knew what would come next. Walter had been waiting for an opportunity to segue into a conversation about Althea. He smiled at Regina as she raised her water glass and clinked it against his.

Tessa, eager not to be excluded, raised her glass as well, but she was remembering how Ursula had watched as the monks had swept up the colored sand and placed half of it in small bags that were then distributed among the viewers as blessings for personal health and healing. When a young monk presented Ursula with a bag of sand, she recoiled as if his offer had somehow offended her. His expression remained implacable, and Tessa had watched with growing concern, anticipating her mother's penchant for erratic behavior. Sensing Ursula's distress, the monk held her gaze and she relaxed under his too wise eyes. She took the bag of sand and when they left the hall where the ceremony had been held, Ursula gave the bag of sand to Tessa who cherished it until it mysteriously disappeared one day.

"To the monks," Tessa said. "And to the certainty of impermanence."

After their plates were cleared, they ordered one tiramisu and one cheesecake to share. As they waited, Walter took Regina's hand, squeezed it, and then released it. She looked at Tessa and then back to Walter.

"What's going on?" Regina asked.

"Your Aunt Althea phoned me," Walter said.

"Really? When is she coming over?"

Lowering her eyes, Tessa braced for his explanation.

"I don't think that's going to happen any time soon," he said.

"Oh?" Regina looked from her mother to her father again. "And why not?"

"I simply don't think we can overcome our history," he said rather stiffly. He paused while the deserts arrived. As soon as the waiter was out of earshot, Walter handed everyone a fork. Using his own fork as a pointer, he tried to explain. "Althea is unable to move forward, and we simply have to accept that."

"It's Mom, isn't it?"

Tessa froze just as she was raising a forkful of tiramisu to her lips. Her throat felt as though she would choke if she tried to swallow. Her hand, holding the fork, was suspended in mid-air until Walter gently tapped her, reminding her to follow through in some fashion. She set her fork down and lowered her eyes.

"No, it's me," Walter said. "Your mother did everything to encourage me to embrace Althea's overture even when it excluded her."

"Excluded her?" Regina said.

"Yes. Althea made it clear that she did not want to see your mother."

"Why?" Regina eyes filled with tears. She was a disappointed five-year-old. "Something must have happened."

"Nothing happened," Walter said. "Althea is still Althea. That's one thing that will never change."

"I was so sure everything would work out," Regina said.

"Maybe everything has," Tessa said.

She really wanted to tell them both, her husband and her daughter, about the time Ursula took her to the closing mandala ceremony and about Ursula's answer when confronted about the missing bag of sand. And although Ursula never confessed to taking the bag of sand, Tessa knew it was her. She had watched her mother perform her own mandala ceremony one night, throwing the contents of the bag to the wind as though they were her own ashes, and as though this odd ritual might somehow circumvent the inevitable future.

Chapter Twenty-Two

"I think someone's trying to get your attention," Anne-Marie said, pointing toward the front of the salon with her chin. She was busy combing out a client. "Over there by the side of the window."

Tessa strained to see over the reception desk. It was Philip. He was peering through the glass, using one hand against his forehead although there was no sun or artificial light to obstruct his vision. It immediately reminded Tessa of the first time she had met Fran. She had struck the same pose as she crossed the street. But then the sun had been strong, blinding really. Not like today, cold and overcast.

Two weeks had passed since Tessa had spoken to Fran and seen Ursula. Even though Tessa had not been specific about when she would phone, she knew that Ursula was waiting, probably watching the telephone like it was a living thing and could be coaxed into ringing. In the aftermath of Althea's disappointing request, Tessa had thought it best to keep a close eye on Regina for awhile and let the dust settle before stirring up anything new. Even Walter seemed relieved to take a brief hiatus from the tumultuous events that had caused so much upheaval in their lives. Regina had not ventured out with her friends these last two weekends, choosing instead to stay home and watch movies with her parents. They did not talk much about Althea or Ursula or Philip. But now Philip was standing outside Tessa's workplace, insinuating himself in her life in spite of her efforts to keep him out, at least for awhile.

"Do you know him?" Anne-Marie said.

"Yes," Tessa grabbed her coat from the closet and draped it over her shoulders. "I'll be right back."

Her next client was due in fifteen minutes. It had been a fairly slow day, and Tessa had welcomed the two cancellations and the one no-show. Philip started to wave the minute he saw her stand, but he stopped as soon as she came closer.

"Philip," Tessa said. "Is everything all right?"

"I wanted to see you," he said. "I need to talk to you."

"Is everything all right?" she repeated.

"I think so." He peered at her closely as if the answers to his forthcoming questions would be found in her face. "Are you mad at me?"

She thought, with genuine amazement, that he looked so much like their father. It took a moment for it register that there was no reason to be amazed, and then she smiled at Philip, reached out a hand and tentatively touched his cheek.

"No, no, not at all." She shook her head. "I don't know what I am anymore, but I'm not mad."

"Good. So why are you looking at me like that?"

"You look like your father," she said.

"*Our* father," he said. "Ursula told me I look like him too. She showed me pictures."

"Pictures?"

"She has lots of them. In albums and in frames."

"So you said."

"Yup," Philip said. "Lots of pictures of you when you were a baby. You were cute. Really cute."

There must have been letters and phone calls, and perhaps even clandestine meetings between Grandma Lucy and Ursula, mother and daughter. Tessa wondered what words they had exchanged, and she tilted her head, listening, as though she could hear them across the span of years. Once, she had confronted her grandmother, looked her straight in the eye and said that Ursula had finally been right about something. Even a bad mother was better than no mother at all. Lucy dropped the dish she was washing and stood, rooted to the floor while Tessa picked out the shards of glass from the sink and said sorry, sorry, I didn't mean it until the words seemed to revive her grandmother.

"I always thought I was too pale," Tessa said. "Everyone was always making polite inquiries about my health."

"I think you were cute," Philip insisted. "I mean it. So serious looking."

"Well, thank you." She saw that his hands were stuffed deep into his pockets because of the cold. "You must be freezing. It's the first really cold day we've had in quite awhile."

"I need you," he said. "That's what I came to tell you." She had no intention of undertaking any commitment to Philip. It was true they were blood relatives, but they had no shared history to bind them, nor any true common ground to hold them fast. He was a stranger even though he resembled their father. She sympathized with his dilemma and really liked the way he thought before answering a question or asking one. Just like their father always had. But Philip was still a stranger, someone she would have walked by on the street up until a few weeks before.

"You need me?" Tessa said, stiff with resistance. "What exactly do you need me for?"

"To call Ursula." He had clearly considered his answer before making the statement. This was no casual remark. He had deliberated over his words for days before delivering his conclusion. "She's waiting for you."

Tessa was about to tell him that she had waited and waited for Ursula, but he kept talking, sensing that this would be her initial reaction.

"We all need for you to call Ursula," he said. "Ursula and Fran and Regina, and me. I need you to do it. Nothing else can happen unless you do that. It's like time is standing still now." There was such urgency to his words that Tessa held her breath in anticipation of what he would say next. "If you don't call, we'll never know how it could have turned out if you did."

She knew exactly what he was talking about. His logic was compelling, but she felt the burden of his conviction and stood firm. Overwhelmed by Philip's sudden appearance, his expectations were almost too much. Her hasty reaction was predictable, but also inexcusable.

"I understand how you feel, but I have to protect my family right now."

She saw how hard these words reached him and was ashamed of her tactlessness, unpremeditated as it was.

"Philip—"

"No, no, no," he said, holding up his hand. "Don't apologize. I should be the one to apologize, barging in on you at home, and now at your work. It was just bad judgment on my part."

"I'm impressed that you came to see me." She placed a cautious hand on his coat sleeve. "Really I am."

He seemed to brighten at that. Tessa was struck by his willingness to overlook her indiscretion, but she was even more astonished by his frankness. It was in such sharp contrast to Tessa's need to always hold back. Philip was clearly more like Ursula, whose lack of guile had been evident when she was not spinning into some alternate persona. But, even at her best, her judgment was often so skewed that her genial nature could compel her to bring home people from the streets and befriend them as naturally as if they had met at a ladies' auxiliary luncheon. Invariably, the people Ursula picked were interesting, viable individuals who had somehow lost everything. Ursula was fascinated by the lives her friends had led before the streets became home. Eventually she admitted that she was even more fascinated by their freedom. She told that to Tessa. *Imagine what it must feel like to get up in the morning and ask yourself, where to, today? And then you can just turn in that direction.* Ursula would close her eyes and shiver with the thrill of such possibility.

"Tessa?"

She had drifted off for a moment lost in a memory of the day Ursula had slipped away from Dennis while they were in the city. They were having lunch after one of Ursula's appointments when Dennis excused himself to go to the bathroom and came back to find Ursula gone.

"I'm sorry," she said. "I'm here."

"I want to know everything about you," he said.

"About me? Why about me?"

She was cold now and tried to move her arms into her coat without much success. Philip came around and held the coat for her as she slid her arms into the sleeves. Then he wrapped his arms around her and held her fast across the top of her chest. For a moment she was frightened, but then she relaxed into his hold and rubbed his hands.

"You're hands are freezing," she said.

"Do you think any of this was a fluke?" He relaxed his hold, but neither of them moved. "The way things worked out, I mean. The way our lives came to here, to this place. Do you think it could have been different?"

Tessa turned around so that her face was pressed up against his chest. His coat was open, and his wool sweater immediately irritated her skin. Wool had always bothered her. Ursula had washed everything wool in milk, and Tessa did the same, pretending she had no idea where she had learned to do such a thing if anyone ever asked.

"Don't disappear on me," he said.

"I wouldn't do that," she said.

On that day so long ago, she had driven with her father all the way down to Lincoln Center and then back up to the hundreds, combing the streets for a glimpse of Ursula. It was Tessa who had remembered that Renee, one of Ursula's street friends, liked Broadway on the Upper West Side. On 101ˢᵗ Street, Tessa spotted Ursula. She was wearing a purple knitted cap that didn't belong to her. It was a warm Indian summer day, one of the last before the weather would turn. Ursula, laughing and talking animatedly, was pushing Renee's shopping cart. And Renee, who was wearing Ursula's black fedora, was totally absorbed in whatever Ursula was saying.

Tessa knew that her father was thinking exactly the same thing she was thinking: *She looks so happy.* Dennis told Tessa that maybe they should just follow Ursula for awhile. You know, let her enjoy her . . . Dennis searched for a word, and Tessa supplied it. You mean her freedom? He nodded.

They trailed her up to Columbia University. They watched as Ursula waited with the cart while Renee went into a Chinese restaurant to ask for food. The two women sat on a bench in the median, eating and talking. Dennis pulled into a spot near a hydrant and waited. When it grew dark, he turned to Tessa and said how sorry he was that he had been unable to make Mommy better.

"It must have been hard on you," Philip said. "The way she was and all."

"Was?"

He looked at her sternly, but not critically, and that did not go unnoticed. Tessa wrapped her arms around him beneath his coat and felt his ribs through the sweater, noting that he did not feel like a stranger at all.

"I'll call her. I promise."

"Call who?" Philip asked.

It took her a moment to realize that he was teasing her. Just like their father. He had loved to tease. But not that time they had waited for Ursula to end her day on the streets. That night had been different. Tessa had witnessed Ursula's surprise when Dennis approached. And even though Tessa knew that her mother could not see her in the dark, she gave a little half-wave when Ursula looked toward the car. Hidden from view, Tessa watched as Ursula hugged Renee goodbye.

In the car, Tessa waited for Ursula to say something, but she was quiet. From time to time, Dennis glanced over at Ursula, smiled encouragingly, and reached over to pat her arm. She was unresponsive, staring straight ahead without saying a word. Just as they were getting off the exit, she began to speak, not to anyone in particular, but just to speak. "I always thought I would like to die on the streets," she said. "I thought it would be romantic to be buried in Potter's Field somewhere."

Immediately, Dennis looked in the rearview mirror. Tessa knew he hoped to find her asleep. And because Tessa was born too wise for her years, she pretended that she was.

Now, however, Tessa rocked with laughter as Philip laughed with her. Although they were up out of the way of passers-by, it was hard to ignore them as they hung on to each other and laughed in a startlingly similar way—long guffaws interspersed with the occasional snort that seemed uncharacteristic for either of them. When they were sufficiently calm, Tessa walked him across the street to the coffee shop where she and all the girls ordered their sandwiches and coffee every day. He was hungry, and Tessa needed to get back to work. She would be finished within an hour or so. Ava, one of the waitresses, came over to say hello.

"What can I get you?" she asked.

"Nothing for me," Tessa said.

"Tuna salad on rye toast with lettuce and tomato, please," Philip said. "And some dill pickle slices on the side. No coleslaw. And a cherry coke. Thank you."

"Well, I'll be damned," Ava said.

It was the identical order that Tessa gave, often several times a week.

"He's my brother," Tessa said without looking at Philip.

Ava nodded, acknowledging the explanation and went to put in the order. Philip and Tessa turned shyly to each other, still apprehensive about the similarities that bound them and wary of the differences that had kept them apart.

"I thought you wanted to get a tea to take back with you," Philip said.

"That's okay," Tessa said. "I have to get back."

"Okay."

"Do you have money?"

Philip smiled and said, "Why, do you need some?"

She touched his face very lightly. She left the coffee shop, and crossed the street against the light, dodging cars in both directions, but feeling curiously safe because she knew Philip was watching her from the other side.

As soon as she was finished with her last client, Tessa phoned Regina and told her that Philip was coming home for dinner. Could she please put the tray of ziti in the oven, make a salad and set the table? There was no response.

"Regina?" A woman having her hair streaked eyed Tessa covertly from under an aluminum cap. "Can you hear me?"

"I can hear you," Regina said.

"Then, I'll see you soon?" Tessa said as if were up to Regina to decide. "Okay?"

"What should I tell Dad?"

"Is he home?"

"He's on his way."

"I'll try to reach him, but if he gets home before I do . . .," Tessa paused and took a deep breath, "tell him that my brother is coming for dinner."

She could feel Regina's smile. It was expansive, and Tessa welcomed it, felt an exaggerated gratefulness that almost made her cry.

"I will," Regina said. "Don't worry. I'll take care of everything."

"Thank you. Thank you so much."

Tessa tidied up her station, said goodnight to everyone, and took her things and left as though it was an evening like any other. Of course, that could not have been further from the truth because Philip was standing in front of the coffee shop waiting. He must have stepped outside as he saw her leave the salon. Tessa imagined him regarding the front door to the salon with a fixed look as he slowly ate his tuna fish salad sandwich. As soon as he saw Tessa, he began to talk to her from across the street.

"Wait," Tessa said, beckoning him to cross. "I can't hear you." She pointed to her ear. "Come this way. The car's round back."

The moment his foot touched the curb on her side, he picked up where he had left off. "And Ava says that you're a doll."

"That's just what I am," Tessa said. She sucked in her cheeks and made her eyes pop, assuming the deadpan expression of a doll before delivering her invitation. "I was hoping you would come home for dinner. Is that all right with you?"

Instead of answering, he said, "That was nice before when you called me your brother. I liked it."

He was walking beside her, matching his long strides to her short ones and tripping over himself in the attempt. Tessa assumed this meant he was coming home with her. When they reached the car, she

opened the door for him and took a pile of junk off the front seat and
threw it in the back.

"Go on," she said. "You can put the seat back for those long legs
of yours."

He fiddled with the lever. When the seat shot back with a thud
that startled him, he jumped. In some ways, he seemed like a visitor to
this planet. Everything he did gave the impression of being unfamiliar
with the world. Yet, he also seemed able to adapt with uncanny
readiness. Within moments, he was pressing the buttons to the radio,
looking for his favorite station, completely comfortable and so clearly
delighted that she wondered why she had felt the need to ever question
anything about him.

"What do you like to listen to?" she asked.

"Oh," Philip said. "I like Salsa. I listen to all the Spanish stations.
That music fills me up." He snapped his finger and swayed a bit. Then
he looked slightly embarrassed. "I'm sorry. I should've asked first."

"No, no! That's fine. You go ahead."

He found the station, but kept the music low. Its steady beat
thumped, coursing through Tessa in spite of the low volume.
Suddenly, he turned the radio off and said, "Ursula will need you the
most for awhile."

"Well, it seems everyone needs me these days."

"Not just these days," Philip said.

"And what do you recommend?"

"You know what to do. You don't need me to tell you."

Tessa tightened her grip on the wheel.

"Don't be angry, "he said "And don't say you're not because you
are."

"I'm not angry." She smiled. "Well, maybe just a little. You have a
lot of faith in my abilities."

"I have a lot of faith in you."

"Ursula told you about me."

"It doesn't matter what Ursula told me."

Philip was not so strange after all. She chose not to ask him what
he knew or what Ursula had said, or even what he meant by his words.
Better to leave some things alone, to let them move through time with
their own force, unimpeded. Better not to know why someone did not
love you back when you had loved with such a full heart. The answer
was certain to disappoint.

"Do you have a regular job as a carpenter, or do you just freelance?" Tessa said.

"You mean am I gainfully employed?" Philip said.

He was teasing her again, but she resisted the bait. She was learning.

"Yes. That's exactly what I mean."

He ran his hand along the dashboard and stared at her.

"You're pretty," he said. "But you should wear a little lipstick."

"Thank you. I do sometimes. Wear lipstick."

"You're welcome, and I'm sort of between jobs right now. Any kind of manual labor suits me, not just carpentry. For awhile, I was working for a junk dealer down in the city, but he died. I dream about starting my own business."

"What do you like about collecting junk?"

"Other people's junk is amazing. People throw out all sorts of things. You can't imagine the stuff people get rid of." He was warming to the subject. "I found a brand new set of dumbbells. Why would someone throw that out? It doesn't make sense."

"Maybe the person never used them and didn't want them around as a reminder."

He snapped his fingers. "I like that explanation. That's really good. I try to make up my own explanations for things too."

"Do you?" Tessa said. She put the directional on. They were turning onto her block. "Is Fran all right with your goals?"

"Well, she wanted me to go to school," Philip said. "I did for two years, but I never finished. I still take classes."

"In what?"

"Literature. I like to read, and I write poetry," he said. "Not very good poetry, but I try."

"Well," Tessa said. "You have a lot in common with Walter then. He writes not very good poetry too." She pulled into the driveway and leaned over conspiratorially to Philip. "But swear you'll never tell him I said so."

Solemnly, Philip crossed his heart. "Swear," he said.

The front door opened, and Regina stepped outside. She was wearing a thin shirt and a pair of jeans, and she shivered noticeably. Walter came out, too, and stood behind her, wrapping his arms around her the way Philip had wrapped his arms around Tessa earlier. So many parallels between one moment and the next. Regina tilted her head back to look up at her father. She said something to Walter that made him shrug. Tessa noticed that Philip faltered a bit with the door before getting out of the car.

"Don't be nervous," Tessa said.

Philip looked skeptical, but then he bent over and whispered as if he did not want Walter and Regina to hear.

"You know, before, when I said you would know what to do," Philip said, "I only meant that you would know what to do because you're a mother, not because of the other stuff."

Tessa smiled. "The other stuff, huh?"

"Yeah."

They didn't feel like strangers at all anymore.

"C'mon," Tessa said. "Let's go inside."

She followed him up the walk to the house, watching his already so familiar gait, hearing Regina laugh, her apprehensive laugh, and Tessa saw Walter reach out his hand towards Philip.

"Need any help?" Regina said. She was a little flushed and avoided looking at Philip after they exchanged a few preliminary words. "I can carry something."

"Yes, thank you," Tessa said even though she could manage fine by herself. She had nothing to carry. But she felt Regina's need to move away, just briefly, to allow Walter and Philip that opening, and to somehow slow things down a bit, so that they might all have the opportunity to marvel at how they had come to this moment.

Chapter Twenty-Three

Walter and Regina took to Philip immediately, and this made Tessa unreasonably proud even though he had grown up to be without the slightest influence from her. Yet, more than once during dinner, she caught herself smiling for no particular reason. Philip had a way of engaging others that was reminiscent of Ursula at her best. Nothing at all like the Ursula that Tessa had wished would be swallowed up into obscurity, never to be heard from again. Philip was like Ursula when she had a stretch of days in which she always bathed and dressed appropriately, had a conventional meal on the table and could hold forth on subjects as varied as the art of Japanese flower arranging, how to make a really superb rhubarb tart or what was really responsible for Mozart's premature death. Then, she had been engaging, just as Philip was now.

Tessa felt the same pride in Philip as she had felt in her mother the day she came to school on Parent's Day and taught all the sixth graders in Tessa's class how to do bargello. When Tessa had expressed her amazement to her father at dinner that night, he had taken another bite of the delicious pot roast Ursula had prepared and said, "Your mother is full of surprises." Ursula responded with a smile that was bashful, almost girlish. Entirely sweet and innocent, nothing at all like the other Ursula. Tessa treasured the good memories even as they occurred, sensing she would need to call on them to ground her in the years ahead.

But Tessa also saw Dennis in Philip. She saw the kindness and thoughtfulness that their father exhibited even on those days when Ursula tried to convince them that she had been captured by aliens and taken to their spaceship. Even on the days when Ursula made Jell-O molds for dinner with Cheerios inside and then wept inconsolably because Dennis would first thank her and then, uncomplainingly, make them all cheese omelets instead. Tessa had never once seen her father say a harsh word to Ursula or handle her roughly. He was always considerate, always tender, and almost always ineffably sad. As Tessa watched and listened to Philip, she saw how Dennis might have been if his entire life had not been overwhelmed with Ursula's needs and how to safeguard his child.

"So Tessa tells us that you're interested in starting your own business someday," Walter said.

Philip looked to Tessa, smiled and nodded.

"I dream about it," Philip said.

"Have you explored your options?" Walter asked.

"A little." Philip served himself more salad. "I'm not really sure how to go about it."

"Daddy will help you," Regina said. "Won't you, Dad?" She took the salad bowl from Philip and passed it to Tessa. "Dad knows a lot of people."

"That's okay," Philip said quickly. "It's a farfetched idea anyway."

"Farfetched ideas have changed the world," Tessa said. She looked at Walter, confident that he would comply. "Don't you think so?"

"Actually," Walter said, "I was going to suggest—before my women stole my thunder, that there's a guy in my office who might have some advice. Even if the idea is farfetched, it doesn't hurt to talk to someone."

"Thank you," Philip said. "I'd like that."

"Great," Walter said. "I'm on it."

The air fairly buzzed with the smoothness of everything; it seemed almost too good to be true.

"Regina's studying Buddhism in one of her classes," Tessa said.

Regina opened her eyes wide in mock surprise and said, "Well, that was random."

"Not really," Tessa said. "Our mother—your grandmother—was very interested in religions."

"I didn't know that," Philip said.

"You'll get used to it," Regina said. "She never tells me anything."

"You're probably better off," Walter said so matter-of-factly that everyone laughed. "Well, I hadn't really intended that to be funny, but I'm glad everyone got a laugh."

"I like religions too," Philip said. "Mostly I like the customs and traditions." He turned his attention to Regina. "Did you learn about Tibetan sky burials?"

"No," Regina said. "Is it gross?"

"I guess some people would think so," he said.

"Tell us," Tessa said.

Philip went on to describe the rituals that accompanied a sky
burial. A Tibetan monk would pray before cutting a naked corpse into
pieces, stripping the flesh from the bones, and then using a
sledgehammer to crush each bone into fragments small enough to
allow the waiting vultures to devour everything.

"I think I'll skip dessert," Regina said. "And by the way, that's
totally gross."

"Sorry," Philip said. "I just think it's so ecologically perfect. I
mean the vultures get to eat, a life cycle is completed, and it uses no
firewood, doesn't pollute the water and takes up no burial space. How
come we're not that smart?"

"Shortage of vultures in these parts?" Walter shrugged in mock
exaggeration.

They all laughed again. Tessa stood and began collecting plates,
and Philip immediately rose to help her. Together they stacked the
dishes and took the silverware while Regina began to wrap the
leftovers, and Walter filled a kettle to boil water for the coffee. Their
movements seemed orchestrated, almost fluid. No one bumped into
anyone, and each knew what do without being asked. And as Tessa
breathed in the satisfaction of the warmth and the ease with which
both she and her family had made room for Philip, it occurred to her
that after all these years apart, they had all been preparing for exactly
this night.

"Did you know that you're supposed to change your pillow every
three years?" Philip said.

"No, I didn't," Tessa said.

"How do you know that?" Regina said. "Talk about random."

Philip said that a woman in line at the grocery had told him.

"Just like that?" Tessa said.

"People always talk to me. I don't know why. Ursula said the same
thing still happens to her."

Tessa had already decided that she would phone Ursula
tomorrow, but there was no need to say anything about it now. They
were all quite happy enough for the time being. And for the time being
Tessa tried to wipe from her memory how Ursula had called her the
Daughter of Darkness, accusing her of having a soul that was
blackened by her mere association with the Devil's handmaiden, the
name Ursula claimed she had been given in the netherworld. Tessa
would try to stop remembering how her father had seemed to believe
that kindness was an antidote. He had died resisting the reality that one

could do everything he was supposed to do, say all the right things, and still it could not be enough. As Tessa was lulled into a sort of smug contentment about how far she had come, it became clear to her that perhaps it was time to let Ursula come home.

"Come sit with me a few minutes," Tessa said.

"Sure," Regina said. She pulled out a chair and sat, curling her legs beneath her.

Walter volunteered to drive Philip back to Fran's. Regina and Tessa had finished cleaning up, quietly, though throughout it was clear to Tessa that it did not take genius to suspect the Regina had questions that she did not even yet know how to ask. Tessa knew it was up to her to help Regina ask what needed to be asked.

"Do you know how I really envision the perfect world?" Tessa said, continuing without waiting for an answer. "I envision a world where no one would take chances. Everyone would know the future. No one would be sad because no one would remember the past. Everything would just happen in its time and be accepted."

She knew that Regina understood everything that was implied. There was nothing subtle about any of it, no matter how it was veiled in metaphor and sweetened with suggestion. Tessa knew what she was saying, and Regina knew what Tessa meant. But there was still the ritual to complete, the words, like incantations, needed to be spoken aloud if the spell was to be broken. And they had all been under the spell of pretense and deception for too long.

"I know you want us to be a perfect family."

"It doesn't have to be perfect," Regina said. "Just a little less nuts."

"That might be a lot to ask for."

"Is it?"

"I don't know. I wish I knew, but I don't have any answers."

"Then what's the use of your so-called gift?"

"It doesn't work that way." Tessa said. "I've told you that."

"I know. I know. It's just a lot to take in, an aunt who thinks you're a witch, a grandmother everyone thinks is a witch, and now an uncle who seems remarkably sane all things considered."

"He does seem remarkably sane, doesn't he?"

"I really like him," Regina said.

"Me too." Tessa ventured out a little further. "I'm sorry about Althea. I wanted it to turn out differently. I didn't think it was possible, but I still hoped."

"Well, thanks for that." Regina smiled. "I really appreciate it."

"And what about your grandmother? How do you plan to fit her into your world?"

"I feel so sorry for her," Regina said.

"I understand."

Regina leaned her head against Tessa's arm. And Tessa pressed her lips against Regina's head, savoring the sweetness of the moment.

"How would it be in your perfect world?" Regina said.

"We'd just live in the moment. I would find it easy to draw my long-lost mother into an embrace without a thought to what had transpired in all the years between her disappearance and her return. There would be no uncertainty, no questions to be asked or answered."

"But it's not a perfect world," Regina said. "Is that the moral of the story?"

"There is no moral to this story." She smiled. "I'm still working on it."

Regina turned her face up to look into Tessa eyes.

"You're smart and beautiful," Tessa said. "And I adore you."

"She gave me something when I was there," Regina said.

Tessa immediately knew what it was. Regina reached into her pocket and withdrew a shiny silver whistle. It was the whistle Tessa had given Ursula long ago to help her find her way back from the darkness.

"She said it's in case I get lost," Regina said. "She said I should blow it really hard."

Tessa took the whistle, surprised at its warmth. How old had she been when she gave this to Ursula, feeling certain it was the answer to all their problems? She had wanted to make everything perfect, just as Regina had hoped to now.

"I wonder what she'll use now," Tessa said more to herself than to Regina.

But Regina heard, and she brushed away her tears with the back of her hand and said, "She said she didn't need it anymore. She said she wasn't lost anymore."

Chapter Twenty-Four

"I'm here."

Tessa had phoned Ursula. It had been her idea to meet in the salon, although Tessa had invited her home for dinner. But Ursula was immediately hesitant, apologetically explaining that she was not quite comfortable yet with even the idea of such an arrangement. Without further discussion, Tessa suggested she come to the salon around seven.

Now Ursula stood in front of Tessa's station. She had been straightening up her tools, arranging emery boards, separating the coarser boards from the finer ones . . . when Ursula seemed to appear out of nowhere.

"Yes," Tessa said, glancing at her watch and frowning. She had told Ursula to come at seven, but it was a half hour early. "I can see that."

"I didn't want to be late," Ursula said.

"Actually, it's not even six-thirty," Tessa said, hastily adding, "but that's fine." She realized how even the slightest ambiguous word or careless gesture could jeopardize their meeting. "I was just worried that you didn't realize you would have to wait. It's my turn to lock up tonight. Come. Why don't you sit down?"

"Where?" Ursula said, frowning. She followed Tessa's searching gaze as she scanned the empty seats and, before she could answer, said, "I want to sit where I can watch you work."

The heat rose to Tessa's face as she nodded. What a fool she'd been to think she could do this without the past rushing in on her and shamelessly claiming any attempts to be disregarded.

Ursula was nervous. She kept touching her hair and fussing with her pearl earrings. It was obvious that she had dressed carefully. She had applied some pale pink lipstick and just a hint of blush. But the lipstick was the wrong shade for her complexion, and she had not even rubbed the blush in well enough. The red circles stood out on her cheeks like the first signs of fever. Even so, Ursula's poignant efforts to please stirred so much feeling in Tessa that she turned away. She was determined to keep her emotions in check, and already she had been sabotaged by her own intentions. But Ursula was waiting impatiently for a response, touching her hair one more time and adjusting the scarf around her neck like a child worrying about her costume just before she was about to go on stage.

"Yes," Tessa said. "Of course you can watch. I'll just be cleaning up, but it doesn't matter. Let me clear these magazines." Ursula stood silent and brooding as Tessa moved a pile of magazines from one seat to another. "Is this all right?"

Tessa had cleared space on a chair behind her station. The chair had an attached hair dryer. Ursula scowled. She had something else in mind.

"I don't care for it," she said. "I want a regular seat."

Frustrated, Tessa looked frantically around the salon, trying to find a satisfactory spot. There was the chair in front of her station, the one reserved for clients. Tessa felt it was too formal, too symbolic, although of what, she was unable to say, but it was unquestionably where Ursula intended to sit. She was already claiming it, holding on to the back of the chair with a certain proprietary air that Tessa found unsettling.

"Well, there's this chair," Tessa said, pointing to the seat on the other side of her station. "But it's for clients."

Ursula considered this with pursed lips before she said, "Do you have another client tonight?"

"No."

The salon was empty. They closed at five-thirty every Tuesday. It was their only early night, and the only night Tessa was responsible for locking up. It was not a coincidence that Tessa had picked a Tuesday.

"Well," Ursula said, "so it's all right then." She sat down. "Thank you. It's a very comfortable chair."

Tessa stared at her mother, feeling not only foolish, but a bit taken advantage of as well, although that made no sense either. Still, Tessa did not know what to say next, or how to act with this woman who was her mother.

"Would you like to take off your coat?" Tessa asked.

Ursula looked suspicious as she gathered the cloth in both hands, clutching the fabric with excessive force. Tessa wondered if Ursula worried that if she stood to take off her coat, someone might take her seat, like in a game of Musical Chairs.

"I guess," Ursula said, standing very slowly and looking about warily, on the alert for anything unusual. Unbuttoning her coat with surprising speed, she laid it across the back of the chair and sat down quickly. She smoothed down the front of her navy blue wool skirt and fussed very briefly with the buttons on her white blouse. When she was satisfied, she drew in her breath and exhaled, pulling herself up to her full height. "Do I look all right? Not terribly stylish, I know. That's all the in past. Never mind. I don't expect an answer. What could you possibly say? Go on. I'm ready to watch."

"You look very nice," Tessa said. "Very put together."

"Put together for what?" Ursula said. "My hair's just awful. I can't seem to find a style I like. I see you still wear your hair exactly as you did when you were a girl."

"I'm not sure what that says about my sense of style."

"I taught you that if you find a style you like, stick to it. Clothes, hair, the whole nine yards. What does that mean? The whole nine yards?"

"I'm not sure," Tessa said. "I think it has something to do with football."

"I never cared for football," Ursula said. "Your father liked it."

"Did he? I don't remember that."

"Well, he did!" Ursula sounded almost belligerent.

The feeling of cautiousness that had guided everything Tessa said to her mother came back. She had become expert at deflecting potential confrontations, proficient at deceit, and somewhat of a specialist at diagnosis. It was clear that her mother was extraordinarily anxious.

"I trust you," Tessa said. "I really do."

When Ursula looked over at Tessa, there was a moment when Tessa believed that she could forget everything and carry on. *Business as usual.* It had been a favorite phrase of her grandmother's. Tessa surmised it was akin to keeping a stiff upper lip, another concept that totally escaped her. But Ursula's expression was so pained, so replete with regret that Tessa wanted to forgive her everything.

"I tried to prepare you," Ursula said, wringing her hands. "I thought if I gave you the basics you'd be able to go on from there."

In the last weeks before the accident, Ursula had given detailed instructions about everything from how much starch to use when ironing to which books Tessa must absolutely read. *Before you iron your blouses, spray them lightly with starch, wrap them in a towel, and refrigerate them for a half hour or so. The iron will glide over the fabric. Reread Madame Bovary every year,* Ursula advised. Much, much later, Tessa realized that with each bit of advice and information, Ursula had been literally packing for Tessa, trying to give her the information she would need in the years ahead without a mother to guide her. Perhaps, knowing what it was like to live alone in a strange world, Ursula thought that if she armed Tessa with enough knowledge it would be possible to soften the anguish of a mother's betrayal.

"I still read *Madame Bovary*," Tessa said, trying to be generous. "Not always every year, but often enough. It's hard to keep up with everything."

"You have a lot of responsibilities," Ursula noted gravely.

"Well," Tessa said. "I don't know about that. I'm a manicurist. I also do pedicures and waxings, but it's not like I'm privy to any government secrets."

Ursula smiled and shrugged, as though dismissing the idea of any further discussion. But she could not resist the impulse to touch everything on Tessa's table. Ursula needed to anchor her location, to somehow place herself at this exact spot in this exact time.

"Did I startle you?" Ursula said.

"When?" Tessa was unsure if Ursula meant now or years ago. "When do you think you startled me?"

"I don't know. I don't know."

"It doesn't matter." Tessa's voice was soft, cajoling, like the time she talked their cat down from the tree. "It's all fine. Really."

"I still seem to startle people even if I don't mean to."

"To hell with them then," Tessa said. She was pleased when Ursula laughed and added, "You never used to care what people thought."

"I didn't?" Ursula said. "That's impressive. I don't think it's true, but it's impressive."

"Maybe I just saw you that way."

Ursula shrugged. "Can you keep a secret?"

"I think I've kept many."

"What about secrets of the heart?" Ursula said. "Can you keep those?"

They stared at each other. Tessa recalled how they used to stretch out on Ursula's bed and play the staring game. Tessa always won, shouting, "you blinked first," sending them both into peals of laughter. Ursula had always let her win, had blinked so imperceptibly that it would never seem that she was cheating. Yet, staring at each other now, it was certain that Ursula could hold a steady gaze forever.

"Would you like a manicure?" Tessa said, surprising herself. "You don't have to . . . I'd understand."

"I would *love* a manicure," Ursula said. "From you? *Very* much. *Very, very* much."

"All right then," Tessa said. "Let me just get everything ready."

Ursula watched as Tessa sat at her station and took a paper cloth, smoothing it down and tucking it securely under the mat. Next, she took clean tools from the sterilizer, readying the nail clipper, the file, the cuticle stick and the bottle of base coat.

"Would you like to pick a color?" Tessa asked.

"You pick for me," Ursula said.

Glad for the diversion, Tessa scrutinized the display, knowing exactly where to find every shade.

"You always liked red."

"Did I?" Ursula said as if Tessa were talking about an unfamiliar person. "I can't remember."

"Can't or won't?" Tessa said.

There was no perfect time for creating this moment. But it had arrived. Tessa's heart beat madly, and she wanted to cry. Ursula remained calm. She turned away from the display of nail polishes and placed her hands on the table, palms down, in front of Tessa.

"So many colors," Ursula said. "So many colors." She shook her head a little, to herself more than to Tessa. "*Can't.* I can't remember the details, but I remember the big things. I won't forget them." She shook her head again and laughed disparagingly. "No, I couldn't forget the big things even if I wanted to."

"Do you want to?" Tessa felt shameless in her pursuit, like a heckler, and wished someone, anyone, would come to her rescue and stop her. "I have to know."

So much depended on her answer. There would be no demarcation between their future and their past if Ursula answered no.

"I don't believe it's a matter of choice," Ursula said.

"It was just a question," Tessa said.

She spontaneously reached for one of Ursula's hands and then paused. All of Tessa's anger was quieted by the sensation their contact summoned, and it had nothing to do with her intuitiveness or with magic. Ursula's hand was so fragile that Tessa thought she could easily break it if she squeezed just a bit. This was the hand of her childhood.

This was the hand that had covered hers when she learned how to roll cookie dough, how to write her alphabet on lined paper, how to dig a hole for tulip bulbs. This was the hand that had slapped her across the face, tested the bath water, and waved to her as she boarded the school bus.

Images reeled behind Tessa's closed eyes, not unlike the experiences shared by survivors of near death situations. Tessa opened her eyes and looked down at her mother's palm as if her entire past originated there, in the palm of Ursula's hand.

"It's all there," Ursula said.

Then Tessa's tears came. She bent low over the table and pressed her face into her mother's waiting hand. Ursula placed her other hand on Tessa's head and stroked her hair, pulling her fingers through like teeth on a comb, gently, so gently that Tessa could not believe how much grief it caused.

"Tessa," Ursula said over and over. "My Tessa, my angel, my darling girl. Tessa. Tessa."

"How could you have left me?" Tessa sobbed. "How could you have left me?"

Ursula rested her cheek against Tessa's hair and said, "I never left you. You were with me every day."

"I don't believe you," Tessa said. Her face was still pressed into her mother's flesh. "You never thought about me at all."

"What if we went backwards?" Ursula whispered into Tessa's hair. "What if today was then, and we went backwards in time? Would you understand what I did? Would anything have changed?"

"I don't know." Tessa lifted her head and brushed at her wet cheeks with her free hand. "You mean knowing everything I know now?"

"Yes," Ursula said. "Yes, knowing everything."

"I don't know," Tessa said. "I can't understand how you could've left me. I needed you."

Ursula slowly stood, wiping her own palms against her skirt, pacing a little, looking more and more agitated.

"Your father was already dead when I left the car," Ursula said. "You knew that, didn't you?"

"Yes. I never believed otherwise."

"Good," Ursula said. "That's good." She stopped pacing and sighed deeply. "I didn't want it to happen."

"I know that also."

"I tried to resuscitate him, but it was no use." Ursula wrung her hands. "It was all my fault. He was such a good man."

"Did he say anything before he died?" Tessa asked. "Anything at all?"

"No. He must have died on impact. He wasn't wearing his seat belt." She slumped into the chair. "I don't think he felt any pain."

"I hope not," Tessa said. She winced, thinking about what must have rushed through his mind in those final seconds. "You should have trusted him."

"I was afraid for the baby. I didn't want him to be born without arms and legs or something worse. It would be hard enough just having me for a mother." Ursula's laugh was coarse. She stopped herself and looked ashamed. "Your father didn't care. He just wanted the baby."

"He loved you," Tessa said. "He loved all of us."

Ursula looked so miserable then, her dark eyes widening with pain and her entire body shuddering at her memories.

"I'm sorry," Ursula said.

"I know." She took Ursula's hands. "And after all that, you had the baby. What happened?"

"Where to start, where to start." Ursula shook her head. "I was homeless for a time. You can't imagine what it's like to be homeless in the rain. Dreadful, dreadful."

"I'm sorry. It must have been awful."

"I was very ill then. I was off my meds, pregnant and homeless. It was such a sad time for me."

"Why didn't you come home?" Tessa said. "I waited for you. I did everything I could to bring you home."

"I know you did. My poor darling. I know you did everything."

"I don't understand. You could have come home."

"For a time I didn't know I had a home. I didn't even know who I was." Ursula brightened. "But I always remembered you. I think I even told people my name was Tessa." She reached out and gently touched Tessa's face. "You kept me attached to this world."

"Where did you live?"

"I wandered around for some time. People on the street can be very kind." Ursula took her hand away and rested it back on the table. "When I began to show, it was time to get off the streets." Her face flushed, with embarrassment it seemed to Tessa. "I forgot that I was pregnant."

"I'm sorry," Tessa said.

"I called home from time to time when I knew you were in school. I was afraid you would know it was me on the phone. I didn't want to hurt you anymore than I already had. I really thought I was doing the right thing."

"What about Grandma?"

"She begged me to come home." Ursula lowered her eyes. "I felt so sorry for her." She sighed and looked up. "I never wanted to hurt anyone."

"But you did!" Tessa said more harshly than she intended. "You hurt all of us. You should have come home."

"Do you know what it's like when you take something so far that you have to finish it? No? It was like that for me. I couldn't imagine coming home with a baby I couldn't care for. I couldn't take care of you."

"I took care of myself. And Grandma was there."

"Yes, I know. She sent me pictures of you. I have every school picture, and every picture of Regina. I got a post office box, and she was very good about letting me do what I had to do."

"She lied to me," Tessa said. "And you both mislead me."

"We thought we were protecting you."

"From what? Oh, never mind. How did you find Fran?" Tessa asked grudgingly. "She said it was through a lawyer."

"Yes. I somehow wound up in the hospital. I couldn't tell you how I got there, but it was a blessing. One of the social workers convinced me that it would be best to give up my baby for adoption, and I was eager to do that. I told them everything, well, most everything. I told them I had no family and that I had been on Haldol. I didn't tell them anything about the accident or about you. I never used my real name. I called Grandma with a phone card from pay phones." Ursula paused, seemed to consider the import of her words and added, "You can't even find a decent pay phone today."

"It was a long time ago."

"Yes, it was, a very long time ago."

"Tell me about Fran," Tessa said.

Ursula immediately brightened. "Fran's an extraordinary person. You might not think so to look at her, but she's very remarkable."

"Looks can be very deceiving."

"Tell me about it," Ursula said with perfect intonation.

Tessa remembered how flawless Ursula's timing and delivery could be.

"Fran's lawyer came to see me. He told me that Fran and her husband were older, and they wanted a baby. He said they could pay. I told him I would have to meet them before I would agree."

"And?"

"And he made the arrangements. Fran and Thomas came to the hospital. Good people. If they suspected something was wrong with me, they didn't ask. That impressed me. I was in pretty bad shape then, but I remember their kindness."

"They did a good job raising Philip."

"They did, didn't they?" Ursula shuddered a little. "Though I do wonder. Did he tell you about those sky burials? Yes? Gruesome, don't you think?"

"Yes," Tessa said. "Totally. He does have some peculiar interests."

"Do you think he's like me?"

Her question was so swift and so evidently filled with concern that Tessa immediately regretted her remark. "I think we're both like you in some ways," Tessa said. "And I think we're both like Dad. How could we not be?"

"But in a bad way. Do you think he's like me in a bad way?"

Tessa could have argued that there was no bad way, but she knew what Ursula meant. More importantly, Ursula knew she knew.

"No. I think Philip is just fine."

"Well, that's a relief. One crazy person per family is quite enough."

"I think you overestimate the health of the American family," Tessa said. "I'd say that most families have far more than one crazy person. I could almost guarantee it."

"Thank you," Ursula said. "You're a good girl."

"I don't know about that, but thank you anyway," Tessa said. "It's getting late. I need to concentrate on your nails."

"Do you love your husband?" Ursula asked.

"Yes."

"Does he love you?"

"Yes, Mother. He loves me."

Mother. It had slipped from her lips like the exhaling of a breath. And Ursula inhaled lightly as though the word had released a perfume.

"No matter how sick I was, you still made me feel like a mother," Ursula said. "You always let me be your mother. Even when you were being mine."

"You were always my mother," Tessa said. "Even when I was being yours."

"Thank you." Ursula placed her wrists on the cushioned rest, her hands poised and ready. "I'm grateful to you."

"You don't have to thank me."

Tessa warmed a washcloth in the microwave, wrapping the heated cloth around Ursula's hands before applying moisturizer. Then Tessa massaged both hands, pulling at Ursula's fingers, moving the joints and pressing into her palms with strong thumbs. Ursula relaxed under Tessa's touch. They did not speak as Tessa began cutting and filing, then pushing back the cuticles, and carefully removing some ragged edges before she began to buff the nails in preparation for the polish. When she was done she took a bottle of pale, almost colorless polish with just a hint of pink.

"Is this okay?" Tessa held up the bottle. "Do you like it?"

"What's it called?"

"Sugar Daddy."

Tessa did not have to look at the bottle. She knew all of the colors by heart. Ursula took the bottle and read the name for herself, shaking her head.

"Silly name," she said.

"They're all silly. Should I go ahead?"

"Absolutely," Ursula said.

Slowly and very gently, Tessa applied a base coat, then two coats of Sugar Daddy, and finally a sealer. Ursula watched intently, following every stroke of the brush with keen interest and evident admiration.

"You're very talented," Ursula said. Her awe was unrestrained. "You have such a firm hand."

"I should have been a surgeon," Tessa said.

Ursula missed Tessa's humorous intent, and said, "No. I don't think you would be a very good surgeon. Anyway, you wouldn't have been able to read people. You don't need to go inside them to know what's inside them."

Tessa screwed the bottle of polish closed with more force than necessary. She nodded almost imperceptibly at Ursula's comment.

"I didn't mean to offend you," Ursula said.

"You didn't offend me." She guided Ursula's hands into a nail dryer and pressed a button. "Fifteen minutes."

"What should we do for fifteen minutes?"

Why don't you tell me that secret you mentioned before," Tessa said, trying to sound more casual than she felt. "I'm curious."

Ursula looked perplexed for a moment, but then she leaned over the dryer, getting closer to Tessa and said, "You know. I was never really taken hostage by aliens and forced on their ship."

"Really?" Tessa leaned back in her chair. "You could have fooled me."

For a moment they were both stunned, and then they laughed, together this time. Then, they talked, not about anything terribly important. They just talked, like a mother and daughter.

Chapter Twenty-Five

"Your Regina is a smart girl," Ursula said. Even though her nails were dry, she held her hands slightly aloft in her lap anyway. "And beautiful. Very beautiful."

"Thank you." Tessa handed her a mug of hot tea. It was eerily quiet in the salon, but they both seemed to enjoy the stillness. Ursula had declined Tessa's suggestion to go to the coffee shop. "She's less angry with me than she used to be." She shrugged. "Typical teenager, I guess."

Ursula took several small sips of tea. It was very hot; the steam swirled upwards from the cup, but Tessa had remembered that her mother always liked her tea that way. Hot and sweet. Dennis had liked to tease her about it. There had been happy times.

"I'm sorry," Ursula said.

"Oh?" Tessa's brow furrowed briefly. Then, she smiled, hoping to encourage Ursula to speak openly. "What for?"

"I should have been there for your teen years. It must have been hard to be raised by an elderly grandmother instead of by your mother. Even a crazy mother."

"You weren't crazy all the time," Tessa said. "And Grandma did her best."

"You were confused." Ursula nodded at her own words, confirming their truth. "I left you with unanswered questions. Too many of them."

"I still have a lot of unanswered questions."

"I know," Ursula said. "I know." She raised herself up a bit and drew back her shoulders. "I know a lot more than you think I do."

In spite of herself, Tessa bristled, but she was resolute. This was no time to be hasty. Ursula was not some stranger she had stumbled upon and was eager to escape. This was the moment Tessa's life had been hurling toward since that terrible night.

"I think you know a lot more than you think I think," she said.

Ursula smiled and said, "Ask me one of your unanswered questions. Or better yet, tell me something I might not know."

"I used some of your spells when I first met Walter," Tessa said. "I was afraid I would lose him if I didn't."

"Does he know?"

"He doesn't want to know. Not about the spells and not about me."

"How can he not know about you?"

Tessa sighed. "It's not like that. You know it's not like that. I don't allow it to be more."

Scowling, Ursula set her mug down on the table and wagged her finger at Tessa. "Does it have to be a life or death situation for you to use your gift?"

"Something like that," Tessa said. "I try to keep connected to the people closest to me." She blushed slightly, forcing herself to continue. "Of course, it isn't always possible."

"Which spell did you use?" Ursula said. Her eyes darted furtively from one corner of the empty salon to the other. "We are alone, aren't we?"

Tessa tried to hide her disappointment over Ursula's obvious choice to disregard her last remark, and in her most reassuring voice said, "No one is here except us."

"It's the same with the spells," Ursula said. "You know that, right?"

Tessa saw that Ursula was warming to her subject and knew somehow that if she had questions, now was the time to ask. Ursula was Tessa's door to the past, as well as to the future.

"More recently, I wanted to use one of your spells," Tessa said, "but it was a spur of the moment decision, and I didn't have all the ingredients on hand."

Years seemed to slip from Ursula's face, and she leaned forward conspiratorially as if they were cohorts in some devious plan. "It's hard to keep all the ingredients on hand."

"I should have improvised," Tessa said. "You always did."

"Well, never mind. Which spell were you trying to use?"

"The one to bring someone back into your life for good," Tessa said. As Tessa waited for Ursula's reaction, each one began to make the necessary adjustments to prepare for her next phase of her journey. Instinctively, Tessa planted her feet firmly on the floor, literally bracing as though she was actually headed into a storm. And in much the same way, Ursula began to buttress herself. She set her mug down and gripped the underside of her chair as if she too were about to be raised up overhead and tossed about.

"Nothing is for good," Ursula finally said. "Will is more powerful than anything."

"I know that."

"Who was the object of your spell?"

They both knew that Ursula knew the answer, just as they both knew that she wanted to hear Tessa say it. And Tessa knew it had to be said. It was clear that if the moment was lost, they could be forever stranded in the past.

"You, Mother. You were the object of the spell."

"That's good." Ursula nodded approvingly, took a sip of tea. Then, she looked up and smiled. "It's very good tea."

"I'm glad you like it."

"Regina wants to see what you see," Ursula said. "You need to teach her."

"How can I teach her?" Tessa was unconvinced.

"How can you not?"

"What do you mean?"

"You just have to teach her how to use what she already has, what we all already have."

"And the magic?" Tessa asked. "Should I teach her the magic?"

"No, not the magic," Ursula said. "The magic was just an excuse. I needed it more than the people who wanted it."

"I know."

"Ask me another question," Ursula said. "I'm at your service." She bowed her head and dramatically swept her arms out and around. "Go on."

"Is it so easy to just disappear?"

Ursula looked over her shoulder, still unconvinced that someone was not out there listening.

"It can take some doing," she said. "But you already knew that."

Tessa nodded ever so slightly, for she did not want to remember how Ursula had toiled to make them invisible. Once after Dennis had threatened her with yet another hospitalization, she had said they would run away and hide from Daddy. He would be able to see them only at their discretion. But Tessa resisted. Refused actually, to cooperate. She was afraid that Ursula was lying and would make herself disappear, leaving them behind forever. Ursula mocked her fears, plied her with false promises. Then she stopped. Just like that. Just like she had started.

"Did the palmistry come in handy?" Ursula asked.

"Yes, it did. Thank you. You were right. People love parlor games."

"Everyone wants to know the future," Ursula said more to herself than to Tessa. "I can't imagine why they think the future will be better than the present."

Tessa looked away momentarily and then started to rise from her chair, but Ursula stopped her. She reached out and placed a hand on Tessa's arm, firmly forcing her back into her seat.

"Don't let those girls in the department stores spray perfume in your eyes," Ursula said.

"I won't," Tessa said very quietly. There was no doubting now that what she had felt when she held her mother's hands was certain. "I promise."

"And read Auden. He was a visionary."

"I will."

"Use a teaspoon of baking soda in warm water if you have a canker sore," Ursula said. "Myrrh, either in powder form or capsules is excellent. The best is in an alcohol solution. Use a cotton swab and dip into the solution. It'll smart a bit, but it works. You can get the alcohol solution in a health food store."

"I'll look for it," Tessa said.

"That's good."

"What about the dream, Mother?" Tessa spoke quickly, responding to the sense of urgency that had overtaken her. "Tell me about the dream."

"The dream?" For the first time since she had arrived, Ursula looked as though she wanted to bolt. "Which dream is that?'

Tessa saw that her mother's hands were shaking, but pressed on. She had to know.

"Why didn't you help me?" Tessa said. "You knew what was going to happen that night, and you knew that I knew. Why did you let it happen?"

"Why did I let it happen?" Ursula repeated, sounding incredulous. "It wasn't for me to let happen. It was your dream, your vision."

"But you had the same dream."

"Yes," Ursula said. "I had the same dream."

"Are you saying that I should have done something?" Tessa said. "Are you saying that it was up to me?"

Ursula jumped up, startling Tessa enough so that she gasped.

"Listen to me," Ursula said. She took Tessa by the shoulders. "There was nothing that could have been done differently. Not about that. Not about anything. Nothing."

"How do you know? Maybe we could have prevented that night from happening," Tessa said. She looked up into her mother's weary face. "Maybe we could have been a family. All of us. Daddy and Philip, and you and me."

"Do you really think so?" Ursula said. "Do you really think we could have changed what had to be?"

"I don't know. I just don't know."

Ursula sat back down. She sighed deeply and closed her eyes. Tessa wanted to kiss her on her lips, wanted to press one finger against the beating pulse at the base of her throat.

"Are you going to leave me again?" Tessa asked.

Eyes still closed, Ursula said, "I never left you. I wish you would believe that. I was just trying to be a good mother. For once in my life, I was trying to do the right thing."

"Are you going to leave me again?" Tessa insisted.

Ursula did not answer, but she opened her eyes and smiled, almost flirtatiously, lowering her voice to a whisper and said, "Regina showed me her tattoo."

Tessa nodded. She felt an ache in her lower back, but she was afraid to move, afraid Ursula would disappear. "Do you like it?"

"Very much," Ursula said. "She has a good mind. Who would have thought of such a thing? A crown." She shook her head, laughing to herself. "What a girl."

"You gave Regina the whistle," Tessa said.

Ursula looked momentarily alarmed, as if she had done something wrong. "Yes. Well, I kept it all these years, and I wanted her to have it."

"Regina was very pleased."

"I'm glad. I have so little to give her," Ursula said. "And I thought she might need it herself sometime."

Tessa stared at her mother's hands, smooth now with lotion and topped with nails that had been groomed and painted. Once those hands had shown her how prehistoric people had left their prints on the walls of caves. *They blew paint on their outstretched palms, and left their mark on wall after wall in all the caves. To be remembered. They wanted to be remembered.* Ursula and Tessa covered the walls of her bedroom with golden hand prints. When Dennis came home and found them, he covered his own large hands in the remaining paint and squeezed in his prints wherever there was room, overlapping theirs in some places. Tessa's room stayed that way for a long while.

Then one seemingly average day, Tessa came home and found Ursula crouched in the corner. Her face was covered in a white powder (that Tessa later discovered was corn starch), and her eyes were bright and wild. She had painted Tessa's room bright pink with purple trim to keep away the evil spirits. The hands, she said, were trying to choke her, and she feared for Tessa's safety.

"You've given her so much already," Tessa said. "She's so happy to have a grandmother."

But Ursula was not to be dissuaded from whatever plan she had in mind.

"It's late," she said. "I've kept you from your family."

"You're my family too," Tessa said fiercely, trying not to cry.

Ursula listened, absorbing this information like it was an intriguing solution to a complex problem, but she did not respond.

"Mom?" Tessa asked.

"I'm so tired." Ursula hung her head as though she might instantly fall asleep. Instead, she looked up, smiled and said, "This is a very cheerful color."

Non sequiturs. Tessa nodded, agreeing that it was indeed a cheerful color. Still, Ursula appeared to be in the moment, and she did look exhausted. *Hanging on by a thread.* It was a favorite response when someone happened to ask her how she was coming along. *Hanging on by a thread.* The answer was guaranteed to provoke stony silence.

"May I drive you home?"

"I don't think so," Ursula said.

"Let me drive you home," Tessa said. "It's late. It's not far, and I don't mind."

"I know you don't mind," Ursula said. "But I do. You need to get on home to your husband and your daughter." She seemed to force a smile. "Maybe next time."

She stood and cleared her throat unnecessarily, readying herself for what she had clearly come to say. Perhaps she had rehearsed the words, standing in front of a mirror, testing herself, measuring the pauses for emphasis.

"Even you couldn't have stopped me, Tessa. You couldn't have changed anything."

Then she smiled the way she used to on a really good day, but Tessa said nothing, waiting for the rest. Ursula took her coat from the back of the chair.

"I wanted it to happen," Tessa said in a rush of breath, disgraced by her confession. "I wished for you to die."

"Of course you did," Ursula said. "Why wouldn't you have wished for it?"

Tessa hung her head and said, "I didn't know what to do."

"There was nothing for you to do, Tessa. Your wishing didn't make anything happen. You must know that. I never wanted you to feel responsible. It was my greatest worry. All those years, I worried about it," she said. "I just wanted to do the right thing. For once in my life. The right thing."

"What should I tell Regina?" Tessa clenched her fists into tight balls and tried not to throw herself at her mother's feet, grab on to her legs and keep her from leaving. "She'll be heartbroken if she thinks she'll never see you again. First Althea, and now you."

"Don't be so dramatic," Ursula said wearily. It was exactly what she had said to Tessa when she was a little girl. Even then, Tessa had noted the irony. "She's probably better off without her."

"And what about you? Is she better off without you?"

"She's always been without me," Ursula said.

"But now she knows you and loves you," Tessa insisted.

Ursula waved her hand as if dismissing the validity of love and said, "She's not a child. Give her some credit." Almost haughtily, she added, "I think she's already smarter than you are."

"Why did you come back?"

Ursula looked surprised at the question, but she answered simply. "Because you needed me."

"I've needed you before."

"But this time I was available," Ursula said.

Tessa warned herself to proceed with caution. She was in a familiar place now, but she needed answers and time grew short.

"Are you just going to walk out on Regina's life now?" Tessa said. "Regina loves you. I love you."

Ursula looked away. She seemed to search her memory for something relevant, something she could offer Tessa.

"Children are very resourceful," she said. "Do you know about the children who can only go out to play in the dark? They're sometimes called Children of the Moon. I love that." She looked around the salon as if she had just arrived. "They have to be all covered up even if they go outside for a few seconds. I can't remember what it's called, XP, or something like that. It doesn't matter, does it? The point is that they have to watch from the shadows for the rest of their lives. But they persevere. Isn't that impressive?" Without waiting for an answer, she mused aloud, "Children of the Moon. I don't think I'd mind being called that, a Child of the Moon, would you?"

Tessa felt unable to breathe, faint with uncertainty. It was reminiscent of how she had felt that night, watching her parents from the window. Helpless again, she watched Ursula button every button on her coat before she took her purse and her scarf, hesitating before she touched Tessa's face with the back of her hand.

"Maybe next time you'll give me a pedicure," Ursula said. "I haven't had a pedicure in so long. Bright red. That's the color I'd like."

"Yes, next time," Tessa said. "Definitely, next time. I know just the color."

They were actors now, playing out their roles to perfection. A few strands of Ursula's hair clung to her coat collar as she turned to leave the salon. Tessa wanted to stop her, fix her hair, and flatten down her collar. But Tessa kept her hands at her sides, and did not try to stop Ursula from leaving.

"It's different this time," Ursula said. "It's not like it was that night."

Tessa remembered that Ursula had always claimed to know what she was thinking, had always been able to feel what she felt. "I can feel your vibrations," Ursula would say when she held Tessa tightly and tried to force her to admit that she was angry, enraged really, that she had a mother like Ursula. "I can feel what you feel," Ursula always said. For the first time, Tessa believed her.

"I want you to know that I heard you before," Ursula said. "I love you too."

"Give us a chance," Tessa said. She had to make one final effort. "You came home for a reason."

"I just want to be a good mother, to do the right thing. That's all I wanted then, and that's all I want now. It's the same dream we all share. Isn't that true? Can you see it now?"

Speaking so softly that she was unsure she was speaking at all, Tessa said, "Yes, it's true. I see it all now. It's the same dream we all have."

They hugged briefly without any further exchange of words. Tessa unlocked the front door for Ursula and did not wait to watch her disappear into the night. Nor did Tessa call out after her, no plea, no admonition, no further testimony of love. Immediately, Tessa shut off the lights, one after another until the salon was dark.

The whole way home, Tessa went over everything they had said to each other, sifting through the words, mindful of everything Ursula had said, and everything she had left unspoken. Grateful when she finally pulled into her driveway, Tessa gathered her belongings and locked the car. Shifting her bags to one side, she felt in her purse for her house keys. Her fingers closed on something small and hard. She dropped everything to the ground and unfolded a piece of lined loose-leaf paper. Inside was the peach pit ring she had given Ursula so long ago. The silk cord Ursula had pulled through its middle was still there, tightly coiled around the pit.

You were with me every day. You never left me.

Unwinding the silk cord from the peach pit, Tessa placed it over her head. She looked up. The house was dark, but she saw the blinds in Regina's room move so slightly that Tessa thought it might have been her imagination. But then a long, low sound beckoned. It came from Regina's window, and Tessa recognized it immediately. She would not need to tell Regina about the Children of the Moon after all. Regina was safe. Pausing on the doorstep, Tessa listened. Regina was calling Tessa with the whistle she had given Ursula to help her find her way back home, away from the darkness, and Tessa was sure her mother heard it too . . . calling to her, calling to them all.

The Manicurist

Phyllis Schieber

Also From Bell Bridge Books

The Firefly Dance Anthology

Featuring Phyllis Schieber's poignant short story,
THE STOCKING STORE

In bookstores now

Excerpt

I was seventeen the last time I went with my mother to the Stocking Store. I have more important concerns now than the simple errands of childhood. I am busy protesting the war in Vietnam and listening to rock music. Martin Luther King and Robert Kennedy have both been murdered within a few months of each other. I am devastated by these losses, but I am also in love for the very first time. When I tie my hair back with a scarf, he says I look like a gypsy. Still, I say yes when my mother asks me to accompany her to the Stocking Store. I think she is even more surprised than I am.

I still call it the Stocking Store because I do not know it by any other name. We call the store where we buy all our buttons the Button Store, and the small cave-like shop that both repairs and sells umbrellas the Umbrella Store. I still long for the red umbrella with the pink ruffle and the appliquéd poodle with its rhinestone collar. I often dream about that umbrella. I can see myself twirling it before a crowd of admirers.

These small shops are part of our daily lives. The Cheese Store, the Pocketbook Store, the Hat Store, and the Toy Store are places that need no other identification. But it is the Stocking Store that I love best. It is in the Stocking Store that I first come to know exactly what it is that makes me different from others.

About Phyllis Schieber

The first great irony of Phyllis Schieber's life was that she was born in a Catholic hospital. Her parents, survivors of the Holocaust, had settled in the South Bronx among other new immigrants. In the mid-

fifties, her family moved to Washington Heights, an enclave for German Jews on Manhattan's Upper West Side, known as "Frankfurt-on-the-Hudson."

She graduated from high school at sixteen, earned a B.A. in English from Herbert H. Lehman College, an M.A. in Literature from New York University, and later an M.S. as a Developmental Specialist from Yeshiva University.

She lives in Westchester County where she spends her days creating new stories and teaching writing. She is married and the mother of a grown son.

The Manicurist was a finalist in the 2011 Inaugural Indie Publishing Contest sponsored by the San Francisco Writer's Conference.

Phyllis Schieber is the author of three other novels, *The Sinner's Guide to Confession*, *Willing Spirits*, and *Strictly Personal*.

Visit Phyllis at http://phyllisschieberauthor.com

Made in the USA
Columbia, SC
01 December 2019